MW01136598

State of the Union

Book 1
in the
Phillips Family Chronicles

Kelly Wanamaker

Love you mom, you have always believed in me. Thank you, Kelly

For John, without your help unraveling the complexities of the story, Dusty would still be sitting on a surfboard in the tranquil waters of Banderas Bay.

The author would like to give a huge shout out to Michael Martel (MichaelMartel.com, *Get Er Done*) for taking the time to be the very first person to read my very first manuscript and for encouraging me to send it out into the universe. Thank you to Donna Pomeroy for being the second reader; you are always an inspiration to me. Finally to Stephen and Nathan, who have been cheering me on from the beginning and have, hopefully, smiled each time I've sent another revised, final revision to read through. A mom couldn't be more proud of the men you have turned into.

America will never be destroyed from the outside
If we falter and lose our freedoms,
it will be because we destroyed ourselves

– Abraham Lincoln

Brian
July 16

Captain Brian Phillips gazed across the sun blistered tarmac as the familiar adrenaline rush of a new mission clashed with the incongruousness of stepping off the plane at North Island Naval Air Station in San Diego instead of the tortured deserts of the Middle East. His orders were clear and also unreal.

He sighed and rubbed a hand across the stubble at the back of his neck and rolled his shoulders, pushing away the jetlag fogging his thoughts. He was a Ranger. He would do his duty, finish the mission and take care of his men, the same as every other time. This deployment just looked to be a hell of a lot more difficult.

Gusts of wind carried the cries of gulls chasing the fishing boats returning with their catch. The breeze ruffled shirt collars as his elite team of Rangers sorted out their baggage on the expanse behind him. Brian's eyes felt gritty. It had been a long night spent getting his command ready to deploy and then a six hour flight across the country. He was ready for a hot shower and a bunk, neither of which was likely anytime soon.

He looked over his troops as they came into formation. The men and women of Charlie Company had not been apprised of the mission parameters before take-off and while professional, were subdued and uneasy. Concern was etched into the hard angles of weatherworn faces as they loaded into the waiting vans. This was not how a deployment was expected to begin.

Leaving Coronado Island, they crossed the bridge, pulling into a large warehouse in National City, well within San Diego proper and definitely inside US borders. His troops piled out, assembling in brilliant sunlight streaming through the open bay doors. Brian stretched his long legs and stood, looking over the heads of his soldiers into the interior, where a team of agents in tactical gear emerged from the gloom. Introductions were quick, including his new superior, Immigration and Customs Enforcement Special Agent in Charge, Dan Mobury.

Brian shook hands. "Sir."

As his team wound their way through folding tables buried under piles of gear, picking up vests, helmets, boots and other items they would need for the coming deployment, including the black windbreakers with ICE stenciled across the back, Brian looked over his new superior. He was a small man in his middle years, his graying hair cropped in some cross between fashion and a military high-and-tight. He wore his uniform with a cocky pride that Brian usually saw on untested first-timers; the harsh realities of war quickly bled a man's ego into the sands, replacing it with grim determination. Mobury was obviously a bureaucrat, never a soldier.

"You have been apprised of the situation, Captain?" His voice was an octave higher than Brian was expecting, undercutting the hard and strident image he was trying to present.

"Yes, Sir."

Mobury, his balding pate barely reaching Brian's shoulder, tilted his head back to look Brian in the eye. "I am in charge here. There will be no question of that. Understood?"

"Yes, Sir." Brian towered over him. Exhaustion intensified his annoyance at the arrogant tone in the small man's voice and he leaned in without further comment, letting a little of the warrior bleed through his professional demeanor. Mobury took a step back, crossing his arms.

While Brian didn't like to play these games, he excelled at them. His superiors had noticed and quickly promoted him to lead advance teams through remote villages in Afghanistan, gaining his Captain's bars early. Negotiating with tribal leaders required using his height and bulk as often as diplomacy to keep control of the situation. Mobury broke eye contact and Brian leaned away, his point made; while he was jurisdictionally under this man, these troops were Brian's.

His team dropped their new equipment off and settled into chairs. Agent Mobury hastily stepped away from Brian and to the front. "The President has tasked ICE with the deportation of every illegal inside US borders. He has assigned you, Company Charlie, of the 10th Mountain Division Army Rangers, to assist ICE in completing this mission in San Diego. This operation is classified Top Secret."

A murmur went through the room. Brian watched his soldiers. They were not here to help reinforce the border stations facing Mexico as past military actions had done. They would be operating undercover inside the US. It was going to be a mind-bend for these experienced warriors, trained to take down the enemy, now forced to use that training against US citizens. He saw stony expressions, the neutral faces shouting alarm, easily read if you cared about these men and women as he did.

Mobury, oblivious to their discomfort, raised his voice. "You are in the US. There are laws here. You will not be cowboys. You will not be issued a firearm. The only reason you are here is because the President ordered it. ICE is more than capable of doing its job. Am I clear?"

"Yes, Sir!"

Brian took a deep breath and let it out slowly as Mobury droned on in an unending flow of words. This mission was going to take every bit of the leadership and diplomacy skills he possessed to keep control of the situation and protect both his command and the people of California.

As they loaded back-up, First Lieutenant Justin Johnson, Brian's second in command, caught his arm. After surviving two deployments in Afghanistan, they dropped the formality when they could. "This has shit-show written all over it, Brian. We shouldn't be here. These guys are government, not soldiers. All this secret-squirrel crap, I don't know. It feels wrong."

"I hear you, Justin, but this is the mission." He settled his ice-blue gaze on the wiry man, swinging his pack onto his shoulder. "We take care of our own, do our job and get all of us out in one piece."

"What they have us doing here? It's illegal. The President can't order us onto the field at home, he doesn't have that authority. We go along with this? It could get us in go-to-jail-and-throw-away-the-key kind of trouble." Justin ran a hand across buzzed, blond hair.

"It's the mission. You want to raise your hand and squeak? I already pushed beyond what I should have with the Major. Anything else and they will bury our asses. We have to watch each other's backs and get the hell out of here before it goes south." Brian rubbed his eyes. A headache was building behind his temples.

Justin's face went stony again. "I've always got your back, Captain." He grabbed his rucksack. "This crap just makes me want to hit something."

Brian watched him walk away. Justin was right; this situation was screwed up and had the potential to spin his whole company into a mental rabbit hole. He would do whatever it took to protect his troops from the emotional fallout of engaging against US civilians. He looked over at Mobury strutting around like a rooster. With that and the ever-pleasant, Special Agent In Charge Mobury, he figured it was going to feel like a long deployment no matter how short it turned out to be.

Brian
September 2nd

The first stars pricked the velvet of deep azure as Brian looked up the length of the mainsail, tinged pink with the beginning of sunset and pulling gently in the soft, onshore breeze. His brother Michael was at the helm, angling the small craft towards the harbor, the hills of Corona Del Mar sprinkled with a handful of evening lights and the red and green buoys at the entrance. Brian pulled the main sheet through the cleat, tightening the sail as he watched the small bits of yarn attached along its back edge. They fluttered and fell. He inched the line back out again until they streamed backwards, the sail bellying nicely.

Six weeks into Brian's San Diego deployment, Michael had driven down from his home in San Francisco for one of Brian's rare days off. They had chartered a Bavaria 32 out of Newport Beach for the day, sailing to Catalina and then back into the Balboa basin. Brian was wind-burned and exhausted. They had sailed hard, eking every bit of speed out of the vessel as they raced through the waves, dolphins rushing back and forth through the bow wake. Now, as evening approached, they idled along in the light wind, reluctant to return to shore.

Michael, an older version of Brian, smiled at him. "Reminds me of Dad. He was always fiddling with the sails."

Brian scowled. "Dad only went out with me a couple times. It was mom that taught us to sail."

Michael nodded. The waves slipped along the hull, shushing quietly. "I see it differently now, why Dad was gone so much. I mean, I understand his deployments."

Brian looked across the small cockpit. Michael's features were disappearing in shadow. "Dad had choices. Even when he was home, he still wasn't there. I graduated West Point. I made Captain before most of my class. You got a Bronze Star and a Purple Heart." Brian felt his anger flare. These were deep hurts that he rarely acknowledged. "A fucking Bronze Star. Has he ever told you, even once, that you did well or that he was proud of you?"

Michael shrugged. "He's not that kind of dad, you know that. It doesn't mean he doesn't love us." His hair, cut a bit longer than Brian's, turned fiery red as the sun sank and his brilliant blue eyes watched him over the wheel. "Anyway, I was always there for you."

Brian nodded. Michael had always been there, more like a second father than his brother. He was always responsible, always watching out for them; him, his sister Madison, and their mom, while their dad chased his military career.

He leaned back and forced his anger back inside its box, taking deep breaths of the salt air until he felt calm seep back into him. His body was on a tight trigger from the stress of this deployment, his emotions running close to the surface. He needed today. Closing his eyes and let his body rock gently as the current pulled the little vessel forward. Peacefulness filled his soul. The cockpit felt intimate as the sun started to set; just Michael and him in the expanse of the ocean, wrapped up in a comfortable camaraderie after a muscle wearying day.

He slit his eyes, watching Michael steer, enjoying the look of contentment brushing aside the sharp angles of his brother's face. He carefully composed his next words. He wanted Mike's advice but had to be careful about giving away anything of his mission. "I'm struggling with my superior on this assignment. I think he is dangerous and I'm spending a lot of time protecting my troops from his excesses."

Michael sighed. "Agent Dan Mobury. He doesn't have a good reputation; a little man with a big chip on his shoulder. It is just a matter of time before he steps far enough over the line to be brought up on serious charges. He is a mean piece of work."

Brian stared across the space. "I'm on a top-secret assignment, Michael. How?"

Michael chuckled. "The long arms of my employer. I kept my security clearance from the Marines. Anything to do with any of our families pops up on their radar and I am told. I checked him out after I heard about your assignment. There isn't much I can do except warn you."

Brian looked out over the water. "He's a jackass and I take the brunt of it to keep him off the backs of my troops. Most days I want to deck him, other days he's lucky I don't have a rifle in my hands. He is a dick to everyone under him so I have to run constant interference. What are you doing in civvies if these kinds of guys are running the show?"

"Those kind of people are everywhere, Brian, even in the Marines."

Brian grunted, his eyes on a Bayliner, sleek and powerful, thundering out of the harbor entrance and barreling towards them. Accelerating without altering course, it passed the buoys in a rush, the captain gunning the engines without paying attention to the water ahead. The boat plowed directly towards them, the bow growing large across their field of vision.

"God damn it, fucking rich bastards." Brian edged towards the lifelines, preparing to jump into the darkening water.

Michael sprung forward and hit their air horn; three loud, prolonged blasts, and swung the wheel around, angling towards the shore.

They moved with glacial slowness in the light wind and it became obvious they were going to collide unless the Bayliner swung wide. Twenty yards out a head appeared at the Bayliner's helm, a shocked expression on the man's face. It sheared off and shot by in a blast of sound, the captain's face disappearing in the dusk. Their boat slammed over the wake, sails flapping, as water poured across the foredeck. The powerboat screamed away.

"Asshole," They said together. Brian grinned and settled back down.

Michael swung the helm, putting them back on course. The sails filled and the boat glided forward.

"That was close." Brian said. He stretched his long legs out across the cockpit seats, relaxing his body into the rhythm of the waves. They sailed on in silence as the sun neared the horizon.

At a faint cry, different from the calls of the gulls, he leaned forward, peering across the choppy water. "I just heard something, sounded like someone hollered."

They froze, listening to the swoosh of waves sliding along the hull as Brian peered across the water. It came again, a cry from the shadows between the boat and the shore. Brian grabbed binoculars as Michael started the engine, swinging the boat dead downwind, the sails luffing as the boom swung crazily back and forth, caught halfway in a jibe. As they cleared the turn, Brian pushed the boom out to the side and the wind filled the sail, pushing her faster.

He glanced at Michael. "Every boat horror movie starts this way."

Michael laughed. "Big, bad ring-knocker afraid of the dark?" Ring-knocker was military slang for Academy Graduates, including Brian's West Point alma mater. Michael had come up through the ranks, skipping college, in a move designed more to frustrate his father, a ring-knocker Colonel, than because he couldn't get in, and it had worked. His father rarely talked with him, even less since he had left the Marines a little over a year before. Brian had taken his father's route, enrolling at the academy straight out of high school.

"Don't say I didn't warn you when a zombie comes out of the water, or a guy with a machete. We are alone out here and awfully close to the border." Brian grinned.

Michael raised an eyebrow. "Zombies in Mexico? I've never seen a zombie, not once, in all the times I've been down there."

Brian grunted as he scanned the water. "Two kayaks, just to the left, upside down. That wake must have flipped them." Brian leaned out trying to get a better view. "Cut the engine." The boat went silent.

The cry came louder, a man's voice calling for help. Brian cupped his hands around his mouth. "We're coming. Hang on." He squinted, peering at the two overturned kayaks in the fading light. His stomach twisted. "Michael, I'm only seeing one head."

"Roger that," Michael said, his officer's voice suddenly unmistakable. He brought the boat in close. "Brian, I'm going to put you in the water. I'll pass them up, heave to, and drift down. It'll make it quieter without the engine and give you a space of calm water to get them to me. Find the other head, whatever it takes. Make sure your life jacket is on tight."

Brian nodded as Michael radioed for help. He moved to the lifelines, holding onto a stay until they came up next to the flipped crafts. Diving, he cleared the lines. The water was icy and he drew a deep breath as his head emerged. Five strokes out his life vest inflated, exploding around his chest. The suddenness of it flipped him over and he back-paddled the last few feet.

A man treading water was hanging onto the sharp angle of the overturned bow, his dark hair plastered to his forehead. "I was holding onto her. She just slipped away. I can't find her." He ducked under and Brain could make out his pale arms searching frantically beneath the surface.

He pulled his life jacket off and shoved it at the man. "Put this on."

He sensed the current pulling him to the right and figured it would be pulling on the woman in the same direction. Taking three powerful strokes in the direction it tugged he dove, reaching around through the murky water. He came up, filled his lungs, took another three strokes in the direction the current was flowing and dove again. Twice more he came up empty handed, his eyes stinging from the salt. He knew he wouldn't give up, even as fear of failing this person he didn't even know crept into the edges of his mind. He came up, took a deep breath and went down again.

He had lost count of his dives when his hand touched fabric. He swung around. She was bobbing up behind him from the side, her dark hair floating out from her pale face, nightmarish in the dim light. He kicked back, startled, his heart racing. She floated closer and he grabbed around her waist, pulling her to the surface, her body limp and unresisting. His head broke the water and he swore, flipping over so her face was clear. Even in the fading light she looked blue, especially around her lips. He bunched her hair in his fist and kicked, keeping her face up even though he was sure her lungs were filled with water.

Michael had pulled the man aboard the sailboat and was drifting down, ten yards out. He tossed the man-overboard sling and Brian caught it, wrapping it around the unconscious woman's chest and under her arms, then signaling. Michael pulled the limp body through the water. As her head and shoulders bumped against the hull he ran the line around a winch, hauling her up with the boom. The sling, caught under her arms, pushed the water out of her lungs as she was hoisted and she vomited it out against the side of the boat as she was hauled aboard. Brian, treading water, watched her struggle weakly as she was lowered onto the deck. Relief swept through him. She was alive.

The strengthening current had swept the boat past him during the rescue and in just this short time, it was quickly headed away. He started after, exhaustion pouring through his muscles. With the current's help he slowly made up the distance, stroking solidly in the frigid water, but the cold and the effort was taking its toll. His teeth chattered and he ground them together.

"Mind over matter, I've been through worse in Ranger School." He repeated it over and over, a mantra keeping time with his strokes.

He ploughed through the growing waves. Lifting his head to orient, he realized the current had now caught the little sailboat and was pulling her along faster than he was swimming. The vessel was slipping away from him. Michael was focused on the woman on the deck and Brian knew he should call out but didn't, grinding through the water as shivers, each bigger than the last, crawled up his spine. He would catch the boat, failure was not an option.

Time crawled by, marked by strokes and kicks. He looked up again and while the boat wasn't closer, at least he was keeping even. The water was black around him as the last bit of sunlight faded from the sky. An image of something big coming up from the depths below shot through his mind and made him falter. He shook his head and pushed on. He really had watched too many horror movies and letting his imagination run amok was not helping him win here. The grueling race dragged on as he fought his way forward in the deepening gloom. Finally exhaustion and the cold water caught up to him. He started to struggle, each stroke weaker than the last, until he slowed to a crawl. The boat drifted farther. He took a deep breath and set out again, fighting the pain. He thought about how ridiculous it would be to drown while he was saving a life. Kicking hard, he stroked forward, using every bit of energy he had left. The monsters in his mind told him it

11

wasn't enough. The spasms took over as he gulped for breath, stalling in the water.

Suddenly, a strong hand grabbed him, pulling him close. Michael's arm clamped around his chest and he hauled him through the water, kicking strongly. He had the sling wrapped around his waist, the free end still on the winch, and he powered to the back of the boat, shoving Brian up the swim step in front of him. Brian rolled into the cockpit and collapsed. Michael was there, his blue eyes reflecting Brian's, worry lines drawing his brows together. He wrapped a blanket around him. "Fuck you drowning. Not on my watch." At Brian's grin, he nodded and tousled his wet hair, like he used to do when Brian was little, and turned to the wheel.

Brian watched from a distance, his mind foggy, as Michael, dripping wet, put the boat into gear and swung it around, sending out a call for emergency services as he powered towards the marina. He checked on the women, dropped the sails, put out fenders and readied the dock lines. Halfway in, a coast guard dinghy approached and Michael slowed while they tied on and transferred the rescued couple. The man shook their hands with an earnest look. "If there is ever anything I can do for you, anything, I will." His friend nodded weakly from the deck of the dinghy and mouthed, "Thank you", as they sped away.

Brian was groggy and still shivering but the spasms had subsided. By the time the boat pulled up to the dock, he was sitting up. There was a crowd waiting, who had followed the rescue on the radio, and they cheered as the boat slid into the slip. They helped handle the lines and got them tied up safely. Michael unloaded their gear and they walked slowly to the café at the top of the dock. Seated under the heat lamps along the waterfront, Michael ordered large, hot chocolates. By the third round, Brian's color had returned, and Michael mixed in a little rum from a flask he had tucked into his jacket.

Brian raised his mug. "To saving lives." Michael clinked his to it. Brian took a drink. "I didn't get her name, the girl. How can I check to see if she made it?"

"It's Katie Walsh, and the man who was with her was Joshua Dunn. She works production for Channel 2 in San Francisco. She was just down here visiting. I'll catch up with her in a couple days and make sure she is alright."

"Guess I was kind of out of it." Brian said. The warmth of the rum spread through his stomach pleasantly.

"Dude, you saved that woman's life. I don't know if I would have kept diving like that."

Brian smiled at the praise, it meant a lot coming from his idol. "Ya, well, I wouldn't be here if you hadn't have come in after me. So right back at you."

Michael's face turned serious. "I told you I will always be there for you Brian. Always."

"Dipshit." Brian smiled, breaking the tension.

"Dork." Michael laughed.

The Assassin
September 30

It was late afternoon on a dusty, fall day in San Diego. The driver of the tan, Toyota Camry kept his windows up and the air-conditioning on high as he drove slowly around the community center parking lot. He pulled out and a block down made a U-turn, guiding the car into an opening along the curb. He leaned his head against the back of the seat, occasionally taking a sip of water from a metal thermos, casually eyeing the traffic as it flowed by and the last cars left the center for the day. He turned his head away when the few pedestrians strode by.

Evening approached and the sunlight faded. He checked his watch, the luminescent dial pointing to seven-twenty. Over the next half-hour, the community center began to fill again. Cars pulled through the entry and lined up in spaces, dispelling occupants, singly and in groups of two, three or more, who moved inside. He noted the dark Suburban as it entered and pulled around to the back, out of his line of site. The Town Hall meeting started at eight; everything looked to be on schedule. He kept up the vigil, head leaned back, eyes half closed.

As expected, thirty minutes after eight, three black tactical vehicles arrived; hulking, box trucks, shiny under the streetlamps, with ICE emblazoned across their sides. A transport bus arrived immediately after and parked a little farther down the street, away from the driver watching in the Camry. Agents in tactical gear with ICE stamped large across their backs stepped out of the vehicles. Setting up orange cones to control the entrance lane, they took positions blocking the exit and then waited for the Town Hall meeting to end.

The driver counted out ten more minutes, opened his door and slid out of the car, closing it quietly behind him. Hugging the shadows, dressed in black gear similar to the agents at the entrance, he moved up the sidewalk to the far edge of the community center lot. It was bounded by bushy oleander. He stepped through, well away from the ICE team at the entrance. Easing around the perimeter, he avoided the feeble glow from the streetlights, until he was positioned thirty yards out and perpendicular to the ICE teams. He stepped back into the hedge and eased the Sig P320 in its holster under his shoulder. It was the same model of handgun the ICE agents carried, although his was equipped with a scope for tonight's mission.

He checked his angles of sight and then relaxed, waiting quietly for his quarry.

Congressman Silva

Congressman Carlos Silva left through the back door of the community center and headed to his Suburban. The air was hot and still. The back lot was mostly empty of cars with the last few stragglers from tonight's meeting edging slowly around the building, their taillights making a red snake across the pavement.

"Sir, do you really think a workable solution is possible after the heavy-handed actions of the ICE agents this past week in San Diego?" John Fields, a young, independent reporter who showed up regularly at Carlos' events, trailed him to his vehicle. He had his cell phone out, videotaping the conversation.

Carlos, his black hair shot through with grey, was in a navy suit and red tie. He was tired after a long day at the office and then the meeting here tonight. He just wanted to get home to a late dinner and the love of his life, Rose. As he turned he forced himself to stand up straight though; reporters deserved respect and consideration. He knew their job was a vital piece of democracy. He put a smile on his face. "There has to be John. There is so much anger. The communities here are set to go off, they are just waiting for a spark. If we don't start talking we could end up with California seceding and a civil war." He reached for his door, pulled it open and the interior lights came on, spilling across his compact figure.

"Secession? Civil war?"

Turning back, Carlos set his shoulders. "Look around you, John. These people's great-grandfathers settled this land. Their families have lived in California since before it became a part of the Union. They are proud Americans." He emphasized each point with his hands.

16

"Is bringing in the military and hiding that fact, which is an illegal act, and targeting every person who walks out of a church on a Sunday in a Hispanic neighborhood acceptable? Roughing them up because they don't happen to have identification on them other than a driver's license and holding them all for hours in the sun? Or requiring passports from grandmothers, who were born five miles from here, before they can go home, is that what our country should be doing?"

John looked at him seriously. Carlos liked this one, had talked with him multiple times. "Sir, the opposition would say that if we didn't have a flood of humanity crossing our borders, taking our jobs, and using our welfare resources, this wouldn't be necessary. We need to abide by the laws of this country, including following legal immigration avenues. Checking every person who looks Hispanic is the only option."

The Congressman focused on taking a calming breath as Rose always pushed him to do, but as he exhaled, the calm evaporated. "In their hunt for illegal immigrants, our government has crossed the line. There is now a strong push for California to secede. That is a desperate choice, but California is being backed into a corner where desperate choices are all that will be left. I am trying to build bridges so that dialogue can happen before there is nothing left to say."

He climbed in, pushed the start button and the truck turned over, settling into a loud purr. He felt the anger building up. This whole situation and the relentless push by some in power to vilify every minority was maddening. He was left dealing with the human costs of their political maneuverings in DC. "Let me ask you this, John, Do you have your passport on you right now? Your social security card? Have you personally verified your birth certificate is valid?"

John looked confused.

"I didn't think so. That is what every person with brown skin has to think about whether they are at work, at home and even at church. You don't understand because you don't have to face the fear of randomly having to fight to prove you are a US citizen every minute of every day and knowing if they don't believe you, even if you legally belong here, you might be sent away without even a trial." Carlos took another deep breath. "So yes, I do think secession and civil war are just an incident away." He looked into John's face. "Are we done here?" He was letting his exhaustion get the better of him. This reporter didn't deserve his ire.

"Thank you Congressman Silva. I appreciate your comments, and your honesty." John smiled and reaching out, awkwardly shook Carlos's hand across the steering wheel. Carlos watched the young man walk to his car as he pulled the Suburban door shut. He reached for the antacids in the center consol. Rose kept telling him he needed to stop letting the shit get to him. She was right. Letting off the brake, he put the truck into gear and joined the line meandering out of the lot.

Thirty minutes later, after several calls to staff and one to Rose, he focused on his surroundings; he hadn't moved more than one or two car lengths since he joined the line. He sighed, put the Suburban into park and climbed down. It was muggy hot. Pulling off his suit jacket and tie, he threw them into the passenger seat and closed the door. He noticed the reporter, waiting one car back, hop out, trailing him. Heading around the corner of the building, he passed families in cars waiting like he had been, some having conversations behind the rolled up windows and others illuminated by the glow of cell phone screens.

In the main lot, there was a crush of cars, lines of stationary tail lights and headlights winding up and down the aisles. There had been a good turnout for the meeting tonight; people were scared and angry with the increased ICE raids. Carlos walked by car after car as he threaded his way to the entrance. As he passed, a door opened and then another.

"Good evening, Congressman." A small man in a polo shirt, black hair neatly combed to the side, joined him. Another man, salt and pepper hair at his temples, nodded. A third, in jeans with a belt buckle glinting in the lights, joined, then a fourth and fifth and more, until Carlos had a crowd of Hispanic faces quietly following behind, backing him up as he made his way through the lanes and over the meridians.

When he finally cleared the hedges, he saw what was unfolding and froze. His constituents formed around him, all bathed in the half-light of the widely spaced light poles. The entrance to the community center was chaos, blocked by dozens of ICE agents dressed in full combat gear, batons held across their chests. A dozen more were walking between vehicles, leaning in windows, looking at paperwork with small flashlights, and motioning occupants to move forward or to get out. People pulled from cars stood off to the side, clutching children who looked on with big eyes. The reporter held his cell phone up, catching it all on video.

"Oh, hell no!" Carlos strode forward. He forgot about the following crowd and reached for the first agent he came to, grabbing his arm as he leaned in a car window. "What is going on here?"

The agent jumped and spun towards him, half drawing the firearm at his waist. "Sir, back up please."

"Why are you detaining these people? What right do you have?"

The agent kept his hand on his weapon. "Sir, I said back up."

"Who is in charge here? Who authorized a raid at my Town Hall meeting? How did this happen?" Carlos looked at his name badge. "Agent Cummings."

Agent Cummings looked at Carlos and scanned the crowd, growing as people left their cars. He took a step back, his left hand keying a radio on his shoulder, his right still gripping his firearm.

Carlos saw panic in the agent's eyes. He spun to face his constituents, raising his hands and lowering them, palms down. "Let's keep this civil, gentlemen. I will not condone violence. I will do everything I can to get anyone they detain released. You have my word. Let's just keep calm."

At a tingling in his spine; a premonition, he spun back. Cummings pistol was pointed at his chest. Agents rushed towards them from the entrance. It all came together in slow motion; the fear in the agent's eyes, the angry rumble of the crowd around him, the men at his back surging forward. He saw panic flow across the agent's face as he sighted down his weapon.

"Freeze!"

Carlos took a step back, raising his arms as though to ward off the bullets, the crowd pushing up behind him. He watched it unfold in horror, slowly, seconds drawing out as inevitability pressed its heavy hand against free will, a single, stretched-out breath. Relief surged through him as Cummings' eyes softened, the barrel shifting down.

Two shots hammered out from the right, clear, sharp and loud. Time leaped back to full speed in the heartbeat of sound. Carlos felt himself slammed to the left and was toppling in an awkward fall, the hard blacktop suddenly against his cheek, still warm from the afternoon sun. He heard screaming from a distance, and more shots, and panic around him.

He wanted to say something to stop it all. He struggled to draw a breath. Rose came to mind; he wanted to tell her he loved her. He tried to open his eyes. He couldn't move his legs. His heart was racing, pumping a crazy, accelerated dance; he was suddenly terrified. The blackness closed around him with a heavy weight, a deep calm settling in. He was floating. From a distance his mom called. "Carlos, Carlos, come in for dinner."

The confrontation and the Town Hall meeting slipped away. He slid back through time. He was running home, the lawns familiar under his bare feet, the screen door creaking in just the right way as he threw it open.

His mom, smelling of vanilla and cinnamon, wrapped him in her arms and kissed the top of his head. He marveled at how long it had been since he last hugged her. He smiled and squeezed tightly. He was home.

Justin

Lieutenant Justin Johnson watched the altercation between the Congressman and Agent Cummings from the entrance to the Community Center. Fifteen Rangers stood with batons held across their chests surrounding him. They had been working with the ICE agents for several months, mostly as human traffic cones; standing on the sidelines. It wasn't a bad gig so far, hanging in San Diego where the weather and the girls were happy and beautiful, and it never seemed to get too hot or too cold. It was so unlike the Middle East, where extremes, in weather and women, seemed to be magnified, like looking at a harvest moon on an August night. Aside from the actual work they were doing; separating families and hauling people in, which he relegated to a back corner of his mind as he did whenever he was in a conflict zone, because if you really ever thought about the people you might have to shoot, you couldn't do it, it was damn near perfect mission to be assigned to.

He saw Special Agent in Charge, Dan Mobury open the door of the ICE vehicle, a big, boxy, black, cargo truck, and step to the ground. Justin looked away. The mission was good so far, excepting for Mobury, who managed to ridicule and berate most every person he came into contact with, unless they stood higher on the food chain. They had all learned to dodge him whenever possible and the Cap'n managed to insert himself between Mobury and the team whenever things got out of hand. He wasn't here now though, Justin was in command, and he sent a prayer heavenward that the man would drop over from a heart attack before he found something to deride their team for, forcing Justin to intervene. He wasn't nearly as good at the negotiating as the Cap'n was and would probably end up in the brig if it came down to a confrontation. Mobury didn't like him and he felt nothing but disgust for the bootlicker.

He saw Agent Cummings draw his weapon on Congressman Silva and Justin's focus lasered in as adrenaline shot through his veins. He made eye contact with the other Rangers under his command as the confrontation escalated. At his nod, they started forward to assist. Two shots rang out and Justin's eyes swiveled to the bushes framing the parking lot, sure the shots had originated there. He scanned them closely looking for movement but they were at the very edge of the pools of light and it was impossible to pick anything out. He signaled and two Rangers, although weaponless, peeled off to investigate. The congressman had been thrown sideways and was prone on the pavement. The crowd surged towards the ICE agents, who began to fire.

"Move, now."

His team surged together in a wedge, reaching Agent Cummings as he was shoved to the ground, his weapon snatched from his hands. They pushed back at the mob, hauling the agent out by his arm and retreating a dozen feet as Justin launched a tear gas canister into the space. Two agents opposite them on the other side of the car fought their way towards the entrance. One fired his Sig point-blank into an elderly woman's torso.

"God damn it, put that weapon away!" His order easily carried and the agent, startled, lowered the muzzle.

Justin's team pushed around the hood of the sedan and engulfed both the agents inside the wedge with Cummings, backing up slowly, batons held across their chests. The energy of the mob changed from anger to fear. They wavered and started to run, leaving Justin facing a small group defiantly guarding the body of the Congressman. He had the Rangers, with the ICE agents in their center, back away.

"Any injuries?" Justin looked to his first sergeant.

"Smith has a possible broken arm and Warstein smashed his hand but nothing life threatening."

Justin nodded. The action was done, it was time for the clean-up. "Murphy and Deeves, back up Paulson and Greggory, see if you can figure out where those first shots came from. Sanchez and Bellows, run a perimeter, make sure nothing else is out there. Everyone else, let's get these wounded civilians taken care of. Medics are on the way. Let's get as many evacuated to the street as we can. Remember team, you do not have weapons so do not engage if you see anything. Report back immediately."

Heads nodded and his team deployed. Justin sighed. This was fucked. It looked like the Congressman was done for good and other bodies were down as well. Going to the elderly woman, he gently rolled her over. The bullet entered her upper chest and deep, black blood was surging through the tattered remains of her dress. She was crying softly. "Shit." He put the heel of his hand over the wound and leaned in. She looked like she could be his grandmother. He felt the tears sting his eyes. This was just wrong. They shouldn't be here and this never should have happened.

Special Agent Mobury startled him. "Goddamn it, Lieutenant, what the hell did your soldiers do?" His voice was shrill.

Justin flinched and the woman cried out. He applied more pressure, afraid to move again, afraid he would lose her if he did. Anger surged through him. "Sir, I will report after medics arrive."

"Goddamn you will, stand up and tell me what the hell happened." The timber changed, dropping an octave.

"Sir, this civilian's life is in danger. I will not stop." Justin stared at the blood seeping onto the pavement, refusing to meet Mobury's eyes, knowing if he did, he wouldn't be able to control the rage coursing through his body. Months of suppressing his reactions in the face of Mobury's ridicule for the sake of professionalism had built up. Justin always ran on a tight fuse, close to explosion, and now he was a hair's breadth away.

Agent Mobury yanked his Sig out and shoved the cold barrel against Justin's temple. His voice was ice. "Nobody ignores me. I can pull this trigger right here and you will just be another dead body tonight that no one questions. Now get the hell up."

Justin froze and a deadly fire entered his eyes. The familiar detachment settled óver his thoughts; he would lunge up, dislodging the weapon, sweep his left foot, tripping Mobury and bringing him down then a quick thrust to his windpipe would finish him, and damn the consequences. He felt more than saw Ortez and Hansen push forwards. Hansen, her slender hand pale against Justin's jacket, grabbed his arm, hauling him up and away before he could move on his plan. He fought as they shoved him towards the community center. Special Agent Mobury, anger suffusing his face, watched them, the gun angled at the ground. He shook his head and moved back towards the street. Justin shrugged the two off and then started back towards the woman. Ortez stepped in front of him. "Lieutenant, don't. That man is bat-shit crazy, he will shoot you."

Justin glared at Ortiz, took a deep breath and the fire receded from his eyes. He nodded and turned back. "Rally the team and pull back against the community center. Bring everyone in except for the perimeters."

The sirens grew closer.

Brian

Brian drove as aggressively as he dared through the streets, watching his GPS for the upcoming turn. He and his team had been involved in dozens of raids over the preceding ten weeks and he was familiar with the grid of San Diego. He sped through the back roads. It was clear from the little he heard from Justin that events had gone to shit. He needed to get to the community center before the press did and get his team clear to keep them safe.

Traffic was light, he was there in minutes. As he swung around the corner, ambulances and police cars blocked the street, parked haphazardly across lanes and sidewalks. He parked and moved quickly through the crowd, flashing his military ID. In the chaos no one questioned it.

Clearing the ring of emergency vehicles, it was like the aftermath of a battle in the streets of Afghanistan. Flares created a smoky, crimson light with ambulance lights flashing off the trees and buildings. Medics rushed around performing triage, low to the ground. The sharp smell of tear gas stung his eyes. Trash littered the street. He abruptly realized that some of it wasn't trash, but bodies, huddled over like old piles of discarded clothes. The wail of the sirens covered up sounds of people groaning, of children's terrified cries. He was back in hell.

Peering closely at every face, he hunted for ICE uniforms or anyone he recognized. It was hard in the eerie light. Stepping across the sidewalk he moved into the parking lot and was approached by one of his soldiers in black, blending in with the night around them.

"Sir, a temporary command post has been established over here." He led the way off into the shadows.

The parking lot was filled with cars, lined up in the aisles where their owners had abandoned them; in neat rows, lights on and doors hanging open. A body was sprawled on the pavement; the man's white shirt, soaked black with blood, standing out starkly, his slacks and head fading into the blacktop. He was surrounded by a cadre of men, faces dark in the dim glow from the light poles, body language aggressive. Brian left them alone.

He found his soldiers in a defensive position against the wall of the community center between the circles of illumination. A perimeter with sentries was set and he recognized the low whistle meaning 'friendly contact approaches' as he crossed between cars. He closed in, assessing the situation. His soldiers had removed themselves from the authority of the ICE agents and were operating as a separate unit.

"Lieutenant Johnson, report." He cracked the order, loud and sharp. He had seen troops when the mission turned ugly. His soldiers needed to see someone was in control; someone who cared. The set of shoulders eased. Faces cleared.

Justin, formality replaced between them, stepped forward. "Sir, twenty present and accounted for, two wounded. No dead." He stopped, looking down. "Sir, they refused to let us help the civilians."

"What happened here?" Brian phrased it as an order, not a question. Justin was hanging on by a thread.

Justin did a quick recap, standing stiff. He pointed to the group surrounding Congressman Carlos Silva. "Those civilians have stood over the body since the altercation. We did not intervene. We have secured the area and I have troops in a one block perimeter, operating silently."

27

"Thank you, Lieutenant." Brian looked over his team. Their stony expressions masked the nightmare going on inside their heads. He was feeling it too. This was too much like Afghanistan but it was here at home. They were warriors who kept America safe from enemies but this was not an enemy surrounding them. They were broken, hurt citizens who these soldiers had taken an oath to protect.

He considered finding Special Agent Mobury and then discarded the idea. His duty was the safety and security of his team. The arrival of news vans, with cameramen climbing out and antenna arrays rising from the roofs, settled it.

It would be hours before the ICE vehicles they arrived in were cleared. With few alternatives, Brian sent his team off in squads, in different directions, with instructions to remove all ICE identifiers and stick to the shadows. Collecting up the two that were injured, he walked them back out to his car. A reporter called out to him, chasing along with a microphone. Brian ignored him. They climbed into the car and he flipped it around and sped off.

At the warehouse, Brian called his commander at Fort Drum after sending his soldiers back to the hotel. He was in unfamiliar territory. During and after actions in Iraq and Afghanistan, he had a base to return to. There were teams of soldiers to help assess the situation and relay commands. Here he was alone. He straddled a chair and pulled out his cell phone, thumbing through texts. He called Michael and ended up leaving a message when it rang and rang. He flipped the chair around and stretched his legs out, leaning back. He considered driving back over to see how the situation was developing. After an hour, he unwound his long legs from under the table and stood, stretching his arms over his head and rolling his shoulders. He started pacing up and down the long length of the warehouse.

There was a commotion and the bay doors rolled up. The incident vehicles pulled into the space, one behind the other, fanning out and pulling to a stop. The ICE team spilled out, pulling gear and stowing it on racks. It was a subdued group. Talk was short and to the point.

Brian steeled himself as Agent Mobury came around the back of the truck. "Sir."

Agent Mobury stopped, glaring around the situation room. "Where the hell are your soldiers, Captain Phillips?"

"All present and accounted for, Sir, and released from duty." Brian bit back the rest of his reply. There was no benefit in calling out his commander's behavior towards Justin at this point. He was furious that this man threatened one of his men though and his posture remained stiff.

"Released? Well I'll be god-damned, released? We had a situational fuck up out there Captain, and you sent your little pandy-asses off to bed. Who in the god-damn hell gave you the authority to release them to their comfy, hotel rooms?"

"Sir?" Brian was hedging. There was no way in hell he would have let his troops be in the same space as this man again tonight. He had released them on purpose, clearing them before this shit-show came down.

"Sir, Sir? Get the hell out of my sight. If I wasn't saddled with your army brats this whole damn thing would have turned out differently. My team is professional. Your guys lost their shit and attacked civilians."

Red crept up Brian's face, uncontrollable, blending into his auburn hair as it reached his forehead, the only outward indication of his anger.

Mobury stood in Brian's space, glaring up, inches from his chest. "If I don't come up with a way to cover this, I'll be a fucking janitor in the detainment facility and all for a bunch of army shits that can't get a job in the real world and illegal scum who don't belong in this country anyway. I don't want to see your sorry asses anywhere near my facility, not ever again."

Agent Mobury tried to shove him aside and stomp past. Brian, although he felt childish doing it, held his ground, forcing Mobury to step around. Bending down, Brian picked up his bag and slowly walked for the bay doors, his shoulders tight.

"Captain Phillips?" Agent Cummings stepped in front of him and started back as Brian jerked his ice-blue eyes towards him.

"What is it Agent Cummings?" Brian reined his anger in. Agent Cummings was one of the few here who were decent. He was professional and went out of his way to be kind to the people they detained. It wasn't fair to blast him with the residual fury. That belonged to Mobury.

"I want to apologize, he is wrong. Your team is not responsible. They have been solid back-up all through the last few months and we appreciate all you guys have done for us. I was also hoping you could thank your team for pulling me out today. They saved my life."

Brian nodded his head slightly and started for the door again, fury still rippling through his gait.

"I'll make sure the truth is in my report." Cummings trailed Brian to the door.

It was a little after one when Brian stepped into his hotel room, peeled off his clothes and climbed into a scalding shower. The smell of tear gas lingered on his skin even after he scrubbed several times with the little bars of complimentary soap. He flipped on the TV, watching the evening unfold again and again. A lot of airtime was devoted to ICE and their mission to deport either undocumented workers if it was a liberal commentator or illegal aliens if they were conservative. They delved into Carlos Silva's background and dissected his voting record. They interviewed crying witnesses and took opinions from people passing by who backed up the commentator's position.

Brian was disgusted with the way it was all played for best advantage, depending on how they wanted to sway opinion. The horrors of war felt cleaner to him than the blatant manipulation did here in his own country. He didn't turn it off though and sat glued to the screen, flipping back and forth. He kept repeating to himself, "At least no one is mentioning Army Rangers," and then stopped. That was trivial when people had died.

He received a call from his commander at two-forty-five. The Army was breaking the connection with ICE and bringing his Company home by platoon, as they had sent them out two months earlier; in secret. They would start the first flights out in three hours and everyone would be gone by the end of day. Brian started waking up his soldiers and then packed his kit. He was angry and frustrated, he hoped he would never see Agent Mobury again and he was glad to walk away.

Mobury

Special Agent in Charge Dan Mobury waited for the line to connect. The voice that answered was butter over steel. "What do you need, Agent Mobury?"

"Mr. Capardi? It's about Captain Phillips. I want him taken down. That arrogant bastard messed it all up. I want him to pay."

"That is not the way I heard it Mobury. Seems your guys were a little trigger happy. The Captain is not your problem, we will handle him. You have a mess to clean up."

Dan paced the small confines of his office. "I did what you said. I followed your orders. I'm not going down without taking you, you understand me?"

"Agent Mobury, I would be very careful who you threaten. I am not some city cop you can bully by raising your voice. There will be another project soon. Clean up your shit and be ready." The line went dead.

Dan slammed the phone into its cradle, a chill crawling up his spine at the icy tone of the voice.

Brian

Brian sprawled in a chair in the Fort Drum Officers Club in upstate New York. He had pulled his soldiers out of California safely, leaving San Diego with the last platoon. His Company were all back on base, arguing with each other endlessly. There wasn't anything he could do to make it better so he made his reports, submitted leave papers, walked into a bar in town and started drinking. That was three days ago. Today, he had talked Justin into joining him. Justin wasn't willing to spend the extra money to go off base so they were on round four or five in the Army's version of a nightclub.

He dropped his elbow onto the table and leaned his head against his hand. Justin plopped another round of beers down, the foam slopping over and spreading across the wood-grained plastic. Brian dragged his finger around in it, making patterns.

"Hey, that guy over there is staring at me, I think he has a thing for Rangers."

Brian dragged his eyes sideways. There were about a dozen other officers in the place. He couldn't tell who Justin was talking about. They all seemed to be doing their own thing, singly or in small groups. "I don't want to fight, dude. You're on your own if you start shit."

He picked up the beer in front of him and drank it down. He watched a small bit of foam settle into the bottom of the glass. The room was getting soft around the edges, which was fine by Brian. It was an Army-ugly box with fluorescent lighting and a vast array of round, faux-wood tables with orange metal chairs from somewhere back in the seventies. Music was cranking out of a pair of speakers hung from the ceiling and a lighted ball spun colors around the room. It felt like an after-school dance in the cafeteria, but with beer. Brian smiled.

Justin was sitting across from him now, fidgeting with the knife he always carried on his belt. Brian knew the signs, Justin had held in his anger until they were through the mission. Now he was ready to unwind on someone. Brian was feeling it too. Throwing a few punches sounded good. Maybe it would erase the sick feeling he had in his gut. This hadn't been like Iraq and having it go sideways. This was a mission in secret, here in America, under supervisors who weren't soldiers. It had gone to shit; US citizens had died. Now he and his team carried the shame of that. It felt dirty. He made his way over to the bar and ordered another round.

The incident was a media storm he couldn't get away from. Every time he turned on a screen, they were dragging the event around and pointing fingers. There was a video being played over and over from the reporter's cell phone. Brian watched it carefully, worried, but luckily you couldn't really pick any of his soldiers out in the darkness and chaos. No faces, except his own, and that was just a brief glance when he was walking by the Congressman at the end. No one seemed to have picked up on it.

Brian watched Justin as he waited. He knew he should talk him down but right now, he was halfway hoping he'd get in a fight. Brian shook his head to clear it. That was the beer talking.

At a look from one of the officers, Justin launched himself from the table with a roar, the chair skidding sideways as he barreled towards the bar. Brian had been paying attention to Justin's body language and was expecting it. He reacted, intercepting Justin a pace away, his longer reach keeping Justin's swing from connecting. He shoved a flat hand against the officer's chest, who was leaning forward aggressively, and held him back, looking from face to face.

"Damn it. Enough!"

He felt the pressure ease against both his hands as Justin and the officer backed down. He spun Justin and shoved him towards the door, maintaining eye contact with the other officer as they left. The bartender nodded to Brian and set the beers he had pulled back behind the bar. They hit the door and emerged into a New England fall rain. It fit Brian's mood. He heard his dad's voice, the Commander's voice, in his head with a hint of disdain in it. "Feeling sorry for yourself isn't going to get the job done boy, suck it up and finish."

"Fuck you, Dad," he said.

Justin looked over at him. "What?"

Brian kept walking. There was no fucking way he was going to let his Dad look down on him. He would exceed the low expectations the great Colonel Phillips had of his second son.

They walked into the cold afternoon. Brian knew the right choice was to go home and sleep this off. The sleeting rain made it easy. He steered Justin towards the barracks.

John

John Fields, the reporter from the Town Hall meeting, sat in sweats on the couch, his laptop on the coffee table in front of him, brown hair pulled back in a ponytail, beard long but neatly trimmed. He was surrounded by toddler toys. As he bent to type, a small, stuffed dolphin sailed from the playpen, hitting him on the chin. His daughter Amy, thirteen months and already an expert shot, giggled and bounced up and down, her bright eyes disappearing and reappearing over the playpen lip she was holding onto. Without looking up, John grabbed it and tossed it back, making her squeal. Her little head and hands disappeared as she went to retrieve it.

"Thank you for making me breakfast." Blanca stepped out of their small kitchen, her long, black hair twisted up into a knot on the back of her head. She was wearing a tan business suit with a pink blouse, her skirt hitting just at her knees.

"You look nice," he said.

She smiled. "But do I look like someone you would take seriously?"

He caught her hand, pulling her down to him. "Yes, Baby. You look powerful. You look strong. You look like someone everyone will listen to." He kissed her. "You are going to do great." She stood back up. Amy made kissing noises from her playpen. They both smiled.

"This is a group of powerful women. What if they won't listen to me? What if they don't understand."

"Believe in yourself. You are Blanca Isabella Perez Ortega, you are as worthy as any of them. You will be convincing."

She nodded, the smile fading. "I have to be. Without additional funding I'm not sure if we can get the secession petition on the ballot. We only have a third of the signatures we need with just a few weeks left." She bent over and kissed Amy's head.

"Congressman Silva was Latino. People are not getting upset because they don't see him as American. I will do what I can," she made a face at Amy, "for our baby girl, so she has a better place to grow up in."

"You will get the signatures. The country needs to have the conversation. There are so many things wrong that need to be addressed that are being ignored by Washington. Just getting it on a ballot will get people thinking." He caught the dolphin and tossed it back to Amy, who was giggling. "I will help. You know I have to stay neutral though, for our future. I just need one break to get on with one of the networks and we can afford to send Amy to college."

Collecting up her purse and car keys, Blanca went to the door. "Wish me luck?"

John laughed. "Okay, but you won't need it. You've got this."

She took a deep breath and stepped out the door. John watched it close. He was so proud of her passion. He promised himself that once he got his break he would figure out a way to help her reach her goals. Amy gurgled and he turned to her, playing happily. He hoped he could live up to both their expectations.

He had been asked by Carlos's wife Rose to speak at the public service they were holding for the Congressman on Saturday. Rose knew he had admired both the man and the politician, something of a rarity from reporters covering the local political scene. He wanted to get this just right.

The dolphin hit him in the leg this time. He picked it up, stood and scooped Amy up, swinging her around as she squealed, then hugged her tight. Her hair smelled of baby shampoo and he breathed deeply, the events of that night playing through his mind. Tears stung the back of his eyes at the thought of how quickly her or his life could be taken away. He couldn't seem to distance himself from the sounds, and the smells, and the fear. A few minutes of chaos and panic, shots fired, and a man he had just been talking with lay dead along with three others. It could have been him except for luck. Amy wriggled, done with being confined, and he set her back gently into the pen, grabbing more toys off the couch and dropping them next to her.

He played the video again of his last conversation with Congressman Silva. Carlos' shoulders took up the screen and then he was turning around, his face filling the camera, alive and strong. "Tell me John, is bringing in the military and hiding that fact, which is an illegal act, and targeting every person who walks out of a church on a Sunday in a Hispanic neighborhood, acceptable?"

John hit the pause button. What was Carlos talking about? What military? Damn it, why hadn't he picked up on that when he could still ask the question? He thought about everything he had witnessed, how it all played out. He pulled up the other video, the one of the shooting, skipping through to right after the shots were fired. He watched it through three times, paying close attention to the interaction of the ICE agents. He forwarded to the end of the video when a clear shot of Brian's face came in to view and paused it again.

"Just exactly who are you? And who do you really work for?" Amy giggled and threw the dolphin at him again. He tossed it back, picked up the phone and started making calls.

Dusty

Colonel Scott Dustin Phillips, known as Dusty to his friends, sat comfortably on his surfboard, feet dangling in the warm, salty water, the tide lifting and lowering him in lazy successions. In his early-fifties, he wore his decades of military deployments well. The gray matt of chest hair covered iron. Faint lines etched across his forehead and at the corners of his pale blue eyes that pierced out of his weathered face. Army life had burned off the softness somewhere in his past. He looked as if the brutal sun had sucked it out and left the core of what he was for the world to see; a hard, powerful man who knew how to make tough decisions and then live with them.

There was no awkwardness as he waited on a board in the Pacific Ocean surrounded by kids less than half his age. He had given up questioning his abilities a long time past. He would master surfing as he had mastered everything else or he wouldn't be out here in the first place.

His surfing instructor Sabine, a willowy model from the Ukraine, rode her board next to him, setting up for her next wave. She talked her way through the process for him, giving him the details in a husky, James-Bond-girl accent that stirred his gut. The wave rose up behind her and paddling quickly, she popped up in a single, graceful motion. Stretching out her arms she sailed by him and rode the crest easily into the beach, stepping off her board in knee deep water and turning to wave back at him.

"That was a beautiful sight." Her partner Jessie, riding a board on his other side, called out. Jessie wore her white-blond hair cropped military short and had skin so pale sit looked almost translucent in the bright sun. She was wearing a long-sleeve rash guard, boy shorts and had a smudge of white across her nose, keeping the fierce sun from blistering her skin. She looked like she was about thirteen to Dusty, although he knew she had been running the surf shop with Sabine for years now so had to be much older. They all looked like kids to him anymore.

Dusty nodded. It was indeed a beautiful site, watching Sabine tame a wave of such power with such little effort and such joy.

"You're up," Jessie called.

This was about the twentieth wave he had tried today but he looked back over his shoulder and started counting the sets anyway, waiting for the next big wave to try again. He wasn't the kind of man who gave up easily and he was going to beat this activity into submission before he was done with it. By the end of the afternoon, while he hadn't yet mastered surfing, he felt he had at least made progress.

As the fiery ball of the sun quickly dropped behind the edge of the ocean and the sky and waves lit up in burnt orange, Dusty paddled his board up to his trawler at anchor off the beach of Punta de Mita on the West Coast of Mexico, and climbed aboard, his muscles screaming in protest. Rinsing off on deck he lashed his board securely against the rail, covering it with its tarp so the tropical sun couldn't damage the fiberglass between lessons. He dried off and hung the towel and his swim trunks up to dry. Carefully coiling the hose, he padded over to the cabin door as the first stars emerged from the soft purple of dusk. A pair of swallows darted around the boat and he stopped, naked in the warm evening breeze, letting the moment settle over him.

Physically, he was bruised and battered and laced with a muscle exhaustion that felt deeply satisfying. He had the usual tug on his heart though. While this was a good life, he often felt as if he was missing something important. This dream had carried him through the nightmares of war, always present in sunbathed detail when he closed his eyes, but now he dared to admit the reality of retirement on a boat wasn't as fulfilling as he had imagined. It had only been a few years since he had taken off his uniform for the last time, bought their lovely, 40-foot trawler, *Ealu*, and moved aboard. Already he was wondering what was next. He felt a stab of guilt for not being happy. He reached out and pushed the door open.

Jillian looked up, her freckled face backlit from the computer screen. "How'd it go?"

The room had gone dark around her and the glow of electronics was a soft halo surrounding her hair. Dusty smiled. She still was beautiful, twenty-nine years after they held hands on a rainy Saturday, under a makeshift canopy of umbrellas while she laughed at the disaster their wedding had become, promising to love him through it all. She had kept that promise and he loved her even more now, after all the years of her standing behind him, strong and resilient, holding their family together. He relied on that.

"Well, it was at least spectacular. I'm fairly good at falling. Sabine said that by the end of the next lesson I'd be 'solid' but I think the only thing solid about my surfing will be the sand I keep hitting." He lifted up his arm and showed her the rash running from his shoulder to his hip.

"Ouch, poor baby." She kissed her finger and touched it to his skin. It was icy cold and sent goosebumps across his chest. Desire hit him hard, the result of a long, physical day. He snagged her hand and pulled her up, smashing her against his naked length as she laughed. Bending, he kissed her soft lips, sliding his hands across her until she kissed him back passionately, her fingers twining in his hair.

He slid to his knees and unbuttoned her shorts, easing them down her hips, kissing her bare skin as she pulled her shirt over her head, her breasts falling out, nipples hard. Teasing her with soft breaths until she wriggled, they fell onto the salon couch. He took his time, caressing her favorite places, watching her face as she slipped into that place where she needed him inside her. He slid in and built the rhythm slowly. He knew her, understood her body. He brought her along with him and kept his thrusts just slow enough to keep himself from coming until she was there, her body rippling with spasms and then he couldn't hold on any longer, and let himself go, slamming against her, hard and fast, until they both came together. He kept thrusting slowly as he melted, sending jolts through her, making her gasp, until he collapsed next to her and she kissed his chest softly, holding tight on the narrow cushions.

"Are you hungry?"

"Starving"

She untangled, pulling her t-shirt over her head, and headed into the bathroom. He heard the automatic toilet flush and the water pump run. Stepping back into the galley, she started pulling things out of the fridge. Dusty lay still, watching her.

"I got an email from Madison today. She seems to be happy back at the Academy. She is teaching two classes under the supervision of a professor and then working on a project with him the rest of the time."

It was like he could visibly see the walls going up again after the soft vulnerability they had shared. The space between them expanded. Dusty sighed and rolled off the couch. He turned lights on and grabbed a pair of shorts, balancing against the doorway as he pulled them on. "She should have pushed for a field position; teaching this soon is a dead end for her military career. I told her I would make a few phone calls to get her onto a good career path. Maybe I will still make those calls and get her re-assigned."

Jillian looked over at him for a minute. She went back to the fridge. Dusty waited. She usually said what was on her mind if he waited.

"Well, I'm sure you'll do what's best." She paused. "Would you please talk to her first though?"

"Yes, I'll talk to her. She is just so hard to get a hold of. I hear from her about once a year." He didn't want to talk about the kids, he wanted to hold on to their moment a little longer.

Jillian chopped an onion, throwing it into a pan. "I know, but just let her know what you are doing before, ok?"

He gave up, nodded and smiled as he watched her cook. Jillian had spent the last thirty years making dinner for him, their three kids, as well as their friends, plus various houseguests and any of his soldiers that had needed her nurturing for a time. She didn't know how to prepare food for less than a platoon. Their freezer was always overflowing with soups and casseroles they could hardly even give away. Tonight looked to be no exception as piles of vegetables emerged and went onto the counter.

Jillian talked while she cut up carrots. "I also heard from Brian. He is back in New York, safely, from his last deployment. He didn't sound so good. I'm pretty sure he had been drinking."

The distance between them barely touched intimacy now. Dusty shook his head and sat at the laptop to check his emails, half listening. They used their cell phone as a hot spot so they could get limited internet while they were out at anchor. While he didn't really get much in the way of news or current events, he kept tentative tabs on friends and family back home through social media and email.

"I think I'm going to give up on this," he said as he scrolled through his feed. "I'm sick of all the political posts. Some of our friends are idiots, especially when it comes to believing every fake news story out there." He clicked open his email. "How do I go to dinner with them if I know they are a flipping snowflake or they believe we never landed on the moon or worse yet, are a flat-earther?"

He noticed Jillian eye him across the space and wondered what he was missing.

"I like keeping up with everyone in one place. Did you hear me about Brian?" She said.

The email screen loaded. One of the benefits of life at sea was that his box was surprisingly empty most of the time. Instead of the hundred plus a day he used to get on active duty, it was now down to one or two a week, usually from his mom and dad or one of the friends they had met while cruising. He liked it that way.

"Yes, he's is back safe. Do you want me to talk to him or was he just drunk and calling his mommy?" He didn't approve of the soft streak he saw in his son sometimes. "How come I never hear from any of the kids but they call you every other day?"

Jill looked up at him again, watching quietly for a moment. She sighed and continued chopping celery. Dusty looked at his screen. Today there was a single new email delivered at 2:22 p.m. from his commander, Todd Jennings. Todd was Army, a two-star general, and one of the few military men that Dusty considered a friend. He hadn't received anything from him since they shook hands at Dusty's retirement party. Dusty trusted Todd and that was that. They could pick up their relationship at exactly the place where they had left it, even if twenty years passed. Communication in between was not necessary. But here it was, which made Dusty hesitate. He clicked it open with a touch of foreboding. Todd was to the point, as always.

Dusty,
You are being called back to active duty. You will be attached as an advisor to the First Special Forces Regiment. Your duty station will be here in Washington

DC as my special attaché. You will be Temporary Duty (TDY) for at least six months and will report to me personally.

I expect to see you here at the Pentagon no later than Friday, October 5th, 10:00 am. Vouchers are ready for your travel and housing. My adjunct will forward you details. Pease confirm with him.

Sorry to pull you in from retirement but it's time you got your damn ass off the boat anyway. Give my love to Jillian.

Major General Todd Jennings
Commander Special Warfare Group

"Holy shit." He whispered to himself. "Holy shit, they are activating me." He said it louder this time, re-reading the email. "I'm supposed to be in DC on the fifth, I'll have to fly out tomorrow. We'll move into the marina so you can handle everything while I'm gone. You will be safer at a dock."

He had been through many deployments over the years and was used to the rush to get out the door. He stood up and began pacing. He crossed the room twice and sat back down at the computer. "It says six months. I should be back well before the weather gets hot. I can book a flight out when we get to the marina." He stood up, moved for the door, stopped. "I don't have any uniforms with us. I'll pick something up when I get to the Pentagon."

He felt the hairs on his arms rise and turned to Jillian. She was standing at the counter, a tomato and the chopping knife in her hands, her face desolate. "I'm not ready for you to be deployed again." Her green eyes, luminescent with tears, caught in the soft light. "I finally got you home for good, they promised. The kids aren't home, I will be completely alone." Her eyebrows drew down. "God damn them all to hell!" She slammed the knife on the counter, threw the tomato into the sink, and stalked to their stateroom. Even though he knew she was hurt and angry, a part of him enjoyed watching her naked bum under the lower edge of her shirt as she walked away. She slammed the door.

He sighed and waited to see if she was going to come back out, then went on deck to get *Ealu* ready to leave. Although it tugged at his heart to see her upset, he wasn't about to pamper her temper. She certainly didn't need coddling to get through this deployment. She was tough and he wanted her to stay that way. He needed her to take care of home, like every other time, so that he could go out and take care of his soldiers. She would come around in a few minutes and they would get the boat to a safe harbor so he could focus on leaving in the morning. She just needed her space to get her head around it.

Going into the wheelhouse he started the engine. Jillian came out a few minutes later and stormed up to the bow, the set of her shoulders tight and unforgiving. She wrestled the anchor chain around and got the windlass started, rinsing the chain with the salt water pump as it came aboard. Once the anchor locked into its bracket, Dusty put the boat into gear and motored slowly out of the anchorage. Jillian stayed up in the bow by herself for the next hour, letting the wind wash her anger away. By the time the red and green lights off the marina entrance at La Cruz came into view, she was sitting back by Dusty, holding his hand. She was maybe squeezing it a little too tightly, but he wasn't going to say anything about it. She was back on board and he was glad for it.

Madison

Lieutenant Madison Phillips walked down the long corridor to her office. A window was open and she paused to breath in the fresh air. Outside, the maples were a vivid shade of burgundy, backlit by the afternoon sun. Early October was her favorite time of year in Colorado. The mornings were crisp but not too cold to run without bundling up. Everything felt fresh and it was alive with color. Reds, oranges, and yellows, set off against the deep evergreens, were a last, brief hurrah before the grays and whites of winter took over. She loved each change of the seasons but especially from fall to winter.

Located in Colorado Springs, the Air Force Academy was a collection of midcentury buildings surrounding a central plaza and the window looked out over the expanse. First year cadets made sharp turns on the concrete parade ground as they crossed. The memories made her smile, she was far beyond that now. Graduating at the top of her class, she had done her first tour in the Strategic Air Command missile silos at Peterson Air force Base. She was recently assigned back to the Academy, one of the youngest instructors there. Teaching was her passion, and she had worked every angle to get this assignment.

Currently, she worked closely with Dr. Lang, professor of military history and the one of country's leading experts on unconventional warfare, specializing in how societies were manipulated by their rulers. In a short time they had become trusted colleagues. While he leaned on her for clerical help, her greatest value was her ability to take complex issues and break them down into easy to understand components for people outside the field to comprehend, something that challenged him.

Approaching the conference room Maddy heard Dr Lang's voice, filled with anger. "You told me that the modeling on the Hispanic community was strictly academic and that none of the scenarios would be used in real life. Next thing I see is ICE at a congressman's meeting. He was killed. These are people's lives you are playing with."

Maddy coughed as she entered the room and the conversation ceased. The other occupant, a civilian, wore a custom tailored suit, flashing the unmistakable gleam of a Rolex. Clearly he was not a government type. Businessman or lobbyist attached to some politician maybe. Something about him didn't fit; he seemed a little too composed while Dr. Lang was obviously angry. Colonel Richardsen followed her in, a woman of dark skin, sharp angles, and most importantly, the commander of the Academy. Madison saluted.

Richardsen shook hands with the civilian. "Mr. Capardi, I believe you already know Dr. Lang. Steven, this is Lieutenant Phillips. Mr. Capardi works with the Senate Armed Services Committee."

An hour later, Madison was methodically packing her duffel bag. It didn't take long. She wore her dress uniform; the blue pants, pale-blue shirt and shiny, black loafers were standard at the Academy, as was the blue cardigan tossed over the back of a chair. She had her deep red hair pulled back into a bun, but wispy curls were forever escaping and falling around her face. She hated the uniform and only tolerated it because the Academy was her key to teaching. She smiled. Along with her uniforms, she had packed a flirty, new dress in the hopes she would get a chance to wear it in DC.

She pulled her cell out and tried her mom, then sent a text. She waited then texted both her brothers at once. In a moment, the phone pinged. It was Michael. He had done the military the hard way, from private through the ranks to officer candidate school and finally to a Captain and command. It had been a long, hard climb and then he had just walked away and joined a private security firm. She knew it had to be something big to derail him and she worried, waiting for him to open up. Until he did, she kept their relationship open, always there for him and ready to listen. As always, he texted back immediately.

Maybe she forgot to plug in her phone?

She smiled, Michael was probably right. Their mom, while gifted on the computer and organized to a fault, often forget silly, small details, like plugging in her phone. It was one of the traits that Madison found touching; her mom seemed just about perfect so much of the time and handled every crisis with equanimity, it was humanizing to see these little faults. There was no response from Brian. She missed both her brothers; they had all been close growing up. Most of the time, she and Brian had teamed up against Michael. With their dad deployed so much, he had taken over as head of the household early on. It had made for a tough childhood for Michael. Growing up Army brats had been hard on all of them.

There was a knock on her door. She opened it to a cadet saluting. "Ma'am, Colonel Richardsen would like to see you."

She knocked and entered Colonel Richardsen's office. There were shelves along one wall with books, mementos and framed pictures neatly arranged. The other wall had diplomas and awards, a picture of the colonel shaking hands with the previous president, and several pictures of her career, mostly in flying gear in front of F15s. She had been one of the first, black females to make it through jet fighter training. There was a large, oak desk positioned in front of the window and to its left, a small couch and chair.

"Good evening Lieutenant, please sit down." Colonel Richardsen motioned her to the couch. "Thank you for coming over. I know you need to muster soon, I appreciate you taking the time to see me." Colonel Richardsen steepled her fingers and looked over them at Madison. "So tell me, what did you think of the meeting today?"

"Excuse me, ma'am?"

"What was your impression; of Steven Capardi, of the mission, of the trip to DC."

Madison tapped her fingers on the arm of the chair. "Well ma'am, it all seemed straightforward. Dr. Lang is needed for the briefing." Maddy looked up. "Can I be candid, ma'am?"

The Colonel nodded.

"I felt there was more going on under the surface. Mr. Capardi didn't feel right; there was something off. And I have questions. Mainly, why am I going with Dr. Lang? I am extraneous and I have duties here. We run all of the projections for the project at the Academy. Plus, Dr. Lang was angry with him over how they used several recent projections. It just feels like the pieces don't fit."

Colonel Richardsen sat ramrod straight in her chair and her dark eyes watched Madison over the tops of her fingers. "Trust your instincts Lieutenant. Mr. Capardi may not be what he seems. As to your attachment to this mission, General Todd Jennings, Commander of the Special Warfare Group, requested you specifically. I don't need to point out the uniqueness of an Army General making a request for a junior Air Force Lieutenant. Dr. Lang is comfortable with your presence so I agreed to the General's request. I expect you to report back on the specifics of your role."

She stood up and shook Madison's hand as she rose. "You can call me at any time. I'd like you to check in every few days and give me an update."

Madison nodded. "Yes, ma'am."

"Good luck, Lieutenant."

Madison walked down the corridor turning the conversation over in her head. She was fairly certain the

Colonel's sudden personal interest had to do with having an insider on the upcoming events. Something big must be happening.

She would have to play this all carefully if she wanted to return with her military career intact. Spying on a General, even when requested to do so by her superior, was risky.

Dusty

Dusty stifled a yawn. "Can I get some coffee? The jet lag is kicking my ass."

General Todd Jennings, his solid body in full dress blues, head cleanly shaven to erase a receding hairline, reached to the center of the table and hit a button on the intercom. A voice immediately replied, "Yes, Sir?"

"We need the coffee brought in, bottles of water too, and something to eat." Todd lifted an eyebrow, eyeing the gray shooting through Dusty's dark hair at his temples. "We're getting old Dusty, jet lag never used to bother you."

"Hey, speak for yourself. I was surfing two days ago."

Todd belly laughed. "That's a picture of you in retirement I'd never considered. Colonel Scott Dusty Phillips, hanging ten with the hippies' kids, riding the waves." He chuckled some more. "I'll have to share that with Carol."

"I'm sure she will appreciate my mid-life crisis."

Dusty leaned back in a soft leather chair facing three floor-to-ceiling screens in a war room at the Pentagon. He was wearing scratchy wool slacks in dark blue with a gold stripe down the side and a black sweater with his rank on the shoulder that he'd picked up from the exchange's uniform store on the second floor. It felt surprisingly uncomfortable, especially squeezing his feet into the black leather dress shoes, after so many months of flip flops and shorts.

The door opened and Captain Roberts, General Jenning's aide, followed by wait staff from the deli, entered. They set up on a side table and Captain Roberts took a seat while the other two left, setting up a laptop.

Dusty grabbed a cardboard cup, filling it to the brim. "So what am I doing here Todd? Why'd you call me back?" He returned to his seat, juggling his coffee carefully.

"Hang on a minute with that. Once everyone gets here, I'll cover everything. You'll be up to speed pretty quickly."

Dr. Lang came through the open door, mostly obstructing a tall, slender woman with deep-red hair and flashing blue eyes, distracted by cases and files. Dusty focused on the slightly rumpled man, with a body more used to sitting than exercise.

Todd put out his hand. "You must be Dr. Lang. I'm General Todd Jennings and this is Colonel Scott Phillips."

The woman's head shot up. "Dad!" She started to smile and then flushed red. Placing everything quickly on the table, she saluted. "Please excuse me, General Jennings."

Todd smiled. "No problem, Madison. I don't imagine you were expecting to see your father at the Pentagon today."

"No, Sir." She flashed a big smile as Dusty hugged her.

"I wasn't expecting to see you either, Maddy girl. I apologize for being unprofessional Dr. Lang; I thought Lieutenant Phillips was in Colorado Springs." Dusty stepped back, looking her up and down. There were dark smudges under her eyes but she was probably fighting jet lag too. Otherwise she looked good, happy. He let shook Professor Lang's hand.

Dr. Lang smiled. "I think we are all places we hadn't planned on being today. I'm glad to meet you, Sir. Lieutenant Phillips has been a pleasure to work with. She is an excellent instructor and we are pleased to have her at the Academy."

Dusty scowled and Madison froze, her eyes glued to her father. Oblivious to their personal confrontation, Professor Lang poured himself a cup of coffee.

Steven Capardi walked in, eyes assessing each of them thoroughly. He was in a custom-tailored, Italian suit that carried a faint charcoal pinstripe, over a white shirt and gray tie. Medium height and solid, with thick black hair professionally styled, and the Rolex on his right wrist, he looked in complete control of his surroundings. Close behind, a man and two women, all in civilian clothes, entered together.

Todd stepped to the front of the room. "Welcome Ladies and gentlemen, as you know, I am Senior Officer of the Special Warfare Group." He put his hands behind his back. "I've brought you together because we have a red flag scenario."

Dr Lang stood and videos jumped onto the three screens with charts and graphs. "A poll taken the day after the shooting of Congressman Silva measured the likelihood of California to secede from the US." There was a murmur from those seated. "For the first time, that number inched over thirty percent. Think of it like the tip of an iceberg; there is a hell of a lot more going on under the water that is not visible. Our projections show one more incident and California's secession would be possible."

Shocked faces looked back at him. Lang was facing a think tank with ties to the heart of the government, whose presence here signaled an emergency. This wasn't an exercise. Secession was likely, not just possible, or else they wouldn't be in this room.

"We have run scenarios though our modeling software and we have two issues related to Congressman Silva's shooting. Either would tip the balance towards secession if they become public knowledge."

Madison started a grainy, dark video on the middle flat-screen. In it, the congressman was striding across the parking lot and people got out of cars to join him. The film was shot from the behind the Congressman and clearly showed the ICE agents blocking the exit.

"This is the video of a cell phone recording from the reporter who was present. Please pay special attention to this part where the Congressman is struck by the bullets." In the video the Congressman jerked to the left and fell to the ground. "Forensics says that the Congressman was shot by someone standing over here." Dr. Lang pointed to the Congressman's right, off screen. "There were no ICE agents that could be identified in this section. Two shots were fired. The bullets were the same caliber as the Sig P320, standard issue for ICE agents, but the bullets do not match barrel markings of any weapon logged in as present at the scene."

"You believe the Congressman was assassinated and it was covered up?" Dusty swung his gaze to Todd, who nodded. There were several indrawn breaths from the table.

The video continued through the altercation and the extraction of Agent Cummings and the other ICE agents. Something was stirring at the back of Dusty's mind. "That doesn't look like it is all one team. Some of the agents don't have weapons and the group isn't working together. They are using different tactics."

"That is issue number two and potentially the most important in regards to California. As the Colonel pointed out, there are two separate teams operating under ICE authority on the video. The President authorized the deployment of the Army's 10th Mountain Division to assist ICE in its mission throughout the US."

"What?" Dusty spun his chair, facing Todd, as murmurs came from several members of the group.

A pleading tone entered Dr. Lang's voice and he raised it over the commotion. "They have been providing support for ICE agents since late July. This is the first incident that has happened in over seven hundred raids nationwide. In light of this event the soldiers have been pulled from ICE operations and returned to their base."

Steve Capardi leaned in, his voice conciliatory. "While technically in a legal gray area because it was a direct order of the President, it is politically damaging if this becomes known."

Constance Gill, head of the Council on Industry and Technology, stood. "There isn't any gray area. US troops cannot operate on US soil against US citizens." Heads nodded.

Todd looked around the room, silent, until he had their attention, then motioned and the video continued. Constance sat slowly, glaring at Capardi.

They watched a young man in ICE gear walk up, survey the scene, meet another agent and start across the parking lot, passing near a street lamp. Brian's face jumped into view. There was a sharp intake of breath from Dusty as Madison blurted, "That's Brian!"

Dusty went still and turned icy eyes on Todd. "My son was put into this mess?"

The room was silent. Madison paled.

Todd became a General from one heartbeat to the next, his voice whipping out. "We will discuss this later, Colonel."

Dusty stared at Todd for a long indrawn breath, then tipped his head. "Yes, Sir." He turned his eyes to the screen. The set of his shoulders stayed rigid.

Dr Lang picked up the thread. "Yes, well, legalities and personal relationships aside, this information, if it becomes public, could tip the balance. If anything else happens in the near future, California will try and split from the United States and become a separate country, creating a legal and financial nightmare."

On the video, they watched Brian head into the darkness. It played for a few more seconds and ended.

Constance raised a hand. "Before we proceed, could you please elaborate on the modeling you mentioned, how accurate are these predictions?"

Dr. Lang lit up. "Yes, it is actually quite remarkable."

He nodded to Maddy and she brought all three screens up with a video game. Each one started the same, with images of a baseball game. Thousands of individual spectators were in the stands, cheering.

Dr. Lang rocked on his toes, suddenly animated. "The modeling software is easiest to explain like an extremely advanced video game where the individual data for each person involved is represented by an avatar. We don't usually do a three dimensional representation like this but Madison thought this would be the best way to explain it. On the screen you can see each person is different in the crowd. The computer has data on every single one of them."

In the first screen, the home team won. The avatars went wild. They poured from the stadium into the street. Fights broke out and they started falling to the ground. Maddy touched a few buttons and a police force materialized, the fights stopped and the avatars left.

Dr. Lang was using a laser pointer to highlight statistics running along the bottom of the screen. "The avatar moves through the simulation, acting like the real person it was modeled after. We can run it for a whole city of avatars, and then plan what police presence we would need to keep the peace after the last baseball game of the season."

In the second screen, the home team lost. The avatars filed out quietly and headed to their cars. There were a few altercations but it was minimal.

Dr. Lang paced back and forth excitedly. "This is incredible technology. The program is constantly learning from current events. Each time something happens the details are uploaded and the computer makes adjustments according to how people reacted in real life. Using real-time data, it could identify who purchased every ticket and check arrest records for violent charges. We could collect data as miniscule as what each person ate and how much beer they drank in all of the previous games they attended."

On the third screen Maddy introduced new variables; the umpire made an obviously bad call on the final run and the team lost. The fans turned violent in the stands. She made it rain and they watched some of the fans leave. She dialed up a large police force and they swarmed into the stands, quelling the fights. She had the two teams shake hands and hug each other, she had them punch each other, she flashed messages on the scoreboard. Each time, the fans reacted. The computer kept running totals of how many were involved in each kind of action, from leaving to fighting.

"Where do you get the data for each agent from? How can you know how I will react to a Red Sox Game?" Constance asked.

Dr. Lang's smile flashed. "Good question. The data is gathered from censuses, public records, surveys, social profiles, the websites people frequent, and purchases. Even online video games; we track the characters they choose and the choices they make and add that into the data. Every bit of electronic information we leave behind every time we access the internet, use our credit card or even show up in public records is collected. We now have the technological ability, computer horsepower if you will, to collect, track and manipulate the hundreds of billions of records of data necessary for this type of program to work very accurately. With the increased concerns over homeland security, we have been given legal access to all of it. Teams of psychologists spent years tracking and analyzing how decisions effect actions and have fined tuned the software, making the prediction capabilities astonishing."

He looked around, hoping for more questions, and reluctantly took his seat.

Todd stood. "Almost every simulation we run leads to California breaking apart the United States. This is real, folks. We need an action plan."

Brian

The rain had let up the night before and Brian and Justin walked from the barracks to the officers club in brilliant sunshine. Once inside, they ordered hamburgers and finished them off quickly. Justin hopped up and returned, setting a round of beer on the table. His phone rang. Brian grabbed the mugs to keep them from knocking sideways as Justin answered his cell.

"Hey Martinez?" His deep baritone boomed loudly enough for Brian to hear from the other side of the table, although he couldn't make out the words.

Justin looked at Brian with a grin. "Sounds like a great way to cure what ails me. I'm here with the Captain though. By the way, what is out-numbered?" Justin snorted. "Twenty to eight, that doesn't sound so bad. If the Cap'n wants to come out, we're game."

Brian raised his eyebrows over the top of his beer.

"Cap's in, we'll be there in twenty." Justin drained his beer.

An hour later the squad hugged the shadows under a vine maple. A stone wall with a wooden pole-gate bisected the grassy field before them. Trees lined the meadow, alive with fall colors; red oaks and yellow ash mixed with deep evergreen. Scattered across the two-hundred yard field were hay bales, barrels, some small walls and a couple brush hedges. Brian signaled his point man, Murphy, who crept forwards. Brian flashed a sign with his fingers and two squads, one led by Justin, the other by Martinez, left their position, circling around the edges of the clearing, well back into the trees. Brian, Ortez and Hanson were to provide covering fire for Murphy. He heard the caw of a crow. His troops were in position.

Making eye contact with Murphy, he gave a slight nod. The man burst from cover, running in a tight zig-zag, flailing his arms above his head with his weapon slung around his shoulders, hollering. "Come on you little chicken shits, you got a better chance of hitting me if you stand up. Look, I don't even have my painter drawn."

Six of the remaining eighteen opponents stood up and were immediately taken out by Brian and the other sharpshooters, three before they could even finish raising their paint guns. Murphy cackled a crazy laugh, dodging from side to side as he made his way towards the wall. Brian sighted and fired, hitting a white rock lodged in the wall, splattering blue paint. The signal was sent. The two teams under Justin and Martinez rushed in, catching the enemy from behind, shooting without mercy; in the back, the arms, legs, wherever contact could be made.

Murphy, ignoring the gate, slung his weapon into his hands and vaulted the stone wall, firing as he disappeared. A flag was raised a moment later and he waved, the top of his head visible just above the lip of rock. It was over in moments, the enemy trudged into the clear, splattered in blue, followed by Brian's team.

As evening settled, they trooped into a dive bar close to the course, victorious in a long day of battles. It was comfortable inside. A mix and match of tables and chairs filled the open areas and neon beer signs lined the dark green concrete walls. The bar was a long Formica strip with painted plywood shelves on the wall behind, bottles arranged neatly. Brian ordered a round as they pushed tables together.

Martinez looked at Murphy. "Damn Murphy, you looked like Cap'n Jack Sparrow running across that field like a crazy man, arms flailing and damn near doing circles in the middle of a hot zone."

"Do you see a speck of blue on me? That run is famous. Nothing can touch me when I'm in the zone." Murphy had never been hit after more combat than most and considered it was because of his lucky run.

"Didn't seem quite fair, we cleaned up in every single round. Next time we need to bring more guys for the other team so we've got some real competition. This was too easy." Justin tipped back his chair, stretching his legs out.

"Ya, but we should at least buy them a round for trying." Martinez walked over to two tables surrounded by a football or lacrosse team, from their size. They had been the competition in one of the rounds played earlier. He offered a round on him, a lone, brown face in a sea of white.

One of the players answered, his voice slurred and belligerent. "Army assholes, we don't want your damned beer."

Justin hopped up, his eyes dancing with fire. Brian put a hand out. "Let it go, it's just bar talk. Martinez can handle it."

He shrugged off Brian's hand and plowed forward. "Can't Cap'n, this boy needs some educating." Brian sighed, finished off his beer and started on Justin's. "No reason to waste a good beer." Smiles greeted him around the table.

Martinez said something they couldn't hear and turned to leave.

The man stood up. "Fucking cheating, lazy scum. Go back to your own country, you aren't wanted here. You've probably never been in a real fight in your whole damned life, running away from everything." His friends laughed.

Anger flared through Brian and he slammed his chair back from the table. Dissing the Army was one thing but nobody attacked his soldiers personally, especially not a racist ass. Martinez was a damn fine Lieutenant and nobody was going to call him out based on the color of his skin.

The rangers all grinned at each other and chairs slid back. Reaching the guy, Justin slapped him on the shoulder, then ducked under the swing when the guy punched, tapping him on the other shoulder. The guy took another swing and Justin ducked again, slapping him in the belly. The guy roared and plowed into Justin, locking him in an embrace, propelling him backwards. Justin laughed and dropped down, pulling the guy over his shoulders. The table crumpled under the sudden load. The bar erupted, fists swinging.

Brian was careful to pull his punches, as they all were. Each of them was trained in lethal hand-to-hand and this was just a bar fight. Murphy was laughing as he connected with a solid body blow and Justin just kept slapping and ducking. Martinez was backed into a corner with two big dudes closing in. A quick combination of a Judo roll and Tae-kwon-do front kick and the two found themselves piled into the corner as Martinez turned to face a guy charging him, fists swinging. He stepped aside and let the man tumble into the two, taking a chair with him as he fell.

Brain glanced over and saw Sarah Hanson, the lone female in the group. Though a bit smaller than most in the company, her martial arts skills were unmatched and she was their best sharpshooter. Brian watched as her opponent over-committed, finding himself on the floor, stunned. Hanson stepped in for the kill.

'Sergeant, play nice." Brian's voice cut across the room. She rubbed her knuckles, smiled sweetly at him then grinned as she turned to help Justin, who was slapping another hulk.

Four military police waded into the mess, called by the bartender. They grabbed soldiers and yanked them out to the parking lot. With the appearance of the MP's, the brawl wound down quickly. Brian made eye contact with the bartender, who headed towards him. He looked around. The damage to the bar wasn't too bad. A few busted tables and chairs was it. Everyone was standing up, which was good. Brian stepped over to him.

"Captain, you should know this is the second time in as many days that I've had soldiers busting the place up. Being an old Gunny Sergeant, I've seen my share of shit and am guessing you're last mission went sidewise. Hope everyone came home. Look, I have a deal with the MP's, no charges if I can get some money for the tables and chairs. I get them at the thrift store so it won't take much."

A couple words to the soldiers and a wad of cash was in Brian's hands moments later. He took it in to the bartender for the damage. "Sorry for the hassles, you're right the mission was F'd up."

The old man shook Brian's hand. "Thanks Captain. You got some tough soldiers in your little group. Glad to know there are folks like you walking the wall for us."

Brian left the bar with bitter thoughts. What would that Gunny think if he knew this group of tough soldiers was just involved with gathering up Americans for no other reason than they had brown skin.

The Four

In the hills outside of Silicon Valley, it was still dark without a hint of the sunrise to come. At a mansion overlooking beautifully manicured gardens a conference call was in progress. Three men and one woman sat around the modern, polished marble table perched in chairs selected for conformity to the aesthetic, not for the comfort of the occupants. They each controlled vast resources that would have made them the equal of kings in previous centuries. The conference call snaked across the Pacific to a government office in China.

"We are prepared to offer assistance to the new republic. We find the prospect of increased trade with fewer restrictions to have enormous potential for everyone involved," a voice proclaimed in perfect English with a British accent.

"Then we proceed as planned," the young owner of the house said and clicked off the call. They each eyed each-other across the marble expanse.

"Can we talk about the numbers?" The woman asked.

"The shooting of the Congressman worked in our favor, as expected. We are up by fifteen percentage points. It will not be sufficient however. The predictions suggest the signature drive will fail." The creator of the current version of the predictive software drummed his fingers on the table. "We will need to create another event. I would like to investigate other actions. If you are all agreed, I will run multiple scenarios and see I can find something that will work to push the secession numbers over the top."

Heads nodded around the table. "We are done then."

Without further words, they stood up and made their way to the dramatic front doors.

They were billionaires, young geniuses, leaders of the commercial world and they were not part of their parent's generation. They had set this plan in motion long before and while they considered themselves progressive; this really came down to business. A separate country of California was good for their stock prices.

They had driven themselves here in ridiculously expensive sports cars that waited for them in the long, swooping driveway. They slapped each-other on the back and sauntered out, trailed by bodyguards.

Dusty

It was evening, the corridors of the pentagon were quiet and the war room was a mess of papers, cardboard coffee cups, empty water bottles and errant pens; the detritus of a productive afternoon by powerful people who didn't need to put energy into cleaning up; they had staff. Dusty poked through the remains in the food basket by the coffee and settled on a lonely apple. Taking a bite and turning back to Todd he settled into a chair, tipped it back and stretched his legs out. They were alone in the room.

"Okay, Todd, it's been a long couple days and while it has been great seeing Maddy, I left Jilly alone in a foreign country. So tell me, why did you really call me back? You don't need me for this." He waved around the room. "There are an awful lot of smarter people here than me to give you advice. Hell everyone in this room today, including Maddy, has probably got me beat." He took a bite of apple, watching for Todd's reaction. "Besides, I know how it's done. This is all for show. There isn't anything new that is going to come out of here. You have done all of the analysis a long time ago, probably before the president was even elected. So, what gives? Why am I sitting in the Pentagon?"

His eyes sparked. "And what the hell was Brian doing in this shit show?"

Todd chuckled.

"It is good to have you back. I've missed your no-bullshit approach, everyone else tap dances around me now. As for Jillian, I am sorry. And while we are talking about family, Dusty, I was not responsible for Brian's assignment. This was a direct order from the President. His team just had the short straw drawn for them. He did well though. It could've gone down a whole let messier if he hadn't have been on top of everything. I will do what I can for him."

"And you couldn't tell me because it was some top secret bullshit." Dusty took another bite of his apple, giving himself time to push the anger about Brian's assignment back under the surface. "So tell me why I am here. Todd."

Todd stood up and started pacing in the small space between the table and the door. Dusty waited. He had been around Todd long enough to know the man thought better when he moved. He had never been good at sitting behind a desk.

"You're right, we have done all of the analysis, run all the simulations. Although a few new things came up today I'll have added into the equation, it is nothing significant." He sat down again and pulled a piece of paper over to him and grabbed a pen, inking out a rough outline of the United States. "It's kind of like this."

He crossed off California. "Say California goes. There is a good probability that Oregon and Washington will break away with California. They are aligned far closer with West Coast politics than with D.C. You will need to add Alaska to that group as well. While Alaska votes deep-red the only place they can refine their high-sulfur-content oil is in Washington." He crossed them off too.

"The Northeast block, driven by New York City, has a roughly forty-two percent probability of separating into its own country if California shows it can be done." He drew a line from where New York City was across to the Great Lakes, then made a big X from New York to Maine.

"Things are going to get ugly at that point because as much as the bible belt thinks it's a great idea to jettison the liberal bases of California and New York, they ignore the fact those two areas carry most of the country financially. So, a little bit of time goes by and the government starts to run out of money.'

'Seeing a financial collapse in the near future," he drew a big X through Texas, "Texas jumps ship within two years. What's left is the conservative but financially dysfunctional Midwest and the Southern states. Also, if it were to play out this way, the trillions of dollars in US Treasuries could be worthless, putting the entire world into a tailspin if California's secession doesn't trigger it first.'

'Best case scenario; the new countries work together much like the European Union. Worst case; the remaining government goes into full financial collapse and the different states are absorbed into the new countries that have been created. That is assuming the Chinese and the Russians stay on the sidelines, which they won't."

Dusty whistled. "We are talking about a total collapse of the country, not just the secession of California." He leaned forward. "What about civil war? Would the US fight to keep states that didn't want to be a part of the whole?"

Todd shook his head. "There are lots of scenarios that could happen before civil war." He slammed his fist against the table. "I will be damned if I believe some computer program can predict the future. We both know the best laid plans only survive until first contact." He leaned back in his chair. "Personally, I think people have their heads up their asses. They aren't looking at the bigger picture. No one wins if the US falls apart and California is the linchpin. Damn right we should fight to keep it a part of the US."

"So where do I fit in?"

You've been managing political relationships in regions torn apart by conflict for most of your career. You understand how leaders react when their countries are in civil strife. You are the only one in this room who has that experience. I expect you to see connections that the rest of these civilians and their crystal-ball-prediction-software will miss. You have seen the depths humanity can fall to, so you are who I trust to prepare for the worst."

Smiling, Dusty leaned back, putting his hands behind his head and stretching his legs out beside the conference table. "When I'm done with this, am I going to find a star in a cracker-jack box?"

Todd snorted. "You know that General Star would have been yours if you had been willing to do one more tour in Germany."

"And you know the cost of that little piece of tin was just a little too high. I probably would have lost Jillian; she was fighting breast cancer at the time. I couldn't risk her for another piece of metal. "

"The General's star is possible Dusty. It would mean committing to another chunk of time. Talk to Jillian and let me know."

"Jillian will be good with it Todd. You know she has always supported my career."

Todd nodded and started packing up his laptop. "I suggest we call it a day and talk details in the morning. Tomorrow is Saturday. There are something like forty rallies planned across the United States in support of Congressman Silva and the rights of immigrants. By end of day we should have a better idea of how likely it is that a secession vote will move forward in the California. Let's get a good night's sleep and hit this all again fresh."

He clapped Dusty on the back and they walked out together through the quiet halls.

Dusty met up with Madison an hour later for dinner at a small Italian restaurant around the corner from the hotel lobby entrance. He didn't have anything to change into so he wore the uniform he had picked up that morning. Arriving early he took a table and ordered a whiskey, sipping it slowly while he waited. Maddy arrived, sparkling as she walked in the door, laughing with the hostess who brought her to the table and smiling at people as she passed. She was wearing an emerald green cocktail dress with a flared skirt and a thin, silver belt. She had unleashed her curls; deep red, that fell around her shoulders, bouncing as she walked. Other diners, when they glanced up, smiled; she brought that kind of energy with her.

Dusty watched her sashay through the restaurant and saw Jillian as she had been when the kids were little. Jillian had caught him up in her bubble too when they were both younger than Maddy, he a freshly minted Lieutenant out of West Point, and he had fallen hard. He was still ensnared, all these long years later, and he had this amazing daughter now, so much like her mom. He knew he would do anything to keep her safe, to make her happy.

Madison came up to the table and he stood and gave her a hug. She looked at him with Jillian's freckled face but his own ice-blue eyes, Jillian's were a deep shade of green. He wondered for a moment if Jillian found pieces of him when she looked at their children, as he found likenesses of her. To him the boys were twins of each other; same auburn hair, same build, same expressions even, just a few years of growth separating them like a mirror through time. Everyone said they looked just like him but he saw Jilly in their faces every time he looked for it. He wondered if she saw a curve of their face or a gesture and was transported to them as toddlers racing to the door to greet them with hugs and sloppy kisses as he did, if she missed their little hands holding tight around her neck.

He wished sometimes he could go back in time and redo all of the missed moments. He hadn't realized when they were younger that you only got one chance and then it was gone. They only turned three once, only learned to ride a bike once, had a first date, graduated high school, all of the milestones that he had missed, just happened once. He had always thought he had time to make those moments up. Then before he was ready, he sat at a table with a young woman, all grown up, and struggled to let her know how much he loved her, because he had missed all those memories and there was a distance now between them that felt impossible to reach across.

Maddy looked across the table at him. "Dad, you look so serious, what's up?"

He shook his head and forced himself to smile. "Nothing baby girl, just a long day. Did you find the restaurant okay?"

Maddy laughed. "Ya, GPS and a good taxi driver, I can get anywhere."

An uncomfortable silence stretched out.

"So, Dr. Lang. He is a history guy. Didn't you want to go into physics?"

Madison looked up at him. "It was the only position open at the Academy, Dad."

"I could have made calls, gotten you into a good post, maybe over in Europe somewhere, set up for a command in a couple of years, like I did with your brothers. I still can, you know."

Madison looked down at the menu, drumming her fingers against the table with her left hand. Dusty knew that motion from Jillian, knew she was struggling with something. He waited for her to talk. The waiter interrupted and they both ordered. Dusty felt both relieved and frustrated that the moment was gone.

"Wasn't it surreal seeing Brian on the video?" She asked as the waiter left. "Do you think he's OK?"

"Brian is a good soldier and officer, he was following orders. I'm sure there are a lot of people looking out for him right now."

Dusty smiled at Madison as he fought down that stab of anger again. Brian was on the edge of a shitload of trouble, but he'd be damned if he would let Maddy worry. She looked relieved. Dusty made sure to smooth his own features. Returning her smile he changed the subject.

"Have you talked to Michael lately?"

"Just texts. He won't really talk to me. I think his new job isn't what he had hoped."

"No, I imagine not." Dusty winced at his tone.

Madison looked down at the table, her fingers drumming a tattoo again. He felt like he was messing this all up. He needed Jillian here to smooth things over in that easy way she had.

She started the conversation again, switching gears.

"So I sure wasn't expecting to see you here today. That was a shock. It's good though."

She flashed that smile. He would do anything to keep that smile on her face.

"Can I bounce something off of you? You've been in this all lot longer than me and I think I could use your perspective."

He nodded. "Always."

"Capardi, from the meeting today? He came to the Academy. He felt, I don't know, off and he and Dr. Lang were arguing over the modeling when I walked in. The whole meeting was wrong. Then Colonel Richardsen calls me to her office and asks me what I thought of him and tells me basically to watch my back around him. She also asked me to update her on what happens here. I felt she was asking me to be her eyes here. I'm not sure I am OK with that."

Her fingers were drumming a tattoo again. "Dad, I feel like I am playing with fire and I don't know who's lighting the matches. Who do I trust?"

Dusty took a long draw on his whisky as he thought through his answer. "You're right to trust your instincts. There is something not right about Capardi being involved in this. I don't know what his agenda is but I sure wouldn't count on it being the same as ours."

He set the glass down, spinning it slowly on the table.

"As far as Colonel Richardsen goes, your Commander has a right to know what you are involved in so it isn't spying. I would trust that she is looking out for your best interests and that she wouldn't ask you to do something that wasn't above-board."

Dusty said this with confidence. When Madison was assigned back to the Academy he had quietly made a few phone calls, vetting Colonel Richardsen thoroughly. He hadn't told Maddy but he had been impressed with the level of respect with which she was regarded with by those who knew her. She was considered a good officer who took care of the soldiers underneath her.

"That makes me feel better," she said.

The waiter came back with their salads, fussing around until Dusty barked at him to stand down. As the waiter retreated, Madison's phone pinged and then Dusty's phone started ringing, playing 'Eye of the Tiger'.

"Oh my God, Dad, you haven't changed your ring? I put that on as a joke like three years ago."

"It kind of grew on me." He fumbled the phone out of his pocket. He didn't want to tell her he couldn't figure out how to change a ringtone.

"I have to take this sweetheart, its mom."

He blocked his other ear with a finger so he could hear over the busy restaurant. Madison pulled out her phone and was checking texts.

"Hi Sweetheart, what's up?"

"Scott?" Her rich voice filled his head, panicked. His gut tightened up.

"It's Brian. His face is all over the internet. I tried to call him, I can't reach him.'

'Scott, it's bad, they are saying he was there when that congressman was shot last week and that Rangers were illegally helping ICE agents. They got a hold of his military photo. They have video of him at the event. They are making it out like he is a terrorist. I don't know what to do."

"Scott are you there?"

"I'm here, Jilly. Give me a second to think."

"I'm getting pinged from people on my forums. I don't know what to tell them. Scott you have to do something.

You have to protect Brian. Call these people and stop this."

He noted that Jillian was rushing her words. He had rarely seen her rattled and almost never on the phone to him when he was deployed. She handled the crisis and then called him when it was over.

"Okay, Jilly, for now, don't say anything. And don't answer the phone unless it is me. Let me figure out what is going on. Are you good where you are?"

Jillian made a small sound somewhere between a laugh and a sob. "I'm on a boat in Mexico. I'm about as safe from this as I can be. Call me right back." She hung up the phone.

All the color had drained out of Madison's face. "I've got about a dozen texts so far. Dad, they have figured out Brian was there."

Brian

Brian half leaned, half sat on the tall bar chair, a pool cue balanced against his hip, a beer glass at his elbow, his long legs stretched out in front of him and crossed at the ankles. A pretty brunette leaned over the green velvet opposite him, lining up her shot, her shirt dropping open in front, giving him a pleasant view of cleavage.

"Ten in the corner pocket," she said, tapping the cue ball gently.

It slid against the blue-striped ball and knocked it in, bouncing back and setting her up nicely. She came around the table, reaching over Brian as she winked at him and picking up a shot glass on the table, downing it in a quick move, and going to the far side of the table. She leaned over again, her shirt hiking up over a tramp stamp of butterflies on her lower back, bisected by the thin tee of bright pink fabric from her thong, tight jeans molding her behind into a lovely shape.

"Fifteen in the side pocket."

She tapped the pocket in question with her cue then brought it back down, took a moment to line it up again and knocked the cue ball hard, sending it flying across the velvet, ricocheting off the solid-yellow one ball, which careened into the brown-striped fifteen, pushing it into the side pocket she had called. She smiled and came around again, leaning in and picking up a second shot glass. He caught the faint scent of spices from her perfume. She held his eyes the whole time, downing it and setting it back on the table, then she laughed, low and sultry, as she turned away.

"I've almost got you beat, pretty boy."

Brian still had half a dozen solid balls on the table while she was lining up on the eight ball but he didn't mind. She was damn good with a pool cue and he was having a thoroughly enjoyable time watching her play. A few rounds of whiskey and a twenty when the eight ball dropped into the corner pocket was money well spent in his estimation. She moved back around the table and leaned her pool cue against the wall to his right. Putting a hand on each of the arms of his chair, she trapped him, smiling.

"Wanna' get some fresh air, pretty boy?" She drawled in a pretty good imitation of a southern belle.

Brian laughed, breaking the tension, and then reached out and pulled her to him, kissing her thoroughly.

"Aw, Brian, I was trying to be sexy."

"I always want you, Ashley, you don't have to try. Do you really want to leave? We've only been here half-an-hour. You've been talking about this all day. Let's have a couple more beers before we head back."

She gave him an exaggerated pout and he kissed her lower lip. She laughed, then turned and went over to a table with a couple of her friends, sitting down in an empty chair. She quickly got caught up in the conversation.

Brian leaned his head against the wall behind him and watched the room. For a Friday night it was slow, just a few groups of people around tables and a couple of bar flies sitting by themselves. But it was early yet. Things might pick up as the evening wore on. Ashley was animated at her table, telling a joke or a story, hands waving in the air as she talked.

She had stuck to him for over a year now, since they hooked up over a game of pool in a college bar that he and Justin were date-fishing in. He enjoyed spending time with her; she lifted a weight from his shoulders and carried him off with crazy stories or little bits of play acting like just now, or texting when he was in the field, breaking up his day with puns and sweet rambling stories about what she was going through. That was more than worth the hour-and-a-half drive from the base and the hassle of fitting into her overloaded schedule; she was going to Upstate Medical University in Syracuse. Plus, her dad had taught her to play pool at an early age and she was dead on. That was a joy to watch, especially when some guy was trying to hit on her and she walked all over him and took his money to boot.

Today was the first time since he had gotten back from California that it all came together. They had hiked around Tinker Falls, standing together and reaching out to touch the backside of a waterfall, then kissing in the mist.

He and Justin didn't talk about California on the drive over. They joked, and Justin played video games, and Brian was glad for the company on the long trip. At the moment, Justin was flirting it up with a little blonde at the bar, probably pushing hard for someone to spend the night with. He glanced up and said something to the girl. They both collected up their drinks and came over.

"Samantha, this is Brian. Samantha's never played pool. I told her I'd show her how."

Samantha smiled. "Hi Brian"

Brian nodded while Justin dropped quarters into the table to release the balls. He set them up and grabbed the pool cue Ashley had left against the wall. Chalking up the tip with a little blue cube, he handed Samantha the cue, turned her towards the table, pulled her close and put his arms around her as they leaned over the table, talking about the rules as he helped her line up on the cue ball.

Brian pushed himself up and grabbed his beer, leaving them to their game. He wandered towards Ashley who reached out a hand and pulled him close as he approached the table. She was telling a story, something about the first time she had to draw blood and hitting an artery and blood everywhere, when his phone buzzed. It was from Michael. Kissing Ashley on the top of her head, he moved towards the door, answering it as he stepped into the crisp evening air.

"Long time, no hear, big Bro. What's up?"

Michael's voice was hard and he was talking fast. "Brian, that shit here in California where the Congressman died? They've tied you to it."

"What?"

"It's about to blow up."

"Wait, how do you know?"

"Dude, I work for Alegeis, we are the biggest security firm on the planet. They have whole departments scanning everything on the web, watching for this kind of shit. They know you are my brother, so of course you were flagged.'

'The point is, the media's got hold of your name from your pic on that video. They've figured out that you're Army working to detain immigrants inside US borders, which is both illegal and a shitload of bad policy. You are tied to a respected Congressman's death. You are about to become the poster child for racism and for government overstepping."

"I was following orders. They have to know that. I wasn't even issued a firearm."

Mike's voice got softer, "I know Brian. I've been there. The level of anger over this right now is so high no one is going to hear that. They are going to come after you because they can't go after who is calling the shots. You are about to take the fall for them."

"Okay."

Brian looked around. He was in downtown Syracuse, on Water and Montgomery, just across from City Hall, looking at a tree lined street just going through gentrification. Newer two and three-story buildings mixed with colonial style apartment buildings, many of which had been converted to expensive condos. Cars drove by, taking people home, or out to dinner, or maybe to the market. This felt surreal, California seemed so far away.

"I'll get back to base. They'll take care of me; hide me until this blows over."

"Brian, I need you to listen to me. I have my team running scenarios. This is a bomb as far as the administration is thinking, and the political fallout is going to splash all over everyone tied to it like the big load of shit dropping that it is. They are going to run for cover and make damn sure that you are left standing, plastered from head to foot.'

'The FBI is already coming after you with everything they have. They have an adversarial relationship with this White House as well as an ongoing pissing contest with ICE. They will be all over putting you up as the face of illegal acts on US soil to pull the President down. The White House is going to want to make you disappear. The DIA, the Defense Intelligence Agency, will hunt you down. They can pin this all on you as long as you can't say different. They are going to make damn sure you don't ever get in front of a microphone.'

Brian looked up and down the street. It all looked completely normal.

"The Pentagon is going to need you so they can control of the situation. Careers are on the line as well as billions of dollars in the military budget. They are going to make you to fall on your sword to protect the military. CID, the Army's Criminal Investigative Command, is going to be waiting for you as soon as you set foot on base and they will do whatever works for them, not you.'

'They are all going into full defensive mode and you are on the outside. Plus, your face is about to go on every screen in the country. The mob of the public is going to be coming after you with pitchforks."

Brian shrugged his jacket hood up and stepped back into the deeper shadow of the building. Scanning closely, he didn't see anything out of step. His life often depended on his ability to notice anything out of the ordinary. Everything looked normal.

"Brian, I'm not going to let you take the fall. The military played the President's game and the FBI is playing their own game. You aren't going down for any of them."

"Okay," Brian said, "I hear you. I need to disappear. How much time do you think I've got?"

"I've been tracking your phone's GPS. I know you are standing on Water Street in Syracuse. I've got your license plate. I can pull up traffic cams and see where your truck goes and who gets in and out. The FBI has access to more high-tech shit than I do, they know exactly where you are. They might be waiting on a clear plan of action from the top but I wouldn't bet on it. Disappear now. Get clear, get a burner phone and call me when you are moving. Don't call me direct, call Alegeis' main line and get transferred back. It's too easy to trace calls direct to my line. I will work out a safe house and an extraction plan."

Brian nodded his head, "Got it. I'll call you soon, and Mike? I need you to reach out to Mom and tell her that I'm okay. She will be freaking out."

"Will do, and Brian, don't get stupid."

"Ya, fuck off, asshole," His voice was light.

"Shithead." Michael laughed.

Brian hung up.

He spent another minute watching every movement on the street. It looked fine. No cars were occupied along the street, no trucks were in sight, no pedestrians, and he hadn't seen a single car pass by twice. He stepped back inside the bar feeling like his reality had shifted, yet Ashley was still wrapped up in conversation and Justin was over with the little blonde, whose name he couldn't remember, at the pool table. He walked straight to them.

"Hey Brian, Justin's a good teacher, I got one in!" She slurred slightly, a few too many vodkas in by the line of glasses on the side table.

Brian looked at her for a moment, trying to remember her name. He gave up.

"Justin won't be sleeping with you tonight."

He picked up the only half-full glass on the table, handed it to her, turned her towards the bar and gave her a push to get her started. Her shocked face looked back over her shoulder and he made a shooing motion with his hand. She kept walking. He turned back to Justin whose face was a mask of indignation with the red creep of anger burning up his neck.

"Lieutenant! Throw a punch right now and you are out on your ass. We have a situation."

Justin stood up straight, his eyes still cracking fire. "Yes, Sir."

Brian softened his tone. "Justin, the media has put me into the ICE raid in San Diego. The FBI is coming for me, here, now. I have to get out of here."

Justin's eyes widened. "Okay, Cap, what do you need?"

"Take my phone; they are probably tracking it, and my truck, and head towards base. I don't want Ashley caught up in this. I need them to think I am heading back so they don't come here."

Brian pulled out his phone and keys. Justin pulled out his wallet at the same time and handed Brian all of his cash.

"Here, you will need this. They can probably track your cards, you can't use them. Do you know where you are going?"

Brian thought for a moment, "I'll probably head into New York City, get lost in the masses. I can live on the streets; it's not that cold yet. I'll need to be where I can get news and where I have options."

Justin pulled off his jacket, denim with a fleece lining, and handed it to him. "There's gloves and a hat in the pocket, they will help." He also undid his belt and pulled off the case holding his Leatherman-multi-tool. They shook hands. Justin looked him in the eyes, nodded and walked out the door.

Brian shook his head. Justin was the best part of the Army. As quickly as that, he had stepped up and done what was needed, no questions asked. Ashley wasn't going to go as smoothly. He pulled on Justin's jacket over his own, tucked the Leatherman behind his belt, turned and walked over to her table. He interrupted the conversation by pulling her up and kissing her. Everyone smiled; the effect he was hoping for.

He whispered in her ear, "Ash, let's get out of here now," and nuzzled it softly.

She looked up her eyes slightly dazed from the whiskey shots.

"Okay, pretty boy, let's blow this joint."

They made excuses, paid the tab, and Brian was through the door again just a few minutes after he had done it the first time. As they left, the TV screen over the bar was showing the video of Carlos Silva's shooting again with an inset of Brian's face. The announcer repeated his name and rank and the allegations of the US Military operating within US borders. The race had begun.

Brian put his arm around her and forced himself to walk slowly down the street while she leaned against him, like any other couple out for a walk. They got to the corner and turned towards her royal-blue Mustang as two Lincoln Navigators with tinted windows, interiors black in the evening dusk, drove by on Water Street. He swiftly buried his face in Ashley's hair and kissed her ear. She giggled. They crossed to her car and he took her keys and unlocked the passenger door, settled her in, and then slid into the driver's seat.

At Water Street they turned in the opposite direction from the SUVs and he made a couple of turns to get onto the interstate. He shelved the plan for New York City when the sign for Buffalo popped up, and veered onto the entrance ramp. He needed to do the unexpected; sure whoever was in the Navigators would immediately discover his ruse with Justin. Everything was reduced to the next step. He needed a safe place to drop Ashley and her car. He needed to buy a phone. He needed to find a ride out of the area.

A few minutes later as they came up on the fairgrounds. He took an exit at a group of hotel signs and randomly picked one, pulling in. Ashley giggled at the reception desk and insisted they use her credit card. He started to object but he needed to conserve his cash. They drove the car around to the back of the lot, tucking it in the row among others. When they got to the room he kissed her gently.

"Ash, I have to leave you here."

Her forehead wrinkled.

"There is some really bad stuff happening. I need to disappear. I want you to be safe so I want you to stay here for the night." He set her keys on the table.

"Brian, wait. What are you saying?" She reached out for him.

He backed towards the door. "Don't believe what you hear. They are going to say things that aren't true. You know me. Just remember I was following orders. I'm sorry I got you into this."

He opened the door. "Lock up after I leave and be safe. Don't let anyone in you don't know."

"You're scaring me, Brian." She followed him into the hallway.

He reached out and pulled her close, kissing her as he held her tight.

"Goodbye, Ashley." He set her gently back inside the room and closed the door.

He hiked back up to a truck stop just off the highway with a handful of tractor-trailers lined up. The store had pay as you go phones. He went down the line asking for a ride and a few minutes later he was in the cab of an

eighteen-wheeler, making small talk and hoping he had
enough of a head start.

Dusty

Dusty and Madison looked at each other as Brian's predicament sank in. The waiter showed up at his elbow, refilling the full water glasses. Dusty motioned him away while he put puzzle pieces together. Brian was in trouble. He had a pretty good idea of what would happen next; what he would do if he were Brian's commander, who would distance themselves, who would try to silence Brian, who would use him. He worked through the scenarios quickly. It all depended on where Brian was. He needed more information and the best person to get that from was Todd. While waiting for the call to connect, he watched Madison, bent over her phone, texting.

The main door was behind her, twenty busy tables away, and he had an occasional view of who came in as patrons moved around the restaurant. With his back against the wall and the kitchen entrance to his right, a few tables away, he could easily keep an eye on everyone who came and went. After so many years in the field he didn't really need to focus on it anymore, he trusted his subconscious to alert him to anything that needed his attention. It was like breathing, he didn't need to think about it unless trouble showed up. Something caught his eye.

Todd answered quickly, "Dusty, where are you? I take it you have seen the news. I need to send a car to get you immediately. Your identification is flagged. They want to use you to get to Brian."

Through the front glass, Dusty recognized Steven Capardi coming up to the door, scanning the restaurant as he stepped in. Alarms went off as the puzzle pieces fell into place. "Capardi's a spook, isn't he Todd? We are getting clear. I'll call you."

He hung up and dropped the phone to the table. Reaching across he snatched Madison's, setting it down as well. At her startled look, he nodded his head to the door. "Capardi is here. They must have tracked the phones. We need to get out now."

"Capardi is tracking us? Oh." Comprehension flashed across her features, "He doesn't just work on the Armed Services Committee, does he?"

He threw a couple of fifties on the table. Leaving their cell phones behind, they stood up and he steered her towards the kitchen entrance, an arm protectively wrapped around her shoulders, keeping their waiter, busy at another table, between them and Capardi. As they pushed the kitchen door open Capardi's voice rolled across the space.

"Colonel Phillips, STOP."

Dusty pushed Madison and they rushed through, dodging through wait staff and cooks. The kitchen was in an 'L' shape and at the end of the 'L' was the delivery door. Pushing the crash bar and running through, they found themselves at a short ramp to the loading dock and the back alley. Dusty saw an empty rack to his left and pulled it in front of the door as Madison took her heels off, balancing against the rail. She swung them by the ankle straps as they started to run again. Dusty saw broken glass on the concrete and tried to pull her sideways but she easily jumped over the spot, running faster than he expected, forcing him to catch up. They came to the end of the alley and Madison pulled up, flattening herself against the wall, pushing her hair back and leaning carefully around the corner, then ducking back.

"Shit," She whispered under her breath. Then she motioned three adversaries and pointed around the corner to the right.

Dusty nodded, looking around the alley. He stepped across it and jumped, catching a fire escape ladder and pulling it down. The clanging sound echoed up and down the alley. Leaving it extended, he grabbed Madison, and pulled her behind a dumpster, settling flat against the filthy concrete. He covered her with his body, tucking her tight against his chest, while they peered through the wheel space between the bottom of the dumpster and the ground. The smell of old garbage and sour milk made him gag.

Three sets of feet pounded around the corner. One jumped and they heard him catch the ladder and pull himself up, climbing quickly. A second set followed. There was a crash from the kitchen door and Capardi's Italian loafers came in from the right.

"They went up," a voice said.

"We will pick them up on the other side."

They watched his loafers leave the alley, moving towards the street. The men above them on the fire escape pounded up to the top and went over the lip of the building. Quiet settled like a soft blanket around them.

Dusty sat up and Maddy pushed herself into a sitting position after him. They waited, quiet for a slow count of ten. Finally Dusty stood up and helped Maddy get to her feet. They walked to the end of the alley and Maddy peered around the corner again. It was empty. Dusty pulled her back toward the restaurant, stopping to brush her off as best he could, but her dress was wet where it had absorbed the muck from the dumpster. She put on her shoes and they entered the restaurant kitchen again. Madison raised her eyebrows.

"We only need to stay ahead of them physically, Maddy. They will have us on camera pretty much anywhere we go but they are human, it will take time for their bodies to cover the distance to where we are next. They rushed this, just the four of them without back-up. Now we just need to stay one little step ahead. "

Leaving their phones with the manager, Dusty grabbed an umbrella out of the stand by the front door as the maître d' hailed a cab from the corner. They ducked into the back seat, hiding their faces from security cameras under its dome. After a few short blocks, Dusty had the driver stop at the Rosslyn Metro station. Sliding out of the taxi, they rushed across the sidewalk and into the station.

It was brightly lit and still somewhat busy; professionals heading home late mixed with couples heading into town for a bite to eat or to listen to music. The escalator traversed a brightly lit tunnel with sound proofing squares arching overhead. They hung to the left side, quickly walking down the moving staircase, skipping around the few stationary passengers. Dusty felt exposed.

In the depths of the station, they bought tickets at a machine and moved through the gates, dodging the light crowd. An LED sign gave them three minutes until the train into D.C. arrived. A handful of passengers milled about on the platform and Maddy smiled at a little girl with big brown eyes, hugging onto her mom's hand.

"Dad, you don't think they would fire weapons if they find us, do you? All these people could get hurt," she whispered. "I will turn myself in to them before that."

"Let's not borrow trouble, Maddy girl. Patience for another minute, the train is coming. I will turn myself before that happens. I will not be responsible for anyone getting hurt."

He searched for options should their luck run out. There were multiple cameras covering all aspects of the station and platform; there was no way to hide. He figured it would be close as to whether the train or Capardi would show up first.

Their luck held. The train whooshed up and the doors slid open. They stepped on, scanning the few passengers already on the car while watching the platform behind them. The doors seemed to take an eternity to close, but finally did. Dusty recognized the guys from the alley as they rushed onto the platform just a few seconds too late. Dusty waited until Maddy looked away and then flipped them the bird through the window as the train picked up speed.

"Dad, where are we going to go?" Maddy asked.

"The last place they would expect, and the one place they can't touch us, Maddy."

The train sped up and a few minutes later slowed again. Dusty stood up and grabbed Maddy's hand, pulling her after him at the next stop.

"Back to the Pentagon?" She asked.

Dusty laughed, "Into the lion's den, Maddy."

They exited the station, quickly crossed next to a small courtyard with a pentagon shape in marble set into the floor and then into the entrance to the building. Once inside a security checkpoint loomed across the walkway. They both stepped through and approached the counter where a Corporal saluted Dusty at the sight of the rank on his shoulder. They presented identification, his issued just twelve hours earlier. The Corporal scanned them in. He looked at the screen and then looked back at Dusty. He picked up the phone.

"Sergeant, I have an issue."

Madison looked at Dusty.

"You are safe now, Maddy. This is what we want. They can't touch us here."

The door behind the man opened and the Sergeant stepped through and saluted. He looked at the screen and then up.

"Sirs, please step this way."

He led them to a small office adjacent to the reception desk, offering them chairs. "This may take a few minutes, can I bring you coffee?" At the shake of their heads, he turned to leave.

"Sergeant, please contact General Todd Jennings, it is urgent."

"Yes, Sir." He saluted as he left.

They sat for a moment and the Corporal brought a phone in, plugging it into the wall and handing it to Dusty. "Todd?"

Todd's voice filled his head. "The Pentagon. I wasn't expecting that, Dusty. Not a bad choice. Capardi going to be pissed. I hear Maddy's with you. I've ordered the duty Sergeant to release you both to me. I'm sending my car. It should be there in the next ten minutes."

"Todd, about Brian,"

Todd cut him off. "We will discuss that when you arrive Colonel. At present he is still unaccounted for."

"Yes, Sir." Dusty replaced the receiver on the base. "Brian is still out there, Maddy."

"Dad, I didn't get a chance to tell you. Michael texted me at the restaurant. He is helping Brian and he was okay as of forty-five minutes ago."

Dusty sighed, "That's good news Maddy. I don't know how Michael got into it but I'm glad for that. Did he say where Brian is or where he's going?"

Madison shook her head.

"I'll call your Mom and let her know."

He dialed Jill's cell. She didn't answer. He frowned remembering he had told her not to unless she recognized his number. He would have to get into his email to reach her. He handed the phone back to the Corporal, who took it and stepped out of the room. They sat in silence.

The door opened and Steven Capardi strolled in, looked around the room and leaned against the wall, crossing one foot over the other. Dusty noticed his Italian loafers were scuffed and his tailored suit looked rumpled.

"Evening, Colonel."

Dusty nodded.

"We need to find your son."

"I believe he is in California."

Steven nodded his head. "We are picking up that one as well." He casually inspected his fingernails, looking sideways at Madison. "We are going to find Captain Phillips. It's just a matter of time. We know he has left Syracuse. We know he is not headed towards Fort Drum. We picked up his girlfriend. It won't be long now."

Madison kept her eyes on her hands, resting on the table.

Steven looked back to Dusty, "I just wanted to let you know the President has publicly accused him of treason and authorized lethal force. When we do catch him, I can't say how it will go down. We can't have a Congressman's murderer running around loose, now can we?"

Dusty's ice-blue eyes bored into the man.

Steven nodded his head. "See you around, Colonel." He sauntered out.

Maddy started to cry quietly, the tears bubbling over her eyelashes and making wet tracks down her cheeks. Dusty got up and came around the table, standing her up and taking her in his arms. "It's going be okay, Maddy-girl, Brian is going be okay. Don't believe him. He is just trying to get to us to say something he can use to find him. You did great."

She nodded her head and leaned into him. Then she pushed back, wiped her eyes and sat back down. He let her go, wishing he could keep holding her a while longer. He missed the way he used to be able to solve her problems, like the pain of a skinned knee or a fight with one of her brothers, with a hug. Things were so much more complicated now.

A few minutes later the door opened and the Sergeant stuck his head in, "The General's car is here for you, Sirs."

As they emerged from the Pentagon, they both searched for any signs of pursuit. Steven Capardi had called his dogs off for the moment and was gone. Jennings staff car, driven by Captain Roberts, made a short trip through Pentagon City and turned in at the Army Navy Country Club. Winding through the fairways they reached a Georgian colonial three-story with symmetrical square additions at either end. Captain Roberts circled around to the classic carriage portico and dropped them at the main entrance then went to park the car.

It was early fall and the air was still warm and heavy, smelling of jasmine. The throaty bellows of bull frogs in the distance, along with an acoustical version of *Let it Be* by the Beatles, drifting from invisible speakers, filled in the space around them. Maddy took a deep breath and forced her shoulders to relax.

They were greeted by a young woman in a polo shirt and skirt who escorted them to a small conference room. Maddy ducked out to the restroom and after using the toilet, looked at her reflection in the mirror. She was pale and messy, her dress filthy. Pulling a band out of her purse, she pulled her hair back into a ponytail, then reapplied her lipstick and touched up her eyeliner where it had smeared. She brushed her dress again, straightened the belt, then took a deep breath, let it out slowly, nodded to herself and walked back to the conference room. She felt better being ordered. It gave her a needed feeling she had control of some small part of this nightmare.

A plate of sandwiches and cookies was sitting on a side table with water bottles and sodas. There were two flat-screens on the walls and the general had both of them up and was switching between news programs and internal communications.

Todd's wife Carol, petite and elegant, rose from the table and came around, enveloping Maddy in a hug, keeping her arm around her as they turned to Todd. She was almost a grandmother to Maddy after all the years Dusty and Todd had been deployed together. She had loved Maddy since the day she held Jillian's hand at the hospital when Madison made her first appearance while Dusty and Todd were in Afghanistan.

"I'm glad you both made it here, let me bring you up to speed," Todd motioned them to the table as Captain Roberts came into the room, saluting and sitting behind an open laptop.

Dusty started to ask about Brian and then decided to sit down. Todd would tell him everything he knew, he was confident of that.

"As far as we can tell, at approximately six-thirty this evening the first references to Brian appeared. The news programs followed a few minutes later. Since then, it has been posted by pretty much every media outlet on the web with different takes on it depending on the political slant of the organization. The Russian bots have picked it up and are producing thousands of social media posts. It is safe to say that the cat is out of the bag. The White House is in full damage control. There will be a press briefing in a few minutes. We expect them to disavow any knowledge of the operation and for the military to take the brunt of the responsibility, along with ICE."

Dusty interrupted. "Todd, Capardi caught up with us at the Pentagon. He flat out said they were pinning this on Brian, including the murder of the Congressman, and that the President had approved an arrest using lethal means if necessary. They are making Brian out to be a terrorist operating independently."

Todd raised his hand to stop Dusty and picked up the phone, stepping outside the room as he dialed. They heard his raised voice in the corridor. A few minutes later he stepped back in.

"Your information from Capardi is correct Dusty,"

Madison drew in a sharp breath.

"I have done what I can, but I don't know if it will change the story the White House puts out. We need to find Brian quickly, before anyone else. That is the best outcome I can manage. If he is under our control, we can spin the story to help him."

"So he is still unaccounted for." Dusty looked over and upon seeing the panicked look on Madison's face said, "He is resourceful, Maddy, he will be alright."

"Yes, as far as we know, he hasn't been detained. He was at a bar in Watertown when this broke and the FBI followed his phone out of town heading towards Fort Drum. They are still working at finding him in the hills outside of Syracuse. If he makes it to base, CID will take him into custody and contact me. We can then extract him to a safe location."

Todd glanced at his notes. "Witnesses say he left with an Ashley Smith."

"That's Brian's girlfriend." Madison said.

Dusty raised an eyebrow.

"Dad, they've been dating for like a year, you had to know. General Jennings? Steven Capardi said they had picked up Ashley and were holding her."

Todd ran a hand through his hair. "Is there anything else I need to know about this conversation you two had with Capardi?"

"He was just fishing, I don't know what was true and what was said to rattle Madison," Dusty said, "I think you've got it all though, except about him going to pick up Michael next. Who does that asshole really work for anyways?"

Todd started pacing. "Officially, he works for Senator Reynolds of New York. Before Reynolds, he was one of the top field operatives at Tredis, the black-ops firm that initiates and enforces deals in lots of places around the globe for high-net-worth individuals and private companies who don't want to get their hands dirty. The President had a long history with Tredis before he took office. Capardi has considerable pull, especially within the DIA and with Homeland Security, much more than a senator's aid normally would have. We assume he has the President's authority behind him and we know he has worked with the CIA in several political situations outside the US. I think it is a safe assumption that he has access to the US intelligence network and is using it on the President's behalf."

"I'm pretty sure the guys he had with him tonight weren't DIA," Dusty said, "they weren't very professional."

"It could have been lower level Tredis guys. With the current adversarial situation between the President and the FBI, that is the only organization we can assume he is not able to manipulate. We just don't have enough information at this point."

"Can you reach out and see if they really are holding Brian's girlfriend?" Madison asked.

Todd stopped pacing and sat down, "Let's let this play out a little longer before I make that call. They aren't aware of how much we know, so I'd like to play my cards close for now. I promise I will do everything to get her released in the morning if they are holding her. Dusty, you should probably call Mike and let him know they are coming for him."

Dusty picked up the phone.

Michael

Michael sat at his desk at a small interior office at Alegeis' San Francisco office. Two of his walls were glass and he looked out over a handful of empty, half-wall cubicles to a late afternoon sun, hazy with wildfire smoke. It was just after five on the West Coast. There were two people sitting in chairs across from him, both combat-tested soldiers who had come with him from the Marines. He trusted them completely; they had served through multiple tours together and he knew they would always have his back. Laptops open, they were typing, clicking and scrolling, working to change the narrative that was unfolding across the internet.

"Your Mom is something," Carey said, "she is putting out stuff faster than I can repost it."

Michael smiled. It had only been a handful of hours since she had first heard the news and Jillian had already started this campaign to change public opinion about Brian. She had always been their rock, no matter what happened. This was no different. She would protect them any way she could and social media was her forte.

She had first started when Michael was in middle school with a couple of groups, creating a place for Army spouses to come together and support each other, then Navy, and Marines and Air Force, then parents of teenagers, and kids who needed help with homework, and it just kept growing. Every time she thought of a group that needed a voice she set up a network until she was moderator of dozens of groups and websites with hundreds of thousands of followers. She had a voice that reached across all age groups and across the political spectrum.

She was using it now to keep a focus on who ordered the Rangers into the field with ICE, on how soldiers didn't have a choice in where they were assigned, on conspiracy theories with Brian as the victim. It was a furious war of words she was waging against the news outlets and they didn't even realize they were fighting, sometimes picking up her memes or posts and quoting them as the race for information ramped up.

Carey and Matt, sitting across from him, were both reposting and adding to Jillian's story, working to turn public opinion away from Brian. He hoped it was working.

The phone on his desk beeped, he picked it up.

"Hey Mike," Brian's voice was loud with heavy, road noise behind it. "I'm out of Syracuse and a good chunk of the way to Buffalo. Is there anything you can put together for me there?"

"Can I call you back on this number?"

"Sure, I'm sitting in the cab of a truck. It's the driver's phone. We are about thirty minutes out." Brian cut the line.

Michael scribbled the number that showed up on his receiver and started looking up Buffalo on the internal company intranet. They had several safe houses and a couple of connections in the system. Buffalo was on the border with Canada and a regularly used route for clients who needed to cross the border quietly.

His phone beeped again. He answered.

"Mike, this is Will down in tech-support. That last call you got? Pretty sure it was being traced. I also wanted to let you know we just got an order from on high to monitor your line. If you hadn't introduced me to my future wife, I might not have told you." He laughed. "Lucky you, I'm not as fond of them as I am of my bride."

"Thanks Will, I owe you one."

His phone beeped a third time.

"Michael, this is Dad."

Mike hesitated. "Yes, Sir?"

98

"Mike, I'm here with General Jennings and Maddy. I understand you are helping Brian. Do you know where he is?"

Michael looked out the window. "Who's asking?"

"What? I am Mike. If you have information, tell me, don't play games."

"I don't know where he is at the moment." Which Michael knew, while technically true was skating close to the line.

"If you find out where he is, Sir, what are you going to do?"

"We need to bring him in. The President has authorized lethal force, we can't take chances. CID can take him into custody and keep him protected. You need to get to a safe place as well; they tried to pick up Maddy and me this evening."

"Dad, Maddy is safe, right? You said she was with you."

"Yes, she is fine. Can you reach Brian? Can you tell him to call me?"

"I will do what I can. Has CID been tracing my calls?"

"I don't think it would be CID Mike, people working with the DIA found us this evening by our phones. They are trying to get to Brian through us."

"I'll call you in a few minutes." Michael cut the call off. He looked at Carey and Matt. "We've got a problem."

The Truck Driver

The tractor trailer Brian was riding in approached Buffalo after a long stretch of dark highway. The lights of civilization started miles before the city itself would be reached; a few houses here, a building there, gradually increasing until they became a steady stream coming up on the windshield as the truck neared the city limits. Three cars with police lights on flashed by on the opposite side of the highway, crossing on the grassy median between the East and West lanes after the truck passed them and roaring up behind it. One came up on the left hand lane and passed it by, the second pulled up to the driver door and the third tucked in behind the truck, boxing it in.

None of them were marked police vehicles; they were using emergency lights tucked behind the rearview mirror and in the back window. The car next to the driver's door motioned for the truck to pull over while the one in front tapped the brakes. The driver swore, downshifting and slowing the truck gradually until he was able to ease off onto the pavement along the side of the highway.

Agents climbed out of all three cars with weapons drawn, approaching the truck cab. The driver rolled down his window.

"Can I help you?" He asked without opening his door.

"Sir, we need you to step out of your vehicle," the agent closest to the window replied, his breath making puffs of steam in the October night air.

"Like hell I will. Who the hell are you? Why did you stop me?"

The agent passed up his credentials. "I'm US Deputy Marshall Les Williams, Sir. We are searching for a terrorist spotted leaving Syracuse in a truck a little over two hours ago. We will need to search your vehicle, Sir."

"I haven't seen a fucking terrorist and I'm pretty damn sure you need probable cause that it was my truck. Otherwise it is a random stop and you have no right to search it." He looked at the ID. "Deputy Williams."

Williams pulled out his weapon and pointed it at the driver's head. "Step out of your vehicle now."

The driver looked down the barrel of the gun for a minute, slid the Berretta he had been holding in his right hand between the front seats, and opened the door, slowly climbing down.

"This is a violation of my rights."

Two agents swarmed up the ladder and into the cab, while the third had him unlock the sleeping compartment and all of the storage lockers. The two agents returned shaking their heads. Deputy Williams pointed his flashlight beam at the two containers the truck was pulling.

"Those are sealed when I pick them up, you can check my logs."

Deputy Williams nodded, checked the date on the seals, and pulled out a cell phone. "Sir, the target is not here. We are releasing the driver."

He looked over. "You can go, Sir."

The driver climbed back up and slammed his door while the Marshals piled back into their cars and drove off. He adjusted everything and made sure his handgun was still in place. He started the truck back up merging onto the highway, a grin crossing his face. He hadn't seen a terrorist; there was no damn way that kid he had given a ride to and dropped off back in Batavia was a terrorist. Plus he had just screwed with the Government. He was a happy man.

Brian

Brian stamped his feet in the cold dark, just outside the parking lot for Batavia Downs, waiting on the person who was supposed to take him to a safe house. The track was just outside of Batavia, a small town about twenty minutes outside of Buffalo. The casino and harness race track wasn't far off the highway and an easy landmark to find; it was lit up like Las Vegas, the neon at the entrance driving back the night. He was working now to stay off any video cameras where his face could be recognized. He was sure the parking lot was monitored and it was possible whoever was searching for him had access to those camera feeds.

A seventies vintage, cream Continental with a tan vinyl roof, its classic hood stretching forever, rolled slowly up to the lot, the oval opera windows in the back seat embossed with the gold stenciling of a Diamond Jubilee edition. The car shined like a mirror, from the chrome spoked wheels to the gold plated emblem on the hood, and reflected the neon from the casino entrance in muted symmetry. The driver, dwarfed behind the wheel of the big car, waved. Brian stepped up and the doors made an audible click as they unlocked. He climbed in.

"Man, this is a sweet ride." Brian patted the padded dash.

The driver, hunched over and looking like he had been dusty old when the car was fresh off the assembly line, smiled. "Thank you. She's been a good friend for a long time." He peered at Brian in the darkness of the interior, "Son, you don't look nearly as scary as they are making you out to be on TV."

"Thank you? Sir."

The old man started cackling, wheezing through his laughter. "I'm Ben Wilks and don't call me Sir, I worked for a living; I was a drill sergeant for a mess of years and a First Sergeant for awhile after that. You can call me Ben or Top."

Brian nodded.

"I've watched too many soldiers pay the price for idiots who don't even know how to put on a uniform. You weren't responsible for that mess in California and I know they are trying to hang it on you. Don't you worry now, they aren't ever going to find you here, they forgot about me a long time ago."

He put the car in drive and slowly turned it around in the big parking lot. They headed out to the street, made a right turn, went two blocks and turned in at the sign proclaiming them to have arrived at the New York Veteran's Assisted Living Facility. They drove around the main buildings, nicely maintained and well lit, and pulled up at a little cottage tucked away at the back of the gardens. Ben pushed the button on the opener and the garage door swung up, a bright square in the night, revealing a neat and orderly garage. He pulled the big car inside until a tennis ball on a string affixed to the ceiling bumped his windshield, cut the engine and pushed open his door. Brian opened the other side, it was a heavy and he was surprised Ben could manage it, he looked pretty frail.

Ben unlocked the door into the house and they entered a little kitchen that let on to a small but well organized living area. The walls were lined with shelves with pictures of Ben; as a younger man in uniform holding a young woman, and with several of kids at different ages, and a few of Ben and his sweetheart aging. There were medals and certificates, and books, and small treasures from around the world, a few obviously from his time spent in Korea and Vietnam. There was a couch with a small coffee table in front of it, a recliner with a small table holding a Zane Gray western and a TV remote. Everything had its place; neat and ordered with that unmistakable military discipline feel. To Brian it felt like stepping into an old pair of jeans that fit exactly right.

"Have a seat, Captain," Ben fussed in the kitchen for a few minutes as Brian sat on the couch, and came out with a beer for Brian and some potato chips in a bowl he set on the coffee table.

"Thank you, Mr. Wilks." Brian watched him settle into the recliner. "So, how did I end up here, if you don't mind me asking?"

Ben started laughing again, a long wheeze. "Probably wasn't what you were expecting, I'll bet. My great grand-niece Carey Lynn, or maybe she is my great, great grand-niece, I never can keep it quite straight, anyway, my sister's son's, daughter's, daughter, yes I think that is right, called me a little bit ago. She's out in California, out of the uniform since she lost part of her leg in Afghanistan, but doing okay. She calls me a couple times a year. She's a good kid.'

'She asked if I could look after you for a spell, said that you were in some trouble. I saw that story they are putting out about you on the TV tonight so when she said your name I knew I had to come get you. You could be one of my own boys that I brought through basic and I've seen this crap ruin good soldiers too many times. I figured you needed some solid advice from someone who knows the ropes. You can talk about it or not, son, either way. You are safe here and I will do what I can for you."

Brian felt his shoulders relax. He asked about Ben's family, then they got onto sports, then about his military career, and finally he was telling Ben the whole story. He started from when he was first deployed in California and the stresses of keeping his Company solid while working under ICE supervision, and finally got to the whole evening where the congressman was shot and then everything until he was let out of the truck in Batavia. Ben listened, nodding his head and letting out a sigh now and then. Brian felt like a huge weight was lifted off.

He wrapped it up and Ben nodded. "Well Son, this here is how I see it. When you get into the Army you end up doing a lot of marching. See, in civilian life, you don't do any marching, you can wander wherever the hell you want, dodging cars and stepping over shit and going wherever you get the notion to. But once you sign up, you are a part of a squad and a platoon and a company and so on all the way up to the top. So you do a lot of marching, with your leader in front of you and your squad beside you and behind you, so now, you don't get to wander any which way you want. Now as you are walking, the same shit is gonna' come up as it does in civilian life, but you don't get the choice to step over it, or around it, because you have your squad around you and everyone above you, and your country back home, depending on you. You can't get out of the way.

The only choice you have is to keep on marching, putting one foot in front of the other no matter what shit comes up before you, or what shit you step in. It comes down to luck. See everyone is marching together, so sometimes you step in shit, or your company steps in shit, but sometimes it's the guy two company's over that gets it. You just never know. You have to trust though, that they will step in it if it is in front of them, just as you will, because otherwise everyone is lost.

Now, one day, you might step in a big pile of dog shit; smelly, nasty, all the way up to your knees. You can't stop so you keep on marching. Pretty soon you realize it smells like hell for a little while but it eventually drops away and it hasn't really hurt you any. On another day, you might be marching on a mountain and you step onto a loose boulder and go down. Your squad pulls you back up because you are a team and even though you are hurt, maybe even kinda' bad, you keep on marching. And you are there for your squad because you made a promise and they made a promise to you.

Then one day, you are marching in your line, not able to get out of the way, your luck runs out, and you step onto that landmine. You here it click as you step and you know this is it. You tell everyone to keep marching, you say your prayers and you take that next step, because that is the only choice you have. As soon as you move your foot, that landmine does what landmines do, taking you with it into eternity.

So if you get my drift, it seems you have stepped into something in the line of duty. Trouble is, until a little time has passed you won't know whether it is a nasty smelling pile of shit that will drop away or whether you are standing on a landmine that is gonna blow you into a whole 'nother adventure. So all we can do is get you settled in here, get a good night's sleep and see where things stand when the sun rises a few times."

Brian put his head down and massaged his temples. He was exhausted. He was worried about Ashley and he knew Ben was right. There wasn't anything he could do but to keep on marching and see how bad the shit turned out to be.

John

John Fields, reporter at large, deposited little Amy on the bedspread and crawled back under the covers, trapping her in the space between him and Blanca, still half asleep and making little groaning noises every time Amy pulled on her hair or tried to climb over her. The dawn light leaked through the bedroom window blinds, playing over both of his girls in slats of soft orange and dusky shadow. He felt the urge to bolt the bedroom door and lock all three of them in forever, safe; where bullets from the bushes couldn't take them away and leave him alone. He loved the two of them more than he had ever loved anything in his life. The reality of how fast they could be taken away, as quickly as Carlos had been alive and then gone, was haunting him.

"Blanca baby, are you awake?" He whispered, gently tucking stray hairs behind her ear.

"Mmm hmm," she opened her eyes halfway, looking up through her lashes at him.

"Baby, will you marry me?" He pulled her hand to his lips and kissed it gently.

Her face drew up in confusion as she opened her eyes wider, pulling herself awake.

"What?" she asked in a soft voice.

"Baby, let's get married. Let's make this real. I don't ever want to lose either one of you. You are my whole world. I never thought I could feel this way, this strongly, but I do.'

'I love you.'

'Marry me."

He kissed her forehead and leaned back, tugging gently on Amy's leg as she crawled towards the end of the bed.

Blanca sat up slowly, pulling the covers up against her chest. Her dark hair was a tousled mess surrounding her black eyes, the blinds throwing soft bars of shadows across her cheeks.

She looked at him and laughed, sweet and happy, and then she turned serious, "On three conditions. First we have a real wedding, where my parents can come and our friends are there and Amy is with us. In the church. A real wedding, not sneaking off like we are ashamed."

Amy crawled back up and burrowed into her arms, giggling and babbling. Blanca pulled her close. "Second, you promise we will buy a house as soon as we can afford it. We will raise our babies in a house in a nice neighborhood with a yard and close to a school so they can walk. And third and this is hardest. You promise me now that we will be married forever, that you will not change your mind when it gets rough or if I get old and fat. You promise me that we will make this work, no matter what."

He reached out and collected her and Amy both into his arms, pulling her into his chest, kissing the top of her head. "I promise you, Blanca."

She looked up at him, smiling. "Oh, and I keep my own name. I don't want to be Blanca Fields, White Fields is a terrible name. But Amy can keep it, Amy Christina Perez Ortega Fields is good, she can become anything with a name like that."

John smiled and held them close while Amy wiggled, working her way out of his grip. She scooted to the end of the bed and eased off feet first, falling the last few inches and landing solidly on her diaper. She laughed and started exploring the floor, tasting shoes, shaking car keys, and using the dresser handles to pull herself into a standing position, and then trying to take a step, while John made gentle love to his new fiancé.

Thirty minutes later he climbed into the little grey Nissan in the parking lot of his apartment complex. It was a little after eight on Saturday morning and the place was deserted. He swung his laptop into the back seat as he got in. He was expected at the TV studio at nine. They wanted an on air interview for Week in Review, a nationally syndicated political program to talk about the military operating inside US borders against US citizens. He had finally gotten a big story. Well, two actually. The whole leap from Carlos Silvas' death to the military connection had propelled him onto the national stage. He planned on leveraging his fifteen minutes of fame into a position with one of the networks if he could. Hopefully his career would take off and he'd be able to buy a house for Blanca sooner than he had thought possible just a week ago.

After the interview he was heading over to Balboa Park, San Diego's museum complex. They were holding Carlos' memorial in the plaza that afternoon. He was one of the speakers.

There was already talk of violence and he had asked Blanca to stay home with Amy. He didn't want them getting caught up in anything if it turned ugly. He hoped she would listen to him in this because Amy was involved. Since she had been born, Blanca was fiercely protective of her, so he was pretty sure she would stay home with her. Otherwise she would certainly be at the rally. She was both passionate and fearless. He knew his argument this morning to keep her from coming to the rally was manipulative but he couldn't bring himself to leave them today if he couldn't leave them safe. He started the car and pulled out of the parking lot.

Blanca

Blanca came out of the apartment an hour after John and bundled Amy into her car seat. She tossed in a diaper bag and started the engine, looking at Amy in the rearview mirror.

"Hey Amy, Amy. Ready to go see Nana? You get to spend the whole day with her and Abue so I can keep you safe and still be there for daddy when he speaks. We are so proud of him, aren't we little angel?"

Amy giggled as Blanca backed the car out of the space, put it into drive and pulled out well after John was on his way.

Dusty

It was close to eleven on Saturday morning in the Pentagon. Dusty looked around the room at the same group of people he had sat with the day before, with the notable exception of Steven Capardi.

Dr. Lang was going over the early poll numbers from the morning in a monotone and Dusty was struggling to stay awake. It had been a late night. Once they heard that Brian was at a safe house the pressure eased. They stayed at the club until after the eleven o'clock news broadcasts from the West Coast wound up. Afterward, they headed to Todd's house for a couple hours of sleep before returning to the Pentagon. Captain Robertson stopped by their hotel, collecting up their things and checking them out. Dusty had picked up his new uniforms on the way to the conference room this morning; they had done a rush on the tailoring, but he felt more formal in his dress blues.

Dusty refocused on Dr. Lang.

"So after a small uptick in the President's approval rating after the press conference when he targeted Captain Phillips as a non-military shooter, we saw a significant downward spiral after a large swell of support for the Captain in social media swung public opinion. We are trying to understand how the backlash came into play so quickly.'

'The President's approval rating now stands at an all time low. If you look at the numbers just in California, it has dropped to below twenty percent. Californians, by a four to one margin, are not behind the President. This an indicator of the success of a secession vote. We are running the simulations now."

Bill Scott, Head of the National Energy Council, looked around the table. "In the past, we have seen this kind of emotional politics fade away as soon as the next big story comes along. They seem to have a shelf life of about two days. Apathy will kill this whole secession debate before it gets moving. We are talking about the President after all. Whether you like his personal style or not, he is getting things accomplished and a large part of the country sees that, even in California. Approval ratings jump up and down all the time."

Constance looked over at Bill. "Can the outrage last? I think it depends on what ammunition they have. If the President would stop his deliberately inflammatory policies, he could maintain some control. We are talking about the possible destruction of the US. We have to do whatever it takes to keep California pacified and to keep a lid on the secession hype swamping social media."

Jennifer Smith, a usually reserved woman with several doctorates in nuclear energy, leaned forward. "I think the problem comes with the President playing ball. He simply isn't going to see the need to pacify. I don't think he considers that the consequences of winning might be that the loser will pick up their ball and go home."

Bill interrupted. "Absent another incident in the next few weeks, I think it is safe it say that this will all blow over before enough signatures can be gathered to get the measure on the ballot. This will be gone by next week and we can all move on."

"So you want to do nothing?" Constance asked, eyes widening. "Haven't you been listening? We have to fight. We can't just let the US splinter apart."

"Yes, we should do nothing. We are Americans. We have to stand firm and say no to California demanding to run their own show. If we agree to their demands, what is to stop them from coming back with more, and then more? No, they need to know the rest of the US will not be held hostage to their wants. They need to come into line if they want to stay a part of our America, we won't beg them, hell no."

Jennifer stood up, leaning both hands onto the table. "Of course we are going to listen, and yes, we are going to use diplomacy. They have every right to be angry. We were using the military to harass, arrest and deport California citizens because they have brown skin. Then our President denies it. So yes, we need to do some ass kissing because, to be blunt; we need California way more than they need us. We can't afford to lose the most innovate part of our country. Without California, this country will fall down hard."

Todd stood up, the general once more, drawing everyone's attention.

"Everyone back down and take a breath. Go get something to eat and cool off. I need your minds not your politics. You all have made valid points. Be back here at 2:00 p.m. and we will wrap it up."

The room cleared out quickly, leaving just Todd, Dusty, Madison and Dr. Lang.

Madison sighed. "I just want the good guys to win and to wake up to a sunny morning with the smell of pancakes drifting through the house."

Dr. Lang had his head down and was rubbing his temples. He lifted his head and looked across the table to Todd and Dusty.

"Well Gentlemen, I think we just saw the biggest obstacle the country is facing, played out in this room just now."

At their blank looks he continued. "What will destroy this country won't be the President doing illegal things, although it isn't helping. Pretty much all Presidents have done something illegal while they are in office, it is almost impossible to accomplish anything otherwise.'

'No, what we witnessed here is the sharp division of the left and right; the loss of the middle ground. That is what will drive the states apart. We have seen it in history a hundred times and the final result is invariably destruction. When neither side can see a place to stand in the middle, then there is no place to negotiate towards. One side can never pull everyone on the other to them, nor can they become the sole decision makers, ignoring the other viewpoint. You can't have two completely divergent power systems in play. It just can't work, it is unstable and it will pull them both down.'

'In the past, even when we were divided, we used diplomacy to work our issues out to a centrist solution. We relied on both parties to temper the excesses of the other. That is the true beauty of the American system of government. Sometimes the country was more left leaning, sometimes right, but never far from center. We trusted each side to be able to give a little to reach a consensus. Now, there is no trust left. We are where we were at the beginning of the civil war and the echoes of that war still color much of our political landscape today nearly one hundred and fifty years later.'

'If we can't find a way to get everyone to accept not getting everything they want; like spoiled children, so politicians don't face losing their seats because they are willing to meet in the middle, then there is no point in keeping the US in one piece. The country we will become will be significantly flawed; either fascist or socialist, but no longer a republic.'

'When they make death threats to a senator representing their own party, just because he voted against a particular piece of legislation, even if he has a lifetime of public service, then perhaps it is time to separate and negotiate as countries instead of trying to work together. It's like a bad divorce; it is painful, but since there is no longer any love to soften the hard edges, and no middle ground to work from, and a loss of respect on both sides, then the only option is to break apart. As a country, if we can no longer meet in the middle, then maybe it would be best if California were to secede. It may be the only way to save what we have."

They all sat quiet for a minute and then Dr. Lang pushed his chair back and stood up. "I'm heading to the cafe; I really need a cup of coffee. Maddy, would you like to join me?"

She looked up at him. "I'll be along in just a minute if you could save me a seat?"

The silence was a weight in the room.

"Sir? I hate to break into your thoughts; I just wanted to ask about Ashley, Brian's girlfriend? Have you heard if she is ok?"

Todd looked up from the tabletop. "Ashley? Yes, she is fine. They picked her up yesterday evening. Brian hadn't given her any information and she didn't have any way to reach him so they released her."

"Thank you, Sir." She stood up and walked to the door. "Can I bring either of you anything?"

"No, Maddy girl, I expect we will be following you over there shortly."

Dusty and Todd looked at each other.

"Damn, I wish you had left me on my boat. Being in the middle of this shit sucks."

Todd started laughing. "I need you here just for your honesty, Dusty. That's the main reason I pulled you back, not the collapse of the world."

Todd switched back into a General.

"So what are we going to do about your family? I heard through connections that it was probably Jillian who worked the social media campaign so effectively last night. And Mike has squirreled away Brian so well that no one in either the FBI or the DIA seems to be able to locate him; quite an accomplishment. While I'm impressed with their results, I'm uncomfortable that they seem to be working independently from both the military and the government. We need to bring them into line."

Dusty's brows drew down, "Jillian masterminded what? She's in Mexico. On our boat. I don't think she had anything to do with this. She turns fifty this year, she's hardly some technical kid out fucking shit up on the internet. It's Jillian for God's sake." He started chuckling.

"I got the information from two different sources, Dusty. She's moderator of something like forty social media groups, she has tens-of-thousands following her, and she runs websites on everything from raising kids to cooking on a boat, to dealing with military deployments. Both sources agree that the vast majority of the counter messages started with her."

Dusty sat open-mouthed, his mind working furiously backwards. How much time did Jillian spend on the computer? Quite a bit, come to think of it, she was always sitting at the table with the laptop open when he walked through the door. Why didn't she tell him about it all? Had she tried and he didn't really listen? Did she give up at some point? She always asked what he was up to, what his day had been like when he came home. He rarely asked about hers.

"Your expression is priceless. This would be funny, Dusty, if I didn't have to answer for it to the Joint Chiefs. I've known you a long time; we've had each other's backs in some pretty hairy situations. I know what a selfish SOB you can be so I get that you had no idea what Jillian was up to, but I need for you to call her off. This is causing big issues for the President. I may not agree with what he is doing and I am working behind the scenes to protect Brian as well as his career, but we have to play ball or I will lose my leverage."

Dusty nodded. He understood.

"And Dusty, I know you and Mike aren't seeing eye-to-eye, especially since he left the Marines, but we need to get to Brian. It is critical that we get him into custody before anyone else catches up with him. They will soon, it is only a matter of time, they have the resources. You need to get Mike to talk."

Dusty nodded again. "I hear you Todd."

He ran a hand through his hair. "I think I need to take a walk."

He walked through the corridors, miles of tiled walkways wrapping in circles around the Pentagon's central courtyard, so he could think it all through. He wasn't sure how to approach either Jillian or Mike. They had done what he wasn't able to and he wasn't sure he wanted to call them off. He was proud of both of them. His heart had jumped when he heard about the reversal of the President's ratings. He couldn't believe it was Jillian's doing but it made sense looking backwards. Of course she would have used all of her resources to protect Brian, as he should have done. He always had put duty first, trusting that Jillian would take care of the family when he couldn't, and once again, she had come through for Brian.

So what now? He was a soldier who had spent a lifetime following orders, even if he didn't agree with them, but he had never had to put his family directly into the way of gunfire before. He didn't know how to square his responsibilities to his family with his responsibilities to his the President. He couldn't see a way to do both.

He turned abruptly and walked towards the cafeteria. He needed more information and Madison was very likely the person who had it.

The Assassin

The driver parked the tan, Toyota Camry at the edge of Little Italy in San Diego, a street of tourist shops, bakeries and restaurants just east of the downtown high rises. He exited the vehicle dressed in dark-gray casual slacks, a polo shirt and a light, gray jacket. He discreetly checked the holster with the Sig P320 under his arm and adjusted the jacket to hide it completely. Today he had a neatly trimmed beard and round glasses, his brown hair cut short. He looked much like any of a dozen tourists who wandered the neighborhood on a Saturday. He strolled up the avenue, paid for street parking at a little kiosk, and returned to the car, putting the sticker inside the driver's side window. He headed off again, stopping to look in shop windows, as he worked his way in the general direction of Balboa Park and the planned memorial. It was several miles but it was early morning yet, he had plenty of time.

Michael

Michael Phillips raced through Carmel in the passenger seat of a Lamborghini, dressed in a dark, navy suit with aviator sunglasses and a blue tooth in his ear. The driver, in his late twenties and an internet billionaire, handled the wheel with ease, putting the car through its paces on the winding canyon roads. They flew past famous people's houses as Mike practiced his breathing exercises, mindful of radiating calm as his employer slammed the gears up and down. He had shifted duty assignments with one of his associates so he could drop off the radar for a few days. There was strict secrecy pertaining to which team member was with which client, providing the perfect hiding spot in plain view. Further, tech billionaires had advanced electronics to keep them off of government grids. Mike was safe for the moment, at least from the FBI or DIA, or whichever other alphabet soup agency might be looking for him. He wasn't so sure he was going to survive this drive though.

His client braked hard and skidded up a driveway, careening around a corner towards a sixties modern structure overlooking the canyon they had barreled through.

He smiled at Michael. "We're here!"

He slammed on the brakes, bringing the car to a jolting stop and climbed out. Mike followed and surveyed his surroundings, looking for threats. He had assumed, as they left Silicone Valley, that they were off to visit a secret lover, either male or female, he wasn't sure which way his client leaned, and didn't really care. His client seemed anxious, amped up in a nervous kind of way and Mike figured he was on his way to a hook-up and a little excited and maybe a little unsure. In the last few months Mike had noticed that while money took away a lot of problems, love still was tricky, even for the super wealthy.

He let his eyes rove over everything, trusting his training to pick up anomalies that could signal danger for his client. He stepped forward, blocking the most likely sniper paths with his body as they walked the last bit up the driveway. As they reached the door, it was opened by a bodyguard dressed similarly to Mike.

"You are pleased to enter," he said in a strong Russian accent and Mike went on full alert. This wasn't what he had expected.

Mobury

ICE Special Agent In Charge, Dan Mobury, looked across the parking lot behind the Navy Hospital, located just across the highway from Balboa Park, where Congressman Silva's memorial was to be held in a short time. The fleet of urban assault vehicles designed by the military for bashing in doors and breaking through barricades; vicious, indestructible six-wheeled tanks, minus the gun turret and the tracks, were lined up before him with a sea of agents, garbed in black combat gear, ICE stenciled in large, white letters on their riot shields. He smiled. This was his day.

Despite the congressman's shooting, which he had been able to blame on the oversized Boy Scout from the army, Dan Mobury was still on top and in demand. He had spun his version of that altercation, painting the Rangers as the problem, to his superiors, who didn't question the situation too closely so they could keep their own hands clean. In the usual turn of events, they nodded understandingly and handed him a bigger and more demanding position under someone else's supervision. This was how his career in law enforcement had gone; his knack for self preservation combining with the desire of those above him to pass the problem along to the next department, instead of dealing with his obnoxiousness and the union hassle. It had ended up in a string of promotions starting with the police force and ending up here, years later, with the Southwest field command of ICE.

His dad had gotten him onto the force and then using the lessons taught to him at the end of a fist or back of a hand, he had manipulated each step up from the ashes of the last job. He was just vicious enough and smart enough to make those around him uncomfortable but not so far outside the lines to get them to actually take action against him. It was easier to just move him along and wipe your brow in relief as he left for the next desk.

Today was the culmination of all those years. Today he was running the largest ICE action in the history of the department. He was in charge. He smiled to himself, throwing out his chest and standing a little taller so he would be seen as an equal by the man he was with.

Steven Capardi, dressed in custom tailored khakis and a soft blue, button-down shirt with a thin tan pinstripe, and his signature Rolex, stood with him. "You must have brought in every ICE agent on the West Coast."

Steven stood casually with just his eyes moving quickly, like a falcon watching for his quarry. Dan had the feeling he could have told him how many agents in the mass in front of them were left-handed. He shivered. This guy made his skin crawl.

"We were able to bring in four-hundred-and-seventy-eight from an eight state region, as the President requested. This is the largest operation we have attempted so far and we are doing it without the help of the Army thanks to last week's fuck up. We are focusing all of our resources in eight states on just this one demonstration here today."

Dan looked up at Steven, watching for a reaction. "It is my belief the President is trying to make a few statements here. First, that ICE can field an enormous amount of power without relying on the Army. Second, California answers to the US government first and foremost. ICE is raiding today, here, to show the President is in charge, not the California legislature, and third, which I think is most important, to send so many illegal sons-of-bitches running back across the border that the news media can't help but cover it."

Capardi's eyes just kept taking in everything around them. Dan looked down. He clasped his hands behind his back.

"What is your plan, Agent Mobury?"

"Well, we are expecting a turnout, on the top side, of about fifteen hundred people, probably less. Although he was a congressman they did a formal eulogy in Washington earlier this week so we shouldn't have many important people in the audience, just his community supporters. Between police, security guards and ICE there should be about three of them to one of us. With this level of force, we will keep from having a repeat of last Saturday.'

'As the rally gets underway we will move the tactical vehicles up through the parking lots. Busses will be stationed at four parking areas to evacuate detainees. We have performed hundreds of raids, although none on this scale, so we expect it to go smoothly."

Steven made a slight inclination of his head. Dan smiled. Clearly Capardi saw he had this under control.

Blanca

Blanca found an empty place to pull her crossover into in the lot behind the Science Center at Balboa Park. She walked to the Prado, the half-mile long walkway that connected an assortment of museums at the heart of the complex. In addition to the regular crowds of tourists, there was already a sizeable gathering for the Congressman's memorial, many wearing black armbands with a white peace symbol inked on. It was overcast, making for a pleasant walk as everyone moved towards the Museum of Man at the North end of the mall.

It was a little before noon and it was already crowded. She could feel the energy building. When she got to the square in front of the museum, she worked her way through the crowds to the booth. Christina and Oscar were behind the table, handing out black armbands and asking for signatures for the proposition to secede.

Christina came around and gave her a hug and then kissed her cheek. "You made it Chica; we were starting to think you wouldn't."

She pulled an armband over the sleeve of Blanca's white blouse. Made out of a thin spandex, it easily stayed in place, the white peace symbol standing out sharply.

"I had to wait to watch John. He had an interview on TV this morning. I couldn't miss that. I left Mama's just as soon as it was done."

"How was it? Did he seem nervous?"

"He did so well. I'm proud of him. He's finally got the break he's been working so hard for. I never thought I would see him on TV. I saved it so I can show Amy when she is older. And Christina, he asked me to marry him this morning."

"Aw, Chica, congratulations." Christina pulled her in for another hug.

Blanca collected up a clipboard with a proposition signature page and moved behind the booth with Oscar. It was a challenge getting support with the mostly Hispanic crowd. Many of their parents or grandparents had struggled to make it across the border. The US had been a candle of hope, a bright light offering jobs and a better life compared to the poverty of their home countries. They were unwilling to give up on the dream, even in the face of the racism and the economic inequality that was thrust on them. Succession, if it happened, would not be easy. The disruption to nearly every person's life in California would be the norm. Everything from taxes to schools to military would change. It was going to be hard but not as difficult as the brutal discrimination they faced daily now. She just had to convince people of that.

Blanca sighed as another older gentleman turned away. Secession ran against a lifetime of bias, even though the federal government was making it painfully clear that Latinos were not welcome in the US anymore. She wanted to scream. They just wouldn't do what was best for their community, especially if it ran against what they felt the government would want them to do. They patiently waited for things to change. It was a cultural thing and nearly impossible to fight against.

Noon came and went as the crowd continued to grow, a heavy press of bodies that pushed against the booth. The organizers of the memorial were collecting everyone here at the North end and then planned to march back to the fountain in front of the Science Center, where the stage was erected, in a show of solidarity. It looked like a lot more people were showing up than they expected. Already the crowd spilled down the Prado in both directions with more coming up the pathways from the parking with the event start still an hour away.

Oscar finally suggested they put everything away and participate fully in the rally since no one could get to the booth anyway. They had collected several hundred signatures, which was good, but far short of their goal. They quickly folded up the table and carried it to where Oscar had a special pass to park the van, then returned to the square, edging through the crowd until they were back on the main thoroughfare.

Working through the crowd, Blanca noticed how somber this gathering was and eerily silent, just a word here or there. They showed respect for a Congressman who was one of them, who had fought for them and had been murdered trying to protect them. There was a strong underlying outrage visible in the set of shoulders and tight expressions; he had been killed by immigration agents in a raid at a Town Hall meeting, an obvious slap in the face to the Congressman and their community.

At a word shouted from the steps of the museum, the crowd turned and moved towards the Science Center. The stretch was already filled with a sea of black armbands so thousands upon thousands of silent mourners merged together, compacting as they neared the Southern end of the Prado. It was a ten minute walk burned into Blanca's memory; the press of solidarity and angry energy, the mass of armbands with the beautiful symbol of peace worn proudly. Standing with a crush of people who felt as she did; who were tired of being treated as less because of their heritage, who believed they had a right to be there, in that space, no matter what they looked like or what country they, or their parents, or their grandparents, came from.

The leading edge came up against the front of the circular fountain at the Southern end of the Prado where a stage, draped in black, had been set up. A row of TV cameras and reporters stood to the right, with their backs to the Science Museum. A podium was on the stage with the US and California flags on stands behind it and a row of folding chairs to the right for Congressman Silva's wife and today's speakers. As she squeezed forwards, Blanca stood on tip-toe trying to get a glimpse of John. She abandoned Oscar and Christina with a wave and threaded her way closer to the stage. Being small was an advantage as she ducked under arms and pushed between shoulders.

John

John Fields sat on the stage, looking down the mall. It was a sea of mostly brown faces stretching all the way back to the bridge crossing the freeway underpass, half a mile away at least, and it was spilling sideways into the courtyards and promenades that lined the Prado; tens of thousands of people. While he smiled casually to the other speakers, his heart was beating a crazy rhythm inside his chest. He was a journalist, he expressed through the written word, not in public like this. His hands were sweaty and smudging the notes he had for his speech. He wondered what a panic attack felt like, and if he had one, what the hell he would do. He wanted to throw up. There wasn't any way to get off the stage though without being noticed.

His eye picked up a hand waving. Between all of the serious, armband clad audience, an arm was waving ten rows out. He focused on it, following it down, and there, with shoulders to either side of her small face, Blanca was peeking out. He felt a rush of love for her. He hadn't realized how much he wanted her there.

She smiled and mouthed, "I love you."

He smiled back.

The first strains of the national anthem started to play though the sound system and a stunning Latino women in a red dress stepped up to the mike, singing it to perfection. John vaguely recognized her as a Hollywood star, but couldn't place her name.

A middle-aged woman in a deep, maroon suit with matching heels stepped up next, "Good afternoon, Ladies and Gentlemen. I am Congresswoman Carmen Ruiz, and I welcome you here today. Thank you for coming on this sad day to show respect for your fallen leader and support his wife Rose and their family. I worked closely with Congressman Carlos Silva in Washington and I wanted to let you, his community, know that he will be greatly missed in the aisles of Congress."

She continued on for quite some time. He kept his eyes steadily on Blanca, emptying his mind and relaxing his shoulders. He heard his name as Congresswoman Ruiz introduced him. His heart banged against his ribcage. He took a deep breath and looked one last time at his fiancé, walked to the podium, set his speech down in front of him and adjusted the mike higher as he was quite a bit taller than Congresswoman Ruiz. He took another deep breath and looked out over the crowd. He saw sadness, compassion and support from every face. In a wash of empathy that dropped from the top of his head down through his body, he felt like he was one with this community. He belonged here. Suddenly comfortable, a small, sad smile crossed his face.

"Thank you for having me here today. My name is John Fields and I was the reporter who was with Congressman Silva last Saturday after the Town Hall meeting. Some of the last words he uttered were in support of you, his community, and I am humbled to be here to share with you how much he influenced my life.

"We stand here, surrounded by buildings influenced by Mexican architecture. We stand on ground that was set aside and designated as a park by the Country of Mexico well before it ever became part of the United States. It was named after Vasco Nunez de Balboa, a Spaniard who was the first European to cross the continent. I can't think of a better place to celebrate the life of Carlos Silva, Congressman, husband, father and grandfather. Like this park, his family traces its roots back to before California was a part of the United States. He was proud of both his heritage and of his position within the US legislature. His passion was for San Diego and he often spoke about the incredible strength this community has because of its diversity.'

'Congressman Silva believed the immigrants crossing the Mexico-California border are a resource of knowledge and culture that he welcomed and celebrated. He worked to create avenues for citizenship and also for visas so that everyone who made it here could legally stay. He understood how difficult the passage was. Many of you here today owe him a debt that can never be repaid, and he never wanted you to."

John paused for a moment, his speech in front of him on the podium, as the reality of the situation hit him full force. He looked at the thousands of faces before him. He felt the weight of their concern over the future, reflected on strong, serious faces. He found Blanca, smiling encouragement. Realization forced its way through his consciousness. This was his community. He wasn't different. He wasn't an outsider. It didn't have anything to do with the color of his skin or where he was born. He felt his heart shift. These were his people now. His baby girl was growing up Latino and he was proud of that.

His community was hurting. His wife and his daughter deserved better than neutrality from him, they deserved his voice, standing up for them. He took a deep breath and turned his notes over. He stood up a little taller, squared his shoulders and started again, speaking what he felt, conscious that the cameras were flashing his image across the world, casting this decision in stone.

"On the night Congressman Silva was murdered, yes that is a harsh word but I believe it to be true, on the night he was murdered I watched some of you stand up with him as he fought against tyranny, and I watched you stand over his body with respect, keeping him in your hearts until his wife Rose arrived. You were my heroes that night.'

'Now I call on you to stand again, to take up Congressman Silva's cause and to fight against the illegal actions of our President. He may deny he ordered it, but be assured; it was with his direct order that US Army Rangers, specially trained in urban warfare, were hidden amongst the immigration agents who have harassed this community, killed your neighbors and assassinated your elected leader. Not only was this illegal, but it was morally wrong.'

'It is time to fight. It is time to say no to racism disguised as immigration raids. It is time to say they will not murder our voice. It is time to say that we belong here and that using force to push us out will not happen. It is time to resist!'

'Resist!"

John rose his two fists into the air over his head and watched as the crowed rippled and then returned the salute, thousands and thousands of hands raising in a silent, two fisted salute of solidarity. He felt tears sting his eyes. He bent to the mike.

"Thank you."

Congresswoman Ruiz stepped back up, looking flustered. "Thank you, Mr. Fields."

He understood she was about to soften his statement with conciliatory words and his stomach turned sour. This was how it always went, a call for justice followed by the cautious politician, making it seem a little outlandish, a little too risky. He looked at his feet.

Before her next words, a commotion broke out behind the stage. It quickly moved into sight by the Natural History Museum. Dozens of swastika banners overshadowing angry white men, heads shaved, wearing an assortment of camouflage, body armor and combat boots, as they rushed across the avenue from the arboretum and shoved towards the crowd. Waving flags, bats and firearms, screaming epithets and 'White Power, Illegals Go Home', they formed a wedge to plow into the heart of the audience. Vicious, violent, they threw themselves at the mourners with rage. John watched, frozen.

The TV cameras swung to cover their entrance. Police officers in riot gear rushed to get between and separate the two groups. The crowd in front of John rippled back and then surged forwards and to the left where the protesters were approaching, like an unruly snake, and he watched Blanca get carried closer to the edge. He stood up.

Congresswoman Ruiz took the mike. "Everyone, please, keep calm. Don't let them interfere in our celebration of Congressman Silva's work."

Her voice boomed out of the sound system, blanketing the area, "Turn your backs on them; let them hold no power over us today. Turn your backs."

The cameras swung back to the stage, catching her imploring speech. It would be played back throughout the primetime news hour that evening.

"He stood for peace. I know you are angry, do not let it overwhelm you. Be strong. Their hate and evil have no place here. Not at his memorial. Stand for peace. Stand against hate. Turn around!"

John watched Blanca, he saw her stop and plant her feet. He watched her turn around, turn her back to the alt-right marchers and tug on the arms of those around her to do the same. They turned and then others did as well. Soon the ripple turned into a wall of faces, rigid shoulders facing away from the police in riot gear and behind them the chanting alt-right marchers. She looked tiny and fragile in the line. He swallowed. She was a fierce light and he was so proud of her in that moment, even as he was terrified for her.

Congresswoman Ruiz continued, "Let us pray so that the evil has no power here."

"Our heavenly father who art in heaven,
Hallowed be thy name,
Thy kingdom come,

Thy will be done,
On earth as it is in heaven,
Give us this day our daily bread
and forgive us our trespasses,
As we forgive those who trespass against us,
And lead us not into temptation,
But deliver us from evil,
For thine is the kingdom, the power and the glory,
Forever and ever, amen."

The crowd, tens of thousands strong, took up the prayer, drowning out the chant of the protesters. It moved from the front of the rally to the back a half-mile away. John stood in awe at the power of the words, sure this moment would never leave him.

As the prayer ended, in a horrible twist of fate, Special Agent in Charge Dan Mobury, sitting in the command van, signaled for the approach. The ICE urban combat vehicles arrived in a well executed maneuver so they appeared at each exit point to the long mall simultaneously. Agents disembarked, dressed in full combat gear with batons held out. A ripple ran through the crowd. Angry shouts rose from the more than ten-thousand people now trapped in the mall. Like something alive, the crowd recoiled from the points where the vehicles pulled in and roiled in confusion.

Special Agent Dan Mobury's precise and carefully controlled raid, without tactical information about the increased size of the crowd and the Nazi counter-protesters, went sideways in the first seconds of contact. The Nazis turned to face the assault vehicle pulling behind them. Disengaging from the mourners, they stood firm against the new threat, yanking assault rifles out of their gear and setting up a defensive line.

An angry murmur passed through the crowd as they recognized the ICE tanks were there for an immigration raid. It rippled back and forth, building, until the calm, respectful mourners exploded into a mob.

"Resist!"

The cry was taken up by thousands of voices and the sinuous snake of the mob struck out towards the vehicles as hundreds of angry rioters roared down on the agents.

The shooter, in the dark grey slacks and a light grey jacket, stepped from under the portico of the art museum halfway down the mall. He had waited patiently all morning, blending with the tourists, for the perfect moment of incline; that point at which a mountain goes from stable to avalanche. He was close to where a tank had pulled in. He moved behind a pillar, stepping around it into a flower bed, and emerging on the other side. Raising his Sig P320, he sighted, fired twice in rapid succession and a man went down, blood splattering onto the mourners surrounding him. The shooter stepped back behind the pillar and then to the other side, sighting and shooting again. Next to the tank, an ICE agent dropped.

The shots echoed up and down the mall. Everything froze for the beat of a heart, and then chaos erupted. By the stage, the alt-right attacked the ICE agents, the unmistakable rattle of machine gun fire raking over screams of panic from the mourners. ICE agents up and down the mall pulled out their firearms, shooting at the crowd coming down on them. There was no place for the thousands of mourners to go. The mob rolled back and forth through the space while people at the edges started to collapse as bullets found flesh. The ICE agents, panicked, emptied their magazines into the wall of people and struggled to reload. The mob charged towards them, overrunning the check points, pummeling the agents with fists and feet as they poured through the openings and the park, running for safety.

John, standing on the stage, saw it all unravel. He stood frozen when the first four shots were fired and then was running for Blanca, leaping off the stage and shoving his way through the mourners. He lost sight of her face at the roar of machine gun fire as the crowd reversed around him, retreating towards the stage. He struggled to keep his footing and pushed forwards. The edge of the crowd was pinned against the wall of police officers in riot gear, now facing towards the alt-right protesters, protecting them from the gun fight between the ICE agents and the Nazis. He couldn't find Blanca.

A police officer dropped, hit by a bullet, and he rushed forward as the man slumped, catching him. Gently easing him down onto the grass, he rolled him over. The shoulder wound was spurting deep, red blood and John put the heel of his hand against it, leaning in. The officer looked up at him and grimaced, trying to smile.

"Thank you, man. Damn that hurts."

John looked around for help. All he could see were the backs of the police officers above him and the crowd ten yards off now, closer to the stage. Gunfire was loud, both in front of him and from different points down the mall. The police were lobbing tear gas canisters into the Alt Right group and the sting of it hit his eyes, making them water.

"Help me," He roared, "Somebody help me."

The mourners were shying back from the gun battle, the peace signs on their armbands standing out in sharp contrast to the events unfolding. A small woman pushed forward and grabbed two men near the front and pulled them along with her to his side.

"I am a doctor," She said, falling to her knees beside him.

Blanca

Blanca heard the first shots and froze. Then the automatic weapon fire and the yells as the Alt-Right advanced on the tank behind her sent her scurrying with the rest of the crowd toward the stage. She came up on the edge of it and an older man in front of her tripped, sprawling. Taking a sudden giant step over him, her heel came down on his arm, throwing off her balance. She went tumbling and felt another body crashing close by. Terror shot through her. She frantically searched for a way to get out from underfoot, from being trampled in the panic. She pushed herself to the stage, lifted up the edging and crawled underneath, shoving herself between the triangular joists. The fabric dropped down behind her and the light went dim. Curling into a tight ball, she wrapped her hands over her head, sobbing.

The mourners push up against the stage and then footsteps pounded over her head as they fled towards the Science Center. Gunshots thundered with screams of panic and furious yelling. The tear gas stung her eyes and throat. She cowered down, as afraid as she had ever been, forcing breath in and out past the sobs, her heart beating frantically.

"Help me. Somebody help me." John's unmistakable voice carried across the chaos.

She lay there, frozen. She couldn't bring herself to move from the safety and invisibility she had found. She started sobbing again. She couldn't make herself crawl back out. She couldn't even uncurl from her fetal position. She held her arms over her head and rocked. John needed her and she wasn't strong enough to go to him.

She thought of Amy, of Amy growing up without John. She thought of all the things he would miss, from her first steps, any day now, to walking her down the aisle. Her resolve solidified. She wasn't going to let her baby girl grow up without her daddy, the man she loved.

Fighting back the burn of tear gas and stilling her sobs, she pushed herself back to the edge of the stage, lifting the fabric with a shaking hand. There was space around the stage now. At the sharp retort of a pistol, she backed up.

Taking a deep, stinging breath, she forced herself to wiggle out from between the joists into the open, crawling along the stage until she came to the end. There was no cover left. The crowd had fled leaving the grass littered with bodies. The concrete of the mall had more. The gunfire was sporadic now but the tear gas was strong, drifting over her in waves. She pulled her black armband off and held it over her face. She could barely see through the smoke and her tears but scanned each body, looking for John's ponytail or anything she could identify.

Twenty yards away a group huddled on the ground. The police moved off and confronted the last of the alt-right in a sudden eruption of intense gunfire. Ducking, she recognized John as he leaned back. She stifled a cry. Pushing up, she ran, huddled over, keeping her eyes fastened on him, praying that focus would keep her invisible. He looked up just as she left the shelter of the stage and relief broke across his features. He half-crouched and rushed to intercept her.

Catching her part way across the grass, he pulled her down, covering her with his body, as the sound of bullets zipped by. He hugged her so tightly she thought her chest would collapse. He was alive; she could feel his heart hammering against her shoulder.

"Are you okay?"

"Baby, are you okay?"

"Yes." Blanca answered first and frantically felt along his chest, searching for injuries.

"I'm okay, Blanca." He kissed her forehead and smoothed the tears off her cheek with his thumb and then tucked her against him and held her close until the last of the bullets stopped.

Mobury

Special Agent Mobury stood helplessly watching the mourners stream around his agents and flee into the park. Teams had been overrun and others had stepped back behind their vehicles, letting the mob escape by them. He would deal with those traitors later. He was with the team that had run up against the Nazi counter-fire and had been pinned behind the vehicle through most of the firefight. His agents had called for backup across the board but the extra manpower had been with him. He wasn't about to give them up in that chaos.

The Nazi's had been a surprise. Although he supported much of what they espoused, especially their stand on immigration, he was frustrated that they had interfered and made a mess of today. He watched with bitter satisfaction as they went down, some with wounds, most taken into custody.

Sirens were approaching. The smoke and smell of teargas and sulfur from the gunfire was quickly clearing, blown away on the light afternoon breeze. As far he could see there were bodies. Most were clustered in front of the assault vehicles but others were also down, perhaps trampled in the panic or hit by a stray bullet. He didn't know and didn't really care. What he saw was one less brown skin taking up space in his country.

Looking out at the disaster this had descended into, he knew his career could be over if he didn't maneuver quickly. Everything he had spent his life working for would be gone. It was like high school; never making the team and facing his dad's ridicule for it. He thought of all the girls who had only seen his short stature and his high voice and turned away. He had vowed to prove to them all wrong but this day was just another disappointment, another reason for his old man to laugh. He couldn't bring himself to give a shit about the people who were bleeding and dying. Most of them were probably illegal anyway, otherwise why would they run. They had ruined this, the biggest immigration raid ever held, and maybe ruined him as well.

The police had rounded up the Nazis and had them handcuffed on their knees. The grass they had been fighting on was blood soaked. He stepped over and around bodies as he made his way to the stage, looking with detachment at the scene in front of him. There were hundreds of bodies sprawled on the grass from what he could see, and he certainly couldn't see the whole mall. The ambulances were arriving up at the North end. The tanks that had been blocking the road had been pushed to the side to make room.

He looked around for Steven Capardi, but of course, he was gone. Near as he could guess, Steven was even better at wiggling out of a situation than he himself was. He admired him for that. Capardi wouldn't get his hands dirty in this; it would all fall on Dan if he couldn't manipulate the circumstances to make it look better.

A young man approached the stage, looking up at him. Dan recognized him as the reporter who had taken the video. He had just been on the TV that morning talking about it. Dan stared at him.

"I saw you at Congressman Silva's murder, didn't I? You were running the show."

John hopped up on the stage, towering above Dan Mobury. Dan noticed a small Hispanic woman was with him, tugging on his arm.

"You are goddamn right I was, and here too. This was supposed to be the biggest round-up of illegals ever, the highlight of my career. This was fucked up by them." He pointed at Blanca.

John stood still, the red creeping up his face. He lunged forward and punched Dan in the mouth with a right hook that barreled into him, hurling him backwards over a chair. He landed heavily on the stage with the chair crashing on top. John started moving towards him but Blanca pulled on his arm, and he turned away, stepping back off the stage.

Dan struggled for breath and then shouted at John's back. "Don't think this is over. You and your whore are going to pay. You hear me? You goddamn race traitor!"

John and Blanca kept walking away. One of the news cameras was still pointed at the stage and the cameraman focused in on the faces of both John and Agent Mobury as they separated.

Michael

Michael was standing against a paneled wall in the den of the mansion in the hills outside of Carmel. His client sat with several of the house's occupants watching a screen that wrapped around the end of the room. Except for the intrusive electronics, the decorating was obviously undisturbed 1960s American modern including shag wall-to-wall and pokey chandeliers set in odd places. The occupants definitely were not. The conversation rambled between Russian and English and Mike was surprised to discover his client was fluent and following along comfortably when the language shifted.

They had been here for several hours and the bullet fragment that was lodged in Mike's hip was throbbing from standing stationary. He was shifting his weight, attempting to ease the ache, when they picked up Balboa Park on a passing satellite and it jumped huge onto the screen, crystal clear although it was viewed from space. Even with light clouds covering parts, he could easily make out thousands of people lining the mall like a black sea spread between the buildings.

He assumed they were tapping into a concert or something; a voyeuristic rich man's game, until he made out the tanks approaching along the walkways. He leaned forward, feeling the adrenaline spread through his system. Logically, he knew he was hundreds of miles away but his body was reacting to the upcoming confrontation as though he was in the center of it.

"Wait for it," Vasily said and they all leaned forward.

Suddenly chaos erupted in the crowd and it bent and streamed like water, recoiling and surging. After a few minutes of agitation it bled out along the walkways like a flood forcing its way through cracks in a dam, leaving the trail of bodies on the pavement looking like broken dolls discarded haphazardly. Everyone watched the aftermath as it wound down.

"Yes!" The man said, "That went off perfectly, no?" He looked around the room with a smile.

Michael slammed a mask of indifference onto his features, working to blend into the background.

His client stood up. "Yes, Vasily, that should move things along."

Vasily stood as well, shaking hands with Mike's client. "Then we shall plan for the future. Yes?"

Mike followed his client to the door and covered his exit, using his body to shield him as they made their way to the car. His client drove rapidly through the neighborhood streets and then slowed as they reached Monterey.

"It's different in real life, isn't it? I mean, I know you have losses in war, that there is a cost. I just never thought about the people who would be hurt. It was numbers and angles. If a system is pushed here it will respond over there. It's different when it's real, when you see the people on the ground. It's harder to stay the course, even though you know it is for the better."

Michael watched the city roll by.

"I really feel all Californians would be better off on our own. We have a vision. Of course it will help our businesses, otherwise I wouldn't be doing it, but more than that it will help the people. We will boost the California economy. We will create jobs. We believe in a government that takes care of everyone, not just us wealthy ones. It will be colorblind and equal for everyone. I might be young but I have the resources to make this happen.'

'Did you know California is the fifth largest economy in the world? We support the rest of the country, yet their regressive leadership takes our capital in taxes then cuts what little federal funding they give back when

143

we disagree with their backwards policies. They are old men who don't understand tech companies or how millennials have changed the playing field. Hell, they aren't even on the playing field anymore. They got lost in the last century and want us all to stay in it with them."

He was silent for a few moments and when he started talking again his voice was softer, almost below what Michael could hear. "I really wasn't ready for real people getting hurt and killed. This was way more catastrophic than the plan. I'll have to rerun the models and see if I can figure out where they deviated."

Michael kept his eyes on the road. He had just witnessed a horrific act of terrorism and treason. As disillusioned as he was with the military and the government, he was not a traitor. He would report this immediately; he just to work out the avenue to do it. His client appeared to be a kid, younger than he himself was, but was also wealthy beyond imagining. He had the resources to make Michael disappear and by letting him witness this, had sent the message that he was untouchable and could shift politicians and countries as he wished. Mike closed his eyes for a moment while he kept his mask up. What had his life come to, babysitting monsters?

Dusty

The war room clock showed fifteen minutes after five. Dusty was sprawled out in a chair and Todd was pacing as Madison packed up her laptop, unplugging and wrapping up cords. The door opened and Captain Roberts entered, saluting Todd and Dusty.

"Sir, there is video coming in from California that you need to see."

At a nod from Todd, he switched screens in the room to TV mode. He flipped through channels, quickly settling on one and turning the sound up. Scenes from the massacre in Balboa Park filled the screen.

"Oh, my God," Madison said, "Oh, my God," she whispered again.

It clearly showed ICE agents firing into the crowd and people falling to the ground as thousands of people rushed to get past the tanks at the exits. They cut from the pre-recorded to live coverage from a helicopter. Emergency vehicles and personnel swarmed the mall littered with people, wounded or dead, you couldn't tell. They went to interviews of witnesses and cut it with more live footage. They showed the plea from Congresswoman Ruiz for peace, cut with the black tanks approaching to block the exits, the agents firing, and the anger on the faces of the alt-right counter-protesters, screaming and chanting.

"Oh, my God, we did this to our own people." She paled. "I think I need to throw up."

She moved quickly for the door, leaving Dusty, Todd and Captain Roberts staring at the screens.

Madison came back, her hands shaky. She slumped into a chair. Captain Roberts gave her a sympathetic smile, handing her a bottle of water. The news program they were watching cut to more live footage from a helicopter, this time of LA, of a riot, swelling; thousands of people rushing through city streets, smashing windows and turning over cars. They watched it all unfold. Todd sank down into a chair as well.

Dusty grabbed the remote and turned the sound off.

Todd sighed heavily, rubbing his eyes with a hand. "Well, that changes things."

The news program switched to the briefing room of the White House and Dusty turned the volume back up. The President's press secretary came to the podium.

"Our thoughts and prayers go out to the families of those killed today, especially those in uniform. While the President was unaware of the immigration check planned for today, he will investigate those members in the audience of Congressman Silva's memorial who attacked the ICE agents and started this terrible tragedy. He will not stop until each of these terrorists has been brought to justice.'

'The President would like to be very clear in his disappointment in the rioting. No further civil disobedience will be tolerated. Martial law is immediately invoked for the state of California. Curfews are imposed. The National Guard has been deployed to assist in bringing order to the areas under threat. There will be no questions taken at this time." He stepped away from the podium as reporters hollered questions at his retreating back.

"He had no knowledge, my ass." Dusty threw a pen across the table and it skipped off and hit a wall. "They had to bring in that equipment from ten states away, there is no way they have that many assault vehicles in San Diego. This required clearance from the top. Of course he is going to deny it, because it went to hell, but if it had worked, he'd be taking all the credit he could get his hands on."

"Dusty, you will not repeat that sentiment outside this room. Am I clear?"

Dusty stared at the General for a long second then nodded his head and looked away. "Yes, Sir."

Madison sat, trying not to be noticed. She was unsure of what she could add in a room with the General and her father, a Colonel. Growing up, General Jennings had been like a god. It was hard to feel comfortable saying what was on her mind in either of their company, let alone both of them together. She looked over at Captain Roberts, equally silent, standing beside the door at parade rest. He sent another sympathetic smile her way. She figured he probably understood how she felt, working with General Jennings every day as he did.

Dusty had turned the sound back off and the screen captured her eyes; the scenes of violence making her feel queasy. Her dad stared at the table but with an undercurrent of energy, as if he might fling himself up at any moment on an important mission. General Jennings looked serious and as though his mind was far away. He glanced up, met her eyes, and leaned forward.

"Well, we will obviously reconvene the focus group. In the meantime, Dusty, you will fly Jillian here so that we can put a lid on the social media aspects of this, locate Mike and get him contained and get Brian back to his base.'

'Madison, I will call Colonel Richardsen and extend your stay here, and Dr. Lang's as well; his knowledge on the modeling software is invaluable right now. You will be on temporary assignment here at the Pentagon until this crisis is stabilized."

"Yes Sir."

"Now if you will excuse me, I have calls to make. I need to find out how the hell this happened and start damage control."

As they made their way to the food court, Dusty and Madison could hear the news playing in nearby offices, going over the events in detail. Arriving at the cafe, the TVs at intervals around the room all had some version of it playing. Dusty and Maddy picked up a couple of sandwiches and went to a table away from the screens.

They ate silently.

Maddy looked at him. "Dad, what did he mean by bringing Mom here?'

Dusty hesitated. He hadn't been able to talk to Maddy before they reconvened. He felt like he was walking on eggshells now, wanting to phrase it all carefully so that he could get the information he needed without worrying his little girl.

"Well." He paused and started a different track. "Did you know your mom ran a whole bunch of social media stuff?"

Madison looked at him, her forehead wrinkling. "Well, yes, Dad, she's been pretty popular since before I was in high school, it's kind of what she does. Why?"

Dusty looked startled.

"Oh my God, Dad, did you not know? She is kind of famous in some circles. You guys live on a boat. How could you possibly live in that small of a space and not know who she is?"

Dusty looked down at the table, feeling his face start to flush. She asked a good question. How did he not know?

Madison started drumming her fingers against the tabletop. Dusty noticed it was a white laminate and that her hands stood out sharply against it. He waited to see what she would say. This much he knew from Jillian.

She took a deep breath. "Dad, I love you. I always will. But sometimes you can be a bit thick when it comes to us, your family."

She took another really big breath and then rushed on. "Do you know I fought to get assigned to the Academy? That I really want to teach and I am really good at it? Do you know how hard it was to do that knowing how much you wanted me to go into a field command and climb to the top ranks of the Air Force? I agonized over the decision to follow what I want and not what you think I should do."

Tears welled up in her eyes. Dusty's heart flipped over at her anguish. He looked at her as he would a young officer, not as his daughter. She was strong, and confident. She knew what she wanted. She wasn't the little girl he had scooped up and swung around in circles to make her laugh anymore. She was telling him something he had missed completely. His mind flashed to Jilly asking him to talk to her before he made calls to move her out of the Academy. She had understood how blind he was and tried to protect Madison from his stubbornness. He dropped his head.

"Dad, I'm not really cut out for the military. Everybody who knows me sees it. I can do it, I can do it really well, but I just don't fit in. I would be miserable in a unit giving orders. That just isn't me. When I get up in front of a classroom, everything flows. I am comfortable, in charge. I am good at breaking things down so they are understandable. I really love putting together the coursework and then seeing it come together for my students. I feel like I am making a difference in the world. I need you to support me instead of always putting down teaching like it isn't good enough."

He felt lost. This conversation wasn't going anywhere near the direction he wanted it to. Maddy needed her father now, he understood that much. But he had never had to deal with the emotional side; Jillian always handled that. He didn't know what to say.

Reaching out, he took Madison's hand, "Maddy girl, it's kind of like when I went away on deployments and I would always think of you like you were on the day I last hugged you, but months and months would go by and I would come back and still see the younger you, not the girl you had grown into. I am proud of you. I will make it a point to watch you teach so I can understand. Can you forgive me?"

149

"Yes, Dad, but it's not about forgiveness. I just want you to see me. See who I really am."

"I hear you Maddy, I promise to try and even though I don't say it enough, I love you."

He looked down at the table again. It seemed like he had come up with the right thing to say. He hoped so. These conversations felt like quicksand. He never knew how to step.

Madison smiled. "Okay, then, tell me what's up with Mom. And don't hold stuff back to protect me, I'm a big girl. I can't give good advice if I don't have all the information."

"I'll try. Todd, General Jennings, thinks your mom has been using her social media presence to shift opinion about Brian and in the process, shift blame onto the President. He thinks she is the source behind the drop in the polls. He wants me to stop her and bring her here to keep an eye on her."

Maddy sucked a breath in through her teeth. "Oh Dad, I'd bet money that she did, she is so good at that kind of stuff and she is doing it for Brian. I can't imagine she would be very open to letting it go though, what did she say when you told her?"

"Well, that's a part of the problem, I haven't yet." He looked down at the table again.

"Dad? You have talked to her since the restaurant, right?"

"Well, we left our phones there, and I told her not to answer strange numbers, and I don't usually call her until the mission is complete so she probably won't be expecting anything."

Madison interrupted. "Dad, we are surrounded by about a thousand secure lines and computers, we are in the Pentagon. You could have texted or emailed, you should have. She has been worried sick about Brian and you weren't there for her. She figured out how to help him on her own because you dropped the ball. I don't think you should try to stop her now. That isn't really fair or the right thing to do for Brian."

Dusty nodded. "I know Maddy, but General Jennings gave me a direct order. I don't have a choice."

Madison looked at him. "Dad, we always have a choice. You taught me that. Those ICE agents today, they had a choice, no one forced them to shoot. They each made their own decision to pull the trigger. Being in the military doesn't give you a free pass when it comes to making a decision to do the right thing. Even in contradiction to an order. You can make the choice to follow an order but it is always your own choice."

"Maddy, you know that isn't how the military actually works. Yes, I can refuse an order but the consequences can cost lives. If you stop following orders, the whole system falls apart. I order men to their deaths sometimes. I know it, they know it. They don't pick and choose which orders they follow and which they choose not to because they are fighting for something greater than themselves. Neither can I. I received an order, and even if it hurts those I love, I will follow it."

"You would pick the President's public image over the life of your son, of Brian?"

"Goddamn it, yes, if I have to. I'm a Colonel, Maddy. I can't be less than that." Dusty was loud enough for conversation to stop at tables around them.

"Well at least I know where the hell we stand in your world. I see now why Mike and Brian don't trust you." She slammed her coffee mug down and shoved her chair back.

"Goddamn it Dad, this isn't love." She walked off.

Dusty stared at the empty chair in front of him. The comment about Mike and Brian had hit a nerve. He took a deep breath and stood up. That couldn't have gone more sideways. He wasn't expecting his conversation with Jillian would go any better. He decided to walk his anger off first and then find Todd to see if there was any way to compromise.

Jillian

Saturday afternoon found Jillian asleep on the trawler *Ealu's* salon couch, her laptop open next to her. She had drifted off a few hours earlier after a night furiously working all of her groups and contacts. With the help of Carey and Matt, Mike's associates, plus her friends online, she felt she had made some inroads into keeping Brian safe. She hoped so. She had done all she could.

The radio crackled to life, pulling her to consciousness. "*Ealu, Ealu, Ealu,* this is Marina La Cruz."

She recognized Maria's voice, the administrative assistant at the office. Sitting up, she pushed her hair out of her face and went to the radio. "This is *Ealu,* go to channel 09?"

She flipped to 09. "*Ealu* here, what's up Maria?"

"Jillian, there are some men here looking for you. They are in the officina talking with Jorge, the manager. They are from the US and they are in suits."

Jillian wrinkled her brow, no one wore a suit down here; it was way too hot. Maria's English was fairly good but maybe Jillian was misunderstanding something. "Who are they? Did they tell you?"

Maria whispered into the mike. It sounded loud and raspy on Jillian's end. "Your government, they showed me their ID."

Jillian understood. In Mexico, a visit from the authorities was a very serious affair. "Thank you Maria, *Ealu* back to 22."

This was bad. Madison had texted her from Carol's phone about Capardi chasing them. Jillian had laughed off Madison's warnings, thinking she was safe. She realized now that she wasn't as invisible as she thought, docked at one of the few marinas in the area her husband had just flown from. Of course they had found her quickly. They probably knew where she was all along.

This couldn't be a friendly visit, not with her internet war and her son on their most wanted list. In a foreign country they could do whatever they wanted to her. She was suddenly scared. She had to get out now, had to run before they came down the dock.

Pulling on clothes, she grabbed her passport, all the cash they had on the boat, her laptop, phone, wallet and the file of important papers that they kept in the navigation station, cramming it all in a bag. She slid into her flip flops as she flew out the cabin door. It locked behind her.

It was a beautiful, sunny afternoon with a light breeze. The marina was quiet. The only way off the dock was by the office which would put her right in their path. Scanning quickly, she pulled the cover off Dusty's surfboard, dropping it into the water. She grabbed her straw hat, clambering over the side of the boat onto the dock. Throwing the bag onto the front of the board, she took a paddle off of *Ealu* and carefully eased onto it, kneeling over the bag. Pushing off and paddling away as quickly as she could, she put as much distance between herself and the dock as possible.

Pulling the hat low over her red curls, she hoped to look like just another boater enjoying the day. About a hundred yards across the channel there were docks for the local fishermen and beyond that, the streets of the town. If she could get into the neighborhood, she could hide in any one of dozens of restaurants, condos or hotels. She doubted they'd have the resources here to search for her and she had friends who would help. She bent low and paddled faster.

Glancing over her shoulder half-way across, she saw three men in suits walking down the dock to *Ealu*.

Arriving at the boat, instead of knocking, they swarmed aboard and she heard the crack as they busted the door lock. She winced, angry that they would hurt the trawler, and then chastised herself for how silly that was. Everything on the boat was replaceable.

She was almost to the fishing docks when they came back on deck. One of them spotted her and yelled. She rushed the board in between two small pangas, the fishing boats bumping up against the sides of the surf board. Tying the board's ankle strap to a dock line, she climbed into a boat and then onto the dock, pulling the bag with her. An engine started up; the three men were in an inflatable dingy with an outboard engine, taken from another boat, and were steering it around the end of the *Ealu's* dock. She looked back one last time and ran, flying across the parking lot between the fish market and a storage yard, then up a long flight of uneven stairs to the road.

As she approached the street, she dropped her bag into a yard behind a bougainvillea bush; it was heavy and slowing her down. She looked back, the dinghy had made it across the channel and the three were running across the parking lot behind her. She took off, turning right as she hit the street.

She ran down the cobblestones, trying to keep her sandals from sliding and turning an ankle. She sprinted the last half a block and turned into Sabine's driveway, looking back. They weren't to the street yet. Opening the side gate, she whipped through, closing it after. A quick duck around the house brought her square into Molly, their black Labrador, who rushed up to give her sloppy, wet kisses. She sank into a chair on the shaded back porch, breathing heavily. Catching her breath, she knocked on the slider door, but no one answered. Sabine and Jessie were probably still at the surf shop.

She settled back on the chair to wait, tucking it up against the house under the palapa roof where she couldn't be seen from the beach at the end of Sabine's yard. She was safe here. Even if a local saw her run by and turn in, they would never tell the policia, especially not men in suits speaking English. Everyone would simply disappear before they got close, not answer doors if they knocked, or not understand them if they couldn't get away, even if the men's Spanish was completely legible. It was just how things were done.

Dusty

Dusty hung up the phone. He had tried calling three different times and Jillian hadn't picked up. He was back in the war room by himself. He hadn't seen Madison since she left the cafe and Todd had retreated to his office. Without his laptop, which was back at the hotel, there wasn't much he could accomplish. He was watching TV on the huge screen; a luxury after three years on the boat without cable. The commercials annoyed him though. He had not missed the endless commercialism that was normal in the States.

He dialed Mike's number, which clicked through to his company Alegeis. The operator put him through to Michael's secure line. He answered on the second ring, "This is Mike."

"Hello Mike, it's dad."

"Hello Sir." Mike was cold and distant, as he so often was in their conversations.

Dusty was tired, he hadn't slept much in the last thirty-six hours, and a headache was beating at the back of his eyes. He really didn't want to fight through this conversation. He realized he shouldn't have made this call until he had slept but it was too late now. "I was just checking on you and Brian. Is everything going okay?"

"Yes, Sir, Brian is secure. I am fine. Look, I'm right in the middle of something, can we have this conversation at another time?"

Dusty was stunned at being put off. "No, we need to have this now. I need to get Brian back to his base in New York. I want you to tell me where he is so I can arrange for him to be brought in." He realized as the words came out that he was backing Michael into a predictable corner but he couldn't take them back after they were said.

"No, Dad that is not going to happen. I am not going to let Brian get screwed by the government like I was. There is no way I am going to give him up to you or anyone else."

"Michael, you are my son and I am telling you what I need to have happen, you will obey me in this."

"Do you hear me?"

"Michael?"

"I am not a child you can order around anymore. Who the hell are you working for Dad? Because it sure as hell isn't for Brian. The military screws its own all the time. I'm not letting him get screwed for this asshat of a President. Why the hell are you?"

Dusty took a deep breath. How the hell did his kids push his buttons so fast? He was a Colonel. Everyone jumped when he walked into a room and he never lost his temper with subordinates. Why was it so hard with his own family, why were his damned kids so stubborn?

"Look Dad, I'm really angry right now. I'm in the middle of some shit that is company top clearance only. I'll call you later."

Dusty heard the phone disconnect. He slammed his receiver down and sat staring at the table. That conversation hadn't gone well either. Maybe it was a good thing he couldn't reach Jillian, he wasn't sure he could take another family blow-up today. He turned up the volume on the TV and scrolled through the programming until he found a college football game. He leaned back, took a handful of deep breaths to calm down and tried not to think of anything for awhile. He couldn't focus on the game but the background noise kept his thoughts from screaming so loudly in his head.

Michael

Mike hung up the phone and leaned back in his chair, letting his head thump against the wall. They had driven back to his client's mansion in Palo Alto, South of San Francisco. Mike had made it a point to make small talk to put his client at ease. He closed his true feelings up in a box in the back of his skull and kept them locked up there.

He had desperately wanted to tell his dad what was happening and get his advice. Hell, he really wanted to dump it in his lap and let his dad handle it so he could walk away like he used to as a child, but he knew his phone calls were monitored. He had already risked everything by referring to it at all.

He took a few deep breaths. Why did his dad have to push his buttons so fast? Why couldn't he react like an adult when they talked? He respected his father, quite a bit actually, it was just when they interacted, all this negative shit floated up and he ended up acting like a damned angry kid. He understood how his father viewed authority. Even the president, no matter how crazy his actions, would always have Dusty's support. He was hard-wired that way. Mike respected him for it. It just stung when duty came before family.

He had been wracking his brain all afternoon, trying to figure out how to get a secure message out. He was at a loss. Even though the government had a lot of top shelf surveillance equipment and tools to find out what people were doing, his client had access to hardware that was in a whole other league. He let his mind wander over the problem again hoping an avenue would present itself.

John

The buzz of the cell phone slowly pulled John out of sleep. Blanca was tangled up in his arms and the covers, her long hair massed around her forehead and tickling his nose. After the rally, they had picked up Amy from her parents and then came to the apartment, both of them mostly silent. They spent the evening hugging Amy and pretending that everything was normal until they tucked her in, then they fell into bed together, ripping at each other's clothes and smashing through sex, a hot, rough affirmation of living. Blanca had started to cry, the sobs building up as he held her close and he cradled her well into the early hours of the morning, stroking her hair and murmuring over and over again that she was safe and that he loved her. They both finally fell asleep, the exhaustion overcoming everything else.

He reached out with one hand, blindly tagging along the bedside table behind him until he got hold of the phone and pulled it to where he could see the screen. He swiped it with his thumb and held it to his ear. "Hello?"

"John Fields?"

John cleared his throat and focused on the call, "Yes, this is John."

"This is Janice Small with CBN's Morning Chronicle. We'd like to get you to the studio this morning for an on-air interview. Is there any way you could get to our Burbank station in the next half-an-hour?"

John gently disengaged from Blanca's tangle and looked around the room in the predawn darkness, giving himself a chance to wake up. "I'm easily a couple hours out from Burbank on a good day. Is there anywhere else I could get to?"

"Just a second." The line click onto hold and a jazz rendition of Pink Floyd's *Dark Side of the Moon* album filled his ear. "Mr. Fields? Can you meet one of our vans at the plaza in front of the Science Center? We can use the mall as a backdrop."

John winced. He didn't really want to go back there today. He didn't really want to go back there ever again. "Sure, I will get there as quickly as I can."

He hopped in the shower and ten minutes later softly kissed Blanca, smoothed her hair back out of her face, peeked in at Amy sleeping flat on her back in her crib, scribbled out a quick note on where he was going and locked the door behind him. The dawn was just beginning in a faint, deep azure along the horizon as he drove out of the apartment parking lot and turned towards Balboa Park. Focused on his upcoming interview, he didn't notice the black ICE vehicle parked in the back corner of the lot.

Mobury

"Commander, I have eyes on subject one, leaving right from the lot. Shall we intercept?"

"Negative, unit seven. Target is still in the apartment. Prepare for infiltration now."

Blanca

Blanca snapped awake as a large boom echoed through the apartment followed by a splintering crash as the front door burst inward. She looked frantically for John, grabbed his t-shirt discarded on the bed, pulled it over her head and jumped to the crib, snatching Amy up as her bedroom door burst open. Armed men in black swarmed into the room, checking the closet and bathroom while they held her and Amy frozen, looking into the barrels of automatic weapons.

"All clear," An agent announced into the microphone on his shoulder. They all stood for what felt like an eternity, Blanca looking desperately between the different agents as she bounced Amy in her arms to keep her quiet.

Special Agent in Charge Dan Mobury strolled through the bedroom door, his eyes blackened and ugly from John's fist. Blanca sucked in her breath as she recognized him, terror flooding adrenaline through her system, making her dizzy. She blinked slowly, willing herself to wake up from the nightmare as Agent Mobury strolled up to her and then, a brutal smile spreading across his features, backhanded her hard across the face. The force of the blow spun her into the dresser, smacking her head against the corner as she collapsed onto the bed, Amy slipping from her arms. She lay on the bed, stunned, as Amy began to wail.

Blanca tried to crawl towards her as Agent Mobury hauled her back by her hair and then punched her squarely in the face. She felt her nose crackle and blood poured out. Sagging to the floor she reached for Amy, who had escalated into a high pitched scream.

Agent Mobury turned and stepped towards the toddler. Agent Sean Cummings, just entering the room, crossed the space and inserted himself between them and scooped her off the floor, cradling her carefully.

"I'll just take this little one out to the social worker." He left the room quickly, putting his body between his superior and the child in his arms.

Mobury kicked Blanca and pain exploded in her ribs and then blackness closed in.

Cummings

Shushing the baby and bouncing her gently, Agent Cummings moved out of the apartment building and to the command vehicle. An older man in khakis was inside filling out paperwork. Agent Cunnings passed her to him and then signed the forms and passed them over as well. As was normal, the paperwork took forever. When everything was completed and in order the man took Amy to his car, belted her into a car seat in the back and left. Agent Cummings could hear Amy's wailing as the car drove away. This kind of event made his stomach turn over.

He returned to the command vehicle to check the feed on his body-cam, spinning it back through the last few minutes to make sure the handoff of Amy to the social worker was recorded accurately. He switched to the active camera feeds on the other agents. They had all been manually switched off. Worried, he made his way back up to the apartment, past doors that were hastily closed as they saw him approach.

Blanca

Blanca slowly swam up through the blackness, coughing and gagging. She was drowning and realized it was her own blood, running down the back of her throat. Lying sideways on her bed, her face was in a pool of thick, sticky goo with her hands zip-tied behind her. Every breath she took shot fire through her chest from ribs cracked by Agent Mobury's steel-toed boot. She heard groaning and realized it was coming from her own mouth. She tried to sit up. Her head swam as she struggled.

Her first thought was of Amy and she swiveled around, panic spiking through her. The room was a shambles, every drawer emptied onto the floor, the crib mattress shoved against the window, the closet ransacked, their lifetime of positions strewn underfoot, smashed and broken. Agent Mobury was standing at the bedside table and glanced at her as she moved. Looking directly at her he let go of her crystal music box, a gift from her grandfather when she turned fifteen, and it smashed against the windowsill, the little shards of glass tinkling on the table as it fell.

"Where's Amy?" she said, her voice stuttering. She cleared her throat. "What did you do with Amy?" She looked around frantically and realized she expected her baby girl to come crawling out of the closet or from under the bed. Amy was not there. She sucked in breath and then gagged as the pain flooded through her lungs.

""Your brat is gone bitch." He moved to the edge of the bed, looking down, the cruel smile still playing across his face. He was enjoying this.

"Did you think you could get away with standing up to me? An illegal in this country? That you could hide your dirty secret? It took me all of five minutes to find your fake birth certificate. You scum don't deserve this country. I am sending you back to the shit hole you came from and you will never be allowed back." His smile widened and his voice dropped to a purr. "You will never see that brat of yours again."

The blur of words sharpened as fear skimmed along her spine. "What? No. No, that isn't true. I was born here. You can't do this to me. Give me back Amy." The last spun out as a plea, her voice collapsing as the pain from her ribs jolted her breath out. She curled around herself as a sob escaped.

"You fucking illegal whore. You scum are the reason I had to tap dance to save my career. I've turned things around though so I decided to take care of a little unfinished business. Go ahead and scream." He said it next to her ear as she cringed away. "No one is ever going to listen to you, bitch."

He grabbed her elbow and easily shoved her onto her stomach, her face buried in a pillow, and his knee forced her legs apart as he undid his belt buckle.

"No, no, no no, Oh God, oh God, no!"

She thrashed and screamed, the pain from her ribs exploding through her chest, her breath catching and ragged as his hands grabbed her hips and pulled her across the sheets, his knee forcing hers wider against the bed. He wrapped his forearm under her pelvis and pulled her tight against his crotch, using his free hand to force her butt cheeks apart until he jammed his penis into her anus, then forcing himself in again and again, ripping her tissues, causing jolting pain with each thrust. With one final thrust he came, standing up on his toes, his body going slack. Smiling, he pulled out, slapping her buttocks hard so that she smashed up against the pillow with a whimper. He hummed as he did up his pants, walking out of the room. She heard voices in her living room and someone laughed. She curled up in a ball, her shoulders pulling against the binding.

The door opened and someone moved across the room. She tensed as they came near. They dragged her around by her elbows onto her back as she yelped in pain. She looked up through the mass of her hair and saw another agent in black, leering at her as he fumbled with his belt. She kicked out and caught him in the stomach. He doubled over as the air wooshed out of his lungs. She thought he would leave until he stood back up, smacking her hard across the face. Through dizziness nearing the edges of unconsciousness she felt him manhandle her legs apart and force himself inside, rutting on top of her until he came.

She drifted away, only vaguely aware as someone else entered the room, laughing with the man already there, and then she was raped again. She didn't have anything left to fight with and she laid there, letting them do whatever they wanted, her mind drifting in empty blackness.

Cummings

Agent Cummings stepped into the room after returning from the command vehicle. As he walked through the apartment, his commander, Agent Mobury, smugly tasked him with getting the prisoner ready for transport.

"Jesus!" he said under his breath as surveyed the bedroom. He purposely turned each way to get the whole scene on camera. He made his way across to where Blanca lay abandoned on the bed, her face bloodied and swelling, her nose smashed, her hair in a tangled, bloody matt spread across the pillows. Her hands were still fastened behind her back and she lay awkwardly, her legs akimbo and blood seeping from her crotch. Her eyes were open but unfocused. She was breathing so shallowly he was afraid she wouldn't make it.

He touched her shoulder and she moaned 'no' and cringed away.

"It's alright, I'm not going to hurt you," he said, anger building in his chest. He got up and went into the bathroom, grabbing a washcloth and wetting it under the sink. He came back into the room and gently started to work the blood off her face. She came around and pushed him off, weakly trying to fight, until he helped her sit up against the headboard. He cut the tie holding her hands behind her.

"Where's my baby?" she whispered.

"Safe. She is with social services. They will take care of her until you can get this straightened out."

He got up and rummaged around on the floor until he found a pair of sweats. They were obviously way too large to be hers but he handed them to her and helped her pull them on as she struggled to bend through the pain in her ribs. He noticed tears were tracking down her cheeks but he didn't think she was aware of it.

"Jesus. Those fucking animals!"

He tried to stand her up. Her knees gave out and she slumped back onto the bed, whimpering softly. He reached down and picked her up, shushing her gently, just as he had Amy a little while before. He carried her out of the bedroom, fury building inside, making eye contact with each of the agents in the next room as he passed. He saw defiance on their faces and even a smile from Agent Mobury, but no shame.

"You guys are fucking bastards. She's a fucking human being, regardless of where she was born."

He carried her out of the building and set her gently in the back of a waiting sedan. She slumped sideways. He closed the door, returning to the command center vehicle. This was it; he made the decision he had been struggling with for months. He would see this woman safely through the process and across the border. Then he was done. He would turn in his badge and be finished with ICE. Fuck their brutal inhumanity; he wanted no more part of it.

He made sure the video from his body-cam uploaded and sent a copy of the file to his desktop in case he needed insurance against Mobury. He drummed his fingers for a moment, fury washing over him in waves. Picking up his cell phone he called for an ambulance. He knew Mobury wouldn't make a scene over the girl in front of emergency workers. The man would never jeopardize his reputation in front of anyone he couldn't control. She would still be deported but at least he could get her to a safe place first and get her medical care.

He had never disobeyed an order, even when Agent Mobury stopped the Army guys from giving medical attention to the woman who had subsequently died during the Congressman's shooting. That choice haunted his dreams most nights, but today something broke. This girl could be his daughter or his niece or anyone else he knew. He saw the violence done to her that Mobury and others justified simply because she was born on a different side of a line.

Agent Mobury had finally found the place buried deep in Agent Cummings that said 'no more'. Mobury had touched his moral compass, silenced under layers of justifications built up over years facing questionable ethics day in and day out as part of his job. This was wrong and there would be no more.

He stepped out of the tactical vehicle as the ambulance wailed up. Agent Mobury and the rest of the team came out of the apartment building. At the look on his commander's face and the slow rise of red washing up from the man's collar to his forehead, he knew this small act of defiance was going to cost him. He didn't care.

Blanca started fighting again as they tried to pull her from the car, lashing out deliriously. The EMTs manhandled her free, strapping her to a gurney, and checking her vitals as they loaded her into the ambulance. Agent Cummings climbed in after her and pointedly pulled the rear door closed as another agent made to join him. The EMT looked on with raised eyebrows but Cummings leaned back against the wall, closed his eyes and listened to Blanca call over and over for Amy in soft, whimpering tones. He swore an oath to himself; there would be no more.

Brian

Brian woke up to sunlight streaming through yellow, lace curtains in a small daybed with a yellow print coverlet. He stretched slowly, his feet hanging off the end of the mattress and his head against the wrought iron headboard. Next to him was a sewing machine on a wide desk, square against a wall covered with homemade nooks full of sewing and crafting supplies, all neatly organized and labeled. When he had first come in, the room, although dust free and vacuumed, had the feel of being long abandoned. He suspected that when the sergeant's wife had died many years ago, this room had simply been put on hold, waiting in limbo. He felt like a giant, oversized intruder on her world, awkward among the small knickknacks and furniture. If he turned around too quickly, he was sure he would catch her watching from the corner, raising her eyebrows as he barely missed knocking over a vase or floor lamp.

He and Ben had spent the greater part of Saturday watching the rioting unfold on the news. They both sat in shocked silence as the coverage of the rally played out. At the video of the bodies lying battered and broken all across the length of the mall, Ben swore softly.

"I'll be god-damned. I never thought I would see the likes of this again. I marched in Selma. I was there when we were overrun on the bridge, when the police beat up women and old folks. I went on and marched with Dr. King, God rest his soul. I hoped never to see anything like this happen again. This is a tragedy."

They had watched the TV for the rest of the evening, each walled up in their own thoughts, and then gone to bed early. Brian had a hard time falling asleep, the images from the riot filling his head.

He had finally drifted off and then slept soundly, exhaustion shutting down his system. He woke clear-headed. It was time to go back to his command and his soldiers. He had troops he was responsible for. He wasn't going to hide out while events moved on around him, that wasn't who he was.

Unfolding himself from the small bed, he stretched, his fingers brushing against the ceiling. He pulled on his pants and collected up the few items he had; the multi-tool from Justin, his wallet and sunglasses, and quietly opened the door into the hallway. The smell of coffee hit him, and bacon, which brought out a smile. Ben wasn't the sort of person you could get up earlier than, not unless your duty started way before dawn. Ben was pouring a mug of coffee as he entered the kitchen and turned and handed it to him.

"Good morning, son. It's a fine day today." At Brian's nod he turned back to the stove, "Course any day I'm above ground I term a grand fine day, but the sun is shining and it looks to be warming up a bit so I might not be far wrong."

Brian tasted the coffee, bitter and strong, and it hit his senses with a welcoming jolt. Ben pulled strips of bacon out of a pan and then cracked eggs into the grease. They crackled and sizzled. Brian took another gulp of the coffee. It burned his tongue but he didn't mind. Ben reached into the oven and removed the pan of hash browns. He dished up some potatoes, bacon and a couple eggs and handed the plate to Brian who carried it over to the little table. Ben followed him. He bowed his head. Brian did as well.

"Lord, thank you for this food."

Brian let the silence flow into him. The sun hitting a cut glass decanter was sending tiny rainbows across the table and a bird was chirping somewhere close by. Other than that, it was the most quiet he could remember it being in quite a long time. The food was warming his belly and a part of him sang out that he could just stay here, wrapped up in this peaceful little cottage in a veteran's home in New Jersey. No one would ever find him.

"Top," he said, "I need to go back to my command. I have to face this head on."

Ben was quiet for a few heartbeats then he sighed. "Yes, I kinda' figured you would, you're that kind of man." He quietly finished up the food on his plate and then leaned back with his coffee in hand. "I was thinking things through last night. I figured you'd probably bring this up and I wanted to see you straight."

He took a sip of and studied Brian over the rim of the mug. "Who've you got in your corner?"

"Well, my dad, he was a Colonel before he retired, and General Jennings I think, he was as close to an uncle as you can get while I was growing up. My commanding officer, he gave me the orders to go, and my command, they all were with me, I know they have my back." He trailed off as he realized what a short list it was that he could count on.

"Well, son, lining up on the offense, you've got the president, who has put a price on your head, the DIA, who your brother thinks is lining up with the president, the FBI, who want you so they can maybe pull the president down, a good chunk of the military who's top commander is the president and whose careers are at risk, plus every beat cop between the Atlantic and the Pacific. Oh, and let's not forget about the whole population of the United States, if this latest nightmare yesterday hasn't driven you out of the spotlight. It looks like this shit you stepped in is a little more than ankle deep and is going to be a bit harder to shake off than we'd hoped."

Brian nodded, looking down at the table as he traced the grain of the wood with his finger. "Well, not the best odds I've had over the years."

Ben broke out in wheezy laughter. "That's putting it a little on the light side." He chuckled some more and stood up, grabbing the coffee pot and bringing it back to the table. He poured some of the rich brew into Brian's half-empty cup and refilled his own.

"So what are we going to do?"

Brian smiled appreciatively at the "we". As quick as that, Ben had taken a share in the responsibility.

"I don't know, Top, I'm not even sure how to get a hold of General Jennings. I could maybe call my dad. I imagine they are watching his phone though. They are probably watching all my family and Ashley too. I don't even know if she ended up okay." He slumped into his seat.

Ben reached over and slapped his shoulder. "Your girl is fine son, stop borrowing trouble and focus. People are trying to use you to play politics. We have to deal with that first. No one is gonna' bother your family or your friends if we get you off the chessboard."

John

John Fields sat on a tall stool in front of the Science Center at Balboa Park, the long mall stretching out behind him. The stage was still set up but tattered and surrounded by bundles of flowers and candles with notes and teddy bears arranged with photos of loved ones. The emptiness and chill of the morning was haunting. He couldn't shake the fact that five-hundred-and-seventeen people had died here yesterday with thousands more injured. Deep brown stains quilted the paving stones and the mall was covered in dropped clothing, litter and the medical scraps from the EMT crews. Areas were cordoned off with teams of forensic investigators snapping photos and taking measurements. Groundskeepers were out in the distance collecting personal items for return. They were trying to restore a semblance of normal to the park.

John felt sick. He looked away, focusing on the camera in front of him. The microphone crackled to life in his ear.

"Welcome, John Fields. Thank you for taking the time with our national audience this morning. We've just been watching a clip of your speech and striking an ICE agent. Could you tell us what it was like on the ground? How did it feel hitting the agent, who we have identified as Dan Mobury, Field Director for the Southwest Region? I think many of us were on your side in that moment."

John felt ridiculous talking into the air; he hoped he didn't look as silly as he felt. "Thank you for having me. I certainly hadn't planned on hitting him but he was in charge of this tragedy and the raid where Congressman Silva was killed. I think I just kind of lost myself."

"Well I think many in the nation cheered you on when we saw it. Your speech was very passionate. Do you feel any responsibility for the events that followed after exhorting the crowd to resist?"

John paused, he hadn't thought of his part in this. The weight crashed down on his shoulders and he felt tears welling. "God, I hope not, I sincerely hope not."

He took a deep breath. "Well, I spoke from the heart and echoed what many in this country have felt but didn't have a voice to be heard. At the same time I can't ignore the chants; I heard my words thrown back at me as the gunfire started." He began to say more but words wouldn't come. He sat there staring into the camera, willing his emotions to stay behind a wall until this interview was over.

"This has had a profound impact on the nation. I think we are all in shock that it could have even happened. Tell us how it unfolded,"

He looked away. His eyes focused on the memorials and he felt the sting of tears. He looked back."Well, it was a lot more crowded than I think anyone expected. Nazi protesters showed up, then the ICE vehicles blocked the exits and shooting started. It was crazy after that. I saw a police officer shot and I went to help him.

'At the end, I found my fiancée, Blanca. I had been terrified she was hit, but she was ok. We were trying to figure out what to do when I ran into the Agent. He was just so cavalier and condescending about everything. I couldn't leave him strutting around after everything. He was responsible for all of this. It was one of those shocking, terrifying events that are kind of hard to put words to." He trailed off. This wasn't going as he hoped; he sounded weak and scrambled.

"You were the one who first said that the US Army was involved in immigration raids. Now that the President claims Brian Phillips was working alone the night Congressman Silva was killed, do you want to revise your statement?"

John paused. How sure was he that the Army was working alongside ICE? He had based everything on the comments from Congressman Silva. Did he believe him? "The Army was there. They are trying to cover their tracks now. Brian Phillips wasn't even present when the shooting occurred. I was there, I saw what happened. He showed up well after. He was not responsible. They are just pinning it on him."

"John, the coalition that is collecting signatures to create a separate country of California is claiming your girlfriend, Blanca Perez Ortega, is promoting secession. Do you share her views?"

"I am very proud of Blanca. California has already separated from the United States in culture and politics. It's just a matter of making it official. Look at the cost we've paid. I am sitting where hundreds of people were murdered yesterday in a massive show of force that went terribly wrong. The President is blaming it on the victims. The United States doesn't deserve us. It is time to do this on our own. Yes, I support her. If you haven't signed the petition yet, I'm asking you to please do it today."

There was silence in his ear. "Well, yes, thank you, John Fields, for speaking with us. Next we have," the voice was cut off.

He looked at the cameraman. "I don't think she wanted to hear that last part."

He took the earpiece out and shook the cameraman's hand. He and the two technicians were alone out here. It was weird to have just talked to millions of people when he was pretty much all by himself. He went through it all in his head as he drove back to the apartment. He hoped Blanca had taped it.

He had been inundated with calls asking for interviews on his way over and had turned his phone off. He was getting his ten minutes of fame, all from hitting that pig of an Agent. It was a horrible reason but he was glad he had let himself go, the man deserved at least that for orchestrating it all. Turning into his apartment complex, he was surprised to see people standing in the lot. He recognized several from other apartments and he started breathing faster. Blanca's parents were huddled together and his stomach dropped. He slammed the car into park and leapt out.

The apartment manager caught his arm. "We've been trying to reach you. I called Blanca's parents from the number in your file. The immigration agents came this morning. Blanca has been picked up."

"What? How? Wait, this is a huge mistake. They can't take her." He looked from face to face. He turned to Blanca's parents. They looked shrunken, their clothes boxy on their small frames. Her dad held her mom around the shoulders. She was crying quietly. "Can they?"

"She didn't know, we never told her. We tried to cross the border when I was pregnant but she came early. We crossed when she was three days old. We almost made it. She was almost born a US citizen. I never thought such a little bit of time would make any difference. Her birth certificate wasn't real. We hid it from her so she would never be scared." She started sobbing and leaned into her husband's shoulder.

"You never told her?"

Her father shook his head.

"Wait." John's heart leaped. "Amy is a legal citizen. Can they deport her when her baby is legal? They can't deport Amy so Blanca can't be deported either, right? Amy needs her. They wouldn't deport a mother when her child needs her, right?"

The manager pulled John to the side, lowering his voice. "John, they took Blanca out in an ambulance, she was beat up pretty bad from what I saw. Amy wasn't with her; I think she was taken by social services. The Agent in charge told me to tell you that Blanca, not the words he used, got what she deserved. I'm sorry I couldn't do anything."

John's knees gave out and he sank to the concrete. He sat there with his head in his hands, his heart racing. He had done this to her. He was responsible for Agent Mobury coming here, into his home, hurting Blanca and taking their child. She would be deported. He caused all this with one stupid punch, for what? To make his ego feel better? Why hadn't he listened to Blanca and walked away. Tears welled up. What did he do now?

He was a reporter. He should start making calls, figure out where she was and what to do. He couldn't move. He slumped there, thinking over and over; this is my fault.

Dusty

Dusty watched a hummingbird make its way from the bushes along the fence to the flower shaped feeder Carol had in the backyard of the General's mini-mansion well outside of DC proper. The chill was still giving way to the morning's brilliant sunshine. He was sitting by himself at a garden table on the porch, littered with the remains of breakfast for the four of them; Todd, Carol, Madison and himself. He was sipping the coffee in his cup, mostly cold now. Carol's two Corgis, short and rotund, were busily inspecting every inch of their manicured yard, following each other from flowerbed to flowerbed.

He was sitting quiet and letting his thoughts run without forcing them into any particular direction, a problem solving trick he used. He breathed in deeply and relaxed, focusing his gaze on the path of the hummingbird, hardly registering as the housekeeper, Rosalie, cleared away the breakfast dishes and refilled his cup.

There were lots of random puzzle pieces all heaped up inside his head, from Jillian and the mess she was creating on the internet, to yesterday's tragedy and the ensuing riots, Mike's outright defiance in helping him reach Brian, the involvement of Capardi, to Brian himself; his assignment that had gone so wrong, his current whereabouts, the president landing the whole blame on his shoulders, and how to help him. Overlaying everything, the dead or alive ultimatum weighed the most heavily. He was scared and furious and ready to take down the president himself to protect his child. He worked to acknowledge his feelings while letting his mind steer clear of the emotions, so that he could find a solution that would see them all through this safely.

They had retrieved their phones and Dusty had called Jillian multiple times with no answer. He was a little frantic at her lack of response. Was she angry and avoiding him? Was she hurt and lying on the boat unable to reach the phone?

This wasn't like her; they had been through so many deployments and by mutual agreement, they always put their arguments on a back burner while he was gone. It was like closing the refrigerator door on leftovers and coming back months later to see if there was really anything left worth re-warming. There usually wasn't. It was a survival tactic they had learned to rely on at the beginning of his career, otherwise their relationship would have fallen through the cracks long ago, like so many of the soldier's around him had.

Why couldn't he reach her now? He set that thought and emotion aside and let his mind move on.

Brian was the biggest concern. He was angry that Michael wouldn't give up his location, thinking he could do a better job of protecting Brian than Dusty could. He set that emotion aside.

If he couldn't find him, was there anything he could do to help the situation. Jillian had created an all out internet war on the establishment to change public perception, what could he do? A memory from West Point came to the surface, his commander in his face after Dusty had failed a training mission. "You are the leader Cadet, you need to be doing the highest level task needed to complete the mission. You are down in the weeds and your whole team failed. Get your head out of your ass and lead!"

He ran through the whole situation again, from the first time he saw Brian's face on the video, and then he ran through it again. Something was tickling his senses, something he was missing. Suddenly it clicked. He abruptly stood up from the table, startling the hummingbird who zipped off over the fence. "Madison. Madison, I need to see a replay of the tape Brian is in. There was an assassin. Brian couldn't be the shooter if we can prove that." He strode through the patio door letting excitement creep into his soul.

Madison and Captain Roberts sat next to each other at the dining room table, laptops open in front of them. They both looked up, startled and guilty.

Dusty stopped. "Its Sunday, Captain, what are you doing here?"

"Uhm, well sir, I just had some charts to show Madison." He hastily shut his laptop and started to stand up.

"I'm sure whatever it is can wait for tomorrow. You both need the down time. The General doesn't expect you to work that hard son, whatever it is can wait. Go home. Get some sleep."

He watched the red creep up Maddy's face. He was obviously missing something. He was goddamn tired of missing cues with his youngest child. There was just too damn much on his plate. He looked back and forth between them. "What the hell are you doing that you look so guilty about."

Maddy's jaw dropped open and the flush went all the way to her hairline. "Excuse me? I am not a child anymore." She stood up. "You will not talk to me that way. Owen has actually gotten through a puzzle in a game I've been working on and I had asked him to show me the mods he used, if you must know."

"Who the hell is Owen and why the hell are you playing video games when Brian is in trouble?"

"Uh, I'm Owen, Sir." Captain Robertson nodded to Dusty and turned to leave. "I'm sorry for the confusion. I think I'll just head back to town. Thank you Madison for taking the time with me."

Dusty felt Carol's hand on his arm. "Well this is a little awkward. Dusty, may I introduce you to Captain *Owen* Robertson." She laughed gently. "Owen, before you leave, could you please help me in the garden? I have a huge bag of birdseed Todd brought home for me that I need moved to the shed."

"Of course, Ma'am." He set his laptop aside and went out the back door.

Maddy and Dusty glared across the room.

"Dusty? Todd would like to see you in the study. Maddy? Why don't you come along and help me out back. Have you seen the chrysanthemums I planted? They are filling in beautifully." She steered Maddy out the back door after Owen.

Dusty stood still. He had just unloaded his stress and worry on these two kids. He was glad for Carol's quick understanding and deft redirection. He hadn't noticed the friendship developing between his daughter and the Captain and he couldn't believe he'd missed getting the Captain's first name. He rubbed his eyes and moved into the study.

Todd

Todd sat at a big, walnut-burl desk watching the news.

Dusty strode through the door. "My God, children are a pain in the ass. I've never had half the trouble with troops as I do with these three pups I whelped. How the hell do they get under my skin so goddamn fast?" Dusty reached for the decanter of scotch and poured a finger into a tumbler placed on the tray, lifting the bottle towards Todd. He waved it away. Dusty sat in a club chair to the side of Todd's desk.

Todd gave him a side-eye. "I've found it helps if you know the name of the boyfriend."

"You heard that? Sweet Jesus, he can't be a boyfriend that fast. I'm not some damned fortune teller. And who the hell does he think he is chumming up to my damned daughter in the first place.

"He's a good soldier Dusty. Maddy is safe with him. He did ask me if it was okay to see her. Carol got wind and invited him out today. Before you throw him out, remember it's an hour and a half drive from the city. That's a damn long drive on a Sunday. He sure as hell isn't here to help Carol in the garden."

Dusty rolled his eyes."Young love."

He took a sip from the glass, his face appreciative. Dusty had always liked a good scotch and Todd thought this brand went down like caramel-flavored, smoky fire. It was a good fit.

"Do you have any more information about who shot Congressman Silva? Have they made any progress on that front? I think that could clear Brian."

General Jennings sighed.

"I'm glad you are sitting, I think you are going to need that scotch." He clicked the TV off. "Dusty we need to have a discussion."

Dusty's eyebrows drew down. A laser focus immediately replaced the smile that had softened his features. As Todd expected and had witnessed countless times, Dusty switched from a friend and father to a leader accepting mission details from one breath to the next. He could count on Dusty to be professional and handle this situation as a Colonel. It was what he needed from him now.

"As you well know, as officers we sometimes have to make decisions in a no-win situation. You and I have both made these decisions and never made them lightly."

Dusty gave a curt nod.

"We have to talk about Brian and what needs to happen. I see where your thought process is going. It would clear Brian if we found the shooter but we cannot move forward on that. The FBI picked up the investigation from the local police suggesting a conspiracy at play. For national security reasons, they want that quiet. You will leave it in the hands of the FBI."

As Dusty started to object, Todd waved him to silence and continued. "There is more to this situation though. There is also the political backlash of military involvement with immigration enforcement within the US.'

'I'm going to be totally blunt with you. We've been friends for a big part of both our lives and you need to know how this is going to play out. I am speaking to you as your Commanding Officer. The President does not want Brian cleared. This is not open for debate. It is a direct order.'

'The President is shutting this down. He was already very much in the gray when he called on the Army to assist. This could be a turning point in the upcoming elections. He cannot afford to be implicated in the congressman's death. Brian as renegade is the politically expedient way to accomplish it."

Todd watched Dusty's face as he continued. The steel blue eyes burned out at him and anger etched into the hard angles of his jaw. This was the man the enemy saw; implacable, brutal, terrifying. General Jennings was one of the few people who could have this conversation with this man. He focused on controlling the situation.

"He will be expected to fall on his sword to protect the current administration, assuming we can get him into a courtroom alive, which is my goal. He will be called on to say he was there on his own, not part of a military action and not under orders. They will work out a plea bargain giving him minimal jail time. When this all is behind us he will receive a presidential pardon that will clear his name. That is the duty he is being called for; to take the fall to protect his President."

Red flooded up from Dusty's collar, suffusing his face. As it reached his hairline, he threw himself out of the chair, slamming the tumbler down and leaning over the desk.

"How dare you tell me I have to sacrifice my son and potentially my entire family for the political benefit of that morally bankrupt son of a bitch sitting in the Oval Office.'

'Is this why you brought me back? Not for my experience or my professional judgment; to contain the situation? You knew I would do anything to protect my family. You knew I would open up this cesspool and shine a light on all the filthy maneuverings they want kept secret. You wanted me back on active duty so you would have control. You brought Maddy here too, and you want me to bring in Michael and Jillian. How far are you willing to go to silence this situation?"

Dusty's words crashed against the General.

"God damn it, Todd, I trusted you. You know me better than anybody. My family is everything and they are destroying Brian. I have done everything you have asked on every mission, every time, no matter how hard or what the cost was. Do not ask this of me. Do not demand I go down this path with Brian and my family."

Todd's voice cracked across the room. "Colonel, are you through? You know it is how this has to play out. This country was built on the foundation that civilians are in charge of the military. You have known this since you took your oath, your family has been taught it since the beginning. Yes, the President is an undisciplined bastard that works in the grey area and sometimes abuses his power, most leaders are, but we both took an oath to protect that office, no matter who the person is that sits in that chair.'

'Don't for a minute think I don't agonize over this. Brian's once outstanding career is over simply because he drew the short straw and ended up in California at the wrong time. Yes, I had to use you to follow my orders from the President. Now we have to deal with that. Given the choice of either seeing him shot dead in the street like a common criminal or maybe, just maybe, saving his life by trying him for treason, I would rather see him alive. His name will be cleared at the end of it all. I would just like to see him live to see it."

Todd's voice went to steel. "This is how it will happen, Colonel. You are under orders and I will not accept anything less than complete loyalty from you."

The words ricocheted around them both. Dusty stood stiff, hands clenched into fists at his sides. He breathed in deeply and let it out slowly. Complete formality dripped from his next words.

"Permission to be dismissed, General?"

Todd nodded. Dusty saluted, performed a crisp turn, and walked out.

Dusty

Dusty strode down the driveway and turned at the corner. He kept walking, the miles of suburban streets unwinding beneath his new leather shoes, until the anger, resentment and betrayal began to ease. It was late afternoon when he slowed down from the military stride that ate up the miles. His heels were blistered from the stiff leather and he had no idea where he was, just a general direction from where he had started. He kept walking until a small neighborhood park appeared, bringing his long march to a halt at a little park bench overlooking a pond. A dozen Canadian Geese clamored for territory. He lowered himself onto the wooden slats and sat, staring into the water.

How on earth was he to negotiate between very clear orders to sacrifice Brian and his need to protect his child from an unjust charge of treason without compromising the very core of who he? Was Maddy's stinging accusation accurate; did he need to do what was right, even if it went against a direct command? What about responsibility; was it his place to call out the hidden agenda of the president and possibly change the course of the next elections? Would broadcasting of the military's involvement with immigration enforcement be the tipping point that pushed California out of the union? Could he be the traitor who put his family above the welfare of the nation?

He leaned over and put his head in his hands.

Was disobeying orders even possible for him? Or would he quietly fall in line, give his son up to be tried for treason, keep quiet about the shooter in the bushes, be the loyal soldier while his son paid the price with his career, his freedom and possibly his life. He had never wavered in his duty, not in all the long years of his career. The military for him was always black and white. Shades of gray were only used as excuses for not doing what was right. How did he negotiate his path now that he was caught in the myriad of shades before him with no black or white to be found?

He took a deep breath. He knew the answer in his head and he knew the answer in his heart. He had to choose between them and he wasn't sure if he could withstand the consequences of either. Would he ever be able to look in the mirror again knowing he was a traitor either to his country or to his child?

A car slowly approached the park and stopped. An unremarkable woman in a plain suit and low heels stepped out, walking over to Dusty and taking a seat. He was aware of a light scent of soap with a metallic hint that suggested she carried and had cleaned her weapon recently. He didn't look up.

"Good afternoon, Colonel Phillips, we think you might like to talk with us."

Dusty sat quiet.

"How far have you followed me?"

"We didn't have to. Your cell phone is in your pocket. We just let you walk it off and waited for you to stop."

"Look, I don't know who you are but I can make some guesses. I don't like being played this way. I'm in a piss-poor mood so it's probably a lot better if we end this here." He stood up.

"Colonel please, sit back down." She said it with strong authority. "What I have to say will only take a minute and I believe you will want to hear it."

Dusty lowered himself back on the bench.

"I am Agent Amelia Wilson with the FBI. We were able to secure a wire tap on General Jennings home as he is harboring the family of a declared terrorist. I know about your last conversation and the plans the president has for your son Brian.'

'We believe the US is being compromised by special interests in California who want to see a secession vote succeed. We believe they have ties to the White House and are manipulating events to make this happen. Your son Brian was caught in the crosshairs. Please understand, we have no interest in unseating the current President, only in understanding the bigger game that is in play and stopping the participants. We would like your help in doing this.'

'We know you will need some time to think this over. I will reach out again soon. Thank you for taking the time to hear me out."

With that she stood up and moved down the path. When she got to the edge of the small parking lot she climbed into the passenger side of a black sedan and departed. Dusty sat in the quiet of the early evening and watched the sun sink beyond the little pond. He didn't think this day could get worse. He pulled his cell phone out of his pocket, called a taxi to the park's address and then heaved the phone into the pond, startling the geese.

Jillian

Jillian woke up in a luxurious bed in a beautiful resort with five pillows, she had counted, propped and tossed around her from a night spent twisting and rolling over in a vain attempt to sleep. As she drew the curtains open. Four floors below the sun sparkled off the azure water and the ocean spread out before her to the horizon with nothing breaking the endless waves. She could travel all the way to China if she chose just by undoing the mooring lines of their boat. She and Dusty were free of the strings and commitments that held most people to the ground. She stretched, flipped on the TV and padded into the shower. There was a lot to do today.

When Sabine and Jessie had returned to their house the afternoon before, Jillian was still sitting quietly in the backyard with the dog. Once the girls were home, she dumped the whole mess on them. More than a few bottles of wine were emptied as they sat in the kitchen discussing options.

She left her backpack in the bushes, just in case they were tracking her phone or had left it there to catch her when she returned. It felt silly thinking along these lines. It was something out of a movie, not her life. Jessie offered to have a friend collect it up in the morning. One of the other couples they boated with owned a timeshare in Puerto Vallarta proper and a quick phone call got her an anonymous place to stay with free wifi; her computer work would be impossible to trace to a specific location.

They waited for dark, pulled Sabine's jeep up to the front door and she ducked into the back seat while Jessie pretended to load the truck. It was a forty minute drive into the city. When they arrived at the resort, Sabine collected the keys and Jillian, pulling a hoodie tight over her curls, raced up the stairs to the room. She had watched the news cable channels all evening, shocked as the replays of the massacre were shown over and over with commentary, interviews and the latest updates. They didn't have a TV on the boat and the onslaught of images was overwhelming. She tried to sort through everything for tidbits that related to Brian. He was forgotten for the moment in this new tragedy, which was good, but it was such a horrible event to be grateful over.

Sabine was sending a delivery this morning with one of the laptops from the shop and a pre-paid cell phone. Until then Jillian was watching cable and trying to enjoy the surroundings. She came out of the shower toweling her hair and caught the image of John Fields on the screen being interviewed on Morning Chronicle, in front of the long sweep of the mall. Sitting cross-legged on the end of the bed, she pulled a pillow onto her lap and leaned forward as he talked about hitting the Agent. She had seen clips so she was familiar with the incident but when he talked about Agent Mobury running the operation for Congressman Silva's shooting it caught her ear. When he said, quite clearly, that Brian was not responsible and had not even been present, she whooped, jumped up and danced on the bed. She finally had an answer to protect her boy from a court martial and firing squad.

John

John Fields sat on the carpet of his bedroom staring dully at the blood stains on the bed. He didn't know the next step or even how to begin. He had tried to call and find out where Blanca and Amy had been taken but it was Sunday, no one could give him any information. He felt his world collapsing and had finally sent her parents home. They were completely distraught and Blanca's mom couldn't stop sobbing. He ushered them out and shut what was left of the door on anxious faces peering from the neighbors apartments; he just couldn't handle it right now.

The sight of Amy's crib empty jolted his heart. He was lost, the center of his existence; his family, had been ripped from him in violence and the evidence was all around him in smashed and broken belongings. He picked up a broom. He was still hoping things would work out and Amy and Blanca would be home in a few hours. He didn't want her to come back to this.

The broken music box, which was so very important to Blanca, caught his eye. He sank down, silent tears rolling down his face. They weren't coming home. It was his entire fault and there wasn't anything he could do. He cried until no more tears would come and then sat staring vacantly at her blood for hours.

Every few minutes his phone would ring and he would glance at the screen, hoping it was from her. It never was. There was an almost steady stream of new numbers; probably more press, or people glad he had spoken up, or haters threatening to hurt his family. They didn't know that none of it mattered. His world was shattered.

The phone buzzed again as he looked dully at the number. It was from Mexico. He stared, the potential importance not registering, then in a flash it clicked, Blanca was being deported to Mexico. He grabbed it, praying for a miracle.

"Blanca? Baby? My God, baby, are you alright?'

There was silence, then a woman's voice, "John Fields?"

John slumped, it wasn't Blanca.

"Yes but I don't want to talk right now, I'm really sorry." He started to hang up.

"Please, please talk to me; you can save my son's life. I heard your interview. I'm Brian's mom."

He lifted the phone back up. "Look, I'm sorry but I just can't."

Jillian heard the anguish and the pain through the line. She had been through so much tragedy as soldiers in her husband's command had not come back or had come back terribly broken. Calls to loved ones sounded like this; the grief flowing through the phone.

She dropped her voice, soft and gentle like she was talking to a frightened child. "John, why don't you tell me what's going on, what's happened. Maybe I can help."

Caught off guard by the gentleness, John broke. The tears started again and he sobbed.

"They took her. They took Blanca and my daughter Amy. They hurt her first. There is blood everywhere. I can't find her. No one can tell me where they took her and I don't know if she is okay. I just can't think. I don't know what to do."

"Oh honey, I am so sorry. Where are you now? Do you know who took her?"

"I'm in our apartment, it's all torn apart. ICE Agent Mobury came. I hit him yesterday. He came and took them while I was at that stupid interview and he hurt her because I hurt him. My god, this is all my fault. She is being deported and Amy is somewhere in a huge social services system and it's all because I lost my temper."

"John? This can all be sorted out. It's going to be okay. It's not your fault. Sometimes people are crazy vicious but it falls on them, not on you. Did they give you a case number or give you any way to call?"

"No, they were long gone when I got here. She doesn't even know her birth certificate was fake. They took Amy separate. She's scared and alone. I don't know how to help them or where to even start."

"Okay first, let's take care of you. You can't help them in the state you are in. Are you sitting there staring at everything torn apart?"

"Yes, I tried to clean it but I, I just couldn't."

"Oh honey. Okay, I want you to get out of that space. Do you have a friend you can stay with tonight?"

"I don't know, maybe."

"Well let's at least get you out of the apartment and into your car. Maybe you can sit at a Starbucks for a bit or find an inexpensive hotel. And then I'm going to need you to eat something. Can you do that?"

John pushed himself to his feet. He looked around. "Ya, I'm leaving now."

He walked out and then pulled what was left of his door closed.

"I can't even lock my door, they busted it apart." Everything threatened to collapse down on him again.

"It'll be okay honey, just keep moving. A door is a small thing."

He walked to the parking lot, squinting against the sun as he emerged. The afternoon was warm and kids were playing in the grass. Moving helped. He fished the keys out of his pocket as he made his way to his Subaru. "Okay, I think I'll be okay now. Thank you."

"Things are going to get better John. We will find your fiancé and your little girl. We will get her a good lawyer and stop all this government crap dead in its tracks.

Just get through this hour and then we can focus on the next one. That's all it takes; little steps."

"Thank you for calling. Did you say you were Brian's mom? I don't know who you are talking about."

"Yes, I'm Brian Phillip's Mom, from Congressman Silva? You said something about him being innocent and I want to talk with you about that, but not now. First let's take care of this. I'll talk to you in a little bit."

With that the phone went silent. John sat in the car collecting himself and then he started it and pulled carefully out of the lot. Brian's mom had been right. He would find a way to help Blanca and Amy and bring them both home.

Cummings

Agent Cummings stayed with Blanca through the emergency room process then took her to the deportation center. They sedated her in the ambulance and she slept through most of the hospital procedures; wrapping her ribs and setting her nose, stitching up lacerations on her forehead, performing a pelvic exam and cleaning her up. He insisted they do a rape kit and take extensive samples and made sure the kit would be processed immediately. She was either asleep or groggy through it all and he hoped she would forget most of it. He stayed with her, feeling in her place, the degradation and humiliation his fellow agents, if he could call them that, had done. While the ER doctor and the nurses were professional, she had shown up under ICE supervision. There was no sympathy, just expedient procedures. She became faceless while Agent Cummings stood by, anger flooding through him at how deeply they shattered her life.

Agent Sean Cummings was a quiet and methodical man that had a long fuse before he got angry but once he was, he would be remorseless in his retribution. He was the kind of man who followed procedure. He paid attention to details. This was why he was in the position he was. He was extremely good at getting the cases he worked closed and through the court system because his evidence was clean and his paper trail was always flawless. Joining ICE after 9/11 when the bureau was newly formed had been his first step out of college. Recruited in the fight against terrorism he had excelled at chasing the electronic footprints of radicalized immigrants, bringing them to justice both before and after they attempted their efforts at destruction. He spent the vast majority of his career behind a computer or following up on crime scenes, working the clues.

He had been happy fighting the good fight against America's enemies and bringing down the bad guys in a race of time where he often felt like he won. He was the quiet hero who stopped bombs from going off in crowded subways because he traced the reckless ramblings of fanatics and tied it together with purchases of fertilizer or tips from concerned neighbors. No one outside of ICE or the FBI even knew the trouble he had helped avert. He liked it that way.

Over the last few years though, the job had changed. More frequently he was working illegal immigrant raids where they were simply questioning large numbers of people, looking for anyone whose paperwork didn't match with the records. They brought them in to the large detainment centers for due process, where judges could decide if they could stay in the US. It was stressful and frustrating. He rarely felt like a hero as he separated children from parents and sent loved ones off to spend weeks or years in detainment, waiting for a trial in a backlogged system. There was little investigation involved and he was no longer asked to find out who might be a threat to the US. He was just rounding up immigrants, some documented, some not, and bringing them in for deportation hearings. His genius for tracing terrorists had gotten buried in the bureaucracy of the administration's current agenda against illegal immigration over the southern border.

Even this had not brought him down too much. He was still enforcing the laws he had sworn to uphold. He treated every person with respect and care, trying to see their humanity, and making a difficult situation easier with professionalism. He was making a difference in a quiet, efficient way. He looked people in the eyes, listened to them and he explained what was happening. He learned Spanish. He carried teddy bears in his trunk for the kids who were caught up losing a parent or sent to separate detainment facilities. He followed up where he could, checking on cases he was concerned about, making sure people who had thought they had legal status found lawyers, and helping parents get reunited with their children when they were released or deported.

That was until he was assigned to the team under Dan Mobury. Arriving at the office in San Diego, he had been shocked to find a culture of vindictiveness and hate mongering. The cadre surrounding the Agent in Charge, his trusted right hands, ran roughshod over the rest of the team, bullying when they could, ignoring protocol and breaking the law whenever it suited them. There was viciousness in Mobury that made Sean cringe. The Agent in Charge truly seemed to despise the immigrants they brought in, laughing at their anguish and inflicting unnecessary physical and emotional pain through meanness and cruelty.

He discreetly made alliances with a number of the team members, working to do what good he could. Within a month of his assignment the soldiers from Brian's company showed up and the situation eased. Dan had a new audience and was focused on proving he was a fit supervisor of soldiers. He suppressed the rages when the young Captain was around and quieted the hate talk, putting up a false front of competence. Sean and his comrades breathed a sigh of relief and went back to the work at hand, grateful for the help and the break. It was all going smoothly, if in a disjointed kind of way, when the event at the community center occurred. It had only been a handful of days since the soldiers had pulled out and already Dan and his goons were back like a flock of raucous vultures returning to feast.

Today was the final pebble that would start their avalanche. He was determined to bring them down, meticulously and with an unquestionable chain of evidence. The country he served could not allow people like this to be in positions of power. He would see to it that justice was served.

As they were driving to the detention facility, Blanca started awake and looked around with frightened eyes. Cummings glanced in the rearview mirror. "Are you hungry?" He asked, and at her tortured look said, "I'm not going to hurt you."

"Where's my baby?"

He pulled into a hamburger drive through. "Amy is being taken care of. She is with social services. I made sure she will be fine. I have to take you to the detention center. Your birth certificate was faked. Even if you didn't know it, you still are required by law to leave the country until you can return legally. You will have a deportation hearing in front of a judge where you can state your case, but realistically, I have not seen one case like this be given leniency. It might be better for you to sign a document saying you are willing to forgo your rights and be immediately deported and save months in detention. You can be reunited with your child in Mexico right away. It is your choice but I would recommend getting this done quickly."

In the rearview mirror, he watched the tears well up and stream down her face. He pulled up as the car in front of him moved and ordered them both hamburger combos. Sharing food, even across the large interior of his government car, always made situations calmer. Everyone who sat behind him seemed better able to assess their situations when they had food inside of them and the simple act of offering it made him more of a friend and less of an aggressor. To help her he needed her to trust him a little bit.

She was quiet while they waited for the food. After it was handed through the window he pulled around and parked where they were clearly visible to everyone enjoying their lunches. He wanted her to feel safe, that his intention wasn't to further assault her. He handed back a bag and drink. Opening up his, he glanced in the mirror instead of turning around, giving her as much space as he could.

As she unwrapped the sandwich he saw her face hardening up. The fire was returning. She was getting angry. This was good. She had some hard decisions to make and anger was a strength that could get her through this.

"Were you a part of that?" She said.

"No, I was out taking care of Amy. If I had known it was happening, I would have stopped it." He said it as a simple fact. He knew he would have.

She nodded, looked out the window, took a bite of burger. "I need to call John." Her eyes looked at him stonily.

"They should give you access to a phone at the detention center."

She nodded, looked back out the window. Sean let the silence drag while he ate his burger, watching her in the mirror. She ate slowly, concentrating on each bite. She was tough. He was glad to see she wasn't broken by this, instead she was furious. It radiated from her.

"Before we get to the detention center, I would like to get a sworn statement from you. I can't imagine how difficult it will be for you to talk about it but I promise you, I will use it to get you justice."

She looked terrified and vulnerable. Then her eyes hardened up again and she nodded. He let her finish eating and then drove to a police station. He showed his ID and asked the desk sergeant to borrow an interview room and a technician. They set her up and she told the events in front of a video camera, her voice shaky, tears welling up and falling unnoticed down her cheeks. She broke down twice and couldn't finish her sentence but each time she took a deep breath and started the hard part over. When she was done they printed up a transcript and she signed it with a police officer as witness.

He could tell the pain medication was wearing off. She started to curl up on herself and breathe heavily. She didn't stop though and he felt confident as they left that he had a solid link in the chain that would pull Agent Mobury under.

He took her to the detention center. It was Sunday evening. He checked her in and watched as they escorted her into the facility. He knew the desk guards, chatting with them amiably. Finally, as he was leaving, he asked them to take care with her, that she was important to a case he was building. He hoped all of his easy conversations with the desk guards over the months would help her now.

He headed home. It had been an extremely long day and he was emotionally exhausted. Pulling into the driveway, he looked through his front window. His two girls were watching TV and his wife, Melanie, was looking at her phone, their big, orange tabby curled up in her lap. He smiled. This is what kept him grounded and why he could keep going day after day. He was keeping them, and all the other families across the US, as safe as he could manage.

He opened the door to squeals as the girls raced to him for a bear hug. He held them closely while he bent over and kissed Melanie, thinking about Blanca, how he hadn't been able to keep their family together today, and how shattered he would be if the same thing had happened to him.

Brian

Brian had the hood up on the old Continental. He was stripped to the waist in the chill air and leaning carefully over the engine to keep from getting any oil on his only pair of jeans. He didn't really need to worry, Ben kept the engine spotless. He was checking everything before they left. The garage door was up and spilled light out into a square along the concrete driveway where a long-haired, black cat was pouncing on bugs attracted to the brightness.

The plan was to drive him back to his base with Ben. Top didn't know anyone in service anymore but he still carried weight as a retired First Sergeant and long-time drill sergeant. He was sure he could talk Brian in safely once they reached the gate. They decided to travel after dark to reduce unwanted attention.

Brian had helped around the house and in the garden all day, doing what he could to ease Ben's load. The old Sergeant's wife had been a social worker at the veteran's home and they had let Ben stay on as a groundskeeper, in their little cottage, after she retired. As he aged, the home had hired a professional service that mowed the lawns and did the big jobs but Ben kept up with all the planting and pruning to keep the acreage tidy for the soldiers who were lodged within the big building. Brian was sure he was in his nineties but taking care of his soldiers gave him purpose and kept his mind sharp. He had a list an arm's length long of jobs needing finishing. Brian worked hard all day trying to get as much crossed off the list as he could. It felt good to be doing chores that helped someone and that didn't require life and death decisions. It was pleasant to work hard in the cold fall sunlight and let his muscles eat up the stress of the last few weeks.

They had bumped into a couple of the residents during the day and Ben had introduced him as his niece's, or was it grand-niece's, or great-grand-niece's friend and winked at him while the residents tried to help him sort out the relation, skirting the issue of who Brian really was. Brian smiled and shook hands, thinking about the unending sameness of these old soldier's lives. He figured he could arrange a couple trips over here with his troops to help when the world quieted down. It would do everyone good and he had come to really like talking with Ben. He had wisdom about the army and about life that was grounding.

The phone rang inside and Brian heard Ben answer. He wiped his hands on a shop towel as he heard him come to the garage door.

"Phone's for you, son." Ben moved over and looked under the hood.

Brian knew Ben would re-check the oil and fluids as soon as he left the garage. He smiled and went into the house.

It was a rotary phone from the seventies with a round dial for making calls. It hung on the wall in the kitchen with a long spiral cord attached to the handset, which was sitting on the counter. Brian had only seen them in movies. He picked it up off the counter and stretched the cord so he could sit at the little table. "Hello?"

"Hey, Bro." Mike's voice, as always, made Brian feel safe. He had been there for as long as Brian could remember, watching over him.

"Hey, what's up?"

"Just seeing how it's going. 'You doing alright?"

"Ya, it's quiet here. It's been good." Brian took a deep breath. He knew Mike wasn't going to like this next part. "I'm going back to my unit tonight Mike. I need to get back to my soldiers and my leave runs out at 0800 tomorrow. If I'm not back on base by morning formation I'll be AWOL."

The line was scratchy but he could hear Mike let his breath out slowly.

"I hear you bro, I'm just not sure what to say. If you go back they are going to arrest you for treason. I don't know how that will play out, but if you don't, you will be running all your life. They will find you eventually, you can't keep hidden for long, and then you will look even more guilty. It's a rock and a hard place and you don't have anything to negotiate with."

"Mike, I didn't do anything wrong. At some point, the truth is going to have to come out. I was following orders that I believed to be lawful. I was assigned there with the whole of my company. There has to be a paper trail. I have to believe I can win if I am brought up on treason charges. I will get a chance to tell my story."

"This is your choice, little bro. I will do everything I can from outside if it comes to it. I love you, Jerkface."

Brian nodded his head. "Me too, Asshat. Tell mom I love her and give Maddy a shove. I'll try to call you if I can."

He stood up and carefully placed the receiver back on the wall unit while wiping his eyes with the back of his hand. He knew deep inside this was the right way to go. He would go back to base and get this straightened out. He trusted his Colonel. He felt sure he wouldn't let him get charged with treason.

Michael

Two thousand miles away Mike shook his head. He prayed desperately that Brian would actually live long enough to tell his story. It was more probable he would be silenced before it ever came to telling the truth. He looked around the little café. It was late afternoon and he had just wrapped up at work. Picking up a prepaid phone from a drugstore had been his first stop, his next was here. He had a double espresso at his elbow and had ordered a sandwich, which was taking a bit longer. Taking a deep breath, he dialed his dad next. The phone went straight to voicemail. He hung up and tried Maddy.

"Hello?" Her voice bubbled into his ear.

"It's me, Maddy, are you okay?"

"Oh my gosh, it is so good to hear your voice, Mike. I have been so worried. Have you heard from Brian?"

"Brian is good. Listen, do you maybe know where Dad is? I tried to call him and his phone just goes to voicemail. I never thought I'd say this but I could really use his advice right now. I think I have a way to help Brian but I might need his help myself."

Maddy got quiet and when she spoke, sounded near tears. "Oh Mike, he and General Jennings had a big blow-up this morning. I could hear pieces of it from out in the garden. He was furious; yelling furious. I've never seen him like this before. He left the house and I haven't seen him since. General Jennings hasn't come out of his office all afternoon. It is so awkward. I want to leave but I don't really have any place I can go. I hope Dad comes back or calls soon."

Michael paused, racing through his mind for any memory of his father yelling. When Dusty was angry it was whip fire in his voice but he rarely even raised it, let alone yelled. He never had to, his quiet voice was terrifying. It was so far out of character that it didn't seem possible. His father never lost control. Not ever, not in all the time he had known him. Being in control was something Mike tried to emulate. It was what Phillips men did. They stayed in control.

He didn't know what to do with that information or what it meant, so he put it aside. There wasn't anything he could do; Maddy was safe and he had Brian to worry about.

"Ok Maddy, I need for you to find him and tell him I'm going to do something to help Brian but I'm going to need him afterwards. Tell him that I'm asking him and that he will know what to do. And Maddy? I love you little girl, I will always do everything I can for you and Brian. Always know that."

"I love you too, Michael. But what is going on. How can I help aside from telling dad cryptic messages? Don't leave me out of this, let me help."

"I'll tell you more as I get it figured out. Talk to you later." He hung up and watched the barista bring over his sandwich.

There was a solution to get Brian off the President's most wanted list and give him the time he needed to get the treason charges cleared. The idea had occurred to Mike as he talked with Brian, but it had to happen now and it had to be splashed all over the news. Brian just needed everyone to have enough doubt about his part in all of this for the lethal force option to be rescinded until he could reach safety. Michael could do this for him. He gulped his sandwich down, drained the last of his espresso and went to his car.

The barber trimmed his auburn hair into the military cut that he used to wear exclusively. With glacier blue eyes like his father's, he suddenly was an older version of Brian. Smiling, he tipped the barber. He drove to the Channel Two News station. Stepping through the mirrored, front doors he entered a glass-walled cubicle with a security door. A guard waved him through a metal detector and clicked the inner door open.

"I'm a friend of Katie Walsh, my brother and I are the ones who rescued her from drowning a few weeks ago. She is in production here and I'd like her to help me get my story out. I'm also the guy from the video when Congressman Silva was shot. I'm not a terrorist and I didn't kill him. Everyone is looking for the wrong guy; I'm his brother. He wasn't even there that night."

FBI

The grids lit up like a Christmas tree when Michael called Maddy from the cafe. Within moments, the FBI was triangulating his location, as were the US Marshals and Homeland Security. It alerted Alegeis, Mike's employer, and his supervisor called in Carey and Matt when they couldn't reach him on his company cell phone. FBI teams scrambled to the café to apprehend him in case he was foolish enough to still be there. With him gone, they were left questioning the barista. His phone, identified from the call, was located in the gutter just outside the café where he had discarded it before getting into his car. With little to go on they began the detail work of looking through street cams and canvassing for witnesses who might have seen the direction in which he left.

A call came into the FBI from the TV station an hour later. Michael was turning himself in as soon as his interview was over. All of the teams rerouted and converged on the Station 2 newsroom.

Michael

The cameras went dark and Michael felt drained. The adrenaline was wearing off and the seriousness of his position was overwhelming. He sank down in his chair. He didn't regret his decision, he would give his freedom for his brother without question; the reality of doing it was just long and tedious. The FBI had been alerted and he was sure they would show up momentarily if they weren't here already. There was nothing left but to tell his story to them, at least the part about the meeting with the Russians, and wait for the fall out.

He heard footsteps approach. Neatly dressed, the gleam of the Rolex on his wrist, Steven Capardi stepped around the camera and into the light.

Michael looked up. "Are you the FBI?"

Steven laughed. "No, they follow the rules a little too closely for my taste." He strolled over and dropped into the interviewer's chair, lounging back in it. "I met your father and your sister recently. Your whole family has quite a resemblance."

Mike nodded.

"I don't suppose you will tell me where your brother is?"

"It doesn't matter now. I turned myself in. He can't help you."

Capardi chuckled. "Well, we both know the honesty in that statement. This charade will fall apart in a couple of hours, so I have to ask myself, why you would turn yourself in for your brother. What's the benefit?'

He leaned back, put his elbows on the armrests and steepled his fingers, eyeing Michael across the top of them. "Either you know something or you are giving him time for something. I can't think of another reason a smart guy would be here. You know, I looked your record up; enlisted to officer, distinguished service, Purple Heart, honorable discharge, looks good on paper. You seem smart and loyal. Someone smart and loyal wouldn't be here, would they?"

Michael felt the small hairs on the back of his neck stand up. There was something off about this man. While his face was animated, his eyes were dead.

"Lots of rumors swirling around you, seems like principles got you your Purple Heart. Shot by our own side, man, that's rough. You can't seem to let issues just go by you without calling them out. Doesn't fit with the world today, though."

Capardi leaned his head back, looking up at the studio lights, tapping the tops of his fingers together. "So I'm asking myself if someone who is willing to get shot and give up their career over somebody else's off-the-books deal" he paused and his eyes cut to Michael, "seems like the type of guy to go on the record with a whopper of a lie, especially one pretty full of holes. It doesn't quite fit the picture, does it?" He smiled, slow and mocking. "So what are you playing at, Michael Phillips?"

Michael felt anger rising up through his stomach. He had had enough of the lies and innuendo about his discharge. He was about to retort when voices approached from the corridor. Capardi suddenly leaned forwards, his intensity ratcheting up noticeably. "Loyalty to your employer over honesty might be your best play here. Bad things happen to people who can't keep secrets. But, as we both know, you should have already learned that lesson."

Michael froze. Long years of military training took over. He was aware of the exits, he was aware that this man was lethal, even without an obvious weapon, he was aware of the conversation out in the hallway coming closer. He planned his next move, a quick feint right and a jab to the throat.

Capardi stared for a second and then rose. "We'll talk later, if you survive long enough to do it."

He walked out of the room, passing a group of four agents just entering the space. They flashed their FBI identification. Michael stood, shaken. He didn't know who he could trust. He changed his plan. "I have something to say, but I have some conditions. I want my father, Colonel Phillips, with me before I say anything. I want immunity. What I have to say is critical to US security. You will want to talk to me."

In spite of everything they fought about, he could always trust his father. That much he knew beyond doubt.

The Assassin

The driver of the tan Camry received a text. He was sitting on his balcony overlooking the San Francisco skyline, dominated by the triangular TransAmerica building's silhouette. He frowned. He didn't usually accept jobs close to home. It was risky and he despised risk above anything. This was a client he couldn't say no to though. He packed what he would need and headed to the basement's parking garage. In the car, he pulled up maps of the city. Last minute missions like this one were stressful. He preferred to have time to work out all of the details, reducing or eliminating unexpected issues. Things always had a way of going sideways but with good advanced planning he could keep the variables to a minimum. With rushed job like this though, he would need to think quickly and clearly to accomplish the goal and extract himself without becoming entangled in the aftermath.

He drove calmly to his destination area, going with the flow of traffic. There was rioting in the city again this evening so he avoided the areas engulfed in turmoil, sticking to the big freeways until he was almost on top of his target. He exited, made a couple of turns, and found a place to park on a busy street filled with people hurrying to get home before the President's imposed curfew. Pulling on a black leather jacket and a tweed beret, his sniper rifle concealed inside a keyboard case, he looked like a musician heading to or from a gig in one of the jazz or blues bars that lined the street. He locked up the car, paid for parking and set off.

The sun was setting, casting a pink reflection off the glass-walled reception area of the Channel 2 Newsroom as he scouted his location. He noted two different government vehicles with agents sitting quietly in front of the building, with another agent at the entry. He turned down a side street and approached the building from the back, where an additional agent was stationed. He considered angles and likely exit points. He frowned. On this side, the station faced a mostly empty lot being excavated for a basement. Surrounded by a chain link fence, it was not workable. He looked at trajectories. The streets around the building were lined with parked cars and low buildings, none of which offered clean lines of sight.

The small park to the side was his best option. He was glad for the curfew; the park was empty, which would make his exit easier to accomplish. On the down side, the location was less than ideal. He would have to guess which side of the building they would exit on as he couldn't cover both at once from any point in the park. Even then they were challenging angles with obstructions. He strongly disliked not having the ability to pick his environment. There would be significant uncertainty in this operation.

He considered his target, thought through the process and the standard procedures of the FBI, and settled on an exit. As the dusk of evening set in he checked his exit routes, located the best observation point, well camouflaged with bushes, and settled in to wait, opening his keyboard case and assembling the sniper rifle.

Jillian

Jillian was still ensconced in the luxurious hotel room overlooking the silhouettes of palm trees, a ribbon of white sand and the dusky, blue waters of evening, currently topped by a fiery-orange sky. She wasn't paying any attention to the beauty though. With the news on in the background, she worked her magic on the laptop. While she hadn't been able to locate Blanca, she had narrowed down the possibilities to several holding facilities in San Diego. She had spread Blanca's story, along with the video of John punching Agent Mobury, down all the lines of her giant social media spider-web. It was trending. A fund had been started to help bring Blanca back home and already it had well over $100,000 in donations in just a few short hours. The nation was angry over the massacre at the rally and wanted to be able to do something. Jillian was giving it to them.

She worked on Brian's story, posting over and over the part of the interview where John said that Brian wasn't present when the Congressman had been killed. It was trending as well; people were crazy over the conspiracy angle. She was finally feeling like Brian could escape this; that she could bring enough pressure to bear on the President to get him to back off the treason and terrorist charges. She had the momentum building. It was challenging to keep the interest up in light of the weekend's events, but she was working it hard.

John Fields had spoken with her twice more. She felt confident he was moving again and might come out of this more or less in one piece. He was focused on finding his daughter. She had been taken to a foster care family immediately and while he had reached the social services officer who had picked her up, there wasn't anything he could do before her case was brought before a judge. He at least knew she was safe.

Maddy and Michael had been messaging her over the internet all afternoon so she knew all three of her babies were safe. She also heard that Dusty had blown up with Todd and it worried her deeply; it was so completely out of character. She left messages all over for him; all he had to do was log into a computer to see them.

Her frustration was building. He had not contacted her since the restaurant. They were supposed to be a team and from what she could see, she was carrying all the weight on her shoulders without even a phone call from him. She had run out of excuses to make for his withdrawal and now it just hurt. In the back of her mind, she wrestled with her life; was she happy in a relationship with a man who gave back so little, even though they lived in a tiny space almost on top of each other? She pushed the little voices aside. She had a job to do.

All together, while she was exhausted, she was winning, but it was difficult doing this from thousands of miles away in another country. She wanted to be there, to hug Brian, to stand in front of him and take the body blows aimed at his chest. She knew when they joined the service that they were beyond her protection; that bullets could find the soft skin she had protected since before they were born, but she kept that walled away next to the fear for Dusty every time he was deployed. It was the only way she could survive their choices.

Michael's familiar timber caught her ear and she looked to the TV where his face filled the screen. Shocked, she jumped for the volume control and his voice boomed out, her sweet little boy, looking strong and in control.

"I was the person on the video at Carlos Silva's rally, not my brother Brian. You have been looking for the wrong one of us. I am not in the military. I was there as a personal security guard for one of the attendees."

Jillian's mouth fell open. "NO! Oh, my baby boy, don't do this for your brother." She watched in horror as he hung himself for treason in his brother's place.

"Oh no. Please baby, don't take this on you." She couldn't stop him and his words continued on. The tears welled up and rolled down her cheeks. "My brave, brave boy, don't do this. Not this."

The cameras cut out and the newscaster was there, talking about what this meant, how it affected the events playing out. She stopped listening. Her mind reeled. What did she do now? His story would unwind and Mike would be in hellishly deep trouble when it did. It was a grand gesture, a brave one. But Lord Almighty it was a stupid one. Why were the fearless ones always so stupid? It complicated everything and it put him directly in harm's way.

This turn of events sunk in slowly as she sat there, the tears sliding down. She was completely defeated. He had unwound all of the work she had done on the internet the last three days. In taking the blame from Brian he had put the bulls-eye on himself for treason but without the military to protect him. He would be charged as a spy, or a murderer, or a terrorist. He would take the fall. She couldn't unsay everything she had posted so far. She couldn't rework this for her other son.

Leaning sideways onto the bed, she curled up into a ball and let all the tears from the last few days sink into the pillows. This was all too much. It was more than she could fix. She felt so alone and needed Scott to hug her and tell her it was going to be alright but he, as always, was off being a soldier. She cried until there were no more tears; letting it all unwind until the sobs quieted.

She couldn't let this derail her. Taking deep breaths, she slowly counted to a hundred, only focusing on the numbers and the air flowing in and out of her chest. She climbed off the bed, washed her face, ran a comb through her hair, made herself a cup of tea and sat back at the laptop. She messaged Maddy and got Michael's location, booked a ticket on the next flight for San Francisco and reserved a hotel room. Picking up the cell, she reached out to Sabine and Jessie, asking them to pick up her bag with her passport from the neighbor and bring it over. She didn't care if the CIA tried to pick her up when she arrived at the airport. She was flying back to her boys and she didn't give a damn who got in the way. Sitting in Mexico was no longer an option.

Sabine and Jessie collected her up forty minutes later. Jillian returned their laptop and they gave her hugs, her bag, and a ride to the airport, dropping her off in the loading zone. With her red curls tucked up under a baseball cap, she looked like any tourist on their way home from vacation as she stepped through the glass doors silently sliding open in front of her. The evening was sultry and the air-conditioned coolness hit her damp skin in a tingly wave.

Check-in kiosks were to her right. She quickly scanned in her passport and waited. Instead of printing her boarding pass, the machine stayed frozen as the minutes ticked by. She looked around nervously. Across the lobby, where decorated, oversized piñatas hung from the ceiling, she saw three men in suits quickly working their way through the mass of luggage, sunburned tourists and Mexican nationals heading home.

She looked back at the screen, willing it to move, to print her ticket so she could dart away. She looked back at the men closing in on her and glanced back down before they made eye contact. She couldn't wait any longer. Grabbing her passport, she turned away and tried to lose herself in a large crowd heading for the security area. It was a short handful of steps when she felt a hand on her arm.

"Excuse me, Senora. You are Ms. Phillips?"

She looked up into the dark brown eyes of a Mexican Federal Agent in a crisp white uniform shirt with bars on his shoulders. Her heart stopped. "Yes?"

"Please come with me." He gently took her elbow and veered her off towards a security door. She glanced back towards the group who had been approaching but they had disappeared into the crowd, just as she had tried to do. He steered her through the door and down a corridor, passing several offices. They entered a larger break area with a long Formica table lined with plastic chairs, scattered with paper napkins and empty soda cans. They were alone.

His expression was formal but a kind smile softened it. "Please do not be concerned, Ms. Phillips, my department was asked by your government, your FBI, to have you escorted back to the USA for your own protection. We get calls like this sometimes and we make calls like this sometimes. I will escort you through our airport and make sure you board your flight safely. When we land I will accompany you until you are safely in the protection of your FBI."

"Gracias, Senior." Fighting back the tears, she looked away. What the hell did she do now?

There was no way to unwind this. Booking her flight had obviously tipped everyone off. She hadn't really thought this through in her rush to reach Michael. There was nothing to do but accompany the agent as he walked her through the back areas of the airport where they emerged close to the international gates. He escorted her onto the flight before everyone else, taking the seat next to her at the very front of the economy section. She leaned her head back and closed her eyes. She would be back in the US in a couple of hours. Until then there was nothing she could do but wait.

Dusty

The bar was carved mahogany and boasted two centuries of service on its pocked and scarred surface. The back bar matched with rows of glass bottles in front of deeply recessed mirrors, illuminated with reflected light from two massive, ornate chandeliers. Dusty nursed a whiskey as he leaned his elbows against the rich grain of wood. His stool was deeply padded and his feet rested on the long brass rail that ran the length of the bar. It was dark and comfortable, a retreat for the working class. Dusty was surrounded by off-duty cops, janitors, fire fighters and warehouse workers on a quiet Sunday evening after the game crowd had retreated to their apartments and rented rooms. He ordered a Rueben with fries and washed it down with another whiskey, the liquor burning in his gut. The blackness radiated from him in heavy waves so that no one approached him. He was alone in the crowd.

The TV in the corner was on. Over the seventies rock music playing from the old-fashioned juke box against the wall, Dusty caught Mike's voice, drawing his eyes to the screen.

"I was the person on the video at Carlos Silva's rally, not my brother Brian. You have been looking for the wrong one of us."

"God damn it!" He roared, slamming down his glass and startling the crowd around him. He dug a couple twenties out of his wallet and threw them on the bar as the bouncer approached him. Waving him off he left the pub, grabbing the first taxi at the curb. It was a thirty minute drive. The anger radiated from him and the driver's face showed worry in the rear view mirror. The rage was followed by guilt and then anger again.

He almost slammed open the front door when he arrived but caught himself and knocked hard, waiting until Carol opened it. The Corgis barked at him, sensing his mood.

She shushed them. "Dusty, we heard. I am so sorry this is happening." At the fury lighting his eyes she stepped aside and waved him past. "Todd is in his study."

Maddy stood behind her. He stormed by, her red and tear-stained face not registering as he shoved open the study door.

Todd

Dusty slammed into the office. "God-damn it, you tied my hands. I could have stopped this. I should have stopped this. Before Mike sacrificed himself I could have changed this. You brought me out of retirement to control me, to keep me from telling things like they were, to keep me from helping Brian. You played me and I allowed it. Now both my boys are paying the price."

Todd rose from behind his desk, tall and mighty, every inch a general. "You will not question my command Colonel. You are under orders. They have not changed. Michael stepped into this by his own choice."

Dusty went icy and they stared at each other, two titans, both commanding utter respect, neither willing to bend. The silence stretched until Carol stepped to the study door. "Todd, I'm sorry to interrupt but this can't wait. You have a visitor. This is Agent Amelia Wilson with the FBI."

Amelia strode through, stopping at the desk edge and holding out her hand. "General Jennings."

Todd stared at her hand. "What are you doing in my home Agent Wilson?"

"I am here because Colonel Phillips is here. I will stay here until he leaves with me. He is instrumental in an investigation we are involved in." She stood her ground.

"He is an officer in the United States Military, my subordinate. You have no jurisdiction over him in this. He will not be leaving with you."

Agent Wilson turned to Dusty. "Colonel Phillips, I need you to come with me. I am sorry that I have to put you in this position. You are a good man who makes the right choices and you have been protecting our freedoms for most of your life. You have gone in and done what was required when others were running away. You are a decorated hero and you have raised three children that all have gone into the military as well. Your commitment to this country should never be questioned this way. In any other situation I would find a compromise, except this is too big for compromises. This conspiracy is shaking the very ground the country stands on.

'We need to understand what is happening in California and your sons can testify. Each of them has been witness to separate events we believe are linked. Michel will not speak about what he knows without you present. He also can locate Brian. We must have his cooperation or we will be forced to arrest him and charge him with espionage and possibly murder. It will not go well for him. He will face the death penalty. I cannot help him if you do not come with me."

"As long as you are active military, you are under military authority. While I can arrest you for national security reasons, I won't. I ask that you come on your own volition. If you choose to stay here, I will respect that, but know that you are very likely signing Michael's death warrant and possibly Brian's as well. If you come with me, we are prepared to assist and protect both of them, as well as any other members of your family that are involved, even if it is unintentional."

Todd swung his steely gaze to Dusty. His voice whipped across the room. "Colonel, you are under orders. Let there be no question here. If you leave here with this agent, you are disobeying my direct command. You will be brought up on charges, stripped of your rank and will not see your family for a very long time."

Todd knew Dusty. They had been on multiple missions through hell and had returned. Dusty had given the military thirty years of trust. Thirty years of unbroken oaths. He felt confident that his orders to this man would be followed. Dusty always came around, even when he strongly disagreed with the action. It always came down to his oath. Dusty did not ever break his word. He had sent men to their deaths before. It was part of the command. Dusty would put the country above his personal life. He always had. His moral fortitude could be counted on.

"Dusty," He reached out to the man, not the soldier, "this is as hard as it gets. Your boys are military. They understand the choice you have to make. I am under direct orders from the President, the Commander in Chief. You are as well. As men, we make choices. It defines who we are. You have had to make the hard decisions throughout your career. Men have died because of your orders. You know the right choice here. Protecting the President comes above our own lives."

Dusty

Dusty stood infinitely still. His mind raced; a thousand thoughts and images colliding.

It had come down to this; a choice between his boys and his word. It was irrelevant that Brian was being framed by the very government Dusty was protecting. It was irrelevant that Michael had put himself into this position to protect Brian. It came down to is own personal code. Underneath it all, it was black and white. Maddy was wrong. "I was following orders" was not just an excuse, it was the code and it was a man's word. It is what kept the military moving and Dusty understood that because keeping his word was at the very core of who he was. He knew what he should do.

His mind filled with the faces of each soldier that had died under his command. He remembered them all, each clearly etched, forever young, forever laughing or serious, tired or serene, depending on how he knew them. He stood still while his lifetime of missions paraded across his vision; places, choices, comrades, enemies, wins, losses and through it all the commitment to his country. It was what kept him going against all the hardships that this life threw at him. It was what made the sacrifices mean something, all those dead young soldiers. It all flooded through him. The sounds, the feelings, the heavy sorrow when his soldiers died, the knowledge in his gut that he was always doing what was right, always protecting his country for his little family back home, so they could grow up safe.

Jillian crept into the picture. Her joy when he walked in the door safe, her steadfast love, the way she cared for his soldiers and their families, holding them all together, all the time, the way their three kids were her everything. He knew if he chose his word over her boys

226

she would never be able to forgive him. This was the one moment they could not overcome. She would turn from him in anger and sorrow. She could never understand placing his oath above protecting Michael or Brian. It was not something she could ever do or fathom another doing. He would lose her.

His children's faces were before him, fleeting moments from babies onward. Their little hugs, Maddy laughing, Michael serious and earnest, Brian trailing Mike around like a smaller copy, boy scouts, camping, homework, the loss of a first girlfriend, teaching Michael to knot his tie for prom, graduations, military, WestPoint, Colorado Springs, Maddy's first assignment, all of it crushed him like a weight against his chest, especially the guilt of missing so much of their lives and the sorrow each time he had to leave them again. He had given so much for his country. They had given so much for this country. This wasn't fair.

Finally he remembered a single moment. He was standing beside Michael's cradle as he held the precious little bundle that was his first born son in his arms for the first time. He had looked into that little face, a reflection of his own and Jillian's, and he had sworn right there, to this tiny, perfect child, that he would give his own life if necessary to protect him. That he would give anything and everything to see him safe. That single memory, that single oath, carried down through all the years in between.

When it all was weighed and measured, that was the oath that took precedence here, for him. He would not break that oath. He would choose the oath of his heart over the oath to his country. It was his only choice. The only one he could make. He hoped God would forgive him. He knew General Jennings never would.

A deep sadness crept out of his soul. He reached up and undid his shoulder boards, the eagle showing proudly in the silver thread, setting them gently on the edge of Todd's desk. It was infinity hard to let them go.

"Sir, I resign my commission. I have no other choice." He saluted, made a sharp about face, and strode from the room, trailed by Agent Wilson.

Todd

General Jennings stood rigid, sadness and bitterness creeping up from his soul as well. For his duty to his President he had just been forced to break one of the best soldiers he had ever known and had also lost one of the best friends he had ever had. Today the price paid defending his country felt extremely high.

The Four

The four in California gathered once more. The signal to meet had gone out as soon as Michael Phillips alerted the FBI. They arrived in their ridiculously expensive cars to an older mansion perched in the hills overlooking the broad expanse of the Pacific Ocean. Built in the thirties, at the height of the golden era of Hollywood when celebrity was a thing of grandeur, it was ostentatious; a modern castle with sweeping gardens and gothic arches surrounding sparkling pools. The young owner refurbished all this lovingly to its original splendor. It also boasted a recent underground addition, built at considerable cost, completely secure from electronic surveillance. They were safe here from the prying eyes of rival corporations or government agencies, whichever might be interested in their conversations.

There was an elevator down, a 1930s era swanky box rescued from the demolition of a New York City hotel and it exited into a series of rooms decorated to match the house above. Dark wood paneling and burnished silver fittings, a collection of Edward Hopper paintings, small tables with exquisite tiffany lamps, a rosewood radio box with a cloth covered speaker and deep leather side chairs with tall backs in mahogany, the image created a time capsule of 1930s Americana. It was a time when the country was struggling to recover from the excesses of the roaring twenties and the great crash, a time when workers were wrestling the wealthy elite for their place in the economy, a time that ushered in the idyllic fifties, where the middle class had a seat at the grand table that was America in its finest moments.

It seemed the perfect setting for this group at this moment. They were intent on bringing a strong middle class back to California's shores but this time it would be diverse, not singly for white, protestant men. They believed the deterioration into poverty of the middle, those who had created the nation with their industry and raised their children to believe anything was possible, was ultimately the undoing of the great United States. The separation of resources to the point where ninety percent of the wealth was controlled by less than half a percent of the population was a travesty to them, even though they were the new ruling class who benefitted from it. Their goal was to reestablish, through political manipulation and a combined effort of some of the earth's most profitable companies, a new world order that worked for everyone, not just those at the top. They were committed to unwinding the greed that had possessed the US government; the plundering of resources for corporate and political gain, the lessening of protections for workers and the decreases in salaries and benefits that eroded working families to the point where their children were not only unable to sit at the grand table but were fighting for scraps tossed out the scullery door at the end of the evening.

This was their ultimate goal, to start with California and then spread this new socialist Democracy across the world. They had waded out beyond the soft shores into the hard currents of revolution where wins and losses were counted in lives as well as dollars. It called for hard decisions. They were here to make them.

Three men and one woman sat in high backed leather armchairs facing an immense fireplace, a replica from the iconic film Citizen Cane. They were all under thirty-five, young leaders, and they were alone, bodyguards and wait staff left in the mansion above.

The owner of the house started. "I am concerned about what Michael Phillips will say to the FBI. It was a mistake to have him present with the Russians."

Michael's client answered, "I made the call. They needed to see I was comfortable with witnesses. It was a power play."

"Did you know his brother was with ICE at the Congressman's shooting?"

"I did. It was why he was with me. I wanted to stay in the information loop. It wasn't a coincidence."

"Did you expect him to turn himself in?"

"Did I think he would take the hit for his brother? No, honestly, that was a surprise. I knew he was loyal but I calculated the odds were relatively small that his conscience would prevail given his history in the military and his personality profile. I think if the President, that idiot, had not accused his brother of treason, then he would have stayed quiet.'

'In his military career he was witness to a cover-up that put him at odds with his immediate supervisors in a deal with oil contracts in Iraq. He took a bullet after turning them in and whispers of friendly fire circulated before he resigned his commission. He has a pretty big grudge against the US and I was fairly certain his loyalty to me as his employer would outweigh his allegiance to his country. It was a risk I had to take. I needed him."

"And now?"

"It is out of my hands. The Russians will not put themselves in jeopardy. They have called in their guy. Michael Phillips won't get the chance to talk to the FBI."

The room was silent except for the quiet crackle of the fire in the fireplace. The reality kept hitting each of them as the plan progressed. The optimism at the beginning was slowly replaced with grim fortitude. They were too far along, there had been too high of a price already paid, to shut it down now. This wasn't a new product line that could be abandoned if the costs got out of control but a revolution, with a price in human lives. They were uncomfortable but they believed that was a good thing. Leaders should always feel the pain of sacrificing lives. It meant they were still in this for a good reason and not motivated by greed.

They wanted to change the world. They were going to fund the new country of California with the utmost confidence that they could pivot their own companies to take advantage of the changes coming. They believed they would never struggle, even in this new society, because they were capable leaders. They believed what they were doing was right.

The woman spoke, "We were correct, the incident yesterday, as horrific as it turned out to be, has created enough momentum to get the proposal on the ballot. The more the government cracks down on the rioting and is heavy-handed with the people involved the more minds are turned towards a separate California that is not controlled from D.C. The current administration is playing right into our agenda with their military Gestapo stuff. As long as the media keeps showing clips of protesters being beaten and dragged away by National Guard in riot gear, then secession will happen according to all of our modeling. Anger is a great motivator for change. The funerals will start soon from the rally yesterday. That will keep this all fresh. There should be daily news coverage of spouses and children in tears."

Michael's client said, "How did these old idiots ever get into power? Are they really so stupid that they can't see the damage they are doing to their own cause?"

"They used the modeling software to manipulate the election. It has surfaced that they had access to all of the personal data for tens of millions of voters. It is naïve to think it a coincidence that events just happened at the right moment to sway the vote to the current President. Of course they manipulated public opinion. It was just surprising the other side didn't do it better.'

'As far as damaging their own cause, perhaps they think it is in their best interests to have a secession vote. Or maybe they are planning a counter campaign. We don't know at this point. The current Administration is as volatile as there has ever been"

The owner of the mansion said, "We can't underestimate their ability to manipulate the masses, they are the original masters."

They all nodded.

"We also need to make damn sure we break these modeling programs."

They all smiled at the irony.

The owner looked around. "Did you see the reporter at the rally? The one who punched the ICE guy? His girlfriend was arrested this morning for being an illegal alien. The story is trending. I think we should lend it some weight. It could be powerful in moving the Latino vote off the sidelines. I will run the models on both her return and her martyrdom. If her return is beneficial we should make that happen."

The four puppet masters nodded. As society's new Gods, they were secure in their right to social manipulation for their own benefit.

"She was working in San Diego with the secession proposition office there. She is already one of ours, already working on the measure. If the models play out, I will donate a million through a crowd source that is already created to bring her back across the border. It will lend weight to the idea that everyone is behind secession, even if they are not. A million dollars does that." He smiled.

The woman said, "We could put her up as one of the new leaders. Give them someone to rally behind."

The owner nodded. "If she checks out, and if the modeling software backs us up, I think that would be ideal. She is young, beautiful, wronged by the government and she is trending. It is everything we could want."

The third man, quiet until now, shook his head. "Maybe we could want a little experience? Maybe put our efforts into leaders, not celebrities?"

233

The owner looked at him. "Lets follow the modeling. It has been exceptionally accurate so far. If it thinks the young woman will serve us now then we can figure out true leaders when we get to that point."

They all nodded.

"So we are all agreed so far. Can we discuss the upcoming conference with the Chinese?"

They sat for an additional hour deep in conversation and then broke. There was a lavish spread on an ornate dining table off the ballroom once they returned upstairs and, as usual, they refrained from any electronic communications until they were done eating. The conversation was light and they headed to their cars early. The drive home beneath a sweep of sparkling stars above the deep blackness of the Pacific Ocean felt more peaceful then the reality they were wrestling with.

Michael

At the Channel 2 studio, the evening stretched out and Michael was eager to be on to the next step. The adrenaline from his confession had faded. The bureaucracy of it was now dominating the process as they made arrangements to transport him to a safe location. He was antsy and frustrated.

Clearance finally came through to move. They were transferring him to the FBI offices in San Francisco where he would wait until they had reached his dad and could bring him across the country. They decided to leave through the back as a collection of reporters had descended on the lobby, clamoring for a chance to interview, or at least get a picture of, America's most wanted. The footage of his interview had been picked up at the national level and had ricocheted across the nation. By tomorrow his face would be known around the world in place of his brother's. He prayed desperately that it was enough, that Brian would be safe until he made it to Fort Drum.

They handed him a flak jacket and helmet in the corridor to the back exit of the newsroom. Donning them without thinking, as he had so many times in his military career, he did a quick inspection and automatically reached to check his weapons. He looked up chagrined at the smiling faces of the three agents surrounding him.

"Done this a few times, haven't you."

"I don't suppose any of you would loan me your weapon? I'm feeling kind of naked."

"Would if I could. Your sorry ass isn't worth my job though."

Michael smiled. "You do a good job with this, I might be able to pull a few strings, get you a real security job. I have a few connections. You could give up this dog and pony show and I could add a zero on to your paycheck."

All three agents chuckled.

"Maybe I like dogs...and ponies."

Another agent grinned. "He meant to say, "My Little Pony" not ponies. He and my kindergartner talk about them all the time."

Michael smiled. He missed the camaraderie of his unit. This was comfortable.

He felt himself sliding into an amped-up nervous like he often was before going out on a mission. The three agents around him were sharing the energy. It was the kind of wound-up he would get when he know the generalities of what to expect but didn't know what was actually coming at him. His body was on high alert, ready to fight if needed, aware of everything around him.

The agents accepted him as equally competent and they unconsciously moved down the hall as a team, deployed in a triangle with Michael in the middle. An SUV pulled up at the exit door and waited.

The radio signal triggered the agent in the lead waving them forward and pushing the bar on the heavy metal door. Swinging it open easily, he took three steps forward. Michael followed, an agent on either side of him. A large, fluorescent light hung overhead and lit up the side of the building brightly, leaving everything else in shadow. Michael found their goal; the open door of a black Lincoln Navigator parked a half dozen yards from them. They started forward.

He had a premonition, maybe he caught a glimpse of something or a smell, he wasn't sure, but he shrugged down, trusting his soldier's sixth sense. The bullets came a hair's breadth later, the first slamming into his helmet, easily penetrating the Kevlar. His shrug was just enough for the bullet to skim across his skull instead of exploding it, then exit out the back. The second caught him in the neck as he was dropping, the blood spraying in an arc as the force swung him to the right. He collapsed against the concrete as consciousness faded, the blood from his neck pumping out in a dark pool on the pavement.

Everyone froze for a heartbeat as the shock hit. The SUV bumped backward over the curb breaking the trance. One agent piled onto Michael, working frantically to stop the bleeding. The other two ducked then faced the park, putting themselves into the line of fire. As the car slammed to a stop they hauled Michael in, one of the agents climbing in on top of him. The driver floored it, skidding out of the lot and around the corner. The other two agents took up defensive positions behind a Ford Explorer parked along the sidewalk while the second Lincoln Navigator rocketed around from the front of the building, barreling to a stop, the two agents ducking as they exited the vehicle. They all converged on the park, keeping low but moving fast. The shooter had disappeared, dropping the rifle alongside the keyboard case he had carried it in. They searched the surrounding area but he was gone.

Dusty

Dusty stepped out of Todd's office and looked up to see Maddy and Carol waiting. He finally noticed Maddy's tear-stained complexion with worry furrowing her forehead. She looked a mess standing slumped, in sweats, with dark shadows under her eyes and her beautiful curls pulled back into a tight, messy ponytail. His heart lurched. His little girl was hurting. Opening his arms, he pulled her close, holding her in a bear hug like he used to do when she was small. She clung there and he felt her shoulders relax. He was her daddy and he could still make some small thing better. Her hair smelled softly of lavender and he closed his eyes, breathed deeply, and held this one child of his tight.

She pulled back, standing straighter. "Dad, what did you do, your shoulder boards are gone."

Dusty just nodded. He turned to Agent Wilson. "Agent Wilson, this is my daughter, Madison. Agent Wilson is with the FBI." Maddy shook hands, the soldier replacing his lost, little girl.

The front door stood open and another agent stepped through. "Ma'am? I think you need to see this." He motioned Agent Wilson over. She stepped out the door.

Carol put her arm around Maddy's shoulders. "How about a cup of tea, or maybe something a bit stronger?" Maddy nodded and Carol left to the kitchen.

"Oh, Dad. What are we going to do? How can we help Michael?"

"I'm hoping Agent Wilson can, she has said as much. Michael has asked me to be with him before he will talk so I will be flying out immediately. I resigned my commission to go. Will you be alright here?"

Shock and sympathy flooded her eyes. In an instant she grasped the decision he had made; taking off his rank, and understood what that meant to him. "I'll be okay."

Carol stepped back with three glasses with scotch swirling around ice cubes. "I thought we could all probably use something." She passed them both a glass. Maddy made a face as it burned its way down.

Agent Wilson stepped back through the door. "I have some difficult news. As your son Michael was leaving the TV station just now they were involved in an altercation. Michael has sustained injuries. They are in route to the hospital."

"Altercation, did he get in a fight?"

Agent Wilson softened her voice. "No, Madison, he was shot twice, once in the head and once in the neck. They are doing everything they can to save him."

"Oh my God, no!" Her hand flew to her mouth and she let go of the tumbler. The crystal pirouetted as it fell, raining drops of scotch across the hardwood floor, shattering as it hit. She bent down to retrieve the broken pieces of glass, tears blurring her eyes.

Carol stepped in. "It's okay, honey." She put her arms around her, pulling her back up.

Dusty felt a punch in his gut and he leaned his hand against the wall. He closed his eyes, trying not to let the fear and guilt swallow him. He allowed himself three deep breaths of time, and then he forced himself up straight. "I need to be on the next flight to California."

Agent Wilson nodded.

"I need to reach Jillian."

Agent Wilson nodded again. "Your wife booked a flight earlier this evening, shortly after Michael's announcement went out, but has not reached the airport yet. We expect her to be in custody within the next fifteen minutes. She will be accompanied to California by the Mexican authorities and we will meet her at the gate. If she is not aware already, she will not be apprised of this latest development until she lands. It is a three hour flight and we do not see the need to give her this news when there is no action she can take."

Dusty nodded. "I can leave now."

Madison looked at Carol. "I need to go too."

Carol nodded and took her hand, drawing her into Todd's study where she quickly told him the news. Todd sat in silence for a moment and then rose and came out. "I am sorry, Dusty, truly sorry."

Dusty nodded. Anger tore through him. He did not trust his words.

Todd turned to Maddy. "Madison, I can and will release you, but you will need to contact your commander and arrange leave. You can stay here until the arrangements are completed and we will drive you to the airport. I imagine your father needs to leave immediately."

Agent Wilson nodded. Dusty and Madison shared a look, communicating everything in a heartbeat, and then he turned and walked out of General Jenning's home. He knew a thirty-year chapter in his life was over; he would never be under Todd's roof again. He climbed into the waiting sedan and they drove him to Ronald Reagan airport where he and Agent Wilson boarded a GSA jet for California.

Capardi

Steven Capardi made a bet with himself. Brian was going back to Fort Drum to turn himself in; it would be the safest place and in Brian's mind, the right thing to do. He immediately notified the team he had on standby in the event Brian would try it, making the call as he left the TV station. There were only a few reasons that Michael would have created a distraction and giving his brother time to get back to base was the one that made the most sense.

Steven Capardi wanted Brian. He wanted him as a bargaining chip to keep Michael from talking and he wanted Brian silenced. The fate of the United States hung on his ability to manage all of the conflicting events playing themselves out across the country. He'd be damned if one family was going to throw a stick into the spokes and knock everything into the ditch. There was way too much at stake for loose ends to be running around.

There was a flurry of unusual activity that lit up the surveillance boards of the FBI office in upstate New York. They had been monitoring cell phones, computer records, homes, offices, radio broadcasts and multiple other communications of suspected terrorists, spies and people who might be considering harm, all legally obtained with court orders, plus local law enforcement radios, ICE, DIA and Homeland Security communications. Algorithms did the bulk of the work, slogging through millions of pieces of information and alerting the operatives only if something out of the ordinary was reported. Tonight multiple hits began popping up relating to Brian Phillips, catching the attention of the agent assigned to monitor the traffic. He quickly identified the contact person if Brian's name pinged and dialed Agent Wilson, who took the call from the tarmac awaiting take-off at Ronald Reagan International airport in DC.

"Send a team to the main gate and make sure they get there in front of anyone else. It looks like someone got a heads up that he is heading back to base. Keep me in the loop."

Brian

The big, old Continental ate up the miles, covering the distance between Batavia and Fort Drum in smooth comfort. In the dark interior, Brian was at the wheel and Ben enjoyed playing passenger, telling story after story as the hours elapsed. Traffic was light; they were well past the rush of weekend travelers heading back into the big city, commercial trucks were their only company. They had left the house around nine and it was nearing midnight when they pulled into the small town of Waterton, close to the main gate of Fort Drum.

They talked it through and decided to have Justin alert the base commander. Justin answered on the third ring, groggy from sleep. He listened as Brian explained what he needed.

"You just want me to call the commander? That's all? I got your back, whatever you need."

He made the call to the commander first and then made half-a-dozen other calls. He shrugged into his clothes, grabbed his keys and headed out the door.

Brian waited with Ben in the old Continental for fifteen minutes. He needed time to let the Commander reach the front gate but he weighed that against the likelihood that Justin's phone was monitored and he had just broadcast his plans. The minutes ticked by. Ben talked about his grand niece, Carey, and the injury she had received, losing her leg to an IED. Brian focused on his words, willing the time to pass. A nervous energy stole through him. He was ready for combat.

He looked at the old clock face in the dashboard. It was about time to leave, these were his last minutes of freedom. He would face a court martial and be tried for treason. He knew he was alone in this and with the

President's word against his, there was little he could hope for; a life spent behind bars maybe. It was better than a firing squad but the idea of giving up the rest of his life made his stomach hollow. Running wasn't an option; he knew that about himself now. It was just that his hand didn't seem to want to start the car.

He turned to Ben. "I can't thank you enough, Top. In case this gets hairy I want you to know how much meeting you has meant to me. You are the best part of the military and I appreciate everything you have done."

"Don't get sappy son, keep your mind on the mission." Ben looked out the window, not making eye contact.

Brian understood. He took a deep breath and forced his fingers to put the key into the ignition. The big car purred quietly when it turned over. He put it in gear and pulled out of the parking lot. The neon of the pre-military base collection of pawn shops, fast food eateries and gas stations lit the night.

As he pulled out, Justin's distinctive truck drove by on the single main road through town, the black primer dusky under the lights. It was a beater truck but Justin was fond of it and it couldn't be missed; he did the repair work himself and just sprayed more primer over the dents and scratches. Brian immediately turned and pursued, angry that he hadn't followed directions. The whole point was to protect his idiot XO and the rest of his company; he didn't want it to be for nothing.

Brian flashed his lights.

Justin pulled over into a grocery store parking lot, empty after closing time, and Brian pulled in behind him. He was just reaching for the door when another truck pulled up behind him, and another, and another, plus a mustang, an older Chevelle, and then a Harley. His soldiers piled out, singly and in groups, as more vehicles arrived, boxing them in. Each one was filled with his troops, faces he knew clearly, people he worked hard to protect during each mission; the ones who kept him awake at night worrying about them. They all showed up, every single soldier in his company, all pulled out of sleep or from the arms of spouses or the company of friends, from video games, books, parties or bars, they all dropped everything and immediately left. This officer belonged to them. They were proud of him and of who they were under him. They were Company Charlie and Brian was their Captain.

They each climbed out and headed towards the shiny Continental. Opening the monstrously heavy door, Brian slid out from behind the wheel and stood, his troops surrounding him.

Justin came up first. "You aren't going in alone, Captain."

"Hell no!"

"We're here for you, Sir."

The words echoed around him as they each saluted and stepped up, forming a protective barrier between him and the street as more cars arrived and more soldiers got out, an ocean of Army fatigues spreading around him.

"What's the plan, Captain, how do you want to handle this? We've all got your back." Justin said.

Brian nodded, feeling the tears sting his eyes. He looked out at his company, the men and women he had brought through two tours of heavy combat on the other side of the world and the action here in the US that had, in ways, been worse. He wasn't too proud to admit he had been wrong. He was not alone. He had his soldiers and he would gladly stand trial for treason to protect them. They believed in him and trusted him. This group, that he would give his life for without question, had his back.

He stood up straight, "Well, I guess it's time to find out what's in front of us."

Charlie Company

The FBI teams sent by Agent Wilson, with the help of the local police force, set up a cordon just in front the main gate to Fort Drum, blocking incoming traffic. Under the guise of a drunk driver checkpoint, they stopped and checked each car that approached; flashing lights into the interior to make sure Brian wasn't missed if he showed up. They had been at it for almost an hour now and had only stopped a handful of cars; the majority of the post's inhabitants returned to base well before midnight on Sunday evenings.

The DIA team, keeping to the shadows and out of sight of the FBI, flanked the road a quarter mile before the checkpoint, tracking each car that approached through infrared and running license plates for anything unusual. A flurry of traffic leaving base a few minutes before had them on edge. They were waiting for radio confirmation, relying on the agencies computer systems to track down what was happening. Presently the radio crackled to life.

"We've got multiple cell phone calls mentioning Brian Phillips being placed in your immediate vicinity. Be on the look-out for an older Ford truck, black primer, license plate FBW-3914. We have video from a grocery store web cam, two-point-three miles away, showing Phillips entering the vehicle. The cell traffic puts him in route to your location. He will be there shortly."

Two trucks, one the black-primered Ford, screamed by the DIA vehicles a moment later and upon reaching the point where the FBI cordon was visible, slammed on their brakes and drove across the median, bouncing back up onto the road on the other side and reversing direction back past the DIA sedans. The agents looked at each other and nodded. Taking off in pursuit, they jumped the median as well.

Justin gave a minute for the DIA sedans to catch up, making sure they were engaged, then both trucks buried their gas pedals, roaring up to Waterton and cornering at the first side road. They followed one another for a half mile as the road wandered out of town and then split, each going a different direction at a four way stop. The two sedans tore up behind them and split as well, each heading out separately. A mile later Justin made a hard left into a back-roads area he went mudding in. It was a series of forest service dirt roads that wound around a hill, jumping creeks, gravel beds, and small hillocks. His four wheel drive easily slammed through the obstacles, the light from the headlights bouncing around in front of him. He watched in his rearview mirror as the sedan tried to follow. The headlights stopped dead, mired partway through a creek bed at the bottom of a boulder strewn hill. Justin laughed and roared up the next hill, losing the car's headlights behind the trees. He made a couple of turns and was back on the main road again, heading towards town.

Ortez, in the other truck, flew down the small road he was on for a mile, swung up a hill and just past the crest whipped into a driveway he knew was almost a U-turn heading back into the trees. He immediately hit the lights and killed the engine, pulling his night vision goggles down so he stayed on the gravel as he coasted to a stop in the forest. The sedan chasing him shot past the entrance to the driveway continuing down the hill. He gave it to a count of fifteen and then backed out, turning up the hill towards Waterton. His part of the mission was accomplished.

Brian gave Justin and Ortez ten minutes to flush out the sedans waiting in front of the main gate to draw them away before he started in. They had been spotted by every single vehicle coming out of the gate. Rangers didn't miss much, especially on home turf. Once the sedans were engaged in the rabbit hunt, he sent Murphy, their point man towards the entrance on his Harley. He talked to them on his helmet mike as he reconnoitered the FBI cordon, assessing the opposition. Passing through the checkpoint, then the main gate, he alerted Brian that the base commander was now present. He rumbled off to the side of the road, shutting his engine down.

Charlie Company's first platoon started ahead of Brian in a series of trucks. Brian and Ben followed in the Continental, surrounded by soldiers of second platoon. Part of third platoon brought up the rear while the rest were dropped off just short of the barricade by the first trucks in the line, proceeding on foot up through the trees. Brian couldn't miss the irony that this formation wasn't that different from when they escorted dignitaries back in the sand box.

They drove slowly the last half-mile, easily thirty vehicles with soldiers packed in. The caravan came up the road side-by-side, a long line of headlights stretching down the hill with a bump where the Continental was surrounded. The front cars reached and passed through the FBI cordon, pulling off the road afterwards, twenty yards before they reached the post's gate. They flipped their trucks around and parked so their headlights shown back on the checkpoint, bathing it in bright relief.

The Agents, watching the action unfold, gave up the farce of a drunken driving check and stood back, waiting for the bump to approach.

When Brian was just outside the lights he stopped and he and Ben stepped out. The agents and police officers were brightly lit by the dozens of headlights both in front and behind them, bathing the road in white light. Brian stood silently in front of the Continental while the cars and trucks behind him parked. Charlie Company assembled in a circle around them, a hundred and thirty strong. Soldiers rising up out of the bushes and coming in from the trees visibly shook the agents as one of the police officers put his hand on his weapon.

Brian stepped forward. "Let's keep this civil, ladies and gentlemen." He nodded to the lone woman agent standing alongside three male agents and four police officers.

"You are Brian Phillips?" A dark man in a dark suit stepped towards Brian.

"I am."

"I am FBI Agent Gordon Smith. I am placing you under arrest for treason and conspiracy."

Brian looked around slowly and then looked back at Agent Smith. "Sir, you have some balls, I'll give you that, but let's take a moment and look at the situation. This is my Company surrounding us here. They are each and every one of them a United States Army Ranger. I am their Captain. You are surrounded by one-hundred and thirty soldiers who have been on multiple tours in the Middle East and if I am not mistaken, have come to this meeting well armed."

There were nods around him and several jackets were pulled aside to show a multitude of weapons tucked in belts and in shoulder harnesses. "So Gentlemen, and you ma'am," he nodded to the woman agent, "it might be best if you let me pass. I believe my Commander, General Peter Grimm, is approaching us now. I don't much like politics; that is really more in the General's wheelhouse, so if you really want me you can have this conversation with him. I don't think he is much in favor of turning me over to the FBI, but you can ask him."

The General, accompanied by two military police, weapons at the ready, stepped through the line of soldiers and approached the FBI Agents. The General stopped and looked around; at the blockade, at the agents and police, at Brian and Ben, at the surrounding soldiers. His face reddening, he raised his voice and roared, "Stand down and get your asses back to base."

All eyes turned to Brian. He nodded and his troops all fell back into their vehicles and began pulling through the front gate.

The General looked at Brian. "Captain Phillips, you will accompany these MPs onto the base."

Brian glanced at Ben, nodded, and then stepped over to the MPs.

Agent Smith spoke. "Before you leave Captain, you should know that your brother, Michael Phillips, has been shot."

Brian missed a step. He swung around. "What?"

"After he claimed responsibility for being at the scene of Congressman Silva's shooting, he was shot in the head and neck as he was leaving the TV station in FBI custody."

"What? That can't be, I talked with him just a few hours ago."

"If you come with me now, before you are in military custody, I can take you to him. We are prepared to offer you immunity from charges for your cooperation. We need you on a matter of national security."

"He is alive then?" He asked, looking between the agent and the general. The agent nodded. Brian stopped. Immunity from charges rang through his head. His brother's face was there, that look he always gave Brian when he was doing something stupid. He had the opportunity laid out before him to walk away from the treason charges, from a life in prison. He could see Michael. He would get a free pass from this obscenely f'd up mission.

He looked over at Ben who stared back at him and nodded. He thought of what Ben had said. He was a soldier, marching in file, stepping in whatever came up in front of him. It was what held the military together and kept the country and the people you left back home safe.

"I'm sorry, Agent Smith, I'm a United States Army Ranger." He turned and walked off with the MPs.

Todd

The phone rang next to General Jenning's bed, pulling him from a deep sleep to instantly awake, a product of life in the military. "This is General Jennings."

"Todd, it's Peter Grimm. We have Captain Phillips back on base."

"Well that is a positive, thank you for reporting it."

"Hold on General, there is a little more to it. I have the FBI in my command center. They want to take Captain Phillips and his Lieutenant, Justin Johnson into protective custody. They are using 'Imminent Threat to National Security' protocol."

"Peter, the President's charge of treason and terrorism takes precedence. You are not to release him."

"General, I understand, but I have an issue here. I just witnessed Brian's entire company turn out at one in the morning to bring him safely through the gate. I originally signed the orders for all of the 10th Mountain Division assigning them to work with ICE. The treason and terrorism charges are not legitimate and every soldier on this base knows it. Rangers stand up for their own. You know this. I cannot hold Captain Phillips without a backlash. This is the wrong move to make with my men."

Todd paused, considering the situation. "Are you willing to put your star on the line for this General?"

The line was silent. "Sir, with all due respect, I think you have been away from the troops for too long. The beltway and the politics there have changed your perspective; you have lost sight of what is best for America and its military. It's not just what's best for the Commander in Chief. So yes, General Jennings, if the

President requires me to take the fall in place of one of my men, I will do that. I have the morale of every one of my soldiers to consider. They cannot do their duty if they believe they will be brought up on charges for following legitimate orders. I believe we have to release these two to the FB, but it's your call. I will do what is required by the President either way. But I want you to understand the cards that are on the table."

Todd leaned his head into his hands. Dusty would never forgive him if Brian was killed in FBI custody. He would never forgive himself. He had watched Dusty's kids grow up, had been a part of their life. There was no easy answer but he also respected Peter's view on the situation and he was right. Also, if Brian was tried for treason and his JAG defense pulled out copies of the orders sending him to California, the President's position would be worse than it already was. He sighed. How did the situation get to this; where using the military for domestic politics was no longer of limits?

"If you do not put him in custody Peter, then you will have to release him to the FBI. The charges filed against him are from the civilian side. We don't have any authority to hold him unless he has broken military regulations. Also, his brother was just shot while in their custody. Remind him we cannot protect him once he is off base."

Todd paused and the silence stretched. "Go ahead and release them to the FBI. I will talk with the President and see if I can resolve the charges." He hung up the phone, leaned back and stared at the ceiling. Where was the country heading, when he was forced to choose between what was right and what was politically expedient.

Brain

Brian was ordered into General Grimm's office a few minutes later. Justin showed up as he walked in, flashing his classic 'let's take them all on' smile. General Grimm was seated behind his oak desk as both officers approached and saluted, standing at attention as they waited for the General to acknowledge them. He kept writing, ignoring their presence, while a plaque engraved with a giant screaming eagle, from his time commanding the 82nd Airborne, stared mercilessly at them from the General's glory wall of pictures and accommodations.

He finally looked up, anger smoldering behind his eyes. "Captain Phillips, Lieutenant Johnson, what in the holy fuck was that circus out at the main gate?"

They both stood rigid, eyes straight ahead.

"In my thirty years in this Army I have never seen such a blatant disregard for Army regulations by such a formerly highly respected group of soldiers. What right do you think you have to use Army property, including Charlie Company, to solve your personal shit-show?"

He swiveled his gaze to Justin. "I could almost excuse the Lieutenant, having received his ROTC commission at some left-wing, public college. Lieutenants get a certain amount of license to be brain dead anyway; but you!"

He glared at Brian. "You come from a top-shelf, military family with a sterling reputation. Did you find some class at West Point called 'How to be Stupid and more Stupid'? I am of half a mind to send you and your entire company to the worst shit hole I can find on this planet and bury you all in it."

He glared back and forth between them.

"However, the Gods apparently have other plans for you. I am turning both you and Johnson over to the FBI. They have been able to demonstrate to me that you are critical to a situation of national security."

He handed Brian a set of orders. "You both are to go directly to your quarters and wait there until the FBI has arranged for secure transport. You are not to talk to anyone, smile at anyone, or even fart in their general direction. Am I clear?"

"Yes Sir." They both said in unison.

He looked at them both. "Dismissed!"

They saluted, executed a parade-field perfect about-face and left. Once outside Justin's color started to return.

"Damn, I think he chewed just about all of my ass off."

Brian looked over at him. "Try growing up with a Colonel. Did you take care of Ben?"

"Ben and the Sarge hit it off. He got him into the visiting, non-commissioned officer barracks and will have a team drive him and his ride home in the morning."

Brian relaxed. That had been one of his many worries this night; that Ben would try to drive home by himself in the middle of a dark night. He was just stubborn enough to try to pull it off. He could breathe a little easier now. He would miss the old man.

Todd

The effects of the rally turned massacre smoldered all through Sunday, fueled by news broadcasts and social media, until a second night of rioting exploded after the sun set and curfews were enforced, driving ordinary citizens into California's streets in defiance. The news of the riots arced across the internet and sympathizers streamed into downtowns across the country in peaceful protests that turned ugly as the evening progressed. Soon the riots engulfed many of the nation's bigger cities.

Protesters and counter-protesters faced off in confrontations all across the US in a mad turmoil of frustration and anger. The National Guard was called out in multiple states but could do little except stand as a shield between the screaming combatants. The powder keg had been lit. The divisions fueled by years of intense social media campaigns of misinformation erupted into violence. The rally turned massacre was the touchstone. The rage exploded across the broad expanse of the nation. Governors and Mayors prayed for the calm light of morning.

General Jennings, unable to sleep after his conversation with General Grimm, sat in his dark study, sipping a fine, single-malt scotch while watching it unfold on his TV. It fit his state of mind, angry and frustrated at the situation his duty had forced him into.

Dusty

Looking out the port window a little after three am local time on Monday morning as the jet prepared to land, Dusty saw October's wildfires lighting up the hills of San Francisco. From ten thousand feet the riots were invisible, the drama engulfed in the vastness of the metropolis laid out below him. Millions of twinkling lights spread out in a blanket, cross-stitched with the solidly lit bands of freeways, the quilt edged by the fires on one side and the blackness that was San Francisco Bay on the other two.

They taxied to a private hanger where they exited to a small crowd of agents. The smoke from the fires hung in the air and stung Dusty's eyes as he emerged. After briefing Agent Wilson on the plane, covering all that he knew in relation to Michael and Brian, he slept for the remainder of the flight. From years in the military, he still could fall into slumber in a moment, even with the weight of his sons on his conscience.

As he came down the gangway, a figure moved through the agents, the curly, red hair bobbing as she made her way to the bottom of the stairs. Her green eyes peered up at him in an older version of Maddy's face. His heart leaped. He took the last two steps in leaps and wrapped his arms around Jillian, feeling her familiar weight and angles lean in against his chest. She looked up and he saw her eyes fill with tears. She knew about Michael. Radiating tightly controlled panic, it was as though a single feather more could unwind her. He understood; he had felt the same. Only moving steadily forward could keep it at bay. Jillian had been kept waiting for him with nothing to fill her mind but worry.

257

He kissed her forehead and turned her to face Agent Wilson, his arm around her shoulders. She pushed away gently, stood up straighter and shook hands, brushing the curls back off her face in a familiar gesture.

"I'd like to go to my son now," she said. "I don't want to wait for Brian. I need to see Michael immediately."

"I understand, I have a son as well. We will get you there as quickly as we can."

The three climbed into a black SUV. It took well over an hour to reach the hospital where Michael was in surgery; they had to detour around several areas where rioting had spilled onto the freeways. When they got close, more areas were blocked by National Guard troops.

Jillian was quiet throughout the drive, only nodding if Dusty asked her a question. He didn't know if it was because of the agent's presence or if it was more. She would tell him soon enough if she was angry, she was open and honest about her feelings, which was one of the things that made their relationship work. Her bluntness kept the air clear between them. He held her hand and waited. He was just glad to have her back with him, this last week had seemed like months.

They reached the hospital only to be shuttled into a surgery waiting room, a small alcove with a handful of modern looking chairs and a table littered with magazines. Michael was still under the knife and there was nothing for them to do but wait, but at least he was alive.

John

Well before sunrise Monday morning, John sat in a small coffee shop close to his mother's apartment, where he had ended up the night before. Ordering an Americano with cream he set his laptop up. His name was still in lots of news articles, this time attached to Blanca's arrest, and he figured it was probably due to Jillian's work yesterday. She was good for her word and was doing everything she could to get Blanca's story on the front page of everyone's feed. He cleared his phone messages. His mailbox had filled up early the day before, and they were nearly all requests for interviews. Calling them each back, he left messages thinking public support might come in handy to help Blanca and he was prepared to do whatever was necessary to get her back home.

Checking the crowd sourcing fund Jillian had set up for Blanca's legal fees, he about spit out his newly arrived coffee when he saw the amount was up to almost a million-two. Surly there was a mistake. He closed the page and re-opened it, then he tried calling Jillian, but it rang through to a recording in Spanish. He stared at the number, hope flooding through him. With that kind of money he could make things happen. Blanca and Amy would come back. He felt tears slipping down his cheeks. He wiped them away with the back of his hand, avoiding eye contact with the other early morning caffeine addicts. They wouldn't understand how this little ray of hope was a lifeline to a man drowning.

At six-thirty, his phone started buzzing and he set up three interviews with national news programs for later in the day. At seven exactly a call came through.

"John Fields?" The voice was female, crisp and firm.

"I'm John."

"I am Elizabeth Whitley with Brooks, Whitley and Barden."

John Googled it while they talked, it was a very prestigious law firm.

"One of our clients has taken an interest in Blanca Perez Ortega's legal case and has asked us to represent you and your family."

John hesitated. "Why?"

"I can't answer as to what their motives are but I can tell you that we are prepared to bring our whole legal team to bear on your behalf. There will be no debt owed by you or Ms. Perez, I can assure you of that. I am not at liberty to disclose my client's name but his instructions were very clear; to resolve all of Ms Perez's legal issues immediately. Can we set up a time to meet this morning?"

John set up a meeting for eight, finished his coffee and left. In the car he hesitated, looking down at his clothes. He needed to pick up a business suit for the meeting and interviews. That meant he needed to face his apartment. He started the car and backed out, heading towards his neighborhood. Turning the Nissan into the parking lot, he looked at the windows of his home. The drapes were pulled and it appeared peaceful, a lie to the brutal events that had happened inside the day before. He forced himself out of the car then down the hall, dreading each step. He stopped short. His broken-in door was gone, replaced by a new one. The landlord had keyed the new lock to match the one in his pocket. Taking a deep breath he stepped inside.

He stood, holding the door, as the tears started again. The place was back together. The broken glass was swept up. Items were back in their drawers or cupboards, a cardboard box with broken things that might be salvaged was against the wall. He stepped into the bedroom. The bed had been stripped and washed. New sheets and a cover replaced the ones soaked in blood. Amy's crib was neat and her toys were tucked into a corner. Someone had even shampooed the carpet and stacked all of their personal items onto the dresser. The kindness of it overwhelmed him. They had understood how devastating this was and done what they could.

He changed into a suit. A sympathy card signed by all of his neighbors was on the kitchen table. Inside, several hundred dollars was tucked, to help bring Blanca home. He willed more tears away. Most of his neighbors barely made it month to month. The humanity touched his soul. How could a country want to turn away people like this?

He took a sheet of paper and wrote 'Thank You' in big, black letters and taped it to the door as he left. Climbing into his little Nissan, he headed to the meeting with the lawyers.

Michael's Client

Michael's client down-shifted the Lamborghini and rocketed around the corner, skimming the centerline. A different bodyguard sat next to him, holding onto the seat and door handle with white knuckles. The driver didn't care. He needed to think and driving the winding roads through the hills helped. They were several hours out of the city and his problems were not resolving. He shifted and stomped on the gas, flying up a hill.

The projections of the latest generation of modeling software weren't good. The disaster of the rally had not been predicted accurately and the predictions since were frightening. Anarchy and chaos, civil war, a breakdown of society, each set of circumstances they plugged into it came back frightening. He went through the problem from the beginning again as he screamed up and down hills.

The issue might be with the modeling program. It was possible a bug had gotten into this version. Originally the software was created to track internet use and fine tune the viewers preferences based on the sites they visited. At least that is the way they sold it to the public. In reality it was designed to pinpoint users who would be open to a particular advertiser's message. Soon the program was so precise; people felt their conversations were being overheard. His advertisers were happy. They paid him lots of money.

The next was the message. Each person had different likes and dislikes, cultures, backgrounds, personality traits, an unending list of differences that made one message succeed where another would fall flat. How could you pinpoint the message? They started collecting data. Huge amounts of data on every internet user, from the sites they visited to their public records, even phone records of who they called and the relationship of the caller. It provided the answers and trends were developed. As much as people like to believe they are individual, there are thousands of people who make decisions exactly the same. The software shuffled every internet user into groups and then showed them the same messages that worked on other group members. The results were phenomenal and the dollars poured in.

Another program, separate from marketing software, had the ability to run simulations. It was developed for resettling refugee populations ten years earlier and trialed in the real world. The rights were purchased and it was merged with the marketing software.

The politicians pounded on the door, grasping the power the software held. It was too easy. If they wanted to win an election, run the scenario and see what will happen if you talk up different policy points. Or change public opinion to fit your own policies. Every action was weighed and measured. The political parties who bought his software started winning elections. They quickly mastered control through exact manipulation pinpointed towards each individual. The developer became fabulously rich.

This new software allowed human manipulation on a grand scale, unlike anything ever conceived before. Instead of selling products, it gave godlike powers. They could craft society into anything they wanted. They had all of the information they needed to illicit any response they wanted from any group of people they wanted it from and could predict how future events would play out.

It worked. Not on every person every time, but on a grand scale, from cities to states to countries, it was amazingly effective.

The most terrifying aspect of it was human brain's inability to accept a false reality created through electronics. We cannot completely absorb or process visual input as fake. The human brain rejects the idea. The stories seen in social feeds becomes real, no matter how far-fetched.

Like puppet masters pulling strings, leaders manipulated every aspect of people's lives for their personal benefit. At first, ethical leaders worked to put the genie back in the bottle, using the software for good and creating laws to prevent abuse. Unethical leaders quickly stepped in and using the software, pushed the ethical leaders to the sidelines.

This was the software the group of four was using to manipulate the citizens of California to vote to secede. It had done an outstanding job, until it didn't. Completely underestimating the number of fatalities at the rally and the resulting riots that were spreading across the country, after being so right for so long, was the issue. It was being taken out on the Lamborghini as the man punished the machine, as well as the very hills, early on Monday morning. He needed answers and they were nowhere to be found.

Madison

Madison hooked up her laptop to the video feed in the war room. This was her last meeting here; she had a flight booked for San Francisco at two that afternoon. General Jennings had assigned Captain Robertson to accompany her as security and, she assumed, although he didn't say so, as his eyes in California. She was glad for the company though. They were still unsure of who Michael's shooter was or even why he was a target. Until they had answers, she was happy to have another soldier with her.

Dr. Lang entered and nodded at her. "Good morning Madison. I hear you will be leaving us this afternoon. I am truly sorry about your brother."

"Thank you, sir,"

General Jennings and Captain Robertson entered.

"It will just be the four of us today, Dr. Lang." He took a seat at the head of the table and Captain Robertson sat next to Maddy.

"I'll jump right in then. We have an emergency happening. You all are familiar with the modeling software?"

They all nodded.

"Well, General. Since the rally on Saturday, we have run the models under multiple scenarios using every different input we can come up with. Basically we are trying everything we can think of to change the outcome that is predicted. We have been unsuccessful."

"And what exactly does that mean, Dr. Lang?"

"Well, according to all of the projections, the United States is, at present, on a direct course to anarchy. The civil unrest that is happening across the nation will continue to grow, without leadership or a definite purpose, until it consumes the stabilizing forces in our society; the police, National Guard, and government leaders. Then the turmoil will pull down the economy, crashing banks, corporations, and destabilizing the rest of the world. The system is predicting a total collapse in the very near future and we can't find a reasonable path of events and messaging that doesn't point in this direction."

The general blinked. "Dr. Lang, are you trying to tell me that we need to immediately deploy the military to restore order? To get in front of this?"

"No, I am most emphatically not. Those were, of course, the first projections we ran. While it might slow the decline, the military solution would in fact lead us into a civil war with many of the same consequences. At present, the United States will not stand for a military intervention without fighting back."

The General asked, "Are you one hundred percent certain this is the road we are heading down Dr. Lang. There is no error in the calculations?"

"I am afraid the software we, and so many others, are using might be the culprit so I am not sure how accurate it is anymore. We have been manipulating emotions too aggressively and in too many different directions. I believe people have been pushed to far and something has broken in the American psyche. The rally and the completely unpredicted loss of lives, even with the ICE presence, was not supposed to happen or to be so violent. It was a tipping point, the pebble that is bringing the whole mountain down. We are witnessing the start of an avalanche and we have not found an acceptable way to stop it."

The general sat stone faced as he considered all aspects of the situation. "In the past, we have come together in cases of war and national tragedy."

"Yes, sir, we have run those scenarios. A war would have to be on the scale of WWII and I had assumed that scenario was off the table. I cannot recommend attacking multiple other countries to bring our own under control. That is not an option we should consider."

"No, of course not, but what about 9/11. That brought the country together."

Dr. Lang hesitated. "Well yes, we did run that scenario and it did work. However we cannot pinpoint when the next terrorist attack will happen. While we could use the software to manipulate the terrorists into acting, we cannot control the method they would use. It could easily be a bio weapon or nuclear dirty bomb going off in D.C., New York City or LA, which could incite reprisals by our own government. Sir, we cannot put the world on the path to nuclear annihilation to protect the US from itself."

"But you are saying that a terrorist event, an attack from without, would galvanize the nation to turn and face the new enemy together? It would prevent civil war or anarchy?"

Dr. Lang hesitated again. "Yes, that is the likely outcome from a major terrorist attack. But do not misunderstand me. I cannot and will not recommend that we incite terrorists to attack. As I have said, the cost could be much higher than a civil war or a breakdown in our society. It could lead to the extinction of all life on earth."

The General nodded. "Is there any other scenario, regardless of viability, that you have discovered?"

"Yes. A charismatic leader could unite the different divisions, but that option seems unlikely. I cannot see the current President fulfilling that role as he is the cause of much of the strife, or stepping aside for someone else. No other scenarios have played out acceptably."

"I understand Dr. Lang. I will brief the President."

He looked around the table at the grim faces.

"Let's not grow this out of proportion. I have been a part of far too many engagements that were predicted to go one way only to have the predictions turned to shit when it happened for real on the battlefield. People are more complicated and messy than you can account for in a computer simulation. While we will watch this with concern, I will place my faith in the underlying sensibility of the American people, not the predictions of a computer model. We will plan and prepare for the worst but in my experience, the American people have always risen to challenges, not fallen apart over them. If you will excuse me." He stood and left the room.

Maddy looked at Dr. Lane. "Sir, if the modeling software and the actions taken because of it are responsible for the rioting then the work we have been doing is very wrong. I don't want to be responsible for nuclear war or innocent people dying. The information we produce is being used too freely by people who are more interested in their own agenda than the good of the American people. I hoped making it easier for everyone to get along would stop wars and fighting. What do we do about this?"

"I don't have an answer Madison. We are not responsible for what other people do with our data, it is just a tool."

"Respectfully, I disagree. The scientists who first split the atom were partly responsible for nuclear weapons. Without their science, their minds, hydrogen bombs wouldn't have been dropped on Japan."

"Madison, this is different. We didn't create the software and if we weren't doing this work, someone else would be. The software is already out there. We can't close Pandora's box now that it is open."

"So what do you think happened? We never saw any scenarios that predicted anarchy or civil war. Maybe we could have prevented this."

Dr. Lane, relieved to move away from the ethics of it, began to get animated.

"We were asked to run the models for the ICE raids at both Congressman Silva's Town Meeting and for the rally. Both turned out to be much more violent than the software predicted but the science is sound behind the program and the data is solid. It's as though someone else is throwing in critical variables at key points, like the assassination of Congressman Silva. It throws everything off. We never ran a prediction for both a raid and an assassin in the same space, who would even think that might happen? The resulting riots from the rally have become far more violent and aggressive than we even predicted yesterday morning and they keep growing. Unfortunately, reality is following exactly along the revised predicted path now. It is the one time I would really want for it to be wrong."

Maddy frowned. "Could someone else be manipulating the software for their own agenda?"

"It seems highly unlikely. How would they know what we were doing? Or what scenarios we were running and what actions we were taking? It just feels like it would be too much of a coincidence without inside knowledge. No, I think the American people have been manipulated too much. Reactions are getting more and more extreme. We have played God too often."

They fell silent. Maddy's phone vibrated and she picked it up, scanning a message from Jillian. "Michael is out of surgery. He is alive, the bullet that hit him in his neck nicked an artery but they were able to seal it. There was swelling in his brain from the other one. It didn't enter his skull though, thank God. They have installed a shunt to relieve pressure and have put him in a medically induced coma. He is still in intensive care."

Dr. Lang looked up. "That is excellent news Madison. Doctors can do amazing things these days. Trust that they will pull him through this."

Maddy nodded, tears welling up in her eyes. "I hope so, Sir."

Dusty

It was just after dawn in California when they brought Michael from surgery into the intensive care unit. The doctor briefed Jillian and Dusty as several attendants wheeled Mike by, attached to tubes and a ventilator, his head wrapped in bandages, the visible part of his face swollen and bruised. They followed him down the corridor into a glass walled room, one of many, where he was connected to screens monitoring vital signs and the assortment of tubes and needles keeping him alive. The wheeze in and out of the ventilator was the only sound in the room. Jillian started to cry softly and reached for Michael's hand, holding it tightly. He looked battered, close to death. She slid down to her knees by the bed and leaned her forehead against his arm on the sheets.

"He is so cold. My baby boy is so cold."

Dusty stood by the door, a step back from Jillian. He looked at Michael, broken on the bed in front of him. Anger burned, the slow, intense heat of coals stoked hot enough to melt steel. He was furious with the shooter, at the person who ordered it, at the system that forced this situation, and he was most angry at himself. He had sat in meetings, had worried about honor and following orders, had been wrapped up in his own internal drama of right and wrong, when Michael had taken it upon himself and stepped into the line of fire to protect Brian. He hadn't questioned, he had acted.

He would never forgive himself, could never. Looking at the damage to his eldest son, he knew he had to live with being too late. He had been selfish, thinking only of how it affected him and Michael paid the price.

His fury boiled over. He would find the shooter and he would rip him apart with his bare hands. Then he would track down who ordered it, because someone always ordered a hit like this, and he would rain vengeance down upon their souls. He was no longer military; he had given up his commission and was off his leash. Hell was coming after them and they would pay. Turning, he slammed out of the room.

Jillian whipped around and leapt for the door as it closed, flying into the hall behind Dusty. There was an FBI agent stationed just outside the door. He saw both their expressions and stepped back, willing himself into the shadows.

"God-damn you, Scott Dustin Phillips, don't you dare walk away from me again."

Jillian's voice, furious, cut through Dusty's fog of anger and he spun. Never, in all the long years of their marriage had he heard that tone with him. Not from Jillian. Not to him.

She stood, back straight, the fluorescents overhead lighting her red curls like flames, her green eyes flashing and her face puffy and tear-streaked. "I will not do this alone. You will not abandon this family again, not now, not to feed your own damned ego."

Her voice ricocheted up and down the quiet hall, stopping everything dead still. All eyes in the intensive care unit turned to the two of them.

"Do you think I don't know you? That I don't know where you are going? Your damned vengeance does not come before Michael. You will not leave me here to deal with this by myself while you take off to make your conscience feel better. You do not get to do that Scott, not now. I do not care how bad you feel about yourself. You will be here with me and for me and Maddy and Brian and Michael. You will set aside your own damn personal shit for one damned day so that I can lean on you. I need you. Michael needs you.'

271

'I love you, I always will, but I won't do this anymore. Get back into this room and be here with me or don't ever come back."

She stared at him for another moment and then turned. The glass door automatically shut behind her. Through it he could see her fall onto her knees again beside Michael's bed and take his hand back up in hers. From the small heaves of her shoulders, she was crying.

He stood rigid, the fury pounding inside of him. She had no right to say that to him, not here, not in front of everyone. She had said out loud, yelled it at him, the thing that he kept most secret, his deepest fear; the doubt that he was a good husband and father.

He turned to leave, slamming the corridor door open and stalking down the next hall. Several agents were sitting outside the intensive care unit. One got up and trailed him to the main doors and then followed him by several yards as he stormed around and around the perimeter of the hospital complex.

Pounding down the sidewalk, telling himself he preferred being an occasional father instead of a full time one, he realized he had passed too many of the responsibilities of the family off onto her. He hated that part of him that craved the military more than family life. She was right; he was selfish. He often couldn't wait to get back to the thrill of being a soldier, running an op, being a hero. She had just let him know that she knew it. She had bared his soul for him.

The sun crested the buildings, casting bright pools of light and deep shadows as late morning approached. Dusty walked by the emergency room several times, vaguely aware of the frantic rush of people. The riots were overloading all of the hospitals in the area as injuries, some severe, came flooding through the doors. On his last circuit it had started to slow. The sun had brought clearer heads into play and people went home, back to jobs, back to their Monday mornings. It calmed down. The day would be filled with news broadcasts, opinion shows and social media wars. They would keep feeding the banked flames until darkness blanketed the streets again.

The agent trailing Dusty stayed in contact with his team, keeping them apprised of the situation as Dusty walked off his fury and brought his emotions under control. On the latest round, he caught up to Dusty as they approached the main doors.

"Sir, we need you to step inside. Brian Phillips would like to speak with you and we cannot allow him to exit the building."

Dusty stopped, nodded and took a deep breath. Would Brian feel the same way Jillian did? Could he face his son while Michael lay broken upstairs? He turned to the doors, steeled himself, and walked through them with authority. Brian stood off to one side surrounded by agents, his close-cropped, red hair visible over the tallest of them. His steel-blue eyes lasered on Dusty and a brilliant smile spread across his features. Dusty's chest eased.

He crossed the lobby and stopped just short of Brian. "I'm glad to see you, son."

Brian pushed his way through the agents and wrapped his arms around his father, hugging him tight. Brian was taller even than Dusty, both of his sons were, and he gripped Dusty's rigid frame firmly until Dusty relented and hugged him back, relaxing a little.

Brian pulled away. "I was just up to see Michael. He looks like shit. Dad, I would have stopped him. I swear I would have. I didn't know he was going to take my place. He didn't tell me or I wouldn't have gone back to my unit. I would have run forever first."

Dusty sighed. "This isn't your fault son. Not in any way, don't take that on yourself. Michael didn't tell you because he understood you would never be able to run. It isn't in you. He was protecting you. He knew walking away from the military in shame, under a charge of treason, would break you. You would do it because you

273

swore an oath and the President would require you to take a fall, but it would have eaten away at who you are until there was nothing left. Michael did the only thing he could; one grand gesture that cleared your name and put him in your place. He knew he could take it better than you. He didn't give you any opportunity to stop him; there was nothing you could have done."

They stood together, quiet.

"You know mom needs us back upstairs."

Brian went to the elevator bank and a door opened. He stepped inside followed by several agents. Dusty hesitated, unsure if he could step back into the room with Jillian. Brian leaned out, holding the door.

"She needs you, Dad."

Dusty stepped into the small space.

One of the agent's radios crackled and a voice said, "The Bull and Red Fox are on the way up. He's got some balls to face the Tiger again. I'm not sure I would step back into that room."

Brian laughed and Dusty raised an eyebrow, looking back at the agents. One of them shrugged. The doors closed.

No one made eye contact with Dusty as he strode through the Intensive Care Unit. He ignored them, walking straight to Michael's glass walled cubicle. Jillian was sitting on a chair facing the bed, her back to the door, holding Michael's hand. Dusty walked over quietly and placed his hand on her shoulder. She leaned her cheek onto it.

"Thank you, love," she said without looking up. He bent over and kissed the top of her head.

"Did you know your call sign is 'The Tiger'?"

She smiled, still looking at Mike. "I'm sorry Scott. I shouldn't have said that in front of everybody."

"It's okay, Jilly, I shouldn't have left you to deal with everything on your own. I should have gotten through to talk to you sooner. I'm sorry."

Jillian nodded and they sat quiet, the rasp of the ventilator filling the space.

"Mine is 'The Bull' by the way."

Jillian chuckled. "They are very observant. Is it all going to be okay?"

He took her hand and pulled her up from the chair, enclosing her small frame into his arms, hugging her tight.

"I don't know, Jilly, I just don't know."

Jillian

A routine settled in as they waited for Michael to wake up. They lived in a bubble, isolated from the turmoil engulfing the outside world. Madison and Owen arrived and Jillian laughed that they were taking up most of a hotel floor, just like celebrities, by the time all of the FBI and all of the family were accounted for.

She kept in touch with John Fields. Amy was safe in foster care and the hearing was scheduled for the coming Monday. The legal team petitioned for Blanca's release from the holding facility. John kept accepting interviews. There were questions about the switch between Michael and Brian, and John used the platform to talk about Blanca's plight. Jillian worked the social media on her behalf. By the end of the week, she was a celebrity, becoming both the face of the plight of immigrants as well as the poster child for how different California was from the rest of the nation when it came to immigration. John had been able to speak with her several times for short minutes.

The riots kept growing, spilling into the daytime hours, fueled by hate and misinformation. The steady diet of conspiracy theories and biased or fake news, enflaming sentiments over and over in order to push each new whim of the President, the Congress or anyone else with the modeling software, had created a country unable to distinguish between what was real and what was propaganda designed to manipulate them. Each new story was believed; the more impossible and bizarre, the more convincing it was.

The riots reached deep into the heart of the country. The people flowing into the streets had never rioted before. They considered themselves the law abiding fabric of society. They came out because they were saving America from 'those others', believing the person standing across from them was a killer of immigrant babies, part of a child sex trafficking ring or any of an endless stream of manipulated stories and events. They attacked without mercy.

Calling themselves the New Minutemen, in small towns all across America, people got into their cars and drove, ending up in the downtown cores of mega cities, bringing baseball bats and small arms with them. Driving around in packs, they were the self-declared saviors of the American way, attacking any minorities they encountered. Reprisals were heavy with self-proclaimed 'snowflake' protesters blocking the streets and overwhelming the packs of Minutemen, ripping them from their vehicles. There were as many different reasons people were rioting as there were fake news stories. Anarchy reined. It overwhelmed the police and National Guard, who stood on the sidelines, protecting what they could.

The end of the workweek arrived and the nation braced for another turbulent weekend. The intervening days had been brutal. The stock market faltered, each day posting record losses. As fear took hold of investors, the economy began to stagger. People struggled to get to work and wouldn't risk leaving their homes for anything that was not critical. Spending slowed to a trickle. Shipping stumbled, affected by traffic blockages, and production ground to a halt as "just in time" supplies stopped flowing to factories. Security became the driving concern.

In less than a week, all aspects of the country were impacted. More and more, people demanded the government step in and quell the dissidents; do something, anything, to stop the turmoil. The President was silent, operating off the modeling software that predicted civil war if the military intervened, yet unwilling to back down on any of his policies. His cabinet rushed to find an acceptable solution in line with the President's directives, running scenario after scenario through the simulation. The riots raged on.

Madison

Maddy stepped out of the elevator into the lobby of the hotel with Owen close on her heels. They had been within several feet of each since landing in California, except when Maddy closed the door to the bedroom suite she had to herself at the hotel. Their friendship had grown and she found herself inventing reasons to wander into the communal living area even then, hoping he would come out as well. Invariably he did and they talked until late into the night. They kept a professional distance between them. Maddy kept her walls up, not letting him in too far.

During the day, he was always a step behind her, watching everyone around them and acting as her personal bodyguard along with the FBI escort that trailed them both. If she hadn't spent the last seven years of her life in the Air Force living in close conditions, she might have found it stifling. Instead it was comforting. He was a quiet presence she could count on.

Her phone pinged and she checked her messages. Dr. Lang had sent an email through the secure server at the academy. She logged in with her password to retrieve it, sinking down into an avant-garde, asymmetrical couch in the lobby. Owen settled into an adjacent low backed, leather chair and her FBI escort stood to the side, discreetly placing themselves between her and the entrance to the lobby. The screen loaded and she clicked on Dr. Lang's note.

Madison,

My thoughts are with you and your family. I hope all is well with your brother and that he is recovering.

As we discussed, we can sometimes draw conclusions based on the input and scenarios we are asked to run on the modeling software. As you are my assistant and you have security clearance, I think I have a legitimate case for including you in the process. Suffice it to say, I am willing to take the risk if it will keep you safe. I value your assistance and would find myself at a loss if anything happened to you.

I imagine I have peaked your interest so I will dive right in, so to speak.

If you remember the conversation we had with General Jennings on Monday morning, you will understand the implications of being asked to evaluate multiple scenarios involving terrorist attacks on specific locations in California, as well as elsewhere in the US. With each one I have more stridently opposed any course of action in this direction but I am concerned my arguments are falling on deaf ears. I do not know how they would proceed with any such action, or the timing, or even if it is a legitimate concern, but I can tell you that it is a possible threat to your well being while you are on the coast.

Targets seem to be centered on California, specifically the home of the Mouse and the Golden Gate Bridge, as I expect the people in power are more comfortable considering an action on a symbol of the US that is also representative of the constituency that is already in defiance. Please keep this information in the strictest of confidences while at the same time keeping yourself and your family safe.

I trust I will have you back at the Academy in short order as I am at a loss to find anything without you,

Regards,
James

Maddy sat still, considering the information. She glanced at Owen, who raised his eyebrows.

"Is everything okay?"

She nodded and closed out her connection. Trusting Owen was not an option, not while he worked with General Jennings. "I promised Brian I would call his girlfriend, Ashley, for him. I think she is a little angry over being left at a hotel and then picked up by the DIA. She isn't answering his calls. He is hoping I can help smooth things over."

"She'll come around. It wasn't Brian's fault. She will eventually see that."

"I hope it works out, they seem good together. Shall we go see if he is in his room?"

Owen nodded and they headed back to the elevator.

John

John Fields stepped out from under the lights of the set, struggling to find his way as his eyes adjusted to the sudden gloom. A camera operator gently guided him around a light stand and past the huddle of electronics grouped around the stage. A striking woman in a flawless suit and matching heels stepped up, taking his elbow and steering him towards the exit door.

"John, I'm Julie West. I'm a news anchor for Channel Two."

"Hello Ma'am, I know who you are, I've been watching you for years, since you were on the air in San Diego."

"Well, I hope not too many." She smiled.

"Well, no, that's not how I meant it, I mean you are my mom's favorite news person, she's watched you my whole life."

She raised her eyebrows.

"Ok, that didn't sound right either." John stopped talking; it seemed the best at this point.

She laughed as they walked.

"I heard you about your interview today and flew down. I actually have a bit of a problem I was hoping you might be able to help me with. Do you have any way to contact Brian Phillips? On camera, you talk as if you know him or at least have more personal details than I have been able to come up with. I thought you might be able to reach him."

John hesitated. "Why are you asking? His brother was shot outside your building. I wouldn't give out any information, even if I did have it; they still haven't found the person responsible."

"I would love an interview with him, of course, but to be honest, his brother Michael left an envelope with me and I promised to give it to his father. Trouble is, I can't find any of his family. They are all completely off the grid. I'm guessing they are under FBI protection since Michael's shooting."

John nodded. "If you give me your phone number I might be able to help you."

She handed him her card and smiled her thanks as he left the building.

Julie West

Late that afternoon Julie West stepped out of her Mercedes on the top floor of a parking garage near the Embarcadero and was ushered into the back seat of a Lincoln Navigator. Dusty was inside leaning against the opposite door.

"You must be Scott Phillips. You all certainly do look alike," She said.

Dusty nodded, his icy eyes appraising. He reminded her of an adder, poised but deadly. She offered up the envelope. He glanced at the handwriting and checked the seal; it was unbroken. He set it on the seat between them.

His voice came at her, hard and angry. "Did you set my son up?"

"No." She paused, choosing her words. "I don't know how they figured out where he was. It was just after the evening news broadcast though so the place was crowded. It could have been a personal text or call. We have no way to check. I would hope that no one on our staff would do that, but in my career, I've seen it all."

"Do you have any information I can use." He glared at her across the interior of the SUV.

"Not at present. If I do though, I will expect something in return. I want an interview with your son Brian."

Dusty's eyes blazed. "You will not use my son as a bargaining chip. Just so we are clear, I will find out who did this to Michael and I will kill them, brutally. If you had anything to do with it, I will find you."

Julie sat up straight. "I am not worried then. It had nothing to do with me. Threatening me is hardly effective at getting information. I am here because I made a promise, I followed through. I spent precious time tracking you down and I agreed to do it because I respected your son. We are done. Good luck, Mr. Phillips."

She grabbed the handle, opened the door and climbed down. The Navigator pulled away as she slid behind the wheel of her Mercedes.

Dusty

Dusty leaned his head against the back of the seat as the agent drove him to the hotel. Michael's handwriting had jarred him. Waiting by his bullet shattered body, it felt like death stepped closer each day. This might be the last piece of his son he ever received. He had been harsh with Julie West, he knew, but he didn't trust anyone at the station when Michael turned himself in. Someone had alerted the shooter and he was going to find them. Seeing Michael's handwriting had been the trigger, but the anger been brewing for days.

He picked the manila envelope up and ran his hands across Michael's writing. He wasn't ready to open it yet. He didn't know what his son would say from across time. What would his last message be? He held it closely and let the FBI get him back to Jillian.

Blanca

Blanca opened her eyes slowly, willing Amy to be there, for the nightmare to be over. It wasn't. Pain shot through her chest as she struggled to sit up, the broken ribs protesting the slightest movement. An older woman on the pallet next to her looked over with soft eyes and moved to help, putting her arm around her shoulders and easing her up.

"Gracias."

"Da Nada." Smiling, the woman sat back down on her mat, the silver, plastic blanket crackling as she moved it aside.

Blanca was in a small room, the size of child's room, with seven other women, all positioned on plastic mats squashed tight against each other. There was no room between to place a foot, walking was done by stepping on the mats as you made your way to the door. Even so, Blanca felt she had it easier than others. Their cell was one of many lining the walls of the old grocery store that had been converted into a confinement center for immigrants. In the vast center of the space, construction fencing had been arranged into twenty-foot squares draped with plastic tarps, creating a series of cages where most of the detainees were held. She at least had flimsy walls, holding in a little of the heat from eight warm bodies at night; the space was kept at freezing temperatures. The walls also buffered the noise of hundreds of people living together but, unlike the open center areas, they were able to turn off the light at night, enabling a little sleep. Small things, but her existence was reduced to small things now.

The first few days had blended together in a fog of pain. The women in her cell had watched quietly as the guards hauled her in, standing against the edges of the room until they settled her on a mat and left. She collapsed backwards and cried out as her ribs took the brunt of the impact. As she struggled to breath they swarmed over to help, gently lifting her head to place a rolled up blanket as a pillow and tucking another in closely around her small frame. They took turns sleeping next to her, helping her to sit, bringing her water and the mostly still frozen meals that the guards handed out. Trips to the bathroom were a production, with someone standing on either side, helping her to walk the fifty yards to the communal toilets. It was filthy inside, often lacking toilet paper or hygiene products and there was rarely soap. When there was, they quickly washed faces and arms before the guards herded them back into their cell. She still hadn't had the chance to shower.

Time crawled by. With nothing to do they mostly talked. Blanca's Spanish wasn't great and the other women's accents were strong and varied. She could understand much of what was said but it was a struggle as the Mexican Spanish her mother taught her was very different from theirs. She learned names and where they were each from, mostly Central American countries where the violence had pushed them into walking thousands of miles from their villages, out of their home countries and then across the entirety of Mexico to reach the US. They had seen the damage done to Blanca before, they had fled from it. They understood her pain, both physical and emotional. They wrapped her up in gentle care as they had done so many times before to sisters, mothers, friends and children. The days merged together as they all waited for the overwhelmed court system to catch up to them.

The hope and excitement that had accompanied them as they crossed the border; the final obstacle they had traveled so far for, the end of their painfully long journeys on foot, carrying children and everything they owned, slowly dwindled, replaced by doubt and fear. As they realized they could be sent back to the terrifying violence of their home countries, erasing the phenomenal accomplishment of survival and deprivation they had endured for months to arrive, depression set in. They would end up dead, they knew that. It was why they fled, running to the hope of a safer life for their families. How could this great country be so cruel? How could it send them back?

Blanca held them when they cried, trying to explain the complex legal system and gently holding space for them as they realized they had misunderstood the process; that while they had legally sought asylum, they lacked the evidence to prove their case or a lawyer to plead their position. Or they had been lied to by smugglers hired to bring them the last handful of miles across the border and they had gambled everything in desperation and lost.

She tried to explain that Americans were afraid. They thought these women surrounding her, their husbands, brothers, boyfriends and children out in the bigger cages, were possible terrorists, would rape children, would steal and murder. She finally gave up, embarrassed at the vast gap in resources between the people around her and the people who ultimately were only interested in holding onto what they had. The fear was simply a way to hide from the brutal truth.

She just couldn't say those words to these women. She couldn't destroy what little hope they still carried close to their hearts.

Without TV, she wasn't aware of the strife consuming the country or of her developing celebrity. Gripped in fear and anger, a large portion of the populace was rising up against the national government, and as Congressman Silva had predicted, fighting in the streets with those who disagreed. While she sat quietly conversing with this group of women and began to heal; the bruises on her face and body turning to deep purples

288

and blacks and then to amber, she was talked about and argued over in the media and across social platforms. She became the face of the campaign for California's independence.

The signature drive for secession became a phenomenal success. They easily reached the number needed to put the measure on the ballot and with a healthy cushion that brooked no debate.

The Resistance

As the sun set on Friday, tens of thousands gathered in San Diego's Balboa Park in defiance of the curfew. The funerals for the victims of the rally had progressed all week, a steady parade of black-draped coffins splashed across news programs. The crowd was angry. Signs with Blanca's face plastered across them and underscored with 'Free Her' in black, block letters were everywhere, waved by supporters across the spectrum of skin color, age and gender.

Someone produced a list of the three immigration detainment facilities in San Diego and copies in the thousands were handed out. Organizers popped up and the crowd began to split up and head to their cars. Regrouping forty minutes later in front of one of the facilities, they chanted and protested as the guards peered nervously from the doorways. Hundreds showed up and at an unspoken signal, swarmed the doors. The guards backed up and let them in, walking away. Immigrants were not worth their life.

They quickly unlocked doors and cages, emptying the space and letting the detainees disappear into the crowd. Blanca was not there.

Blanca

It was after midnight and Blanca was struggling to sleep, tossing back and forth to get her ribs comfortable when she heard multiple sirens approach. She tensed as the women around her woke up, the edges of their eyes shining white in the dusk of the room. They heard chanting and shouts followed by a loud bang as the front doors of the building were smashed open. Minutes later feet pounded by the door. They all quickly rose and backed up against the far wall of the cell. The door swung open to a handful of men, one of whom flipped the light switch. He looked them over; settling his gaze on Blanca's bruised face.

"I think we've got her," He hollered. Reaching out and grabbing her hand, he pulled her from the cell. She struggled as they ran down the corridor, her breath catching each time she stepped. Her ribs were fire. She looked up as she cleared the building, seeing Christina and Oscar in front of her. Oscar caught her as she stumbled towards them.

"Aw, Chica, you look like shit." Christina pulled her into a hug, wrapping her arms around her and holding her up.

Blanca pushed away, the pain ricocheting across her chest. "Can't. Hurts."

Christina nodded and yelled as loud as she could. "We've got her, we've got her."

The chant was taken up as several hundred people surrounded them. They walked by the handful of police cars who had responded to the emergency calls from the guards. The police let them pass. There were too many protesters for them to intervene safely.

Blanca breathed in the cool, dusty air. The women who had been in the cell with her vanished into the crowd. She hoped they would be alright. She breathed in again. She was free.

Several hours later she was soaking in a scalding shower, letting the hot water draw out the nightmare of the last week and wash it down the drain. She would never be the same again. She felt broken. She would carry around the shame and the pain of what they did to her always. The bruises would fade, her broken nose and ribs would mend, but the scars to her soul were forever.

She stepped out of the shower into Christina's tiny bathroom and toweled herself off. She borrowed leggings and an oversized sweater to wear and pulled them on gently, careful of her ribs. She glanced in the mirror and stopped. She looked like a zombie. Her face was still badly bruised; yellow and brown mottled skin stretched around deep, black bruises under eyes still puffy from crying. Her lips were dry and cracked and her hair hung limp. Frowning, she ran her fingers through her wet hair and wrapped it up into a bun. It was the best she could do. She decided to avoid mirrors until she felt better.

She heard a knock on the small apartment's front door and stepped out of the bathroom as John came through it. She hung back against the wall. She felt lost.

He nodded to Christina distractedly, his eyes focusing on her as he strode across the room. He reached out and ever so gently pulled her into his arms, cradling her carefully. She felt his tears fall on her forehead as he kissed the top of her head.

"I am so sorry Blanca, I am so, so sorry. This was all my fault. They hurt you because of me. I am so sorry."

She leaned into his familiar embrace, willing the tears away, willing herself to be strong. It only lasted a moment. She was safe. The tears started slow and then turned into big, heaving sobs as she clung to him. He held her until it quieted and then steered her onto the small couch, tucking her up under his arm. Exhausted, she listened to Christina tell him about her rescue and she slipped off to sleep. John held her without moving until the sun came up.

Capardi

Steve Capardi arrived as requested, presenting himself to the security at the front gate and then driving his rental up the steep driveway to the angular mansion overlooking bushy, dry hills. Security opened the door as he approached and ushered him into a library off the main hall. Stepping through the double doors, he found himself in a museum of computer technology. He was surrounded by the history of the computer age, from first edition calculators to large boxy home computers with tiny screens, to a pong video table game from the early seventies. First edition gaming consoles, games and controllers were artfully arranged, early laptops, brick sized cell phones with a battery in a separate satchel, portable DVD players; all had a place. Capardi didn't browse, he stood still, focused.

Michael's client stepped in, unconsciously skimming his hand across his treasures as he moved. He took a seat at the pong table and motioned Capardi to the opposite one. Michael's client fished a nickel out of a small dish off to the side and fed the game. He was silent for a moment while he played, the little electronic blip bouncing back and forth, pinging with each ricochet.

"I am paying you a hell of a lot of money to babysit my modeling software the government is using." The machine warbled as he scored a point.

"This current situation is hammering my company's stock. I am losing money. Your job is to protect my investments. You are not doing a very good job." He scored another point.

"I want to review the Town Hall Meeting assignment. The shooting of the Congressman was supposed to expose the military's involvement with ICE raids and drive voters to our side. That was all. Now the rally this weekend and the following riots have overshadowed everything. It has reset the game and I'm bleeding."

He won the match in front of him and the machine let out a melody. He started the next game. "Then the rally was carefully orchestrated so that the white nationalist protesters, that the President supports, would start a small altercation. Only a few shots were supposed to be fired, by our own contact. Saturday should have gone off exactly as predicted. That did not happen. Instead, ICE tried to block the exits and a massacre ensued. How did ICE get into this?"

"I am not the President. I can sway him but he makes his own decisions. I have little control over that."

"I pay you to have control over that. I also pay you to bring me information. I should have known ICE was arriving with that size of a force, we would have come up with an alternate plan. Now there are only a handful of scenarios that will avert a total collapse of the economy. None of them are ideal. Again, being in this situation is not what I am paying you for."

He played quietly for a moment. "I do not want the President to act on any of the options the software is recommending. We are handling this. We are setting up the Mexican woman as a charismatic leader who will successfully calm the populace. It will stop the rioting, restore order and bring stock prices back up."

He looked up at Steve. "The President is not to act. Is that understood?"

Capardi nodded.

"You may go."

Capardi stood and walked out. Michael's client continued playing through a third set.

Capardi left the mansion in Palo Alto and drove to a small boutique hotel in downtown San Francisco. He was expected and escorted to the penthouse. The elevator doors opened into a small, ornate vestibule with a single door into the full floor suite.

A guard stood in front of the door and greeted him in Russian. Capardi nodded and then entered the rooms.

"Hello Visaly, the President needs a favor."

The Assassin

Thirty minutes later, the shooter, ensconced in his high-rise apartment, received his target with the location, date and time of the event where he was to act. Again it was too close to home and again he did not have a choice. Although he had been to the site multiple times, he meticulously researched the exits, vantage points, likely staging areas for the police, and the best methods for completing the mission. He spent the day collecting what was needed; purchasing several pieces at a small hobby shop he had scouted out and the rest from a big-box hardware store. Satisfied with the equipment, he returned the Tan Camry to the rental company and purchased a Honda NC700X off the internet. A motorcycle's nimbleness could prove necessary.

Dusty

Dusty sat alone in the chair of Michael's room, listening to the soft shoosh of the ventilator. He slit the envelope and pulled the pages out, settling the handwritten note on top onto his lap.

Dad,

If you are reading this I am dead, otherwise I would have retrieved it or warned you of its contents. I have enclosed information proving the rally last week was actually a terrorist attack. I need you to get this information to General Jennings or to the FBI, whichever you feel is right. I trust you to keep Brian safe, however you can.

These might be my last words to you so here goes.

I know that we have always had a hard time but stubbornness is inherited, so it is all your fault.

Seriously, I never wanted us to be so far apart, it just feels like we are always on opposite sides of things. In case I don't make it out of this, know that you are the man I try to be. I understand the code you live by. You use it to steer with, every time, and I try to follow that same code.

I am sorry for how distant we are. I always wanted it to be different.

Please take better care of mom. She isn't cut out to be alone all the time and you suck at being there for any of us. The code doesn't leave much room for family. If something happens to me, she will be a mess, she will need you. Don't let her down.

Tell Maddy I said to follow her heart and stop doing what you think she should and tell Brian I made this choice and there was no way he could have stopped me.

I love them and I will be watching out for them wherever I end up.

Please take care of our family dad, keep them safe.
All my love,
Michael

Dusty felt the sting of tears as he read. They tracked paths down the lines of his face and fell onto the words of the letter. He finished reading, head lowered, letting the tears roll down freely, then reached out and took Mike's hand, squeezing it gently.

"I love you too, son. I will keep us all safe."

He met with Agent Wilson a half-hour later. They were seated in waiting room chairs attached together in a row outside the doors of the intensive care unit.

"This is why he was targeted, because he witnessed a terrorist act, not because of Brian."

Agent Wilson looked through the pages Dusty put in front of her. Michael detailed his trip to the mansion on the day of the rally. He gave the address, his client's name, a description of the people present, exactly what he witnessed and concluded with the conversation between himself and his client in the Lamborghini on the way home. It was all laid out with precision; a military after action report of an enemy contact.

She laid it on her lap.

"I will file a court order to begin surveillance on Michael's client. He is incredibly wealthy and politically powerful. We have to be exceptionally careful or we will all end up mired in legal troubles for years. We probably will anyway, he has the pocketbook to litigate endlessly."

She tapped her finger on the pages in front of her while she thought.

"I can have a team move on the Russian connection immediately. We have a fairly accurate idea of who's in the country, who would likely be involved and whether they are operating in California. Michael only has the first name of one; 'Vasily', which might only be a nickname. I will send a team out to the house in Carmel but my guess is they will have erased any traces of their fingers in this. I will be surprised if we get anything. We will be thorough even so."

She glanced at Dusty. "Mr. Phillips, I have to ask you to stand down. We will take it from here. This is our job, it is what we do and we are very good at it."

Dusty raised an eyebrow and his eyes blazed, changing color to a steel grey that betrayed the violence he was prepared to do. Whatever he was going to say, he visibly stopped himself, leaving it unsaid.

He stood. "I need to call General Jennings, he can use this to have the charges against Brian dropped. The Russian involvement in the last few weeks should change the message the President wants to send, freeing him to clear Brian."

"Please don't make that call, let us handle this. It will be more effective if this information is sent through the appropriate channels."

Dusty walked out.

Agent Wilson

Agent Wilson sighed as she watched him leave. He definitely had not agreed to stand down. She would assign an extra detail to him. He was primed to take matters into his own hands and his actions could cause havoc in their investigation. He needed to be watched carefully.

She put in the call for a court order to surveil Michael's client as she reread the testimony, wishing they had been able to protect him so she could have received the information a week earlier. This was a game changer. She talked quickly and hung up. The FBI attorneys would present it immediately, catching the judge at home on a Saturday afternoon.

Dusty

It was late on Saturday when Michael's team of doctors deemed it time to begin the process of bringing him back to consciousness. The swelling, with the help of the stint, had been reduced inside his skull. The electrical activity in an awakened state was no longer likely to cause additional damage. Everyone rushed to the hospital.

As the lead doctor injected a serum into Michael's IV, Dusty, Jillian, Brian and Maddy were all standing hard against the glass walls of the cubicle to make room for them to work. Owen, Justin, and Agent Wilson stood just outside in the corridor.

They were removing his ventilator. Even with the air conditioning it felt stuffy and hot in the small space and watching the long tube pulled from Michael's mouth as he involuntarily coughed made Maddy light headed. The tube came out and the ventilator was turned off. Quiet filled the room. Jillian looked at Dusty with panicked eyes as the seconds ticked by. He squeezed her hand. Time stretched out until suddenly Mike's chest expanded and they all heard him suck in his first breath on his own.

"Yes!" Brian whooped, and then quickly looked to the Doctor. "Sorry Sir."

The doctor smiled. "It's OK. We're glad he is breathing too."

Jillian leaned into Dusty, the tears overflowing her lashes and sliding down her cheeks unchecked. Maddy buckled her knees and sunk down against the wall to the floor. Dusty bowed his head, thanking whoever was listening, a silent prayer sent upward.

"It will probably be several days before he is conscious and awake enough to talk but this is an excellent step." The doctor smiled again as he watched Michael's monitors.

The nurses cleaned up from the procedure and made sure Mike was comfortable. They left the room, leaving the Phillips family alone. They watched Michael breathe.

Brian reached out, squeezed Michael's shoulder and put a hand down to Maddy, pulling her from the floor. He wrapped his arm around her shoulders and guided her out the door, a huge smile spreading across his features. He and Justin high-fived as they went into the corridor.

"Oh Scott, I've been so scared." Jillian leaned her head against his shoulder.

"I know Jilly, me too."

"Do you think he's going to be okay?"

"Of course he is, it'll just be a couple days now," he said, looking away to keep her from seeing the lie. He had witnessed too many head injuries in his career. It was likely Michael still had a very long way to go before he was okay, if he ever got there. He hugged her close and kissed the top of her head. Tucking her into the chair by the bed, he stepped into the hallway.

Steven Capardi pushed his way through the intensive care unit's doors, an agent trailing him. He was in a dark gray suit, perfectly cut, and a brushed-steel tie. His Rolex flashed and his black oxfords, polished to a shine, clicked on the tiles as he struck his heels down with each stride.

Maddy, in sweats with her curls pulled up messily into bun, had spent the last week waiting in an emergency room. They all had, and looked it. She drew in a breath and Brian tightened his arm around her shoulders. Dusty stepped in front of them both.

"What the hell do you want Capardi?"

"Ah, the imposing Colonel Phillips...and his little Phillips kids. I hear one of them has had a bit of a scrape." The mocking in his voice grated. He looked towards Michael and Jillian through the glass. "I did tell you something like this would happen."

He nodded to Maddy. "I'm not here for you today, Chicken-Little."

She looked away as Owen stepped up on her other side. Jillian slipped out of the room. Justin was leaning with his back up against the wall, his legs crossed at the ankles. He had pulled his knife out of its belt scabbard and was flipping it up and catching it.

"Aw Cap'n, want me to take him out?" he drawled slowly, "He don't look so tough."

Capardi ignored him. Agent Wilson stepped between the two sides.

He looked Agent Wilson up and down slowly. "Amelia, isn't it? I came to tell you to cease your investigation into a certain businessman. He is a person of interest in a federal case. He is under the jurisdiction of Homeland Security. The judge has denied your order."

Agent Wilson, standing straight, looked him in the eye. "You have no authority here, Sir. I have jurisdiction within the US on an investigation concerning National Security. You may not interfere."

Capardi slowly pulled his phone out of his pocket. He winked at Maddy while he waited for it to connect.

"I'm with Agent Wilson and it is as expected. Can you make the call?" He slid the phone back into his pocket. "This will probably take a few minutes, what shall we talk about?"

He looked around, nodding at Justin. "Nice blade."

Justin flipped it again. Capardi smiled.

"How about we talk about the little bird you've been helping?" His eyes slid to Jillian. "I hear she has escaped her cage and will be singing a tune about group hugs at the Bridge tomorrow. Wouldn't it be sad if her singing gets cut short by interests who don't want togetherness? Poor little bird, so beat up. Should make the whole nation cry if she goes boom." He spread his hands out in imitation of an explosion.

Agent Wilson's phone buzzed. She answered. "Yes, Sir. Yes, Sir.....Yes Sir."

Hanging up she looked at Capardi as she spoke to Dusty. "The FBI has been ordered to stop the investigation into Michael's client."

Dusty went rigid, eyes blazing. Capardi turned. "Sing, little bird, sing." Laughing he walked out.

"God-Damn it." Dusty said, his anger radiating like a molten forge ready to explode.

"That came straight from the President's desk Mr. Phillips. There is nothing I can do."

"What did he mean about a bird singing?" asked Maddy.

Jillian pushed her hair off her forehead with the familiar gesture Dusty knew well. "Blanca Perez is speaking at Golden Gardens Park tomorrow. The protesters swarmed the detention facility last night and freed her. The Governor wants her to speak and see if she can calm the rioters. The government is desperate, they will try anything."

"It's what the models predicted," Maddy said, "they need a charismatic leader to stabilize California. Coupled with the President's call for calm it was one of the scenarios that played out well." She looked at Owen and then to Dusty. "Dad, the other scenario that stopped the rioting was a terrorist event."

"Excuse me?" Agent Wilson spun to Maddy.

"The modeling software the President uses is predicting a terrorist attack would stop the rioting. Every other scenario they ran ends up in either country-wide chaos that overwhelms everything or civil war."

Everyone around her looked confused.

"Hasn't anyone been watching the news? The rioting? It's everywhere and getting worse. We had to detour a couple times just to get here. I've been so focused on

Michael that I've been ignoring the outside world, but it is huge and taking over the country."

"Of course I am aware, but this is the first I've heard about predictions being so dire, or the solutions being reduced to a terrorist attack. Please excuse me." Agent Wilson stepped through the intensive care unit doors and out of sight, dialing her cell.

"Dad, Dr. Lane said the terrorist event might be at Golden Gate Bridge. That was one of the scenarios his team was directed to run and they use these predictions like a cult following scripture. They don't question the outcomes anymore; they accept as gospel that what the software predicts, will absolutely happen. "

"Maddy, there in no way the President would authorize a terrorist attack on US soil or anywhere else for that matter. That is just plain conspiracy theory bunk. It is not even remotely possible."

"Ok, then what was Steven Capardi just talking about? He made it sound like Blanca was going to be blown up while she is speaking."

"We have no idea if that was what he was referring too. You are jumping to conclusions based on Capardi's ramblings. We could be reading this completely wrong. We know he says things just to get a response. It doesn't make them true."

"But everything he told us so far has been true. He told us Brian was going to be charged with treason and that there was a shoot to kill order on him. He tried to use it to manipulate us but he was using the truth."

Brian tightened his grip o Maddy's shoulders. "Wait, what? There was a shoot to kill order on me?"

Maddy looked exasperated. "Long story Brian, but my point is still the same. He is an asshole and a snake but he hasn't lied so far."

"Dad I have to agree with Maddy. If the President of the United States just tried to have me killed for following his orders, he is capable of arranging a fake terrorist bomb to take out a speaker who heads the secessionist movement. It seems like his mode of operation."

Dusty shook his head again. "We know he was just trying to get you to take the fall, Brian. It's not unusual to have a shoot to kill order on an accused terrorist. That is a long sight away from staging an attack within the US, even against a region causing trouble. Someone is always causing trouble; the president doesn't just take them all out."

The room fell silent. Dusty, Maddy, and Brian all glared at each other.

Jillian broke the silence. "Scott, you say that like it was acceptable, the President using Brian to take the fall. He would have been killed if the situation were just a little bit different. Michael is in a coma. Don't you think your judgment might be compromised when it comes to political leaders, the military and honor? Not everyone is as noble as you. The President put out an order to have Brian killed and you think he wouldn't bomb an event where an adversary will be speaking, especially if it could stop the rioting?"

"Goddamn it. No. I will not accept that. You are jumping to conclusions. A and B do not always lead to C, sometimes there are a whole lot of letters in between."

Dusty crossed his arms and stared at Jillian as she started tapping a rhythm with her fingers on the nurse's station counter. He didn't want to hear what she was thinking, he already knew. The silence dragged on.

"Sir, permission to speak freely?"

Shocked eyes turned to Owen. Dusty had yet to hear him speak except when he had addressed him directly.

Owen looked at each of them. "Steven Capardi has not lied to you in the past so I think we should assume the threat is real. He said 'interests that don't want togetherness'. It seems to me that he could not be talking about the President or he wouldn't have used those words."

He looked at each of them again. Maddy looked away. "I think we should rule both secessionists and the President out as a threat since this event is organized by the secessionists and Ms Perez is also the nation's best chance at stopping the riots, a reason the President would not attack her." He looked directly at Jillian, who finally nodded.

"We need to look at who would benefit from civil strife. Most players in the Middle East want this but they lack the sophistication to maneuver events like this and they need the US to buy their oil to keep their economies stable. China maybe? North Korea? Russia?"

"Russia is already involved. We know this from Michael," Dusty uncrossed his arms, leaning forward, "and they have a professional already here in California."

Maddy nodded. "With the meddling they have already done in elections around the world as well as the US, they have shown they will promote anarchy in other nations."

Owen looked around again. "For the sake of expediency, let's go with Russia. How would they manage it and most importantly, how can we stop it? Because honestly, it doesn't matter who is planning it as long as we can figure out most likely scenarios and stop the attack."

Justin spoke up from his position against the wall. "We also might want to consider how to avoid..." He leaned his head in the direction Agent Wilson had left.

The Ross Martin

Glinting in the Sunday morning fog, the foreign flagged tanker *Ross Martin*, it's massive, four-hundred-foot, black hull looming, tugged against its massive lines on the commercial dock across from Alameda on the Western edge of San Francisco Bay. She had an unusual silhouette; four orange bubbles, ping-pong balls sized for a giant's hand, were set halfway into her decks, rising as high as the forty foot gantries, almost doubling her storage below the main deck. Preparations were complete for her trip across the Pacific; her holds filled with over one billion cubic feet of liquefied natural gas. She had made this journey multiple times without incident, an old workhorse in a fleet of ships owned by national shipping company Malcon, whose roots were deep in multiple countries.

She ran with a tiny crew, battling ocean storms with electronics instead of human hands, her brains a series of black boxes and a satellite connection to her base on land. Her crew only required minimal training as the computer was her captain. They were there for legalities as much as anything, babysitters with little to do except watch the endless ocean swells roll by the great ship. There had been a time when she had not been allowed to travel anywhere as crowded as the bay. That legislation had been repealed when the current administration had come into office on a pledge to reduce government red-tape. It was abolished, like so many other environmental and safety policies, with an eye towards improving the economy and corporate bottom lines. She was quickly repurposed to travel through sensitive areas and had performed her job safely for almost two years.

Now she sat, waiting for clearance to cross the bay and continue to her next port. With her holds full and her crew on board she surged against her bindings, eager to start.

John

Sunday afternoon was chilly and damp, an ocean mist obscuring the grand majesty of the Golden Gate Bridge, enshrouding it in clouds of dingy white. Blanca, in an emerald suit over a pale blouse and matching heels, held John's hand as the moisture laden breeze tugged strands of hair loose from the tight bun at the back of her neck. It teased them across her cheek. They stood on the edge of a stage in Strauss Plaza, just steps away from the Golden Gate Welcome Center, itself perched next to the Southern foot of one of the great engineering wonders of the world.

The stage was positioned in front of the statue of Joseph Strauss, temporarily hidden behind black pipe and drape, so that the columns of the bridge would be prominent over her shoulder as she spoke, providing the mist cleared. As one the symbols of California recognized around the world, it seemed an appropriate backdrop.

After a single day of rest, the league working for secession had flown her and John to San Francisco that morning. She was the new face of the revolution and it was a battered face, eliciting sympathy, but more important, signifying a resilience and tenacity to see this through. They wanted her on display, bruises and all.

As anticipated, the rioting had escalated on Friday and continued, growing as the hours passed. It was decimating city centers. The secession leaders and the Governor both, in spite of their differences, hoped the state would rally behind this young, resilient woman and come together, putting down their hostilities. With the right words, carefully crafted by a team of speechwriters, all vetted through the prediction software, they prayed for a return to sanity. She just needed to stand up and wave, talk for a few minutes and then it was done. The social media teams would take it from there. Reporters and cameras lined the front of the stage. She was the charismatic leader; one of the few scenarios their complex video game had shown would be effective.

The mist curled around them, swirling through hundreds of her supporters, blanketing them in a soft haze as they gathered on the paved plaza. The Golden Gate Welcome Center framed the East side of the space with a café on the western edge. John glanced at Blanca and looked away. This was wrong. Her face was rigid with stoic lines of determination that erased her personality, her gentleness. To him she felt fragile, like blown glass; hard to the touch with a roaring tempest locked down inside. A single blow could shatter her into a million, tiny shards. He was afraid this was too much to ask, too soon. He squeezed her hand. It was all he was allowed to touch since that first hug, except for when the night terrors pulled her out of a drug induced sleep. She had let him hold her shaking body as he whispered comforts he didn't think she could hear.

She pulled her hand away and folded her arms across her chest. "This is taking too long. It's ridiculous. I'm leaving if they can't get this going."

John noticed she had been edgy and angry since returning from the cascading horrors of the last two weeks. She was no longer the women he knew. He caught her eyes. "We are doing this for Amy. Hold on just a little bit, it's almost over. Elizabeth, the lawyer, said that if you were seen as vital for California and the nation, you could get your visa expedited and be cleared of escaping from the immigration facility. Without that, the judge might not release Amy to us tomorrow."

He saw the tears well up in her eyes at the mention of Amy. He reached out and unwound her arms, taking her hand and walking her away from the crowds along a gravel trail edged with wildflowers.

"Just breathe, baby, it's going to be okay."

"Oh John, I just can't do this." She came to a stop and leaned against a railing looking out over the bay, fogged in white. "I don't want to be their puppet. They hurt me. I don't care if it all explodes. I just want my baby and we'll go live in Mexico. They can all go to hell."

John didn't know what to say, his own guilt washing over him. She was rocketing between anger and tears and a mask of indifference. None of it was her, or all of it was, but he didn't know what words would help, what to say to make everything right. He took her hand and walked her a little farther. The physical motion helped. Her shoulders relaxed.

"I'm a mess John, I don't even know if I should be with Amy. I don't want her to see me like this."

John pulled her hand gently until she looked at him. "You are Blanca Isabella Perez Ortega. You are strong, you are smart, you are passionate and I believe in you. Amy has the very best mother any child could have. We are going to buy a house in a nice neighborhood close to a school and you are going to marry me in a church with your parents right in the front row, and you are going to keep your name. Hell, I will become John Perez Fields if you want. We are going to be married a very long time and we are going to have a life Blanca. No one is going to take that away from us. Everything that has happened this last two weeks, it will all just be a story in our past. None of this matters. There is only you and me and Amy. We will do whatever we have to to get her back and then we are free."

Blanca nodded, took a deep breath and gave him a real smile before she put the mask back up. She brushed the tears off her cheeks with the back of her hand and stood a little straighter. John walked her back to the stage.

John saw Jillian. He had asked her to the rally because of her work to promote Blanca. Dusty had insisted on coming to protect her. John had also met Brian and Justin, who were sitting in the FBI van parked next to the café, watching video feeds in case they recognized some detail they had seen before, on the night of Carlos Silva's shooting. Madison and Owen were also wandering through the crowd.

Owen had picked up earpieces at a huge electronics market and John could hear all of their conversations in his ear. It was distracting but also reassuring. It would stop soon enough; they had warned him communication would be cut to his and Jillian's earpieces when the event started. As long as they were by the stage, they would be inside the electronic bubble set up to block most radio frequencies, common now for political rallies, and would be out of contact except by sight.

Jillian had introduced herself earlier and now reached out, embracing Blanca in a hug, even though Blanca was stiff and restless in her arms. Disengaging, she steered them to the side, away from the bustle.

Agent Wilson

Agent Wilson caught Dusty as he circled through the crowd and passed close to the security van.

"Mr. Phillips, I am asking you again, please stand down. We have taken this threat seriously. We have agents on every building surrounding us where a sniper could be placed, we are mixed into the crowd, we are monitoring the roadway going on and coming off the bridge, we are watching everything on video feeds, plus we have swept the area with dogs trained for explosives and firearms."

Dusty nodded without saying anything. He kept walking.

Agent Wilson watched his retreating back. "Mules have nothing on that man." She turned back to the van.

The Assassin

The shooter arrived immediately after noon, pulling the motorcycle up next to a weatherworn building beside the windswept beach, a mile West of the bridge's Southern entrance. Dressed casually, he went inside and sat in the back corner of the coffee and book shop, opening his laptop. Earlier that day, disguised as a runner out for an early morning workout, he had discreetly arranged three tiny remote cameras close to where the secessionists would set up the stage with two more several hundred yards out. They would show the sweep of the plaza. His back to the wall, he was watching the feeds now, switching back and forth between the different cameras. The mist obscured everything, only giving occasional brief glimpses of the activity in hazy white. This wasn't going to work. He hesitated. Should he give up this plan or wait for the mist to clear. He sipped his coffee, straight up dark espresso, double shot, and worked through his options.

The Ross Martin

The tanker, *Ross Martin*, received its final clearance and began the slow process of detaching from the dock. The tug, *Shelley Two*, the *Ross Martin's* escort out of the bay, started up its own massive diesel engines and left its own dock, three miles down the channel from the *Ross Martin,* in a small commercial area that housed the fleet of tugs responsible for maneuvering the big ships safely though the Bay. As she left, a ship's mechanic stepped out of the maintenance building and watched the *Shelley Two* make way.

He smiled. He had been paid enough money to travel back to his home in Croatia and live out the rest of his life comfortably. It was quite a bit of money for depositing a small package under the floorboards of the tug. That pretty much guaranteed it was not morally right, but Anatoly was tired of America, tired of speaking and trying to think in a foreign language, tired of struggling, of being treated as substandard if not sub-human. Even though he was a master mechanic back home he was paid less than even the newest employees working here, certainly not enough to survive in San Francisco without living in a crowded apartment with distant relatives he didn't particularly like.

Since he immigrated, everything had been less shiny than his dreams. San Francisco was dirty and the people were cold and unwelcoming. Food was expensive, housing more so and God help him if he got hurt; his medical insurance barely covered anything. He was ready to go back to his culture. He just wanted to have conversations with people who understood him and dance with beautiful women who didn't look down on him.

Besides, the captain on that particular tug was an asshole that treated everyone in the mechanical department like shit. He felt a little warmth in his stomach helping karma set things right. This afternoon he was getting a ticket home with a payday he could live comfortably on for a very long time. As the tug pulled away he returned to his station, packed up his few personal items and then left the building forever. He would be across the border into Mexico in a handful of hours and then on a flight from Ensenada, with multiple layovers, back to his home in Eastern Europe.

The *Shelley Two* pulled abreast of the *Ross Martin* as the tanker let out two blasts on its ship's horn, alerting neighboring traffic that it was ready to make way.

Blanca

Blanca was introduced and she stepped onto the stage to a chant of her name. The crowd was packed into the space in front of her. She froze. She cowered down and turned to run, to hide anywhere. John was one step behind and when she turned, saw the panic. He immediately reached out and brought her close, pulling her off the stage and steering her behind a column of speakers. Jillian rushed over.

They surrounded her in a wall of bodies while she clung to John, sobbing. "This is too much like last time. They are going to come for me and hurt me again. Don't let them hurt me again."

He slid Blanca's small purse off her shoulder and handed it to Jillian. "There's Valium in there. The doctor prescribed it yesterday."

Jillian dug it out and Blanca took one in between gulps of air. Someone else had taken the stage and was rambling on about secession, glancing over towards Blanca to see if she was going to step back up. John held her until she started breathing more easily.

"I'm not making her go up on that stage. This is killing her."

Jillian nodded. She looked around. "They need to see Blanca for this to work. We need to stop the rioting and for that, we need her."

Blanca pushed away from John. "I want my baby back. I don't care about them or anything else but I have to get Amy back tomorrow. I need to do this for Amy."

John nodded and waved to the stage manager, who arranged another introduction. Blanca stood up straight. Jillian tucked wisps of hair back from Blanca's face. "You are a leader and far stronger than you know, Ms. Perez. You can do this. They will listen to you."

John walked up the steps onto the stage with her, reaching for the microphone, and adjusting it down. He took a single short step back. The crowd roared. Blanca took a deep breath and waved. Her carefully crafted speech was on the prompter in front of her and the Valium was keeping her heart from skittering out of control. "Hello California."

Brian

Justin punched Brian in the shoulder, pointing at the screen in front of him inside the close confines of the van.

"That's an ICE vehicle pulling up. What the hell are they doing here?"

Dan Mobury climbed down from the truck along with a handful of ICE agents, all dressed in the ICE tactical gear. They made their way towards the stage. Brian's anger ratcheted up his spine as he watched the swaggering walk of the small man who pushed people out of his path. This man and the lies he told were ultimately responsible for Michael lying in a hospital bed. He launched himself to his feet, the stool crashing against the side of the van.

Justin reached out and put a hand on his arm. "Focus Captain. This isn't the time to take your eyes off the mission. We can find that SOB in an alley somewhere. For now, our job is finding the bad guy."

Brian hesitated. Picking up the stool and righting it, he eased back down, the anger burning him to the core. Justin was right, the mission came first.

The Assassin

The shooter, fake press credentials hanging against his shirt, moved through the rear of the crowd, adorned with camera bags. He had given up the coffee shop and moved to his alternate plan. He wound through the spectators flowing out from Strauss plaza onto the street. They were enveloped in mist. His cell phone was out and he was watching signal strength as he walked; there were often cell signal blocks set up around political events. He worked his way around, looking for both a clean line of site and a clear signal.

Behind a large family standing close together, bundled up in bulky jackets against the chill wind, he stopped and unpacked one of his bags, pulling out a drone and carefully prepping it for flight. Its spinning blades were eighteen inches across and underneath was a small explosive device surrounded by tightly packed ball bearings. It was essentially a claymore mine, designed to be triggered remotely and decimate anything within sixty feet, and it had the ability to fly.

As a photographer, no one questioned him sending his drone aloft as he maneuvered it deftly. Unfortunately it faded in and out of the fog almost immediately. He frowned and moved through the crowd, following it, trying to bring it low enough to see but keeping it above the signal blackout dome.

Brian

There were two FBI techs in the van with Brian and Justin when Agent Wilson stepped in, their faces all backlit by screens. "Anything yet?"

"We have a possible that just entered the area, facial recognition is running now." The tech said.

Brian looked over. "Can you send it to my screen? See if we recognize him?"

The tech nodded and looked back at his screen. "Wait, we've got a hit, looks like it's 'Alexei Chicherin', Russia National, noted as a person of interest in an assassination in South Africa in 2009 but nothing since then."

Brian leaned over as the tech flipped his screen around. "I don't recognize him, do you Justin?"

"No, but it was dark."

They looked to Agent Wilson.She nodded to the technician who sent a location and description to the agents in the plaza. She opened the door of the van and stepped out. "I'll go take a look."

As soon as the door closed Brian hailed Dusty, Madison and Owen, repeating the information. The tech raised his eyebrows and Brian shrugged and smiled. They all watched Alexei work his way through the back of the crowd, the mist fogging through the picture as it drifted by.

Dusty

"He's getting something out of a backpack. It's a drone, he is sending it up." Dusty could barely make out Brian's voice through the earpiece. It was noisy; the crowd was applauding as Blanca walked onstage.

"The drone is big and it's carrying something. That doesn't look like a camera."

"Wait, I lost it in the fog."

"Maddy, you are closest. He is behind that family with the dad with a red coat and jeans, just to your left."

Dusty moved quickly through the crowd, searching out red coats, looking for Maddy too.

"I'm here. There isn't a guy behind this family that matches the description." Maddy's voice was loud and crisp.

"Wait, he's moving, I've got him...no, lost him again. Damn this fog, it's like swimming through milk."

"Holy shit, he's right here by the van."

Dusty spun and ran for the FBI van. Across the heads of the audience he saw the back door of the van burst open and Brian and Justin barrel out. Maddy's red curls, pulled back into a ponytail, were just in front of him and to the left. She was running for the van and got there ahead of him. He watched her sprint the last couple of steps and leap, tackling a man in a nondescript tan jacket and chinos, holding a controller. Dusty never would have noticed him in the crowd.

Maddy and Alexei rolled through the tackle and Alexei was back on his feet and moving. He reached for the controller as it spun out of his hand but Maddy snagged it first, tucking it in tight like a football, dodging away from him. Alexei sensed Brian, Justin and an FBI agent approaching and took off at a dead run, smashing through the crowd, knocking people sideways and barreling down a short flight of steps to the trail Blanca and John had left, shedding camera cases as he ran. Brian and Justin flew after him, jumping over the people he knocked down, seconds behind. Three agents converged on the trail, pounding across the gravel.

Maddy flipped over and frantically searched the sky. Dusty stopped short next to her. Owen showed up a step behind.

"I can't find it, I can't find the drone. Where is it?"

The crowd around them stepped back and looked up. The situation sank in; a man chased and tackled, a missing drone, a frantic woman searching for it. A voice in the crowd yelled, "There's a drone, it's a bomb, get the hell out of here. Run, run."

Like water from a pitcher, the crowd streamed out of the plaza, pushing and shoving as they fought to get clear. Maddy ignored it all, focusing her eyes on the sky.

Owen shaded his eyes, pointing towards the stage. "I think I've got it, it's high, really high."

Maddy followed his fingers and smiled when she picked it up. As the mist started to clear, burning off quickly, it glinted in the sun. Owen reached out for the controller and Maddy laughed. "In your dreams. This Flyboy gets dibs, Army rat. This is what I do." She started toggling the controls and the drone reacted, spinning one way and then another.

Owen squinted, shading his eyes from the sun. "It looks like it has the payload underneath. Probably has a remote detonation device. But that wouldn't work once it was under the radio frequency blackout area so he would need a way to set it off. He must have known about the blackout, everyone does it. Maddy, keep it where it is until we figure this out. I don't understand his plan."

Maddy nodded.

Dusty glanced at the stage. He could see Jillian's brilliant red hair as she went up on stage to help Blanca.

She felt his eyes and turned, meeting his gaze across the square. Four ICE agents climbed the front of the stage and Jillian faced them as Blanca put her hands out to ward them off.

He started towards Jillian, then stopped and looked back at Maddy, then to where Brian had run down the trail.

Maddy had just tackled a man and was now piloting a drone carrying an explosive device hovering over all of their heads without a clear plan. She needed his direction. Brian had taken off in pursuit of an assassin, the man most likely responsible for shooting Michael, the man Dusty swore to kill, without a weapon. If they caught up, he could be showing up to a gun fight with less than a knife. If anything happened to Brian, he could not forgive himself for staying here. Jillian was trying to face down an ICE threat to one of her newly adopted kids on the stage. She didn't know to get out of the way in case the drone exploded. He stood frozen. He had to choose; his son, his daughter or Jillian.

He heard Owen. "Maddy, could it be a dead man's switch? Was he taking it up over the blackout dome and then just going to drop it? Let it explode when it hit the ground?"

"Shit." Maddy's was focused on the drone. "It's fighting me in the wind. I don't know how long I can hold it up out of the zone. Dad, get mom out of there now."

Dusty looked at his daughter. He saw her as a toddler, running to greet him at the door, her arms soft and chubby around his neck as he scooped her up and as a young teen, tall and awkward, braces glinting as she laughed at something, then at her graduation from the Air Force Academy, still so young and vulnerable. She needed his help here. She was still a child, still his baby girl.

He looked at the stage and then looked back and in a crystallized epiphany, saw her from the outside, the way she looked right now. She was strong, in control, capable. Brian was too. His children had grown up. They were adults, very competent adults. He wasn't helping them by stepping in. He had to trust them to figure it out.

The first step he took away from doing it for Maddy, from being in control of her situation, was the hardest he had ever taken in his life. The rest came easy. His precious Jillian was in danger and unaware of it. He flew across the paving stones.

The Ross Martin

The *Ross Martin* made its slow, ponderous way out of the channel and under the Oakland Bay Bridge, the tug *Shelley Two* maintaining a steady course next to her. Well inside the VTR, the regulated and monitored shipping channels, she edged left just past Angel Island. Clearing the shallows and rocks off the tip of Alcatraz, she lined up on the pass with the foggy Golden Gate Bridge spanning the distance, its pillars poking out of the wispy tendrils of mist that were starting to burn off.

A signal came down from the satellite, unknown to the crew, and she adjusted course slightly more to the right. The engines throttled up, a steady, slow increase in speed because of weight and mass. The control panel beeped repeatedly, a small sound really for the emergency it declared, and the crew came over, tapping the navigation screen and then resetting the focus.

A small bang went unheard under the floorboards of the tug *Shelley Two*, its engines masking the sound of the small explosive ripping apart the water intake valves. The engines kept running as the temperature rapidly rose. Three minutes later an alarm sounded on deck and the First Mate shut the engines down. She was overheating. He radioed the *Ross Martin*. They were on their own for the last two miles.

The Captain of the *Ross Martin* picked up his satellite phone and called his boss. He explained the situation developing on the bridge of the Ross Martin and the loss of the tug. His boss called the navigation center, requesting they check their charting and make sure the tanker was still on an accurate course. The technician on station checked on her progress. She was off by seven degrees. He adjusted the settings and sent them off. He watched the course for several minutes, waiting for her to turn. Nothing happened.

The station supervisor was alerted to the situation. He spoke directly with the Captain on the *Ross Martin,* who tried to change the course settings manually from the bridge only to discover he was locked out of the system.

The *Ross Martin*, carrying one billion cubic feet of Liquefied Natural Gas was on a collision course with the North support tower of the Golden Gate Bridge. There was nothing he could do. He made the call to the Coast Guard, alerting them.

Assembling the small crew they donned mustang suits, the heavy waterproof layers designed to keep them alive in icy water, and their bulky commercial life jackets. They made their way to the stern of the ship, climbed into the lifeboat pod and deployed the inflatable ramp, launching the small craft into the frigid water of San Francisco Bay. Starting the small engine they steered straight back into the bay, praying they made it clear before the blast. The *Ross Martin* continued on her slow majestic course towards the enormous span of the bridge.

Brian

Alexei sprinted down the gravel path and vaulted over the railing at the overlook, hitting the steep slope below on his feet and sliding past short, windswept trees and gnarled shrubs, grabbing branches as he passed and pushing off rocks to keep himself upright. Brian and Justin slid along behind him. At the bottom of the slope a roadway appeared and he turned to the right, sprinting for the bookstore café. Justin and Brian pounded after and Justin closed the gap; close enough to try a tackle. Alexei moved to the left through several strides, running parallel to the edge of the pavement where a series of bollards ran along the water's edge, holding a heavy sea chain at knee height, acting as the barrier between the roadway and the rocks. He took several long strides and then jumped up and to the side, pushing with his foot off the low bollard and propelling himself sideways into Justin as he came abreast. Justin started to tumble and Alexei caught his arm and used the momentum to propel him around in a circle and into Brian as he caught up to them. Releasing Justin, he continued his turn and leaped into his next step, picking up his pace again. Brian and Justin tangled and rolled, both coming to their feet and leaping to follow.

Justin started to laugh between breaths. "That was an awesome move."

"Shut up and run, Lieutenant, he's getting away."

Alexei hit the parking lot first, angling between cars and sliding over a hood. He used a post to swing around the corner of the building sliding to a stop at his motorcycle parked in the gravel. Flipping open the compartment in front of the seat he yanked out a Glock, spinning and facing the corner while he fished the key out of his pocket with his left hand.

Brian and Justin raced up to the corner and Brian, seeing Alexei through the café windows, reached out and grabbed Justin's shirt, yanking him back as he started to go around. A shot, muffled by a silencer into a soft pop, chipped a divot out of the wood at Justin's chest height.

"Shit," he growled.

They heard the Honda engine rev to life and roar out of the parking lot. Black SUVs converged, the FBI had arrived. Alexei drove straight towards them, then at the last moment swerved the cycle onto a walking path and shot back towards the Welcome Center and Strauss Plaza. Brian and Justin raced out and waved down one of the FBI vehicles, climbing in. They spun in a circle and flew back along the roadway to the plaza, dodging cars and people fleeing in the opposite direction.

Blanca

Blanca was partway through her speech, noble words about rioting hurting neighbors and change needed to come through peaceful actions, when the crowd heaved by the small restaurant at the back. As the crowd roiled, Jillian saw her lose track of her words, faltering to a stop. They watched the crowd pour from the area, rushing up the stairs on their right or down the stairs on the left or back towards the parking lot. Blanca stood, looking lost, until John grabbed her hand and pulled her backwards. Jillian rushed to them, helping Blanca take off her heels; she was stumbling from the effects of the valium.

Blanca smiled. "I liked you right away. Thank you for helping us." She reached out and took Jillian's hand.

Jillian looked into her dazed eyes. "Oh child, I wish you didn't have to go through this."

She tucked Blanca's hand into John's and turned, searching for Dusty, catching his eyes across the plaza. Maddy was on the ground, looking into the sky, maneuvering a controller in her hands, Owen stood a step away, looking up also. Closer in, four black-clad men climbed the stage. She heard Blanca cry out behind her and in peripheral, saw her drop into a crouch, shielding herself with her arms. Jillian stepped between them, putting Blanca firmly behind her. John stepped up next to Jillian.

Jillian stood straight. "What can I do for you?"

Dan Mobury stepped forward, a step to close for comfortable conversation, and ignoring Jillian, cocked his head up to look at John. "There is a certain satisfaction in this, another rally, another stage. This time I'm arresting that bitch of yours and I am going to take real pleasure while we are going to the station. We will have lots of time alone with her." He leered at Blanca. "You enjoyed that last time, didn't you, Darlin'? We'll give you a lot more this time around."

Blanca was crouched in a ball, her arms over her head, rocking back and forth. She was sobbing out, "No" over and over as she cringed and swayed.

Jillian saw Dusty sprinting towards the stage. "Get clear, Jillian, get them clear!" He was waving them off to the right as he pounded towards them.

Jillian took both of her hands and shoved Agent Mobury back a step. "Later. We have to move right now." She spun and grabbed Blanca's hand, pulling her up. Blanca struggled against her and John reached around Jillian and grabbed her waist, pulling her off the stage with him and starting down the path. Jillian's FBI escort stepped up between her and Agent Mobury, ushering her quickly after John and Blanca.

Dusty spun by the edge of the stage. "Clear the damned area, there is a bomb." He sprinted after Jillian.

The ICE agents and a handful of technicians, reporters and cameramen hesitated and then took off, separating in different directions across the plaza and out the exit-ways.

Madison

In short order the area was clear, except for Maddy, Owen and Agent Wilson, who had stepped up to help them. She spoke into the air, her earpiece catching her words.

"Get that cell phone block down and get these two protection. We need cover out here, right now. Move, Gentlemen.'

'Madison, let's get you backed up."

Maddy nodded. "I don't know how big the blast will be. I don't know where to send the drone. I'm barely keeping it aloft, the signal keeps cutting in and out. Damn, I'm not sure what's best."

Owen looked around, "Can you get it to the water? Drop it in the Bay?"

"If I can keep it and me out of that damned blackout area, maybe."

Owen pulled out his cell phone. "I can lead the way. I'll watch the signal while you watch the drone." He helped Maddy stand up. An agent ran up and handed them both flak jackets and helmets. They put them on while they eased around the perimeter of the square.

"This might work," Maddy said.

They heard the motorcycle before they saw it, the Honda roaring up the pathway from the beach, its engine fading in and out as Alexie dodged people streaming away and zipped around curves on the gravel path. He came to a clear area and gunned it up the steps into the plaza. He pulled the Glock out of his belt and aimed at Madison as she fought with the controller for the drone. He pulled the trigger twice and then sped by, gunning it again as he lowered himself over the fuel tank and angled towards the parking lot and the road leading to the highway.

Maddy felt a hard punch to her shoulder and started to spin. The second caught her mid chest and threw her back, the controller spinning from her hand and across the paving stones. It skittered into the blackout area and signal was cut to the drone.

"Shit," Agent Wilson fell on top of Maddy and Owen piled on top of them both as the drone fell like a rock, dropping the two hundred feet in seconds, smacking the paving stones. It exploded with a hollow boom, propelling the ball bearings in a circular shotgun blast, ripping apart the curtains surrounding the stage, shattering the windows in the restaurant, and peppering the figures splayed out on the pavement with a barrage of small steel pellets that tore through clothing and flesh. A cloud of smoke crawled upwards into the sky. Silence descended.

The back door of the van was flung open and the two technicians jumped out, running to the huddle of bodies on the ground. "Agent down, agent down, get a medic here, now. Area is secure, hostile left through the main parking lot on a motorcycle."

Brian

Brian and Justin saw the blast from over the rooftop of the Welcome Center as the motorcycle sped up to them. Alexei shot in front of the black Navigator and then through the chaos of the parking lot. He gunned the Honda over a median and into oncoming traffic, swerving around several cars, then cut back over and onto the on ramp for the highway and sped towards the bridge entrance. The SUV pursued, dodging between the cars and the streaming people.

The traffic was stopped on the highway, a mass of parked cars stretching backwards from the entry. State vehicles had been pulled across the entrance lanes to the bridge, blocking access. Alerted to the *Ross Martin's* eminent collision, traffic was clearing from the bridge as sirens echoed along its length. Pedestrians rushed across the one-point-seven mile expanse, trying to get to shore. Alexie gunned the cycle along the side of the traffic lanes and dodged the state maintenance trucks, lying low and opening the throttle once he reached clear roadway. The cycle screamed around the right hand sweep and onto the nearly vacant bridge.

The Ross Martin

From the shore the *Ross Martin* seemed to take an eternity to reach what was to be her final resting place. Her size and the distance from shore made her speed deceptive, a painfully slow collision that stretched out, turning minutes into hours, especially after the small ramp was deployed and the crew evacuated. There was no way to stop the ponderous crawl to impact and no time to deploy anything that could mitigate the damage, although tugs raced to try and intercede. Inevitability weighed down until with a last indrawn breath from onlookers, the leading edge of her hull made contact with the concrete surrounding the North tower, collapsing the bow as her mass ground her forward with a groaning death scream as her steel hull tore open.

There was one second of hope, a prayer that nothing more would happen, and then the first tank of liquid natural gas exploded. A terrible thunder clap echoed across the bay and a fireball engulfed the tower, shaking the cables across the bridges length. The bridge deck swayed and shuddered. The ball of fire coalesced with the last vestiges of mist and rose skyward. A white hot fire followed, engulfing the *Ross Martin* and the North Tower as the remaining fuel in the ruptured tank burned. It took ten minutes for the fire to reach the second tank, setting it off. The onlookers watched in stunned horror as the third and then the fourth followed the first two. Each of the explosions sent up a fireball, rocking the bridge to its foundations, and it only held in place because of the recent earthquake renovations.

The *Ross Martin's* hull slowly began to sink as the firestorm ate up the steel support structure as well as reaching hungry hands towards the tower. Fireboats converged on the ship, standing far enough back to avoid injury while they waited for her to be safe enough to approach.

Brian

Brian and Justin bailed out of the Navigator and ran forwards through the traffic. They had just cleared the roadblock when the tanker hit. Only a few steps later the explosion sent them to their knees. Looking to the right, the length of the bridge was lost in fire and smoke as the fireball traveled upwards. Alexei Chicherin was gone. Whether he had died in the firestorm or made it through to the other side, they couldn't tell. Chaos had erupted at both ends of the bridge. There wasn't any way to stop him now if he had made it through. They left the bridge to the FBI agents and returned to the plaza.

Dusty, Jillian, John and Blanca, along with a handful of FBI agents, were grouped around two ambulances in the parking lot. Maddy was sitting in the back of the first while an EMT flicked a small flashlight back and forth across her eyes, checking their dilation.

"You good, Maddy?" Brian asked.

"Yup, the bruises are gonna' hurt where the bullets hit the vest but I'm good. Owen took the blast. He's gonna' be hurting pretty bad when the pain meds wear off. They are taking him back for surgery for the shrapnel."

Owen grinned at them from the gurney. "Can I date your daughter now Colonel Phillips?"

"Focus on healing soldier. It's going to take more than putting yourself between her and a bomb blast to impress me. You are going to have to make her smile."

Maddy stepped over and kissed Owen's cheek. "You took the bullet for me. That was brave, thank you."

He reached up with both hands, pulling her down, and looking deeply into her eyes, raised his eyebrows.

She nodded slightly and he pulled her close and kissed her lips. When she pulled back, she laughed.

Owen grinned. "I just wanted to get that out of the way. You know, while I'm all banged up and you're feeling sorry for me and grateful I saved your ass."

"You don't need an excuse in the future, I kind of liked that, and I was saving all your asses first, I just got shot. But, yeah, I think I might keep you around for awhile, you come in handy."

They loaded him into the van, the legs of the gurney collapsing as they pushed him in. Maddy turned to walk away.

"I'm glad I saved it, I kinda' like looking at it, your ass, I mean."

"I'll see you back at the hospital." Maddy shook her head, smiling, as they closed the door and an EMT slapped the back of the ambulance twice. It started up and pulled out of the lot.

She looked up to Dusty and Brian's grinning faces. "Don't say a word, not one."

"Aw, Brian don't have 'nothing to say. I on the other hand,.."

Maddy slapped the back of Justin's head as she walked back to sit on the ambulance. "This conversation's done."

The second explosion from the tanker rocked the plaza. They all unconsciously ducked.

Maddy watched the fireball rise over the stage area. "Sweet Jesus, I can't believe they actually attacked the Golden Gate. I wanted to believe you Dad. I really did. But they take this prediction stuff so seriously."

"Maddy, we still don't know that's what it was. It could have just been an accident." Dusty folded his arms across his chest.

"I thought we won Dad. I really thought we messed up the terrorist attack. I fricking got shot. How did we miss the bridge itself? That was the plan all along. This was just a diversion. Capardi gave us just enough to get us running in the wrong direction."

"Maddy you can't be sure. I don't accept the President would do this. We think the Russians were behind the drone today, maybe they attacked the bridge as well. We won't know until it has been investigated."

Maddy made a face. She sighed. "I don't want to fight about it. Let's talk about it some other time."

Dusty nodded.

John looked between the two of them, forgotten for the moment. He put the puzzle pieces together and frowned. He didn't like where his thoughts were going. He determined to dig into it later, after things calmed down and his family was safe.

The *Ross Martin* burned throughout the afternoon and well into the night, lighting up the underside of the bridge in wavering, brilliant orange. She began to melt the tower support and it sagged, pulling the side of the bridge lower, the cables above holding the roadway from collapsing. Oil detainment booms were towed into a large oval around the wreck.

It was an effective and devastating attack. The media ran with it all through prime time broadcasting. It was blamed on a terrorist cell out of beleaguered Iraq and as hoped, it began to pull the country together. People came into the streets with shock instead of anger and as predicted, for the first time in over a week, the rioting ceased and calm descended.

The night stretched on and when Monday morning arrived most everyone went back to work. As quickly as that, it was done. Events would be dissected and argued over for weeks to come; a barrage of social media posts and opinion pieces on the news. People slowly forgot their animosities as this new collective threat drove the conversation. Before long the riots were a part of history and no one believed that they had been manipulated into it all. The software stayed secret and the scenarios kept being run and relied on while California moved towards the vote to succeed. Repairing the bridge commenced.

The President ordered missile strikes on suspect terrorist targets in Iraq and Syria as well as sanctioning the current Iraq government, but it eventually died away as well without much fanfare.

John

Early Monday morning, John pulled himself from a deep sleep. He grabbed at his cell, missing it in the different surroundings. Blanca was curled in a tight ball, her back against his side and she groaned as he struggled to turn off the alarm before she came fully awake. He silenced it and leaned back against the pillow, taking in the hotel room. Sunrise was still a long way off but the hallway light was visible in a thin white bar under the door and it lit the small room in a soft glow. The sheets were crisp against his skin. He had taken one of Blanca's valium when they got in and still felt groggy after a full night of sleep. He considered coffee but the room's air conditioning worked extremely well and it was cold outside of the covers. He turned to the side and gently pulled Blanca into his arms, careful not to wake her. He breathed in the smell of her hair and closed his eyes. He wanted this minute to last forever.

They had gone with Jillian and Dusty to the hospital while Maddy had x-rays. They all sat in the waiting area in front of Michael's intensive care unit while Owen was in surgery. When he emerged several hours later, his new fan club cheered. Jillian had noticed how worn Blanca was and brought them back to the hotel, absorbing them into the suite of rooms so that Blanca would be safe. They had fallen into bed and with the help of the valium, slept through the night. A flight back to LA was booked for seven am.

Today was Amy's hearing. They were meeting the legal team at ten and the hearing would be at eleven. He slowly massaged Blanca's shoulders, willing her to wake without startling. He kissed the back of her head, calling her name softly until she started to move and then scooted back, giving her space. She uncurled and stretched. Turning and seeing him there, she smiled.

"You are far away," She said sleepily.

"I wasn't sure how you were doing."

"Oh John, I'm sorry. This is all so hard. I'm okay right now. I think the drugs are still working, I don't think I even moved all night." She slid over to him and pulled his arm around her shoulders, snuggling against his warmth.

"Are you ready for today?" He asked gently.

"I'm scared. What if they don't let us have Amy? What if they think I'm a bad parent? John, I have to get her back. I can't live without her."

"I don't know, baby. The lawyers are good though. If something goes wrong today, and that is very unlikely, we will just keep fighting until we get her. We won't give up."

"There were women at the detainment center who lost their kids. They were taken away. The judges didn't think they would be good mothers because they brought them across the border illegally and they didn't have jobs. They took them and gave them to parents in the US, let them be adopted. John, they can never get their little babies back."

"That won't happen to us, Blanca. Your situation is different. It will be alright."

"John, they just wanted to die. They cried all the time. They didn't have anything left. It was nightmarish. This country is horrible. I don't want to live here anymore."

He wrapped her up in his arms and kissed the top of her head. "Let's take it one step at a time. Just get through today. We'll figure out tomorrow once today is finished. Maybe we will have Amy and you will have a visa by tonight. Then everything will be easier."

Blanca nodded. "We won't stop fighting for her. Not ever. I won't let them keep her away from us."

"Hop in the shower, Babe, we need to get started. Neither of us wants to miss our flight."

While the shower ran, John stayed under the covers, willing the tears away. He didn't want Blanca to see it but he was terrified that they wouldn't get Amy back. He didn't know if he could handle it if they took her away forever. He imagined those poor families split up and their children adopted out. He wouldn't want to live either if that happened. Facing court today was about the hardest thing he could imagine doing.

They met with Elizabeth at ten and arrived at the courthouse at ten-thirty, dressed in the same clothes they had worn to the event the day before. Elizabeth had managed to get a hearing with an immigration judge to sign a temporary visa for Blanca. One of her associates was there now, pleading in Blanca's defense so that she could be here for Amy. Elizabeth felt sure they would have the visa before Blanca and John stepped into family court and could show it to the judge in Amy's case.

John was pacing nervously up and down the hall and Blanca was perched on the edge of a bench outside the courtroom they were assigned too. Elizabeth had a folder spread across her lap and was intently reading its contents. The minutes ticked by. John sat down and Blanca got up, walking back and forth on the same route. She kept looking up and down the hall for someone to bring Amy. She needed to see her baby.

Figures appeared around the corner, four men walking briskly. John was trying to make out who it was when Blanca cried out. "No, don't come near me." She started backing along the corridor, tripping in her heels.

Elizabeth looked up and shoved the folder aside, reaching for Blanca's hand. She pulled her behind her and asked over her shoulder. "Who are these people?"

"They hurt me." Blanca whimpered, cowering down.

John reached her and wrapped his arms around her from behind, holding her close against his chest. "They aren't touching you today. I promise."

Dan Mobury strode down the hall and stepped up to Elizabeth as his men closed around Blanca and John. He looked directly at Blanca, ignoring Elizabeth.

"Did you really think you could get your brat back? Did you think I would let you? As your arresting officer, I get notified of your court dates. You had to realize I would be coming for you after yesterday. There isn't a chance in hell of you ever even seeing your kid again because I'm taking you in before this even starts."

Elizabeth answered coolly. "No. that is not going to happen. A temporary visa is being signed right now. She is legal."

Dan looked at her and smiled. "Show it to me. If you can't, she is mine."

Elizabeth stared at him for a full minute and then turned to Blanca. "Until I have the visa, there isn't anything we can do. You will have to go with them and I will follow as soon as the paper arrives."

Blanca started to cry. Two of the agents stepped behind John and grabbed his arms, forcing them open. The third reached in and grabbed Blanca's hands as she fought, snapping handcuffs on easily. He yanked her forward and she stumbled in her heels.

"Don't let them do this. They hurt me. Don't let them hurt me!" They dragged her down the hall. "Please, help me. Please."

John struggled with the two agents holding him. "God-damn it, let me go."

Dan nodded to Elizabeth, standing rigid, and glanced at John. "Hold him until we are clear and if it happens to get rough, it's even better." He turned to follow Blanca, swaggering as he walked down the corridor.

"I will kill you if you hurt her again," John yelled as they moved away.

Another group came around the corner moving with purpose down the hall, intercepting Blanca and after a few words, turning her around and bringing her back along the corridor until they reached Dan Mobury. Sean

Cummings stepped up, followed by two men and a woman in black suits, and three police officers. The woman came forward.

"I am Senior Agent Milla Hastings with Homeland Security Internal Investigations. Special Agent Dan Mobury, you and the three men with you are under arrest for the rape and battery of Blanca Perez Ortega. These agents will read you your rights and escort you to a holding facility. Please stand back so my officers can release Ms. Perez."

John shrugged off the agents holding him and ran to Blanca, grabbing her and pulling her close as her handcuffs came off.

Mobury glared at Agent Hastings. "You can't do this. I am the Southwest Field Commander. You cannot arrest me."

Handcuffs were snapped on his wrists.

"Cummings, you bastard. You were in on this too. Arrest him Agent Hastings. He was responsible. He was there. He arranged it all. It wasn't me."

Cummings stepped to Mobury, close in, towering over him. "You are supposed to protect people. You have no business wearing that badge."

"Fuck you, asshole. You damned snitch, you betrayed your brothers. You are a coward and a traitor."

As Mobury turned away, Cummings hit him with an anger driven punch that lifted him off his feet. Mobury doubled over, shock spreading across his features.

"You were never my brother. You are monster and I hope you get in prison what you have been so willing to hand out to others."

Mobury's angry vitriol drained away as the officers took him and the other agents down the hall.

Cummings faced the group in the silence. "Ms. Perez, I am truly sorry for the pain you have suffered. I will see this through. Every one of those monsters who hurt you will be going to jail for a long time, you have my word. On behalf of ICE, I would also like to stay and speak to

347

the judge on your behalf if that is okay with you and your attorney."

Blanca leaned against John, shaking. John and Elizabeth looked at each other. Elizabeth reached out her hand and shook his. "Thank you Agent Cummings, as Ms. Perez's attorney I will accept on her behalf."

John stepped aside with Blanca and wiped the tears off her cheeks. "Take a deep breath. Are you okay?" At her nod he said, "Let's go get Amy then."

Steel was in his voice.

An hour later they emerged with Amy firmly held in Blanca's arms. She wiggled and squealed, alternating between, "mama mamama and da da da da."

John held one of her pudgy small hands in his while he walked beside them out of the courthouse and into the California Sunshine. Crossing the street to a café, they enjoyed their first meal as a family in what felt like forever. As they ate, feeding Amy little pieces of a grilled cheese sandwich, a young man in slacks and a sport jacket approached.

"Ms. Perez? I am Evan Fry with Governor Smith's office. He would like you to meet him in Sacramento this afternoon to discuss how the succession movement and the current government can work together to ensure the peace we are seeing today will continue. I have a car waiting to escort you."

Blanca looked at John. He watched the anger rise in her eyes. She stood up, shielding Amy.

"I am not a puppet for you to pull my strings, Mr. Fry. I will not be used as your tool anymore. This country is responsible for my rape and you took my child away. John and I were almost killed. You can all go to hell. I don't care what happens in this God-forsaken place. You have not protected me, you have used me. We are packing our things and driving to Mexico this afternoon, they want me there."

"Ms. Perez, I don't think you understand. You are the face of the revolution. You are their leader."

"I never asked to be the face of the movement. I don't have to play to your game anymore. I quit."

"Ma'am, The state is changing. The secession movement is snowballing. We need to work with the leader of the secession. That is you."

"Damn it, no! You have used me. You have hurt me. You have made it clear I am not wanted in this country, that I am worth less then you because I was born on the other side of an imaginary line. Now you want me to help you? After everything you have done to me? This country can go to hell."

"Ms. Perez, I cannot image the pain and suffering you and your family have gone through but your Latino community needs you. As a leader, you are in charge and with secession on the ballot, you have the power to make real change. The Governor and the President want reconciliation and are willing to make concessions to make it happen. At least come and talk. You are the current head of the movement. We need to work together for every person in this state. You can always go to Mexico in the future."

John reached out and took her hand. "This is your choice Blanca. I'm behind you either way."

Blanca looked at Amy busily smashing the sandwich into her tray. She finally nodded. She would do this for Amy's future.

"Your country thanks you, Ms. Perez."

Blanca looked at him and started laughing, bitter and cynical.

Jillian

Michael regained consciousness slowly, swimming up through the darkness. Jillian reached out and took his hand. "Hi Love, welcome back." He smiled and drifted off to sleep again. Jillian watched his face and as it went slack, leaned back in her chair. Maddy stepped into the room behind her.

"He just opened his eyes."

Maddy lit up and she came over, taking his hand and peering into his face. "He's back asleep again. I hope he wakes up enough to see me before my plane out this evening."

"So you are going?"

"I have to Mom, I have classes to teach."

Jillian nodded. "How are you doing with all this?"

She smiled as Maddy brushed the hair off her forehead in a familiar gesture. Maddy turned and leaned against the bed, facing Jillian.

"Mom, I don't think I can go back to running the prediction software. It doesn't seem right. I know someone else will still do it, but at least it isn't me. I won't be responsible for helping them manipulate everyone. What they are doing is wrong."

Jillian nodded, watching her daughter's intense expression.

"I can't destroy the software, not only would it be against regulations, but they would just purchase another copy. Someone could maybe send a virus through the data files and destroy them but realistically, that isn't likely to be even possible. I don't know how else to stop this from happening." Tears bubbled to the edges of her lashes and spilled over. She wiped them away with an angry swipe. "It's just a matter of time before they push everyone into doing this all over again. Nothing has really been settled, it has all just been swept under the rug until the next time it explodes. They aren't going to stop playing with people's emotions. It's about wealth, power, and control, not about what is right for the country. I don't want to be even a small part of that, even if it means losing my position at the Academy."

Jillian reached out and took Maddy's hand, pulling her into the chair with her. She put an arm around her and hugged her tight, kissing her forehead as they sat together watching Michael breathe. "Madison, the one thing I know, that I am sure of, is that people eventually see through the games. It may take awhile, but they will begin to recognize the manipulation and stop responding to it. Have faith.'

'You are a leader. Use your voice, people will listen. Keep reaching out to both sides and bring them to the middle where they can talk and negotiate. Help them see the manipulation for what it is; a way to control everyone so a few, powerful people can control all of the resources for themselves. You are strong. Fight back with your words, everywhere you can, pointing out the false stories and the manipulative propaganda. Fight against the hate. The internet is a powerful tool, but it is just a tool. You can use it to make a difference. It is what I try to do with all the moderating I do. It is the only way I can see a path out of this."

Maddy nodded. "Technology may help solve this too. One of my students is working on a system that encodes all of our personal data into blocks on the internet, like having a virtual safe with all of your information locked inside. It is changing the whole game board."

Jillian smiled. "I am glad to hear that. Hopefully it will take awhile before someone figures out how to break into those safes and manipulate the data all over again. Greed is a part of who we are, it isn't going to go away. It is up to each of us to be aware of when we are being played and to control how we react. You aren't a child anymore. We all need to be better than we are now to survive as a country. I believe in you. I know you can make a difference.' She hugged her tight as her phone started to ring, buzzing loudly from her pocket. She pulled it out. 'It's Carol, do you mind if I take this? It could be important."

Maddy nodded. Owen waved at her through the glass wall from his wheelchair and she untangled from her mom and stepped out of the room.

Carol's soft southern accent filled Jillian's ear. "Jillian, great news! Todd was able to get the charges against Brian lifted. He convinced the President that there was too much of a paper trail. The President agreed to switch his story. It is now Michael at the community center on a legitimate protection assignment for his company. There will be no charges for either of them."

Jillian felt the tears sting her eyes. "Oh Carol, that is the best news. Michael is starting to come around, what a great way to welcome him back. His sacrifice meant something."

Maddy

Maddy smiled at Owen as she emerged. "Aren't you supposed to be lying in a bed somewhere?"

"The nurses got sick of me, threw me out. Told me to go find that pretty girl I've been mooning over and tell her to how lucky she is to have me."

Madison raised an eyebrow.

He grinned. "Ok maybe they said for me to tell you how lucky I am to have found you. I'm on pain meds, you know, I can't be responsible if it gets all mixed up."

Madison laughed. "You know I'm flying out tonight."

Owen's smiled dropped.

"They said you could leave the hospital today and I imagine you have at least a few days to heal before you have to be back in DC. Don't spend it here; come to Colorado Springs with me. I'll take care of you. I'm not ready to say goodbye yet, we just got started."

"I'm not sure your dad would approve. I don't think he likes me... Now Captain Robertson? He thinks Captain Robertson is a fine soldier."

"You aren't ever going to let him live it down, not knowing your first name, are you?"

"Are you kidding? Having something on a Colonel, who also happens to be your father, is gold!"

"Will you come?"

He nodded, and pulling her hand up, kissed the back of it. "I would love to get to know more about this beautiful woman I'm falling for. Long distance relationships are tough. I plan to do everything I can to make this one work."

Dusty

Carey was sitting on Michael's bed when Brian walked in, dropping his rucksack on the floor near the door. She frowned, looking back and forth between them. "My God, you two could be twins. No wonder you pulled it off, Michael. I didn't understand how it could be possible."

Brian reached out his hand, shaking Carey's.

"It is really nice to meet Ben's great, great grand something. I can't thank you enough for putting us together. I really enjoyed spending time with him."

"No problem, he called me right after you left, said he had to set you straight but that you were a good kid. He thinks you will do alright. That's pretty high praise coming from him."

Brian looked to Michael. "Hey Bro, my flight is in a couple hours. This is it until you come and visit me."

Mike smiled. "I will as soon as they let me out of here. I think I want to spend a little time traveling before I figure out what I'm going to do next. I don't think babysitting billionaires is calling my name anymore."

"Anytime. I will show you all the lovely sights around Fort Drum."

Michael chuckled. Brian came over and slapped his shoulder. "Hey Donkeyshit, thanks for saving my ass."

"No problem, Dickwad. You weren't up for saving it yourself."

Dusty and Madison walked through the door and Carey, winking at Michael, stepped out of the room, her mechanical foot tapping on the tiles as she walked by. Dusty smiled warmly at her as they passed.

"I like her," he said, "she seems tough."

"She's had my back in some pretty hairy stuff. She is one of the few people I trust in this world."

Maddy walked over and hugged Michael. "I want you to come and see me as soon as they let you out of here. You can stay with me as long as you need."

He squeezed her hand.

Dusty sat down in the chair, took a deep breath, balled up his courage and looked at his children. Three faces, each so similar to the other and to both he and Jillian. They were the result, these strong, decent people, of the love he and Jillian shared. They had created three incredible human beings. The pride he had in his career paled in comparison to this.

Maddy and Brian sat on the edge of the bed and as the silence stretched looking more and more concerned.

He sighed. It was time to say this, as hard as it was. "I've been doing a lot of thinking over the last couple weeks. I mostly want to tell all three of you that I'm sorry. I know that isn't enough for all the birthdays, baseball games and helping with homework times that I missed. I can't ever make that up. There were times when I should have done things differently. I should have picked different assignments closer to home or maybe opted out and gone into government or something and created a better home life for you. I can't undo that. I wasn't always a very good father or even the father you needed, but I always loved all three of you more than my own life.'

'You have grown into amazing adults that I am so proud of. I want you to know that. Know too, I want things to be different going forward. I promise to listen without judging and to let you live your lives they way you want. I will support your choices, whatever they are, because I know you are smart and talented. All three of you are more than capable of making them without my help. I am sure you will still make mistakes but those are your lessons to learn. Just remember, I am here for you always, though, no matter what." He lapsed into silence.

Michael reached out a hand and Dusty took it. Maddy came over and hugged him.

Brian smiled. "Wow Dad, you have cancer or something? Is this like a last testament kind of thing? Cause honestly, before you go, I think you need to tell Michael you love me more than him."

Michael looked over at Brian. "Shit-for-brains."

"Asshat."

Maddy started laughing. "Are you guys ever going to grow up?"

Dusty rolled his eyes. "I'm going to go find your mom."

He hugged Michael, then Maddy and finally Brian on his way out the door, holding them each for a little bit longer than he had in the past. Brian finger bumped Michael and Maddy kissed his cheek as they followed, Brian picking up his rucksack off the floor as he left.

Brian

Brian and Justin made their way through the airport terminal, stopping at baggage claim; Justin had brought back several new throwing knives as souvenirs so they had checked their small rucksacks. As they stepped out to the curb, Ashley's royal-blue mustang pulled up and she flung herself out of the car and skipped around the back of it, catching Brian up and wrapping him in a hug. He dramatically leaned her over and kissed her as Justin rolled his eyes.

"God-damn it, Suh'." She drawled in her imitation of a Southern belle. "If you eveh' leave me in a hotel room again, it bettah' be crazy swanky and have an open bahr' tab."

Brian smiled. "I'm sorry, dahlin' and I neveh' plan to leave you in a hotel room again. Fahgive' me?"

"Awe Brian, I've missed you. It's good to have you home safe. It was scary the way they talked. They were too eager to pull the trigger if they found you."

Justin threw his ruck into the trunk. "Can we get going already? I'm starving."

"You're just lonely Dahlin', we need to find you your own sweetheart." Ashley dropped into the driver's seat. "Where do you want to stop to eat?"

Dusty

Dusty sat in an Irish Pub across the tramline from the South Park baseball stadium. He nursed a Guinness and distractedly watched the football game on the screen set over the bar while he kept one eye on the door. It was dark inside with wood paneling and prints in shades of gray from San Francisco's early days. The pub was long and narrow with the bar stretched along one wall and booths along the other. A very robust mermaid, faded with age, was painted on the build-out containing the restrooms. It smelled of beef pie and spilled beer, but the music was good; soft rock played low.

As evening sun lit up the front windows Dusty recognized Steven Capardi walking through the glass door. Capardi squinted for a moment as his eyes adjusted and then came over to the booth, sliding onto the padded bench across the oak table from Dusty.

Dusty tipped his beer bottle. "Capardi."

Steven ordered a stout as the waitress walked by. "What brings me here, Colonel? Or am I supposed to guess?"

"I'm willing to trade. I want my son off the hit list."

Capardi looked off to the TV and then back. "What makes you think that is even something in my power?"

Dusty took a sip off his bottle. "Do we really need to go there?"

Capardi chuckled. "No, let's let suspicions stay that way. What do you want Colonel?"

"I want to kill the son of a bitch who ordered this. You know my record, I will make it happen, it will just be a matter of how much pain he endures and how long it takes him to die. I've run more complicated ops."

358

Steven watched Dusty like he did everything else; intent, poised to fight. "I can't let that happen."

The waitress came by, dropping off a bottle and glass.

"I know. That's why we're here."

"Are you saying you'll walk away if your son is protected?" Capardi poured the dark brown liquid into the glass, tipping it sideways and filling it slowly.

"If by protected you mean off the hit list he is on, then yes. I don't want him having to look over his shoulder for the rest of his life. I want this done."

"And in exchange, you go back to your boat in wherever the fuck, and forget my client's name."

"My kid's life for his life and I go wherever the hell I want."

Capardi nodded his head. "and the Russians?"

"Call them off. Otherwise I will make this very public. Russia and the President already have image problems. I promise to make it way worse."

Capardi took a drink and set his glass back on the coaster, centering it. "And Michael, is he going to forget names and faces?"

"Michael is going to be a lot tougher. His client ordered him killed. He's taking that personally." Dusty played with his glass, spinning it slowly. "He doesn't have a job to return too either. His client is far too powerful to allow that. Michael will be holding a grudge that I can't answer for."

"What if I could offer him something? He may be a straight up guy but I have places I can use that. He's too smart for babysitting billionaires."

Dusty nodded. It could work. "Do we have a deal?"

Steven nodded. "Done."

They both took another drink.

Dusty looked at Capardi, a smile played in his eyes.

"I probably would have liked you in another situation." he paused. "No, probably not."

Steven chuckled again.

"I've never liked you Colonel."

"You don't ever lie, do you Capardi."

Steven laughed. "I never have too. The truth always works well enough."

"So tell me Capardi, you seem to be pulling strings in all of this; the Russians, this rich bastard, the president, homeland security. In all of this, who are you really loyal too? The deal's done, am I making peace with a traitor?"

Capardi took a slow drink from his glass, watching Dusty over the rim. "I've always been the President's man. I make a lot of money working in the shadows and playing sides against each other. But, in the end, I am loyal to the President. The man, not the office."

"And to that point, why did you tell me about the hit on Blanca in the first place? Did you know about the tanker as well?"

"What is in the Presidents best interest sometimes goes against his plans. A martyr would have sent the secessionist movement into hyper-drive. The President cannot afford to lose California. I cannot afford to lose my good standing with the Russians. As much as I dislike you Colonel, you do manage to always get the job done. The charismatic leader was saved, my contacts were protected and the President is none the wiser."

"Tell me the President did not order the attack on the bridge itself. Dr. Lang ran the predicting software for a terrorist event to stop the rioting, but the President ordering this would be beyond treasonous."

"Colonel, do not ask questions you do not want the answer to."

Dusty dropped his head, taking another drink, the silence stretched. Dusty finally looked up. "Did this all turn out the way you wanted, did it follow the predictions?"

Capardi laughed, a real deep down laugh, surprising Dusty.

"Hell no, the software is a tool and powerful people are idiots using that tool to manipulate the world for their own benefit. It's fucking hell trying to get it all to come out straight. I'd destroy every copy of the prediction software if I could. My life would be a damn site easier."

He stood up and dropped a ten on the table, "Maybe I'll see you in Mcxico sometime but don't count on it."

He walked out the door.

Dusty sat and finished his beer, drinking it slowly. He paid and left the pub, walking out to a chilly breeze blowing off the bay. He shivered. He was ready to get back to his boat in the tropical sun. He was eager to start anew with Jillian, this time actually asking about her day and listening to what she had to say. He smiled and headed for the hospital to say goodbye to Michael.

Get the Next Book in the
Phillip's Family Chronicles

To sign up to be the first to receive the next book in this series and find out if California votes to secede, go to www. KellyWanamaker.com

Kelly Wanamaker

The author, having grown up in the heart of the Arizona desert, now spends the bulk of her time on a small sailboat surrounded by the deep, blue sea with her spouse, John, two big rescue dogs and one small cat. Writing fills the empty hours between ports and the lives of her characters keep her company in the long watches as the stars clock overhead.

The inspiration for this book series comes from a lifetime spent next to two international borders, one in Arizona, the other in Washington, where she raised her four children. Acutely aware of the humanity behind the immigration statistics, she wants to bring the human cost to life in the pages of her books.